HOWARD FAST

An Independent Woman

HARCOURT BRACE & COMPANY

New York   San Diego   London

ISBN 0-15-100271-1

Text set in Fournier Tall Caps
Designed by Linda Lockowitz
Printed in the United States of America
First edition
A   C   E   F   D   B

*To the memory
of a wonderful and
independent woman,
my wife, Bette Fast*

Contents

*I wish to thank
Sandy York and Mercedes O'Conner
for putting my manuscript into a computer
and for editorial help.*

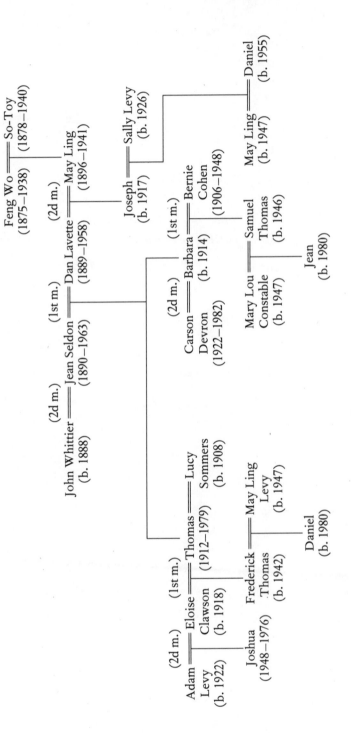

The Lavettes

Feng Wo (1875–1938) ═ So-Toy (1878–1940)

John Whittier (b. 1888) ═ (2d m.) Jean Seldon (1890–1963) ═ (1st m.) Dan Lavette (1889–1958) ═ (2d m.) May Ling (1896–1941)

Joseph (b. 1917) ═ Sally Levy (b. 1926)

Adam Levy (b. 1922) ═ (2d m.) Eloise Clawson (b. 1918) ═ (1st m.) Thomas (1912–1979) ═ Lucy Sommers (b. 1908)

Carson Devron (1922–1982) ═ (2d m.) Barbara (b. 1914) ═ (1st m.) Bernie Cohen (1906–1948)

May Ling (b. 1947) ═ Daniel (b. 1955)

Joshua (1948–1976)

Frederick Thomas (b. 1942) ═ May Ling Levy (b. 1947)

Mary Lou Constable (b. 1947) ═ Samuel Thomas (b. 1946)

Daniel (b. 1980)

Jean (b. 1980)

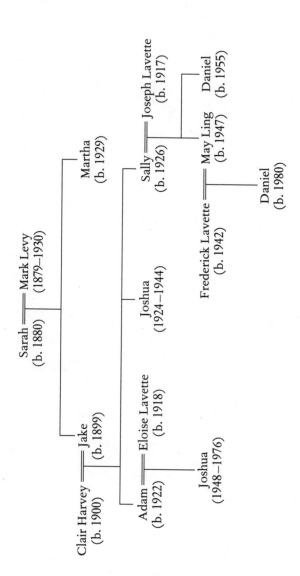

The Levys

The City

1

IT HAS BEEN CALLED a city of hills, draped with dreams; it has also been called the city of illusions at the end of day. Those who live there call it simply the City, because for them it is the only city. It has a rim called the Embarcadero, where the streets swoop down Russian Hill to meet the Bay; and on one of these streets, called Green Street, Barbara Lavette lived. Her house, like the other houses on Green Street, was built to compensate for the slant of the sidewalk, an old house with a tiny porch and a bay window; but on the third floor of the house, one could look out of the guest room window and see the Bay and the Golden Gate Bridge, and count, if one cared to, at least a dozen white sails skimming before the breeze. In the summertime, when the sun was sinking to the northwest, one could stand at this window and see the sun leisurely departing through the Golden Gate.

Today, on a bright June morning, Barbara Lavette was carefully choosing a costume for her lunch with the mayor of San Francisco, Dianne Feinstein. Having run for Congress and lost, Barbara was not unacquainted with women in politics, but she had chosen only two of them for her devotion. Fortunately she had met both, Eleanor Roosevelt and Dianne Feinstein—Mrs. Roosevelt when she visited Dan Lavette's shipyard during the war, an opportunity given to Barbara because Dan Lavette was her father, and Ms. Feinstein during Barbara's run for Congress. They would lunch today at the Redwood Club, a place not unlike the Century Club in New York, where achievement was more highly regarded than wealth.

Costume was important. She thought of gray silk slacks—but decided they were not for the Redwood Club. After all, women were first admitted only a year ago; a black silk skirt six inches below the knee would suit the place better, with a white cotton blouse and a pink cashmere cardigan. Perhaps a scarf as well. The Redwood Club faced the Pacific and they might dine outside.

The Redwood Club was actually built of redwood, a fact that nettled the environmentalists and that had once caused a brief picket line; but that was years ago, and the environmentalists had decided that it was better to let the Club stand, since they had proven their point, than to tear it down and have some other building material used. The dining room had a high-beamed ceiling and a long bar, and the tables were arranged so that the glass windows could be drawn back, leaving the dining area open to the Pacific. Set between Lincoln Park and the Presidio, it was not a long drive from Barbara's house.

Dianne was waiting when Barbara arrived, and she rose to meet her. "You look absolutely beautiful," Dianne said. "You don't age. What's your secret?"

"Luck. I picked some good genes."

"I remember your mother. You look like her, you know."

"More good luck."

Ms. Feinstein was wearing a beige suit. Barbara could not recollect seeing her in anything but a suit. She was a very attractive woman who always seemed to be downplaying the fact that anyone might consider her beautiful.

They ordered white wine before they pored over the menu, then chose crabmeat salads and engaged in small talk. Dianne mentioned that Barbara's son had been chosen for the post of chief of surgery at the hospital, and congratulated her. She appeared to know everything that happened in the City. She turned the talk to Highgate, the winery that had been so much of Barbara's life, asking whether Barbara's nephew, Frederick, were still running it.

"Everyone dreams of owning a vineyard. Freddie's there for life. He wouldn't think of anything else."

"Well, he certainly has done something for California wine. But I didn't ask you here to chat about your remarkable family, as pleasant as that is. Tell me, Barbara, do you still do columns for the *Los Angeles World*?"

"Yes, I do. I love it."

"And Carson?" He was the owner and publisher of the *World*.

"I was sixty-seven this November past. I never believed I could fall in love again, especially with a man I divorced years ago, but it's happened."

"He's married? Forgive me, that's none of my business."

"He is. Not happily."

"Would he let you do a longer piece instead of a column?"

Wondering where this was leading, Barbara nodded. "Ever since my story on El Salvador was mentioned for a Pulitzer, he's been pleading for another. But I'm too old for investigative reporting."

"Good. All the investigating has been done—I have it here with me. Barbara, we're going to take a step that no other major American city has dared to try, and I think we've got the votes to put it through. We're going to ban the possession of handguns in San Francisco."

Surprised, Barbara said, "Even in homes?"

"Everywhere—on the person, in the home. The police are wholeheartedly with us. As I said, we have the votes, except that one or two are a bit shaky. They're under the influence of some L.A. polls, and I want to shake them loose."

"In L.A., the motto is 'A gun in every home.' "

"Barbara, I know that, which is why I want to blast the subject open on the day we vote. They read the *L.A. World* here. I want to shake them loose with the leading L.A. paper on our side. That might be just the shove they need, and I know what kind of force and passion you can put into a story. Let me give you a few facts."

Dianne rummaged through her portfolio. "Here are just a few statistics: In 1979, handguns killed 8 people in Britain, 48 in Japan, 34 in Switzerland, 52 in Canada, 58 in Israel, 21 in Sweden, 42 in West Germany, and 10,728 in the United States. Oh, I am so sick and weary of this murderous plague, and here in San Francisco we can do something about it. I have five solid votes on the Board of Supervisors. The handgun crowd has four, with the National Rifle Association turning handsprings, and I'm pretty sure that we can swing the gentleman on the fence. That will give us a six-to-four majority—and we'll do something no other big city has dared to touch."

"We dreamed of this," Barbara said. "We never thought it could happen."

"It's going to happen, and you can help us make it happen."

"When is the vote? I read something about next week."

"Three days. Can you write it and get it in the paper by then?"

"I think so. You have all the background material?"

"Everything. The vote is Friday. If they can run it in Thursday's *World*, that would be perfect, and that would give the media time to pick it up and quote from it. Just anticipating what you would say, I spoke to three radio stations. Two of them will read your column, in full, through commuter time."

"Bless you," Barbara said. "My dad used to say that I spend

my life spitting into the wind, something no sound sailor does. But sometimes, just sometimes, the wind turns."

"Yes, it does," Dianne agreed.

THAT AFTERNOON, sitting on her desk, Barbara's old Olympia typewriter appeared to welcome her. No word processor for her; she and the ancient Olympia knew each other.

She had just finished a long telephone conversation with Carson, and the idea excited him. "It's about time the City came to its senses," he said. "Build up Dianne in your story. She's a wonderful woman. Tell her I'll give it front page, two columns, with a banner headline. Barbara, this city is an armed camp. Every man and woman in L.A. wants a gun. We run half a dozen ads a day for shooting instruction. You're right on the nose."

"Fifteen, sixteen hundred words—will that do?"

"Write yourself out. If it has to be cut, I'll cut it—very carefully."

"And how are you feeling, dear man?"

"Good. A little stickiness in the chest, but that's the junk food I'm eating—doctor says it's gas—"

"Oh no," Barbara protested.

"I watch my weight, work out every day. I haven't gained an ounce. And I'll be in San Francisco Friday night. Dinner and other things?"

"We'll see."

She was still writing at midnight, her desk covered with stacks of material from Dianne's office: details, statistics, homilies. Her back ached, but the material lured her on: who produced handguns, how they were sold, the political power of the National Rifle Association, the technical changes in guns, the handgun machine pistol, handguns and suicide, handguns and family quarrels. How could she leave out the story of how Dan White walked up to Mayor George Moscone, a man Barbara respected and believed in, and deliberately shot him

to death with a handgun? And Dianne Feinstein—Carson wanted
a lot about her, of course; she won elections, unlike Barbara Lavette.

At three o'clock in the morning Barbara went to the kitchen
for her fourth cup of coffee, and at six o'clock, with the gray light
of dawn seeping through the blinds, she finished the two-thousand-
word piece and fed the sheets into her fax machine, trying desperately to remain awake. The fax machine was a gift from Carson and
it was then so unusual that a local magazine had run a story about
the only household in San Francisco with a facsimile processor.

Then Barbara climbed the stairs to her bedroom, tired to the
point of utter exhaustion. It had been years since she had worked
the night through, and she fell asleep almost instantly. At twelve
noon the telephone rang four times before she could shake herself
awake, pick it up, and respond rationally:

"Ms. Lavette?"

"Yes."

"Felix Colone." Colone was the managing editor of the *World*,
a dyspeptic, skinny little man who had grudgingly accepted Barbara's place as a columnist. "I have to tell you, Ms. Lavette, that
we can't run your story. This is a town where every other citizen
has a gun—and I'm referring not to the ghetto or the barrio, but
to Hancock Park and West Los Angeles and Beverly Hills. In so
many words, your article projects a policy that will do nothing and
only offend."

Taken wholly aback, Barbara shook her head to clear it. There
was no use arguing with Felix. "Let me talk to Mr. Devron, Felix,"
she said coldly.

"You can't. I'm serving in his place. Mr. Devron died last
night."

"What!" Then her voice failed her, and she sat for a long
moment, staring at the telephone. "What are you saying?" she managed. "Is this some ugly joke?"

There was no sympathy in Colone's hard-edged voice.

"Hardly a joke, Ms. Lavette. Mr. Devron had a heart attack after dinner last night. He was taken to Mount Sinai Hospital but they were unable to revive him. He passed away shortly after ten. And by the way, Mrs. Devron gave orders this morning that your column be terminated immediately. If there is anything I can do for you, let me know."

Her hand trembling, Barbara put down the telephone and stared mutely at nothing. She felt the tears begin and she felt the tears on her cheeks, but inside there was only emptiness, as if she, too, had passed away with Carson. Then the anguish boiled into anger. Her Carson could not have died of a heart attack. She knew the man, every inch of his splendid body, every muscle, every reflex. He was the man who had run the decathlon and won the gold in the Olympics. He had been her husband; they were divorced, and after the divorce he fell into a wretched marriage, and then they became lovers. She recalled how he would pick her up in his arms, as if she were a child—and she was no child, but a solidly built woman of five feet and eight inches.

Grief was not new in her life, but this was not simply grief. She was sixty-seven years old; Carson had been a gift of life, as she felt it, the last gift. Her mind raced crazily. Carson's wife had no love for him, but she would not have divorced him or the Devron fortune—which she would have done anything to have without Carson. His death—as Barbara saw it at that awful moment—liberated his wife and took from Barbara all the hope in the world.

She steadied herself as well as she might, found the number of Mount Sinai Hospital in Los Angeles, and asked for Dr. Hazelthorpe. He had practiced surgery with her son, Sam, at Mercy Hospital in San Francisco, when they were both residents; and often Sam would bring him to her house for dinner. She got through to the hospital, told them that it was an emergency, and in a few moments was connected with Hazelthorpe in the doctors' dining room.

"Barbara? Yes, of course I remember you. I was going to call you, but I've been in surgery all morning."

Let it be his excuse, Barbara thought, and said to him, almost bluntly, "I love Carson. How did he die? I must know. Carson was strong and healthy. How did he die?"

"Barbara, this happens to men who appear to be in good health—and sometimes to athletes. As I understand it, Mr. Devron came home from his office and went out to run at a nearby track. He did this several evenings a week before dinner. He collapsed at the dinner table, a massive coronary occlusion. He was dead when the ambulance got there."

"Just like that?"

"Yes, that's how it happens."

"Did his wife call the ambulance immediately?"

"She was at their beach cottage. As I understand it, the butler called the ambulance. Mr. Devron was eating alone. They called me when he came here, but there was nothing we could do. It was too late."

Barbara put down the telephone, her hand trembling. *It was too late.* Everything was too late.

IT WAS AN HOUR AND A HALF LATER that Eloise Levy appeared at the house on Green Street. Eloise was Barbara's dearest and closest friend, but more than that she was a part of the tangled relationship of the Levys and the Lavettes that had begun over eighty years ago, when Dan Lavette and Mark Levy became partners as shipowners. She was a daughter of the Clawson family, as well known in San Francisco as the Lavettes, and she had married Thomas Lavette, Barbara's older brother. She was a gentle, generous woman, and the marriage had been short and cruel. Divorced, she married Adam Levy, Mark's grandson. Her second child, born of her marriage to Adam Levy in 1948, Joshua by name, had fought in the war with Vietnam, lost a leg, and a few years after his return to California, had taken his own life.

She and Barbara were knit, not only by their fondness for each other, but also by the series of tragedies that both of them had endured. Each was privy to the thoughts and hopes of the other, and when Eloise heard of Carson's death on a morning news report, her first thought was to be with Barbara.

Now, when there was no response to her ring, she used the key to the house that Barbara had given her years ago. Inside she called Barbara's name softly and then glanced at the kitchen and Barbara's study, still littered with the books and papers of the night before.

"Barbara?"

She went up the stairs and to the bedroom, opened the door quietly, and saw Barbara sprawled on the bed in her nightgown, face buried in a pillow. Eloise's immediate fear was that Barbara had taken her own life, although she would have sworn that Barbara could not do such a thing under any circumstances. Her mind flashed back to the day when she and Barbara had found her son Joshua dead, his wrists cut.

Her voice rose in a shriek. "Barbara!"

Barbara stirred, turned over, and sat up, her face tear stained, her eyes bloodshot, her hair in a tangle. Rushing to her side, Eloise embraced her, and for a minute or so, the two women clung to each other.

"What time is it?" Barbara managed to say.

"Almost two." Eloise went to the window and drew back the drapes. Sunlight poured into the room.

"Two o'clock," Barbara whispered. "How did you know?"

"It was on the radio. I drove here as soon as I could. Are you all right?"

"As all right as I'll ever be, I suppose. I need a shower, Ellie. I have to get dressed."

"I'll make some breakfast. You have to eat."

"Just coffee."

"No, no." Eloise wouldn't have that. They had the closeness

of partners in pain. She went to the kitchen and fixed bacon and eggs and brewed fresh coffee. She recalled a weekend that Barbara and Carson had spent at the winery, and the walk the three of them had taken up the long slope to the top of the hill that overlooked Highgate, the long rows of vines stretching down beneath them, and the old, ivy-covered stone buildings of the winery nestling under red tile roofs. Carson was almost ecstatic that afternoon, bemoaning the fate that had tied him to a newspaper rather than to a winery and telling the girls that this is where he was meant to be and live; and certainly he could have done so if ever he'd had the strength to break loose from his family. He and Barbara had been married a few months before, and already their union was fraying at the edges. Yet Eloise remembered what a splendid pair they were— Carson, the Olympic athlete, with his tall, well-tuned body and his thatch of blond hair; and Barbara, long limbed and free striding, five feet, eight inches—the two of them dwarfing Eloise's five feet, three inches, Eloise being a round, gentle little woman who almost had to run to keep up with them. They had been so full of youth and confidence and strength; and now Eloise's hair was white, and Barbara's hair was almost white, and death had come to her again.

Barbara, dressed in old jeans and a brown shirt, looked at the platter of eggs and bacon and buttered toast in dismay. "Dear Ellie, I can't eat. I'll have some coffee."

"All right. And then perhaps you'll eat something." She poured coffee for both of them. "And you must come home with me and stay in the Valley with us. It will be good for you. You'll be surrounded with people, and they'll bother you to confusion and take your mind off everything, and the children will be delighted because Aunt Barbara is there..."

Barbara was now munching the toast, carried away on Eloise's river of words.

"Adam and Freddie are battling away like cats and dogs—"

"Freddie and Adam? I don't believe it."

"Oh yes. You know, Freddie takes off every winter for the wineries of Europe, and this time he brought back a case of Imperial Tokay, from the gardens that once belonged to the emperor Franz Joseph. It tastes like elixir of the gods, and he brought a bag of seed. He paid a thousand dollars for the case and another thousand for the seed, and he had to bribe all sorts of people to smuggle them out—which, you know, is typical of Freddie—and Adam says we can't grow it in the Valley and that every California Tokay he's tasted tastes like—well, I won't use the word—and anyway Adam hates sweet wine, and Freddie brought in the argument that when Jake and Clair bought the winery for a song in 1920, the only business they had was sacramental wine for the Jews and the Catholics and the Episcopalians—and it just went on, and for two days they didn't speak to each other—"

In spite of herself, Barbara was caught up in Eloise's outpouring of family gossip. "And are they going to grow it?"

"Heaven forbid! Freddie apologized to Adam—for what, I don't know—and we drank the Tokay every night after dinner, and Freddie gave a bottle to Candido as a peace offering—you know, that wretched business with Freddie and Candido's daughter—and Candido, who never saw a bottle of wine at a thousand dollars a case, won't open it but is saving it for his daughter's wedding. Adam, as a gesture toward Freddie—you know, Barbara, Adam is a very sweet man, and I think his anger at Freddie was more because of the way Freddie treated Carla than about the Tokay—and anyway Adam went to the university and consulted Professor Hermez, the dean of the vintner school, who agreed with him that only the soil around the town of Tokay in Hungary could produce the wine, but pleaded for a handful of the seed for their experimental garden—which Freddie provided—so everything is healed and the professor came to dinner and drank two glasses of the Tokay and declared it one of the great privileges of his life. So there you are."

Eloise was far more intelligent and complex than people gave her credit for, and Barbara didn't know whether she had formulated her story deliberately or not, but it caught Barbara up in the life of Highgate, which was stocked well with her memories, and she said yes, she would come, she'd love to come.

"And you'll be there in time for dinner—please, Barbara."

"Yes, I can be there in time for dinner."

"And you're all right now—enough to drive alone?"

"I'm all right."

"And one other thing. Freddie bought one of those new facsimile machines, the first one in the Valley, so if you decide to stay a while, you can send in your column—'faxing,' they call it."

Smiling sadly, Barbara shook her head. "There is no column, Ellie. The first thing that wretched wife of Carson's did this morning was to call the paper and tell them that my column and my job were over. She must have called from the beach house the moment she heard that Carson was dead."

"No! I can't believe that."

So much had happened. It was only the day before that she'd had lunch with Dianne Feinstein at the Redwood Club; it felt like weeks ago. "Dianne Feinstein has that handgun ownership bill coming up for a vote day after tomorrow. She asked me to write a column for the paper, and I called Carson. He was so pleased with the idea that he asked me to make it a feature story. I sat up half the night with it—the last time I spoke to him."

"Poor dear, I'm sorry, so very sorry."

HIGHGATE WAS MORE THAN A NAME on red wine that was recognized and appreciated the world over; it was saluted as the best Cabernet Sauvignon produced in California, by virtue of twenty-two awards; and to an extent it had made the Napa Valley famous. The winery was still totally a family business, presided over by Adam Levy, Eloise's husband, and by Frederick, Eloise's son by her first marriage, to Thomas Lavette, Barbara's brother. Adam, who

had just turned sixty, had taken over his father's role as the patri-
archal head of the winery, while the merchandising was in the hands
of Frederick, now forty.

Dinner was served at eight-thirty, in the great kitchen–dining
room of the big stone house that was the central feature of the
winery. The kitchen–dining room measured twenty-two by forty
feet, with one end open, and in the Mexican style the walls were
covered with blue tile. The open end of the room had heavy drapes
of coarse wool, handwoven in Mexico, but on this balmy June night
they were drawn back. The whole opposite end of the room was
given to a great iron wood-stove, half of which had been converted
by Clair to natural gas. In the center of the outside wall of the
room, there was a large fireplace, cold now that it was summer. The
dining table was a bit more than twelve feet in length, the top made
of a single redwood plank. It was an old table that had been there
when Jake bought the place, and it had been waxed and polished
through the years to the point where it shone like a gleaming stone.
It stood lengthwise in the room, and on the side opposite the fireplace were cupboards for dishes and an iron band of hooks from
which pots and pans hung.

Adam, white bearded, with a shock of white hair still thick,
sat at the head of the table, Barbara on one side of him, Eloise on
the other; and down the table toward Freddie, who presided over
the opposite end, were Barbara's son, Sam, and his wife, Mary Lou;
Sally and her husband, Joe Lavette, who practiced medicine in Napa;
and their son and daughter, May Ling and Daniel Lavette. Freddie
had once married and divorced May Ling, and now, having ended
his relationship with Carla, Candido's daughter, he was wooing May
Ling, as Barbara saw it, like a rejected puppy.

Once, in writing about her family and its intertwining over the
many decades of Highgate, she had faced their tangle of relationships
in despair. Now, sitting at dinner with the people she knew and
loved best, she was filled with guilt. Carson was dead, his body

scarcely cold in the grave, and here she was, engulfed in sympathy and love.

Eloise, responding to Barbara's gloom, said, "Darling, my mother was Irish and my dad was part Irish, and the wake goes way back into time, and I used to think that the Irish were barbarians to carry on that way, but this is a celebration for the living, not for the dead. The dead will go their way and we will go ours."

Meanwhile, now that she had finished filling the goblets with wine, Cathrena was stirring the steaming pots on the stove; and up and down the table, matches were struck to light the six thick candles that sat in hammered silver bases. Adam lit the last candle, and each at the table reached for the hands nearest, and Adam said, "For food of the earth and the fruit of the vines, we thank thee." The invocation was always the same and had been for as long as Barbara could remember, all the time back to when Jake Levy had sat at the head of the table. Her eyes filled with tears and she covered her face with her hands. Cathrena brought platters of hot tortillas and baskets of bread to the table.

"We'll drink a toast to Carson," Eloise said, raising her goblet. "May he rest in peace and always be remembered."

There was a roast shoulder of fresh ham, bowls of potatoes and turnips and carrots, a baked salmon for those who did not eat red meat, platters of sliced tomato and onion, and Mexican beans *refritos*. The bread was home baked, and except for the salmon, all of the food was raised at Highgate.

Aside from a few bites of the toast at breakfast, Barbara had not eaten all day. After the first bite, she found herself stuffing her stomach with food. The Cabernet kept coming, and after the meat and the salad and the apple pie for dessert, she could barely keep her eyes open.

"I think you have to sleep," Eloise said, and though Barbara protested, Eloise rose and took her by the arm and led her upstairs to her room.

It was always the same small room on the second floor of the big stone-and-redwood house, the dolls and dollhouse still there, things that Dan Lavette had bought for her on the occasions when both of them slipped away to Highgate, on days when his wife, Jean, had other things to do. Now Barbara was half-asleep, full of good food and wine. Eloise helped her to undress, tucked her into bed, and she was asleep almost instantly.

When Eloise returned to the kitchen, there was a flood of questions about Barbara: How was she, and what would she do now without the column that had meant so much to her? It was the first time in months that the whole family had gathered together at the table, an impromptu occasion when other appointments had been set aside because of Eloise's plea that Barbara needed all of them. "She'll be all right," Eloise assured them. "I'll keep her here as long as I can."

Sally, Adam's sister, moved into Barbara's chair so that she could harangue Eloise about the Devrons and particularly about Carson's wife, whom she detested. Sally was given to emotional outbursts. "I met her once, at a party after the opera. I was introduced to her, and when she heard the name Lavette—I was married to Joe then—she looked at me, took her hand away, as if I desired to touch it—I would sooner touch a snake—and if looks could kill, I would have died at that moment. I liked Carson—I always did—but it was his family before everything. That was his weakness, and in that way he *was* weak."

"He's dead, sis," Adam said. "Let him be."

"The grand dame," Sally went on. "El Rancho Gonzales. That was half of Los Angeles before the Devrons took it away from them, and she was the last Gonzales. Carson's mother was determined to unite the two families."

Eloise nodded. "Barbara told me about it. It didn't matter to her that Carson was weak. He was his mother's baby, her child. That's why they couldn't stay married. He was the golden boy of

California—the gold medal at the decathlon, America's hero—but he never grew up."

"For God's sake," Adam said, and pushed back his chair and went to take Sally's seat next to Freddie.

"He can't stand gossip," Sally said. "I love gossip. My heart goes out to Barbara, and I hate status seekers, sadly—but to be snubbed by a Devron! That boggles my mind."

Eloise shrugged. "They do have Kit Carson as a noble ancestor, you know. Barbara used to twit him about that, poor man. And I've seen the old map of the Rancho Gonzales. It was a grant from King Philip I in the fifteen-hundreds—"

"And they came here to get away from their dreadful Pasadena sun, to touch civilization—"

"Do you remember," Eloise said gently, quoting, " 'If you come to live here, be damned but you choose/to live with the Irish and the Jews.' "

"Jack London?"

"Or somebody. Adam liked Carson, but he could never understand a man who drank gin in preference to wine."

At the other end of the table, Adam and Freddie lit cigars and fell onto their favorite topic, wine. "I was wondering why you decided on a 1972 for tonight?" Freddie asked.

"You don't like it?"

"It's a good year, but just a touch too much tannin."

"You've been cultivating your taste. Maybe we should buy some table wine from Mondavi," he said sourly. Freddie was his stepson, out of Eloise's first marriage, to Barbara's brother, Thomas. Adam had adopted him legally and was utterly devoted to him, but they had a natural but easy antagonism.

"That will be the day."

"The fact is," Adam explained, "that we have a hundred cases or so of 1972 in the cellar."

"Do you want to move them? All it takes is a telephone call.

I have a store on Market Street that's been pleading for product."

Adam burst out laughing. "Freddie, Freddie—what in hell am I going to do with you!"

No one disturbed Barbara, and she slept soundly until almost noon of the following day. Stiff but refreshed, she spent about ten seconds under a cold shower, agonizing, and then switched to warm water. She opened the drapes, and the sun poured into the room. How good it was to be alive! Poor Carson, poor Carson, no more in her life, gone away. Well, in November, she would be sixty-eight years old. No one lived forever. Long ago she had given up any reflections on a hereafter. Baptized an Episcopalian, it was years since she had set foot in Grace Church, and she had borne the deaths and the pain that threaded through her past with a passionate love of life. *God forgive me,* she said to herself, *but I am glad to be alive and here.*

She slipped into a printed dress of India cotton and sandals. The long, smooth curves of her body were still much as they had been at thirty, and she used no makeup. She dried her hair with a towel, brushed it out, and went downstairs. Her son, Sam, and his wife, Mary Lou, had returned to San Francisco; Joe and Sally had gone back to Napa; and their children, May Ling and Daniel, had gone to Berkeley, where they lived and worked. The men had finished lunch and gone off to work, and Cathrena was clearing the table. Eloise still sat at the table with a cup of coffee, and she rose and embraced Barbara.

"Did you sleep well, darling?"

"Like the proverbial log."

"You look beautiful."

"As Mother taught me, thank you."

"Breakfast?"

"I make you some eggs *rancheros*," Cathrena said.

"Oh no, no. Just coffee. After last night, I won't eat for a week."

They had their coffee, and then they went out and walked. This was a good time of the year for the vines, the new growth bursting forth from the pruned stems, the whole world around them an explosion of life and color. They climbed up the hillside to a little clearing where there were benches and a stone fireplace for outdoor cooking, and a great live oak to shade them.

"I suppose the funeral will be tomorrow," Barbara said. "Or today?" She had lost track of time.

"Tomorrow, probably."

"Did you ever read Fannie Hurst's book *Back Street?*"

"Yes—years ago."

"I suppose that was the Victorian way," Barbara reflected. "If I remember, he set her up in an apartment, and that was his real life, and his own wife was his respectable life, and I remember how demeaning I felt it was, and then when he died and she couldn't go to the funeral—"

"Fannie Hurst slobbered," Eloise said. "She reached whole new peaks of sentimentality."

"She was no Edith Wharton," Barbara admitted. "But *I* never felt degraded or demeaned. It sounds cheap and unpleasant to be someone's mistress, but at least we never kept it a secret. We tried, but I suppose everyone in town knew."

"Not everyone. This is 1982, and no one cares much about such things."

"Except the *Enquirer*. You remember the story in the *Enquirer?*"

"How can I forget it? Freddie threatened to hit the editor. Can you imagine Freddie hitting anyone? And Adam, my gentle, sweet Adam, declared that if any *Enquirer* reporter set foot on Highgate property, he would shoot him. Can you believe it?"

Both women were laughing now.

"And Carson—dear Carson," Barbara said, laughing and crying at the same time. "He raged that he was going to buy the

Enquirer and fire everyone who worked for it. He said he would sue them, except that there were so many people suing the *Enquirer* for so many millions of dollars that it would take twenty years before it ever got to trial."

"You never told me what his wife did?"

"Nothing, absolutely nothing. She ignored the whole thing. She was not going to let a small matter like that get between her and the Devron billions. You know, they had season tickets to a box at the opera—and so did I, except that mine was a seat in the orchestra—and she came to the next opening."

"Did you?" Eloise asked.

"Ellie, I'm not insane—weird, but not totally insane. He didn't want to go, but she has a look that would freeze boiling water instantly. Carson said that the photographers were all over them, but she never even quivered. Poor Carson."

"And still you loved him."

"Did I? There are all kinds of love, and there are women who hate and fear men, and there are others like myself who adore them and can't live without them. I remember one night in L.A. in a hotel when he got himself gloriously drunk, and when we came up to the room after dinner, he collapsed on the floor, cold out, two hundred pounds of bone and muscle, and I had to get him into bed and undress him. Somehow, I did it—I don't know how, and my back hasn't been the same since, and thank God I'm one of those strong muscular types. But somehow I got him onto the bed, with him gurgling how much he loved me, and I undressed him and tucked him in and crawled in next to him, and all I was thinking was that this was my child, not a man, but an oversized beautiful child, and now he's gone forever—" The tears came again.

They heard Adam's deep *halloo:* "Where the devil are you two hiding?" He came stomping through the vines up the hillside, his long white beard bent in the breeze. In his jeans and a blue cotton workman's shirt, he looked for all the world like some patriarch out of the long past. Eloise, thinking of what Barbara had said, remembered the first time she had met him, in Jean Lavette's gallery. He was a tall, lean, gentle boy, whose face had been scarred and torn in World War II (the scars were now covered by his beard), and she had loved him from the moment she met him. She had been married to Tom Lavette then, Barbara's brother, and he had verbally beaten her to an emotional pulp; and then, under the love and shelter of Jean and Barbara, she had grown and matured. Adam was her world, her lover, her rock—how else could she have survived the suicide of Joshua and become whole again?

Adam stood in front of them now. "Not my idea to break in on you," Adam said apologetically, "but Dianne Feinstein called, and she wants to talk to Barbara, and she wants you to call her right back, and since she's one of my favorite women, I set out to find you. What is it, Barbara? Are you back in politics?"

"Never. It's probably the gun thing."

It was the gun thing. When Barbara called City Hall, they put her right through to Dianne Feinstein. "Dear Barbara," the mayor said, "my heart goes out to you. Carson was a fine, wonderful man. God only knows what will be the future of the *World*, and I shouldn't be delighted with anything. But we took an early vote, and the bill passed six to four in the Board of Supervisors, and we're the first big city in America to ban guns within city limits. We've done it!"

"That's great," Barbara said. "Bless you"—and added woefully, "They killed my story."

"I know. It's her paper now. We won't talk about that. But please come and see me as soon as you get yourself together. There has to be something very good for you here at City Hall."

"Thank you, but my political life is over. But thank you for the thought, and good luck."

The Jewel Thief

BARBARA LAVETTE AWAKENED. It is said that dreams are a part of awakening; that a dream will come in the few seconds of awakening; or perhaps, as she herself had heard someone say, the awakening makes the dream. She clutched at the dream, trying to hold on to it as it faded; and then she heard a ship's foghorn from the Bay, lonely and haunting, and the dream was gone.

She reached for her bedside light and looked at her clock. Two o'clock in the morning, an odd hour. Usually she awakened at four and then lay in bed, struggling for more sleep but rarely achieving it. For a few moments she lay quiet, eyes closed, listening to the foghorn. Then it was joined by another, and then a third—was it a third, or perhaps the first horn answering? The Bay must be thick with fog, soaked in fog, and she could imagine a ship trying to slide through the Golden Gate. It could drop anchor and wait until the fog lifted, or at least until daylight; but recalling her father's years as a shipowner, she knew the price of a ship's day lost in passage.

She dropped into memories. It was not hard to remember her

father, his commanding voice, low and resonant, and still at times amazingly gentle.

Then true awakening came, hard and sharp, and her body responded to the sound of a footstep outside her bedroom door. Barbara stiffened, fear quickening her heartbeat, fear that she tried desperately to control, clenching her fists and easing herself. The old house was full of sounds, boards creaking, boards tightening in the cold air of night, and possibly she had heard no more than that.

She was not easily given to fear; her life had been too violent, too shredded. She had resisted the parade of salesmen who had tried to sell her this or that security system. "I have nothing worth stealing," was her response. She was sixty-nine years old, and she had consistently rejected the notion, offered by her friends, that she should keep a gun in the house.

The sound again, and this time she was certain. It was a footstep, no doubt about that. She leaped out of bed, threw on her robe, and reached for the telephone.

The bedroom door opened, and a voice said, "Lady, don't pick up that phone!" He had a gun in his hand, not pointed at her, but simply held as an exhibit. He was a tall, slender man, blue jeans and a black sweatshirt, a mask with eyeholes, and tightly curled hair cropped close. Dark skin showed beneath the mask. He wore sneakers.

Barbara was herself now. She heard his words against the lonely hooting of the foghorns. Her hands had stopped shaking. She pushed her white hair away from her face and tried to speak calmly.

"What do you want?"

"I'm a thief. What do you think I want? Open your robe."

"Why?"

"I want to see what you look like."

"I'm seventy years old."

"Shit, lady. Do what I tell you."

She opened her robe. Staring appraisingly at her body, visible through the thin nightgown, he nodded. "You're stacked," he said approvingly.

"I have AIDS," she said. She had thought of that invention recently, anticipating the possibility that she might someday face rape. But so had all her friends. The man grinned.

"What the hell, it's San Francisco," he said. "I'm not a rapist, I'm a thief."

"Thank God."

"Where do you keep it?"

"Keep what?"

"Jewels, gold, any damn thing I can sell."

"What's your name?" Barbara asked. She was in control of herself now, wrapping her robe around her and tying the sash.

"Oh, Jesus—lady, you're weird. Fuck my name. Let me get what I came for and get the hell out of here. I don't want to get mean with you. I don't want to shoot you, so don't push me."

"There's a television downstairs."

"I'm not breaking my back with any lousy television. You got any cash?"

Barbara sat down on the bed. She felt that it gave her an advantage, that it was a bit more difficult to shoot or beat someone sitting down—at the same time wondering where she got the notion.

"Suppose my husband came in. Would you shoot him? Would you shoot both of us?"

"You got no husband, lady. Don't fuck with me."

"How do you know?"

"I know."

"There's a hundred and twenty dollars or so in my bag."

"Where's the bag?"

She pointed to a chair. He found the bag, a large brown leather purse with a shoulder strap. Not taking his eyes off her, he picked up the bag and tossed it at her. "Empty it on the bed."

The contents spilled out on the comforter, a change purse, a wallet, an address book, keys, cards, lip gloss, handkerchief, gold pen, small mirror, comb, nail clipper, and a glassine folder of children's pictures.

"Empty the wallet and the purse." He walked to the other side of the bed and flicked on the other bedside lamp as Barbara took the bills out of the wallet and opened her change purse. There were five dollar bills and some change in the purse. He stuffed it into his pocket and counted the money from the wallet, one hundred and twenty-six dollars. Barbara started to rise.

"Don't move, lady. Just sit there."

"What else do you want?"

"Jewelry. Do I have to dump all the drawers, or are you going to tell me?"

"What I have is here in my bedside drawer." She sighed now.

"Pull it out and dump it on the bed."

"All right." Barbara reached over and pulled out the second drawer of her bedside table, and turned it over onto the comforter.

"Don't get euphoric," he said sharply. She looked at him curiously. He was separating the jewelry, four rings, one of them a small diamond set in gold, two plain gold bands, and the third, a large man's ring, heavy gold and carved to look like a leopard. He held it in front of him so that he could watch Barbara as he read the inscription on the inside. There was also a heavy gold linked bracelet, a neckband to match, and a brooch set with small diamonds and rubies.

"That ring was my father's," Barbara said. "I wish you would leave it. The other stuff is worth much more." She had never cared for jewelry, wore it only occasionally, and ignored the advice of her friends that she keep the pieces in a vault.

He weighed the ring in his hand.

"My mother gave it to him. It means something to me."

"It's worth a thousand, lady."

"I'll give you the thousand. You can have the jewelry. I won't call the cops, and I won't ever bear witness against you. Take it as a gift but leave me the ring."

"You are something, lady. Where's the thousand?"

"I don't keep cash in the house. I'll write you a check."

"Oh, lady, lady," he said, smiling. "You'll give me a check—written out to me, of course. And when I go to cash it, the cops will be waiting to pick me up. I wasn't born yesterday. This is the largest crock of shit I ever heard."

"If I give you my word, I'll keep it. You're no ordinary thief. You're an educated man. I don't give a damn about the other stuff, but I care about the ring."

"Lady, I'm a plain street nigger."

"But you use words like *euphoria*. You don't talk like a plain street thug. You try to, but it doesn't come off. If you were a professional, you'd grab the stuff and be out of here in minutes. You wouldn't be sitting here and talking to me. You'd beat me up and rape me and get out of here . . . You don't have to keep pointing that gun at me. I'm not going to resist you. But I want the ring. There's a small leather box on my dressing table, and there's a string of pearls in it that's worth more than five thousand dollars—a lot more than the ring."

The black man stared at her for a long moment. Then he went to the dressing table, opened the leather box, and took out the pearls. The necklace was twenty-four inches long, matched natural pearls, a gift from Carson Devron. In the two years since he died, she had never touched the pearls, never worn them. Two years was not long enough for her to accept the fact that Carson was dead, and she shunned anything that brought it home to her. She had intended to give the pearls to Sam's wife, Mary Lou, or perhaps to Mary Lou's daughter when she was a few years older.

The black man was looking at the pearls, holding the necklace up to the light. "What else did you forget to show me?"

"Nothing else. As a matter of fact, I haven't thought about the pearls for months."

"I don't know shit about pearls."

"Suppose you stop trying to talk like a thug," Barbara said softly. "Why don't you take the pearls and the other stuff and go—and leave me the ring, please. Suppose there's an alarm somewhere in the house?"

"There isn't. I looked around downstairs. And the fog's as thick as glue. Nobody's coming."

"The pearls are valuable, believe me. What college did you go to?"

He was taken aback, off guard; she could see his eyes narrowing through the holes in his mask. "You don't want to know."

"But I do."

"Why? So you can call the cops the moment I leave and tell them to look up every nigger that graduated from—oh, shit, lady, keep the goddamn ring!" He stuffed the jewelry into his pockets and said, "Stand up and turn around."

"Are you going to tie me up? It's not necessary. I'm not going to call the police."

"Sure." He walked around the bed and tore the telephone cord out of the wall and crushed the connecting tab under his foot.

As he turned to the door, Barbara said, "One question, please. Why?"

"Why I'm a thief? All right, lady. I'm a civil engineer. For a year after I graduated, I washed dishes and cleaned toilets. This is easier. Four years of engineering training, and I can pick locks and neutralize alarm systems. Most crooks have the brains of a maggot, so the competition's not heavy. I knew you were alone because I know the story of you and your father. Who doesn't in this town?...Don't go outside and start screaming. The fog's as thick as shit, and maybe you'll meet up with one of the bad guys."

"I don't scream," Barbara said. "How did you get in?"

"I told you, I picked the lock. You don't impress me, lady. You liberal do-gooders give me a pain in the ass. It's burning out there, and you sit here with your fuckin' jewels. So thank you for nothing."

Then he left, and a few moments later she heard the downstairs door slam. She was dog-weary and a little sick inside, her pulse hammering. Thank God he had not tied her up! She thought of going downstairs and seeing whether he had disabled all of her telephones, but then she decided that it didn't matter and she truly didn't care. All she desired right now was to get into bed, turn off the lights, and pull the covers up to her chin. Anything else could wait until tomorrow.

SHE WAS TOO TIRED TO SLEEP, too tired to let go of her churning thoughts. Was she sane, or was she acting out the last thing he had said—"It's burning out there and you sit here with your fuckin' jewels"? He had walked off with the money and at least a hundred thousand dollars' worth of jewelry. Did she care or didn't she care? Long ago, half a century ago, she had taken an inheritance of fourteen million dollars and turned it into a trust, coddling herself with the virtue of what is right and what is wrong. Her grandfather had died, and the fourteen million was stuck in her grandfather's bank, left to her in his will.

Why am I thinking of that? I am an old woman of seventy, and I have just been robbed by a black civil engineer, and I am hiding under a comforter. Who was it that said, "Successful and fortunate crime is called virtue"? Was it Seneca? Who was Seneca? I've forgotten that, too . . . I want to sleep and forget that this ever happened.

"But I have the ring," she said, almost in a whimper.

She would not think about the robbery anymore. But she did think about it; she lived it through again and again. She had experienced a great deal, but she had never been robbed before. She had a feeling of violation, of penetration to the uttermost soul of her being, of having been raped in a way that was worse and more devastating than any physical rape. She had been a liberal all her life; for almost half a century, there had been no good cause in San Francisco that Barbara Lavette had not been a part of—frequently as the leader. It began with the great waterfront strike of the thirties, and it went on from there, one thing after another until it became a commonplace to turn to Barbara Lavette— *So why the guilt?* she asked herself. It was not the jewels; she had been entirely truthful with herself and with the thief when she said she did not give a damn for the jewels. It was what he said and how he said it; and his leaving the ring. She recalled his gesture of contempt as he tossed the ring on the comforter. Any hockshop would have gladly paid a hundred dollars for the ring. What was gold selling for now—four hundred, five hundred dollars an ounce? She tried to recall the sum; she didn't read the financial pages, but the enormous rise in the price of gold was talked about all over the City.

On the other hand, her father's name, Dan Lavette, was inscribed on the inside of the ring, and when she recalled that and realized that it would be worthless to the thief unless melted down, and a conclusive piece of evidence if he were to be caught with the ring in his possession, she was at last able to relax. "Let virtue be what it is," she said to herself, smiling forlornly for the first time since the night began.

She must have dozed after that, and she awakened to the vague morning light. She left the bed and looked out of the window. Green Street tilted down Russian Hill to the Embarcadero, and from her window Barbara could see the last wisps of fog curling before the wind and drifting across the Bay. It was a beautiful sunny day, and for all that she had had so little sleep, she felt renewed and refreshed.

She showered, pulled on a pair of gray slacks and a cashmere sweater, and went downstairs. Nothing appeared to be disturbed, except that the drawers in her desk were partially drawn and the clay jars in which she kept sugar and flour were upended and dumped on the kitchen table. He must have been careful, since she had heard no sound until his footsteps on the creaking stairs awakened her. The phone plugs had been pulled out of the wall and broken, so she was still without a telephone. Somewhere she had an extra phone wire, but that could wait until she had cleaned up the kitchen table and had breakfast.

She had regained her composure, and that pleased her, but the cleaning of the kitchen table and the precise, orderly way she went about boiling two eggs and preparing a bowl of dry cereal made her acknowledge to herself that she was putting off the telephone call. In many ways Barbara was a precise and orderly person, but this time she was purposely slow and deliberate, giving her additional time to consider the question. She had heard that little that was stolen was recovered, and she had also heard that many people preferred to simply let it go and claim the insurance; but to claim the insurance, the theft must be reported to the police, and there was the rub. *Do I or do I not want to report this to the police?* She had told the thief and she had told herself that she didn't give a damn about the jewelry, but the diamond and ruby brooch had been a gift from Carson. Was it callous—or could a lifeless thing have meaning? Why did she plead with the thief to let her keep her father's ring? Why was she so hungry, buttering a third slice of toast and chewing it slowly and savoring each bite of it? Was this indifference? Carson had been her husband, and after she had divorced him, he had been her lover and protector, and this very morning, providing she could get her head together, she would begin to work on the final chapter of her new book, the story of her time with Carson and his death. It was to be published as fiction, and originally she had planned that when the manuscript was finished, she would change the names; but for the last eight months she had evoked Carson daily, reexamining her relationship with him, and had come to the conclusion that she would publish it as she wrote it, and let come what might. And yet the most precious gift

of jewelry that he had given her was gone. When she had offered
to buy the ring from the thief, he had derided her—and still she
could tell herself that she would keep her word, although by now
she realized how ridiculous her proposal was.

"It's burning outside, and you sit here with your fuckin' jewels!"

No, no, no! exploded inside of her. *I am not a racist! I did not
make slavery! I paid my dues. Who are you to judge me? What do
you know of me?*

Angrily she rummaged through her tool drawer, found a spare
telephone cord, and managed to plug it in. She looked at her watch;
it was seven-thirty. She sat staring at the telephone and brooding,
and then she looked at her watch again and it was seven forty-five.
She went into the bathroom, glanced at the mirror, and then brushed
her thick white hair. Her dearest friend, Eloise, had pleaded with
her to dye it the rich honey color it had once been, but after Carson
died she had become indifferent to her looks. Then she went back
to the chair by the telephone, an ancient green velvet upholstered
Victorian chair that she had inherited from old Sam Goldberg, her
father's lawyer and, after Dan's death, her surrogate father. Evidently the chair finally brought her to a decision, and she picked up
the telephone and called her own lawyer, Abner Berman.

"Do you know what time it is?" he demanded sleepily.

"It's a time when honest men are on their way to work."

"Barbara?"

"Yes. And I have a problem. It's a short walk to my house,
and I have a problem."

"What kind of problem?" he wanted to know. "You always
have a problem."

"This is a different kind."

"You always have a different kind. Come to my office in an
hour and bring your problem with you."

"No. I can't talk to you in your office. You're too rich and successful, and the walk will do you good. I have fresh-brewed coffee, and I'll give you toast and eggs."

"Barbara!"

"For two hundred dollars an hour, you can afford to come here."

"I don't charge for house calls. I'll be there in an hour, and just coffee. I'm trying to lose weight since Reda left me."

SO REDA HAD LEFT HIM! Abner was a corpulent, good-natured man of fifty or so, and they had been married for twenty years, and he announced this offhandedly at the end of a sentence, and then hung up before she could question him. No more *until death do us part*; it was all over the place.

Until death do us part was her own curse, and every man she had loved was dead. Well, she had an hour before he'd be there, and she might as well put it to use. But when she sat down at her desk she could not escape the night, and instead of writing she found herself not only reliving the night but probing through her own past.

At nine o'clock the doorbell sounded, and when she opened the door, it was not to Abner but to two men, one stocky and mustached, the other thin and tall. They showed her their open wallets and badges before they announced themselves:

"Inspector Meyer," the stocky man said. "This is Inspector Phelps. Can we come in?"

She pulled herself together and nodded. "Of course. Come in and sit down. You'll excuse me for a moment." Then she ran upstairs and into her bedroom, and when she picked up the telephone, she realized that it was not working, that the connection had been ground under the thief's heel. "Oh, Abner, Abner," she whispered, "for once get yourself over here on time." And then, as she closed the bedroom door behind her, she heard the doorbell ring. *Abner.*

It has to be Abner. She called out, "I'll get it!" And then down the stairs as if her life depended on it, and still with no clear idea of what she would do.

As she went to the door she saw, out of the corner of her eye, the two detectives handling the broken telephone line in her living room. *Fool, fool, fool,* she thought. *Why didn't I get rid of that one?*

She opened the door, flipped the latch, and closed the door behind her, whispering to Abner, who stood on her small porch, "There are two detectives inside. No time for questions, Abner. Just go along with me, please."

"Who have you killed?"

"Abner, shut up. Just go along with me." Then she opened the door and followed Abner into the house, trying to recall the policemen's names: "Inspector Meyer, isn't it? And Inspector—"

"Phelps. I'm Phelps." He still held the telephone cord in his hand.

"This is my friend Abner Berman, and my lawyer," Barbara said, smiling as if it were the most normal thing in the world to have her lawyer at her house at just past nine in the morning.

"Your lawyer?" the Inspector asked.

"His wife just left him. He comes for coffee and breakfast. Would you like some coffee?" she asked, feeling utterly ridiculous. Abner was watching her, puzzled.

"No thank you, Ms. Lavette."

So they knew who she was; of course they would, her name was on the door. She still used her maiden name.

"There was a robbery last night, Ms. Lavette," he went on. "We caught the thief this morning, down on Fisherman's Wharf."

"Really?" Barbara said.

"He had his loot on him." He paused. Abner was studying her, his brow knitted. "Were you robbed last night?" the inspector went on.

Barbara hesitated a long moment, and then she replied. "No."

"Is she a complainant?" Abner put in. "Did she call the police and report a theft?"

"No," Meyer said.

"Then why are you questioning her? Was the house broken into?"

"Not as far as we know. But this?" Phelps exhibited the broken telephone plug.

"It happens." Abner shrugged. "She said she wasn't robbed. That's it."

"Not quite." He reached into his pocket and took out the brooch and held it out for her to see. "Is this yours?" When Barbara did not answer, he said, "We spoke to Swinburn this morning, got him out of bed. Our jewelry expert said that only Swinburn carries this kind of stuff. When we described the brooch, Swinburn remembered it. It was purchased by Carson Devron three years ago, for sixty-five thousand dollars. You don't forget that kind of a buy. Your relationship with Devron, if you will forgive me, was all over the scandal sheets, so I'm not prying. Whether Devron gave it to you or his wife, I don't know, but we will find out when we check the insurance companies. The thief we caught is a smooth and smart-ass operator with a record. He did two years for manslaughter. His name is Robert Jones, and he's not your usual kind of crook, so all this makes me wonder. I'm going to ask you once more, is this your brooch?"

"She doesn't have to answer that—or anything," Abner said sharply. "She's not a complainant, and I think she's had enough for this morning. I suggest you leave."

Phelps was still staring at the telephone plug. The inspector nodded. "Come on," he said to Phelps. Barbara went to the front door with them, managed a weak smile, and closed the door behind them. Then she returned to the living room, looked wearily at Abner, and flopped into an easy chair.

"How wondrous are the doings of men—and women," Abner

said. "I need coffee and breakfast, so get your ass out of that chair, Ms. Lavette. I have to call my office, because we're going to have a good long talk. Is there a phone here that works?"

"In my study." Barbara sighed.

"Thank you." He went into her study and she went into the kitchen and made toast and cracked eggs. Her hands were shaking. When Abner joined her in the kitchen, she asked him whether he wanted bacon.

"I'm off bacon. I'm going to lose weight. No, the hell with it, give me bacon. Today I need it. I'm also off cigarettes, but not this morning. Do you have any cigarettes?"

"I don't use them. I keep some in a box on the coffee table— in the living room."

"I'll get them."

She put the bacon in a frying pan, trying not to think, concentrating on the sizzling bacon. Abner returned.

"Match?"

She handed him a match. He lit the cigarette and sucked deeply. "Ah, small blessings," he said appreciatively.

"Why did Reda leave?" she asked Abner.

"You know why she left. It's been coming on for ten years. I smoke, I eat too much, I'm fat, I'm a pain in the ass. She's still beautiful. She had to leave before it was too late to start all over again. So the other day she picked up and left . . . The hell with that. Let's talk about you."

"Yes, about me. Abner, what's going to happen to me?" She put the bacon and eggs on his plate. "Shall I butter the toast?"

"Barbara, for heaven's sake!"

"Yes, yes, of course. But I am so troubled, I'm so troubled, Abner. What's going to happen to me?"

"I won't have the foggiest notion until you tell me what you've done." He pulled out a chair for her. "Here. Sit down, and then tell me exactly what this crazy thing is about."

As completely as she could, she told him what had happened during the night.

"Why didn't you call the police?"

She thought about that for a while before she replied. "I guess I couldn't send a man to prison—not that man. I didn't know he was a murderer."

"We don't know that he's a murderer. Manslaughter is not murder."

"Then what is it?"

"It could be any number of things. Two men have a fight. One of them dies. It could be self-defense, but not today with a black man. Not here. It could be accidental. Did he intend to kill? Two boxers are in a ring. One of them dies. That's manslaughter, but there won't be any indictment. If they gave him only two years, then there was no intent to kill. I don't know, but I'll find out. Today you lied to the police. Why? You recognized the brooch. Carson gave it to you, didn't he?"

"Yes. But I told you I made a deal with the man—if he gave me Dad's ring, he could keep the rest."

"That was no deal. He had a gun on you."

"Yes. But it wasn't the gun." The gun was not a part of it.

"Was it his college degree, his waiting tables, his cleaning toilets? Is that it? You can't be that naive—not even you, Barbara." Through a mouthful of eggs and bacon, he demanded, "Then why did you call me? The cops hadn't come yet?"

"I was frightened. I didn't know what would happen to me if I didn't report the robbery. I still don't know."

"Do you want my best advice as your lawyer and friend?"

"Of course."

"Then when I finish breakfast, we'll both go downtown, and we'll explain that you were too traumatized by the robbery to respond properly, and then you'll identify the jewels and they'll show you a lineup and you'll pick him out, and that makes their case and it's over. We want to finish it before the media gets hold of it."

Barbara shook her head. "No, Abner, I can't do that. I will not be witness to sending a man to prison. I've been in prison"—remembering the six months she had served in a federal prison in Long Beach. That was long ago, in the forties, but the memory of what had happened was vivid and ugly. She had been one of the organizing members of a committee that had purchased an old convent in Toulouse and fitted it out as a hospital to help the surviving soldiers of Republican Spain and their families. She had given a great deal of money to that cause, and when she was called before the House Committee on Un-American Activities and told to give the names of people who had supported their work, she refused. The result was a citation for contempt of Congress, and then a trial and a sentence to six months in prison. Those six months were burned in her memory.

"I can't," she said to Abner. "I have to live with myself—for whatever time I have left. I'm an old woman. I can't wipe out the life that I lived. I can't bear witness against this man, Jones. I made an agreement with him. I gave him the jewels and he gave me my father's ring. I told him I would not bear witness against him."

"He gave you the ring!" Abner snorted. "Barbara, the ring was yours. He stole your jewelry. How much? A hundred thousand dollars' worth? God almighty—'he gave you the ring'!"

"Don't argue with me, Abner. Just tell me what I must do and what will happen to me. I'm not brave. I'm more frightened than you can imagine."

"Well, to begin, you'll be aiding and abetting a felon—which makes you equally guilty."

"If I gave him the jewelry? Why is that a crime? Can't I give away anything that is mine? How can they prove otherwise?"

"How did he get in the house?"

"He picked the lock," Barbara said. "It's an old lock, the same lock that Sam Goldberg had on the door. When I rebuilt the house after the fire, I kept as much of the old house as I could. The lock isn't hard to pick."

"It's still breaking and entering. Even if the door was open, it's breaking and entering with intent to steal."

"But if I insist that I gave him the jewels?"

"That's perjury. For heaven's sake, Barbara, can you toss away a hundred thousand dollars' worth of jewelry like that? Are you that rich?"

"The jewels meant nothing to me. I kept them in a drawer. There was a linked gold chain I wore, but nothing else. Yes, I wore the pearls once or twice, but nothing else. I wore the brooch only once. If I have to trade it for a man's freedom, fine. Don't try to understand me, Abner. Just be my good friend and my lawyer, and help me get through this."

"You're serious, aren't you?" Abner said softly, a touch of awe in his voice.

"Deadly serious."

"And I'm compounding a felony. Reda walks out on me, and her last words are, 'You ain't worth shit.' That's a hell of a thing to tell a man who can't get it up and who stops trying, and who's too fat for anyone else to look at twice."

"Abner, Abner," she said gently, "you're one of the best men I know. Reda was probably in a rage, and she didn't care what she was saying. We'll talk about that another time. Right now you're my lawyer, and I'm your client."

He nodded.

"Do you want another cup of coffee?"

"Yes."

She poured coffee, sat across the corner of the table, so that she could reach out and put her hand on his; and he was thinking what a fine figure of a woman she still was, seventy and all, tall and slender, her gray eyes clear and bright; and he wondered why he had never found someone like Barbara, and what his life might have been if he had. He sipped the coffee, and asked her whether another cigarette would trouble her.

"I'll get them." She brought the box with her. "They're old and dry."

He lit up and drew deeply. "OK, let's see what we can do. Sometime today, a policeman will be here and ask you to come downtown for a lineup. Go with him. A little irritation on your part, but don't push it. They'll come backed up with a subpoena, but don't make them use it. You're quixotic to begin with, and they probably think you're a nut of some kind. Of course you know what a lineup is?"

"I go to the movies, Abner. I even watch television."

"You say he wore a mask? Did he ever take it off?"

"No."

"Then you have the best excuse in the world for not picking him out. Although that may not wash. You don't give a hundred thousand to a masked man. Could you recognize him, in spite of the mask?"

"I think so."

"How old, would you guess?"

"Thirty perhaps. No older."

"Then recognize him if you can, if you're sure."

"Wouldn't they have found the mask on him?" Barbara asked.

"Not if he's as smart as you say he is. He'd ditch the mask and the lock pick the moment he got out of here, so I wouldn't even mention the mask. By the way, make the recognition easy. I'll be with you, so you don't have to answer any questions. Of course, there's the possibility that he confessed—"

"No, he wouldn't."

"You know a lot about a man you never met before. Well, we'll hope. I'll find out who is defending him, and I'll tell the story the way you want. That doesn't implicate his lawyer. He only knows what I tell him."

"Can you do that?"

"Sure. I can do it without leaving the house. Can you find another telephone cord? I have calls to make."

"I think so. What happens then?"

"The San Francisco cops are not stupid, and this will piss them off no end. They don't like to be diddled. They press for a grand jury, and then you're under oath. If you stick to your story and they can disprove it—then it's perjury. This is very dangerous, Barbara. God help me, I don't know why you're insisting on this. You have no obligation to this crook. You didn't ask to be robbed. You know, the newspapers will be full of this. You're not nobody; you're Barbara Lavette. It means television and all that goes with it, and everyone in town, everyone who knows you, will be talking about it. If this were simply grand theft, the cops would write it off and let the insurance company take the heat, but this is kinky."

"I'm not kinky, Abner. I've lived my life this way, and I'm going to continue to live it this way."

"What else did he take?"

"Some gold bands and a string of pearls—also from Carson. I told Carson that I didn't want jewelry from him, I was not selling my love. What exists of Carson is inside of me, not in some fancy jewelry."

"What were the pearls worth?"

"I don't know. He bought them in Japan."

"Do you know what they were insured for?"

She tried to recall it. "I have the policy somewhere—I think it was ten thousand dollars."

"It gets worse." He sighed. "All right. We'll take this step by step. You talk about this to no one, no one, do you understand—not your family, not your son, no one. Will you agree?"

"I'll be careful," she said.

The telephone rang, and Abner moved quickly to answer it, waving her back. "I'll take it," he said sharply.

She followed him into her study. "This is her attorney," she heard him say. "Abner Berman." He listened and then he said, "You don't have to send a car. I'll bring her down—yes, this morning. Yes, she understands the nature of a lineup." He replaced the phone. "They're being nice. We'll drive down in your car. I don't want to make them wait too long."

IT HAD NEVER OCCURRED TO ABNER BERMAN that he was fat because he desired to be fat, that since childhood he had worn fat as armor, a sort of clown suit that hid a hard-nosed attorney. Barbara knew this, and when he accepted her position and determined to back it up, she felt relieved. On the other hand, Abner had known her for years, had adored her silently, and was less surprised than he pretended to be by her story.

On the drive down to police headquarters Barbara said little, and Abner occupied his mind with how he would handle something he had never handled before and avoid being disbarred in the process. He was not a criminal lawyer. Here was a common robbery that very shortly would be the talk of San Francisco. In spite of his unwillingness to go along with her idealistic and unreasonable nonsense, he had assented to her decision and he would stay with it.

Barbara, reviewing what had happened, had a feeling of sickness. She was digging a hole in the ground from which there might be no escape. Of course Abner found it unreasonable; who would find it reasonable? Blacks were sent to prison every day; it was something she could not influence or change, so why did she persist? If she could not answer that question herself, how could she spell it out to anyone else?

When they arrived at the Hall of Justice, Inspector Meyer was waiting for them, smoking an old black pipe and apparently enjoying the sunlight. He greeted them with a friendly nod. "It's taken some time to put it together and find some look-alikes. If Ms. Lavette will wait in my office, I'll try to make her comfortable. It won't be more than a few minutes."

"Who's representing your guy?"

"Lefkowitz. Do you know him? The perp didn't ask for a public defender. This is one interesting crook. Lefkowitz doesn't come cheap."

Barbara was about to say something, but a glance from Abner silenced her. "You're making a mountain out of a molehill," Abner said. "You know, Inspector, you could drop this and attend to the bad guys. Ms. Lavette makes no complaint. You've got him with a gun, and that should do it—that and the burglar tools. As for my client, you know the Lavette story as well as I do. They're what they are."

"Crazy? Strange? What am I supposed to say, Mr. Berman? Anyway, I can't put this back in the box. Burglar tools? All he had were his keys and a metal toothpick, and his gun, a Mauser, was put together out of plastic, one of those kid toys."

"That still comes within the law."

"With Lefkowitz defending him? Come on. Anyway, it's too late. Some sneak inside whispered it to the *Chronicle*. If the TV crews knew you were here, they'd be all over the place. Let's go inside."

Barbara's heart sank. She could spell out exactly what her son, Samuel, would say; she could hear the words: not *How you are going to explain this farce, Mother,* but *How am I going to explain it? You're not a loose gun, you're not Rambo*—would he say *Rambo?* No, that was unfair. *You're not Albert Schweitzer in the African jungle. You're a woman in your seventies in San Francisco. Do you know what my colleagues will think? That it's genetic. I will tell them it's Joan of Arc—reborn. I am chief surgeon in a normal hospital where they heal sick people*—

Oh, enough! she told herself. *You don't know what he will say or what anyone will say.*

Lefkowitz was sprawled in the single armchair in Meyer's office, smoking a cigar. Meyer had tapped his pipe outside, and now he snapped, "You don't smoke in my office, Mr. Lefkowitz!"

"The place certainly smells of smoke. That's why I took the liberty. Let me apologize. Can I hold it? It's an eight-dollar cigar. I hate to crush it." He was a small man, small and thin with a ferret face and a low melodious voice. He looked inquiringly at Abner.

"Abner Berman. I think we met once or twice."

"This isn't your style, Mr. Lefkowitz," the inspector said.

"No, indeed. My style, as you call it, is corporate thieves. This is pro bono. Your Mr. Jones intrigues me—college graduate, civil engineer, and now accused." He turned to Barbara. "Ms. Lavette? The complainant? I've heard a good deal about you, Ms. Lavette, and I'm honored to meet you."

"She's not a complainant," Abner said. "She's here for the lineup."

"Oh? She's not a complainant?"

"Nothing was stolen from her."

"Gracious," Lefkowitz said softly. "She's not a complainant, so why are we wasting time? I'm a busy man."

"Now, hold on, Mr. Berman. I thought we were over that nonsense. She agreed to come to the lineup," the inspector said.

"Yes, of course. She's a citizen answering the request of the police."

"And what is she going to do?"

"Oh, she'll identify the man who was with her last night—if she can, of course."

"But she's not a complainant?" Lefkowitz asked.

"As I said."

"How interesting, how very interesting," he said gently. "It makes me wonder. A hundred thousand dollars' worth of jewels are enough to make anyone wonder a bit. A generous woman!"

"Too generous!" the inspector snapped.

Lefkowitz was looking at the pictures on Meyer's desk. "Your children? Beautiful children, if I may say so. The little girl with the blond hair—she must take after your wife."

The telephone on the inspector's desk rang. He picked it up, muttered something, and then said, "They're ready."

"Do you intend to go to the grand jury with this?"

"I damn well do."

"But with what, Inspector? No complainant, a toy gun that isn't even a water pistol, a metal toothpick—my word, I carry one myself."

Meyer scowled and let them out of the room. As they walked down the hall, the inspector asked Barbara, "Did he have a mask?"

"Did she say he had a mask?" Abner said crossly. "She didn't say so, so he didn't have a mask. Did he have a mask when you picked him up?"

Meyer gave no answer to that, and Abner said to Barbara, "All you have to do is identify him. That's all. Don't offer anything. Don't say anything."

"Where are the jewels?" Lefkowitz wanted to know.

"In our safe."

They went into a darkened room with a large plate-glass window. Through the window Barbara could see six men, all black, all tall, all slender. Yet there was no question in her mind as to who was the thief.

"It's a one-way glass," Meyer assured her.

The thief stood tall and easy, a slight smile on his lips. He had a long, lean face, high cheekbones, and close-cropped hair. She knew he couldn't see her, but he appeared to be looking directly at her, a quizzical expression on his face.

"The third man from the left," Barbara said.

Meyer picked up a phone and said, "Number three, step forward." And then to Barbara, "You're sure?"

She nodded, and then they left the room. "You don't need her anymore today?" Abner said to the inspector.

"She's not leaving town. She's still the witness."

"She's not leaving town," Abner agreed.

Once outside he said to Barbara, "Take your car home. Lock your door. Don't answer the telephone. Don't answer the door without looking through the peephole. No one goes in. Mr. Lefkowitz and I are going to have a cup of coffee and a short talk—and remember, you talk to no one—no phone, no door except me."

There was a newsstand on the corner, and Abner picked up a copy of a late edition. "Here you are, right on the front page. You know what—don't go home. We'll all go to my office, because my guess is that the TV chicken hawks are already at your house. How about that, Harry? I'll send out for a nice lunch, and you and me, we'll get to know each other, and Barbara can spend her time reading about herself."

THE LUNCH WAS VERY NICE INDEED, chicken salad, rolls, and a plate of varied pastry. Lefkowitz ate his salad, scorned the pastry, which Abner consumed, and prowled around Abner's ornate office—the Persian rug, the leather sofa, the French Louis-something desk, the tapestry-covered chairs, the paneled walls, the television in the oak cabinet, and the great window that looked out over the Bay. It was one of those sparkling days, the fog blown away and sails all over the water, making the most of the breeze and the sunlight, and to complete the picture, a white cruise boat on its way to Alaska.

"There's where you and I should be, Abner, playing rummy and on our way to Alaska. You ever been to Alaska?"

"I been to Alaska, Harry." They were on a first-name basis now.

Barbara was reading the paper and nibbling at her food. The headline read, "Lavette Heiress Claims She Gave a Hundred Thousand in Jewelry to a Thief." And the story went on to say:

> In as bizarre a jewel theft as San Francisco has seen in years, Barbara Lavette, heiress and philanthropist, claims she gave away $100 thousand worth of jewelry to a charming and well-educated thief. Or was he a thief?

> Last night Inspector James Meyer and Inspector Woodrow Phelps, patrolling in the heavy fog, saw a man on the Embarcadero throw something into the water as their car approached. When they got out of their car and walked toward him, he stood still and surrendered without resistance. . . .

And the last paragraph of the story went on to say:

> Was this a blackmail payoff, or was it a theft, or was it a unique part of Ms. Lavette's charitable career? We have not spoken to Ms. Lavette. Her telephone does not answer, and as far as this reporter can discover, she is nowhere to be found.

Abner said to Barbara, "Please make yourself comfortable, Barbara. Alice will switch the calls to me, and there's coffee and cold drinks in the cupboard. Mr. Lefkowitz and I will be in the boardroom. Turn on the TV, and see whether the chicken hawks have arrived at Green Street yet."

In the boardroom, sitting at a long table, Lefkowitz and Abner faced each other. "Can I smoke, Abner?"

"Certainly." He slid a large ashtray down the table, and

Lefkowitz took out the cigar he had been smoking in the inspector's office.

"You're not going to smoke that damn thing?"

"Why not? These things cost me eight dollars each."

"You can afford it."

"Yes and no. What do you do in a year, Abner?"

"Two hundred thousand, if things break right. Now I'm getting divorced."

"You have my sympathy."

"And is it the truth, that this is pro bono?"

"That's right. I'm hard but I'm not mean. I'll fight a corporation to the death, but if I win a judgment, it's not out of people, and the company can afford it. This black kid, Jones, is a phenomenon. He comes out of the worst street in Oakland, no father, one of five kids and a remarkable mother, puts himself through engineering school—fourteen hours a day, waiting tables and working in the school kitchen, comes out a qualified civil engineer. Then a private guard at the school insults him, calls him a stinking nigger, slaps him around, and Jones blows it and lays the guard out. The guard goes down, cracks his skull on the concrete, and becomes very dead. They arrest Jones—this is down in Southern Cal—and they charge him with murder one. I read it in the papers, so I decide to do my soul some good, providing I have one, and I get the charge reduced to manslaughter, and I get him off with two years. Are you Jewish, Berman?"

"No, I'm afraid not."

"Name sounds like it," Lefkowitz said.

"My grandfather was a German. Came out here in the eighteen-eighties on a freighter and jumped ship."

"A lot of good men did. Well, there's an old Jewish legend, out of the Talmud, I suppose, called the legend of the Lamed Vav. It holds that in all the world, there must be thirty-six good and righteous men. The existence of the world depends on them, but no one of the Lamed Vav ever knows that he or she is one of them. That's not letting the right hand know what the left hand does, or something of the sort. I don't volunteer myself, but when I do a decent thing, which is not so often—ah, what the hell!"

"And what is all this Talmudic hearsay leading up to, if I may ask, Harry?"

"They don't have to be Jewish. Maybe your Lavette lady— well, I hear she refuses to press charges, insists that she gave the jewels to Jones. I can understand that. I remember when she went to prison for contempt of Congress, some business about refusing to name names in a hospital they ran in Toulouse—so she knows a lot more than most people do, and I don't find what she's doing so strange. She has plenty of money, and I imagine the jewelry doesn't mean much, as up against a man's life. If she were a complainant, Jones would go down for fifteen years. This way, they got nothing. The talk about a grand jury is puffery. There's nothing they can charge him with..." His low, gentle voice trailed away.

"Has Jones said anything?" Abner asked.

"Not a word. He called me, woke me up. I told him to keep his mouth shut. I'm going to demand his release, and I'll get it if Barbara Lavette sticks to her story. On the other hand, you didn't drag me in here to listen to Jewish *Bubeh meises*. That's Yiddish for 'stories.' "

"No, I didn't. You're good, Harry. Do you ever raise your voice in court?"

"Sometimes. Not often. Juries don't like a man who bullies a witness."

"I agree with you: Jones will walk. You know what I want."

"The jewels," Lefkowitz said.

"That's the deal—one hundred thousand dollars' worth of jewels."

"Abner, I spoke to him. He's ready to return the jewelry. But look at it another way. The whole town knows Barbara's story. She

can't wear that stuff he took. On the other hand, I can sell them
for Jones at top price. It gives him a life, a chance. He can start his
own firm. Someday he'll pay her back. This guy is something. Give
him a chance. Let it stand."

"And how much of it is your fee?"

"I don't deserve that, Abner. I told you it was pro bono. That's
it. I don't get a cent."

"Then I apologize," Abner said, "and I think I believe you,
but his repaying her is an article of faith. I don't buy articles of
faith, and a hundred grand is a lot of money. She's given him fifteen
years of life, and that's a pretty damn good gift."

"Abner, listen to me. Tomorrow she'll be all over the press
and the TV. The liberals will call her a saint. The conservatives
will damn her for aiding and abetting. Nobody will buy the story
that she gave him the jewels. The presumption will be that she was
robbed and that she refuses to send a man to jail. And more im-
portantly, Inspector Meyer, who is totally pissed off by what she is
doing, will press for a grand jury, and the whole question of perjury
will come up. You don't want to put her on the stand."

Abner thought about it for a few moments. There was a lot
of truth in what Lefkowitz said. Lefkowitz smoked his cigar and
studied Abner, and finally Abner said, "Let's leave it up to her."

"Agreed."

They returned to Abner's office. Barbara had turned on the
television. An interview show was interrupted by an announcer who
said, "This is a breaking story. Last night the police arrested an
alleged thief who had in his possession jewelry to the value of one
hundred thousand dollars. The police have ascertained to their satisfaction that the jewelry belonged to Barbara Lavette, daughter of
Dan Lavette, and three years ago candidate for Congress on the
Democratic ticket. Ms. Lavette denies that the jewelry was stolen,
insisting that it was a gift to the alleged thief. We will follow up on
this story on the six o'clock news. Stay tuned."

"Such is fame," Barbara remarked. "Who was it said that fame is the accumulation of evil deeds?"

"Don't put yourself down, Ms. Lavette," Lefkowitz said. "This is salvation, not perjury."

"I wonder. Have you gentlemen settled your difficulties?"

"Just about," Abner replied without enthusiasm. "We don't think there'll be any prosecution of Jones. Harry here wants him to keep the jewelry. I want him to return it to you. We've decided to let you make the choice."

"Can he keep it?" Barbara asked, taken somewhat aback.

"You might have to say under oath that you gave it to him."

"I did."

"My position, Ms. Lavette," Lefkowitz put in, "is that this would give him a new life."

"How much would you want as your fee?"

"Nothing. This is pro bono."

"Then I don't see how we can change anything. I gave him the jewelry. I don't want it back."

"Barbara—," Abner began.

"No, Abner. I don't want to discuss this, and I won't change my mind. It's a beautiful day outside. I want to walk home. I'm pleased that the man isn't going to prison. It's over."

Road 3 *Signs*

DURING THE PAST SIX MONTHS, perhaps half a dozen times, Philip Carter, minister of the First Unitarian Society on Franklin Street, had noticed a tall white-haired woman at the Sunday service. He knew all the members of the congregation, but there were always a few new faces, friends of members and often people who came of their own accord, some out of need and some out of simple curiosity; and when it was possible, he tried to say a few words to the newcomers. But this particular woman usually arrived only minutes before the service began. She would take one of the rearmost seats, and she would leave as soon as the service concluded.

He asked Reba Guthri about her. Reba was the assistant pastor, fiftyish, stout, encyclopedic in her knowledge of the congregation, and Carter's barrier against total confusion.

"Have you ever spoken to her, Reba?"

"Once, yes. No desire to become a member; curious-spectator species. I thought you would recognize her."

"Should I?"

"She's rather notorious—no, no, that's the wrong word. I

don't know what the right word is. She's one of a kind. Her name's Barbara Lavette. As a matter of fact, she was headlines last week, but of course you don't read the interesting stuff. You recognize the name?"

"Dan Lavette's daughter?"

"The same. I made a very gentle pitch to her."

"And what did she say?"

"Perhaps—someday."

"Interesting," Carter said. "When we have time, you must tell me about her."

"We never have time," Reba Guthri said, and turned to the small circle around her and their endless questions and needs.

But Carter found his own answers. Two Sundays later the tall white-haired woman remained standing at one side of the entryway until most of the congregation had drifted away. Then she approached him and said, "Could I talk to you, Mr. Carter—somewhere private?"

"Yes, certainly. Come into my office." He led her into a rather plain book-lined room: a desk, some chairs, and a few portraits and paintings on the walls.

"My name is Barbara Lavette."

He nodded and smiled slightly. She appeared to be ill at ease, and he wondered what he might do to relax her. "Won't you sit down, please?"—pointing to a chair facing his desk. He was a tall, lean man, long faced, with iron gray hair and dark eyes.

"I've been here half a dozen times," Barbara said. "I'm not a Unitarian—well, in terms of religion, I don't know exactly what I am. I was baptized at Grace Church, but I haven't been there for years." She shook her head and smiled. "I must admit that I came here first on a Sunday when it was raining cats and dogs, and I ducked inside and sat down in the last row. I liked what I heard, and I came back several times. I guess you noticed."

He nodded. "Yes, I noticed. As a matter of fact, I asked Reba

Guthri about you. She's my assistant, and she knows everything about everybody, more or less. She holds that I never read the interesting parts of the *Chronicle*. We keep a file of the paper, so I went back and read the story."

Relieved that she wouldn't have to go through the details, Barbara said somewhat apologetically, "I know you don't have anything in the way of confession, but I have to talk to someone about it—and I know I have no right to come and beard you about this—"

"You have every right. Please."

"Thank you. I won't bore you with all the details. This is what was not in any of the stories."

"Would you like something to drink, Barbara? May I call you Barbara? No one here calls me Mr. Carter. I'm Phil to everyone."

"Certainly."

"I have coffee or Coke or plain water."

"I'll have water, if it's no trouble."

He rose from behind his desk and took a cup of water from the cooler. "Please go on."

"Well, as I said, this was not in the papers. The man—Robert Jones is his name—he's a black man, a college graduate and a civil engineer who hasn't worked at his trade since graduation for reasons that are more or less obvious—well, he turned to burglary. He picked the lock of my front door and woke me at two in the morning. No rape or any threat of rape. We talked. I told him where the jewelry was, in my bedside table."

She paused, and Carter said, "Why not in a vault?"

"I suppose I don't care enough about things," she replied, and Carter reflected that she certainly did care about clothes, dressed as she was in a longish pleated beige skirt and an ivory-colored cashmere sweater. "I always felt that if someone needed the jewelry badly enough to steal it, then let him have it or anything else in the house."

She paused again, and Carter waited.

"He said something."

"Yes?"

"I have to use his words. Please forgive me. He said, 'You liberal do-gooders give me a pain in the ass. It's burning out there, and you sit here with your fuckin' jewels. So thank you for nothing.' "

Carter did not react at all to this, and Barbara sighed. "I shouldn't have come here," she said. "I have no right to lay this on you."

"You have every right." She was silent for a long moment, and then Carter said, "But you didn't call the police." There was something in her gray eyes that Carter felt was searching him for what was inside of him.

"No. That's the crux of it. He took everything I had in the way of real jewelry, and that included a heavy gold signet ring. It had a sort of leopard carved on it, which was Pop's corporate seal, and his name was engraved inside the ring. It was left to me in my father's will. I told him—"

"Jones?"

"Yes, I told him that if he left me the ring, he could have the rest."

"You actually told him that?" Carter asked.

"Yes."

"Did he threaten you? Hurt you in any way?"

"No. He had a gun. At least, I thought it was a gun, but it was a plastic toy. You don't think very clearly under such circumstances."

"And the jewelry was actually worth more than a hundred thousand dollars, as the paper said?"

"I suppose so."

"And he left you the ring?"

"Yes. He flung it on my bed."

Carter was silent for a while, and Barbara started to rise. "No," Carter said. "Stay a bit. I think we have more to talk about."

"I'm taking up too much of your time."

"That's what my time is for. You're a rich woman, Barbara, and you can afford the gift—if that was your intent."

"I'm not that rich. My grandfather left me a great deal of money, but I put it into a foundation, and while I'm on the board, I can't use any of it for myself. I earn my own living, books, screenplays occasionally, and my newspaper and magazine work. My house on Green Street was a gift from a dear friend of my father. I live modestly, and I am not an idiot who has delusions that would lead me to give a hundred thousand dollars to a thief. I didn't call the police or make any charges because I could not live with sending a black man like this Jones to prison. I have been in prison, as I'm sure you know. I couldn't sleep or have a day of contentment knowing that I had taken fifteen years of a man's life. The jewels are not worth fifteen years of a human life. But I lied. He stole the jewels, that's the long and short of it. He whimpered that the only work he could find was washing dishes and cleaning toilets. For six months in prison I cleaned toilets!" Barbara's voice choked up. "And I damn well didn't whimper!" she managed, and then stood up to leave.

"Oh, sit down!" Carter said with some annoyance. "You wanted to talk, let's talk. You lied—everyone lies. Without lies, human existence would be intolerable. What troubles you: being a liberal, being decent, losing your jewels? What troubles you: letting down your defenses, talking to a stranger? Would I have surrendered a hundred thousand dollars for fifteen years of a man's life? I don't know; but what you did was an act of decency and morality, and that should end it. On the other hand, there is a hole in your thinking. *You* would not have taken fifteen years of his life if you had called the police. It was his act to steal the jewels, and his moral responsibility. But that doesn't lessen the decency of your action. So you lied. Have you never lied before? Tell me."

Her eyes brimming with tears, Barbara nodded. "I'm sorry, I cry very easily. I cry at animal pictures. Thank you. I have to go now." Carter handed her a tissue, and she dabbed at her eyes. "Thank you for your time, Mr. Carter." And with that, she fled from his office.

IT WAS STILL EARLY IN THE DAY, and she hadn't been to Highgate since the robbery. When Barbara got home she called Eloise, who was delighted. "Can you come for dinner? We're having someone you'll be pleased to meet."

"Who?" Barbara asked.

"No. Let that be a surprise."

Barbara changed into jeans, a pullover, and walking shoes, packed a dress and a pair of black pumps in a bag, and climbed into her Volvo for the drive to Napa. It was little more than an hour's drive, and she would be there by two, in time for a visit with Eloise before dinner. Thinking about her talk with Philip Carter, she felt a weight had dropped from her shoulders. It was not simply what he'd said, but the practical matter-of-fact manner of his approach to her problem. She had not been to Highgate since the theft, fearing the barrage of questions about the incident.

It was a beautiful July day, cool and crisp, with a clean wind blowing from the Pacific and small white cumulus clouds sailing across the sky; and here she was, sixty-nine, and hale and hearty and looking forward to being with people she loved. It was by no means the worst of all possible worlds.

Eloise, still round and pretty in her sixty-sixth year, was waiting for her. She had confessed to Barbara that she was tinting her blond hair. "Adam won't let me grow old." Now she embraced Barbara and admired her jeans. "I can't wear jeans. I'm too fat."

"You're not fat."

"I am, and I will not worship at this American altar of diet. You eat like a horse, Barbara, and you never gain an ounce."

"Thank you."

"Oh, my dear, you know what I mean. You're not dainty. I grew up with the curse of being dainty. 'Oh, what a dainty child! Oh, what a beautiful little dainty child!' I was wearing those damn Mary Janes until I was sixteen. No one ever called you dainty."

"That's true," Barbara admitted. "I was all long bones with a bony face and freckles."

"You should bless the bones. Everyone wants them. Good bones and all that nonsense. We'll put away your things, and then we'll walk and talk. Are you hungry?"

"After what you said?"

In the kitchen Cathrena was making tortillas, rolling the dough into little balls and then patting them out in the old manner.

"I offered to buy her a tortilla machine. She wouldn't have it."

"Because they are no good." Cathrena snorted. "Did God want tortillas to be made in a machine? How many for dinner, *señora?*"

Eloise counted on her fingers. "Eight, I think."

"You think, but you don't know. I cook for twelve."

"She always cooks for twelve," Eloise said as they went outside. "Put this on. The sun is strong today." She handed Barbara a wide-brimmed white straw that she had in her hand. "Now, what is all this about you making a gift of a hundred thousand in jewels to a black thief? I never knew you had a fortune in jewelry. You never wear jewelry."

"Just what you read in the papers. Who's coming to dinner?"

"You tell me the inside story of the great jewelry caper, and I'll tell you who's coming to dinner."

"Darling," Barbara assured her, "there is no inside story. I had a choice between sending a man to jail for fifteen years or insisting that I gave him the jewelry. That left me *no* choice in the matter."

"But why can't he give them back to you?"

"We'll discuss that another time. Meanwhile, let's walk. It's a glorious day. I want to breathe this air and look at the vines and count the grapes."

"Count the grapes, indeed."

"And who is the mysterious guest?" Barbara asked.

"First we'll go to the bottling plant. I have to ask Adam about dinner tonight. He's been in the bottling room all day—can you imagine, on a day like this? Last season, under the influence of Freddie, he agreed to buy a truckload of Sylvaner grapes—you know what Sylvaner is."

"I think I know—is it Franken Riesling? My dear, I didn't grow up with wines as you did."

"Forgive me, Barbara! But few people know what Sylvaner is. Adam has such prejudice against white wine—he keeps tasting and tasting. The wine is delicious, but he feels that it's humiliating to buy grapes from another grower. But we have to. The business is growing, and our acreage isn't."

THE WET CHILL OF THE BOTTLING ROOM made Barbara shiver. Adam kissed her and offered a glass of wine. "Taste it," he said moodily.

"I'm not a good judge of Riesling, Adam."

"Sensible, but taste it anyway."

The wine was very good, fragrant, with a delicate flavor, just dry enough to favor the appetite. Barbara nodded.

"About tonight and dinner, Adam," Eloise said firmly, "we must talk."

"All right, talk."

"Shall I ask Joe and Sally? It's not too late."

"Absolutely not! May Ling is a big girl—how old? She's thirty-six, isn't she?"

"Thirty-seven, poor child."

"What do you mean, 'poor child'? She's beautiful and old enough to handle anything. None of Sally's damn business."

"Adam, Sally's your sister."

"I know who Sally is. Let Harry and May Ling have this night to themselves."

"Whatever you say, sir," Eloise agreed, and then led Barbara out into the sunlight.

"What's all this mysterious business about Sally, and who is Harry?"

"Look at it," Eloise whispered. A butterfly whose wings were a splendid assortment of color had alighted on a vine. "Isn't it marvelous? They are coming back since we stopped spraying and introduced counter-culture. Is there anything so beautiful? And since when do you not know white wine? Every time we have dinner out, you order white wine."

"I met a remarkable man today who convinced me that small lies are entirely permissible. Who is Harry?"

"Freddie's lawyer."

"Come on."

"There's Candido," Eloise said. "He's dying to see you. The local Spanish rag devoted a whole page to Barbara Lavette and the thief. You are something in the Valley."

Candido was laying down the law to two men who were cultivating. He glanced up from his harangue and broke into a wide smile. "*Señora,*" he said with pleasure, "*buenas tardes, mi alegro de verla!*" Then he and Eloise engaged in an exchange in Spanish that amounted to his plea to be allowed to talk to Barbara for the sake of his wife. His wife lived on gossip.

"*Mañana, mañana,*" Eloise said.

"They work on Sunday?" Barbara asked as the women moved away.

"Only at this time of the year. But they have the morning off for church and all day Saturday. It's Adam's one bow to his being Jewish."

They walked on, moving almost instinctively toward the bower on the hillside.

"So Harry is Freddie's lawyer. What has that to do with Sally?"

"He wants to marry May Ling." With no response on Barbara's part, after a few moments Eloise asked, "Did you hear me?"

"Yes—of course, but my mind slipped, and I told myself that May Ling is dead, so how could she marry anyone? I'm getting old, I suppose."

"May Ling dead? Barbara!"

"No, no, but for just a moment, the name meant her grandmother. It's a tangled web, isn't it? May Ling—May Ling my niece is her namesake. The first May Ling was this wonderful Chinese lady, my dad's second wife. I don't think you ever met her, but I knew her very well. She was as delicate and as beautiful as some ancient ivory carving, and my brother Joe is their son. She was killed in the Hawaiian Islands—during Pearl Harbor. I don't think my dad ever got over it. She was the daughter of my father's business manager, Feng Wo, who was also an important Chinese scholar who translated the *Natural Way of Lao-tzu and Chuang-tzu*, which I have been rereading and trying to understand. You know, for the past six months or so I've been writing the history of the family, starting with my grandparents and with Dad's father and mother, who died in the earthquake—"

"Barbara, hold on, take a deep breath, you've lost me. I've been married to Adam for thirty-six years, and I still can't get the family relationships straight."

"Then you'll have to read my book. My grandparents on Dad's side were northern Italian, and Dad's grandfather was French, whereby the name Lavette. Adam's father was Jewish. Adam's mother, Clair, was raised by her father, who was a Protestant of some sort. His family name was Harvey, but she never knew who her mother was. My brother Joe is half Chinese, and he married Adam's sister, Sally; and so their daughter, May Ling, is part Chinese and part Jewish and part all sorts of other things—but you should know all that after all these years—"

"Enough!" Eloise cried.

"All right. Now tell me about this Harry, who is Freddie's lawyer and in love with May Ling."

"That was to be the surprise. His name is Harry Lefkowitz."

Barbara stared at her and asked slowly, "Did you say Harry Lefkowitz?"

"Yes."

"You're kidding."

"No. Not at all. That was the surprise. You're surprised."

"I certainly am."

"Why? A little new blood wouldn't hurt this family."

"How long has this been going on?" Barbara asked.

"Almost a year."

Barbara dropped onto the bench and shook her head dumbly. "He never said a word."

"He's a lawyer. What would you expect?"

"Oh, you're deceitful, Ellie. Totally deceitful, asking me what was the inside story of the theft."

"No. We haven't seen him since then. Freddie saw him and invited him here tonight to meet you."

"Isn't he married?"

"No. He was. His wife died seven years ago."

"But he's old!" Barbara protested.

"No, my dear. He's fifty. You and I are old. May Ling is thirty-seven."

"Let me digest this. You say this has been going on for a year—but you never told me word one about it."

"I'm not a gossip."

Barbara burst out laughing.

"Thank you."

"We're both gossips, Ellie. We love gossip. Gossip is everything personal, sensational, or outrageous, and everything else that's politically incorrect."

"What's happened to you today?" Eloise wondered. "You're actually happy."

"Sort of." She paused and thought about it. "Harry Lefkowitz . . . At first I thought he was a bit slippery—you know, Abner Berman says he has a reputation for defending big corporate thieves—but on the other hand, there's something about him—"

"Freddie thinks he's the smartest lawyer in San Francisco. He doesn't look like much—I mean, when you first meet him—but he grows on you."

"How did it happen? I mean, how did he meet May Ling?"

"Oh, we were being sued over some acreage that Freddie bought—an open tract between Highgate and Spinnaker's place, an acre or two that Spinnaker had no use for and Adam wanted, and then someone called Hernandez turns up with a claim that goes back to 1842—and Harry was here, and he and Freddie began to climb over the disputed land, and Harry fell and sprained an ankle. He was in a lot of pain, and Freddie got him into a car and took him to Joe's surgery in Napa. You know, May Ling acts as his receptionist and nurse—she got her degree last year—and since Joe was at the hospital, she X-rayed the ankle and bandaged it, and lo and behold, Harry was in love. When he learned she wasn't married, he began turning up at Napa every weekend. He takes her into the city on her days off or meets her here. He's been showering her with gifts, and whether he's proposed or not, I don't know. They're both very private people."

"And how does Freddie feel about it?"

"Grateful. He's been avoiding May Ling since the divorce, full of guilt. Anyway, they're second or third cousins, and Freddie is just not made for being a husband, so it's just as well. Or are they first cousins? I simply can't keep it straight."

"But Freddie feels he's off the hook?" Barbara asked. "People are very interesting. And what's Sally's objection?"

"And what makes you think Sally objects?"

"Just the few words between you and Adam."

"You know Sally as well as I do. Mostly the fact that he's a lawyer. Not sensitive enough, not charming enough, and May Ling's two inches taller than he."

"Yes, of course. Sally never got over being a film star." Barbara shook her head. "I'll have a word with her."

They sat and talked until the sun touched the top of the hill. There was a tracery of long, slender clouds that turned the sunset into a mass of shimmering color, pink and azure, with streaks of scarlet that fought the pale pastels.

HARRY LEFKOWITZ COULD NEVER QUITE get over his awe at the Levy–Lavette family. He had never before encountered anything like it, a group of people of so many diverse ethnic origins, and a family history, wealthy without doing as the wealthy do, and all connected by long or short strings to a winery that was more like an antique Mexican–Californian *hacienda* than the American style of big business. Not that Highgate was big business or comparable to such giants as Gallo or Mondavi, but it did gross more than five million in a good year and it hewed to a good quality of red wine that by now was recognized and valued in every wine-drinking country.

Harry had been born in 1934, at the nethermost point of the Great Depression, one of five children of an unemployed garment worker who struggled to feed his children and pay the rent on a miserable flat on Orchard Street, in New York City's Lower East Side ghetto. Harry and his two brothers had worked at every conceivable way to earn money since they were children, gathering and selling old papers, delivering whatever there was to deliver, making pennies for hours of work while his mother and his two sisters took in washing and sewed piecework whenever they could get it. He had graduated high school with honors, had been admitted to City College, which was then free, graduated with top honors, and had gone on to Harvard Law on scholarship. Offered a job in California, he took the California bar and passed easily.

During the years since then, he had married, suffered the death of his wife, opened his own firm, and bit by bit, as so many immigrants to California do, he lost touch with his family. His mother and father died; one sister died of pneumonia; the other sister married and moved to Alpine, New York, and one brother taught philosophy at Tulane in New Orleans, while the other became an auto salesman in Utica, New York. The family was shredded beyond repair.

Sitting this evening at the big table in the kitchen at Highgate, with a lovely woman who was one-quarter Chinese and the rest portioned out of Jewish, Italian, and white Protestant, and all of it combined into very considerable beauty, he felt that this was the most pleasant moment of his life. Adam sat at the head of the table, Freddie at the other end, Barbara and Eloise on either side of Adam, and Lefkowitz facing May Ling and Barbara.

"You never said a word about May Ling," Barbara was complaining to Lefkowitz. "You could have told me. It would have made it so much easier."

"I was being a lawyer. I knew who you were. May Ling gave me your books to read, and I think she told me most of your life story, but I never met you. I like Abner Berman. I didn't want to put him in the middle."

As always, Cathrena had cooked for twelve, the table piled with mounds of the ever-present tortillas, a huge poached salmon, bowls of rice, beans, and broccoli—the continually blooming broccoli that renewed itself day after day—hot bread, and salad greens picked that afternoon from the kitchen garden.

Eloise, heaping the plates, demanded to know what was going on.

"We haven't seen Harry since the theft of the century."

"Not a theft," Harry said shortly.

"I still can't believe you'd defend him against my aunt," May Ling said, "and you knew she was my aunt."

"I was defending him against the state. Barbara—if I may call you Barbara—was not a complainant. It was the cops who wanted to get their grubby hands on Jones."

"The papers said he was a murderer," Adam said. "That's hard to wash away."

"Will you all please listen to me?" Barbara demanded. "Harry took on the man's case pro bono. That means—"

"We know what it means," Freddie interrupted.

"Let me explain what it means. Everyone is not as wise as you, dear Freddie. It means he took the case without payment. And this man, Robert Jones, is not a murderer. He's a college graduate with a degree in civil engineering. A white guard at the university insulted him and then slapped him, and they got into a fight and Jones hit him, and the man went down and cracked his head on a concrete path, and Jones would have sat for fifteen years of his life in prison then if Harry had not taken his case, and that was also pro bono. Am I right, Harry? Since he had no money, how could he have paid you?"

"Harry, why didn't you tell me that?" May Ling said.

Harry, who was an excellent litigator, appeared tongue-tied. He swallowed uneasily, started to speak, and then stopped.

"You should have told me," May Ling said gently. "You tell me about these dreadful corporate swindlers, but you never said a word about Barbara's case."

"And one thing more," Barbara added. "In the true sense of the word, I gave him the jewelry. You know that I never wear jewelry. I didn't even keep the pieces in a vault, for all they meant to me. I had them in a drawer next to my bed. But there was one thing that I did want, Daddy's ring. Perhaps you remember it, Adam. My mother gave it to him when your dad and he formed the shipping company and bought the *Ocean Queen*. It's a heavy ring, and with gold selling for five or six hundred dollars an ounce these days, it must be worth a great deal. I said that if I could keep the ring, he could have the rest."

"Oh, come on," Freddie said. "You were robbed. How can you say you gave him the stuff? That's putting the cart before the horse, Aunt Barbara."

"Not quite," Lefkowitz said. "Abner Berman was willing to go along with Barbara's story, and we had a talk about that. Abner said that if he returned the jewels, there would be no charges. I must say that I sort of agreed, if silence could be taken as acquiescence, but then when Abner and I finished our meeting, I double-crossed Abner and asked Barbara to let him keep the loot. She agreed."

"Not quite that way," Barbara protested. "I had intended to let him keep it."

"This grows stranger and stranger," Adam said. "What did Sam say?"

"He thinks I'm crazy." Barbara shrugged. "His exact words were, 'Mother, if I didn't love you, I'd file papers to commit you.' It was nice to hear him say he loved me. But to expect children to understand one's quirks—well, that's a bit much."

"Hardly a quirk," Eloise declared. "It's simply Barbara."

"And a hundred thousand dollars is a hundred thousand dollars."

"Is it?" Barbara wondered. "According to Abner, Harry has

defended more minority defendants pro bono than any other lawyer who isn't a public defender. How many hundreds of thousands of dollars does that add up to?"

"I've been thinking about Getty," Harry said, in an obvious attempt to shift the conversation. "Nobody reads Veblen anymore and his theories about the conscience of the rich, but did you know that Getty left his whole stake, a billion-point-one, to that museum of his? Based on that sum the law requires that to keep its status as a foundation, the directors must spend at least fifty-one million a year on works of art. Every auction house here and in Europe is dancing with delight. But somehow, in this year of 1984, it doesn't wash. Not with me. Can you imagine how many turkey dinners this billion-point-one would buy for poor kids? He could have wiped out that rotten L.A. ghetto and rebuilt it from scratch."

"I don't see where there's any conscience in that," Eloise said. "The paintings would survive, no matter who owns them."

"Veblen didn't care for the rich," May Ling put in. "He questioned whether they had a conscience. And some of us do read him, Harry."

"I like to think that all people have a conscience," Eloise said gently.

"They keep it in a small pocket, Mom," Freddie said. "Let's go back to this Jones character. He had a gun."

"A toy gun."

"Still, the cops could have gone to the grand jury and indicted him for intent."

"It wouldn't wash, Freddie," Lefkowitz said. "If they did anything that foolish—and I don't know that they could—I'd have six blacks on the jury and laugh them out of court. They were content to call it quits."

"Yet we eat and we drink," Eloise said, "and we're rich."

"If the crop is good," Freddie admitted. "If we don't have a drought. If the price of bottles doesn't go up. If the grape pickers don't go on strike, and if the vintage doesn't turn on us, and if we don't get sued because some crazed kid gets picked up with a bottle of Highgate after he's killed someone—because essentially, Mom, we're farmers, and few farmers get really rich. I know a guy in L.A. who has eight thousand acres in one-crop barley, and with that one crop he has a house that would put the White House to shame, and he owns a dozen high-rises in L.A. But Adam wouldn't go that way, and he's absolutely right. There was a time when I thought of battling Gallo, but Pop sat on me because you don't make good wine that way. We grow our own grapes and the wholesalers plead for our stuff. And what did the old poet say? You were always quoting him, May Ling—"

May Ling smiled. How could she ever dislike Freddie? " 'I wonder often what the Vintners buy/One-half so precious as the stuff they sell'?"

THE SUNDAY DINNER WAS OVER. The sound of the piano came from the living room, Eloise playing Gershwin. Adam would be sprawled in his armchair, listening to the music and counting his many blessings. May Ling and Harry were either there or off somewhere to be alone; Barbara was still at the table, taking a seat next to Freddie, both of them with mugs of strong Mexican coffee. Cathrena had cleared the table, stowed away the uneaten food in the huge refrigerator, and gone off.

"She has Saturday off," Freddie said defensively.

"I know. Tell me, Freddie, how is it with my favorite nephew?"

"Your other nephew, young Danny, is very successful."

"All the glories of the Lavettes. He's dull. Scientists, God bless them, are dull. My brother Joe is utterly dependable but dull."

"And myself?"

"Never dull, Freddie. But you're forty-two years old."

"Meaning, Why don't I get married?"

"More or less."

"And why don't you get married, my dear aunt?"

"I'm sixty-nine years old, and I've been married."

He looked at her with interest. "You're still beautiful."

"I'm not beautiful, Freddie, though flattery will get you everywhere. I never was."

"That's not a majority opinion. And I love you with white hair. It's simply great, and it goes with your eyes. Let me try to answer your very personal question."

"It's my right to ask, by seniority."

"Good enough. It's not that I don't like women, Aunt Barbara. It's just that I love women too much. For me, the greatest thing on God's earth is women. I look at women with joy—almost any woman; you, for example. I find myself walking behind a strange woman on the Embarcadero, for instance—any woman—and I find myself enthralled with the movement of her legs, the way her hips move, the slope of her back—it doesn't matter that I don't see her face, the vibrations are the same. And unfortunately I have no particular preference—it's all-embracing. I watch the Mexican women working in the bottling plant. Mexican women are beautiful. They're passionate, they're joyous—"

"I know all about that, Freddie. You never learn."

"What is there to learn? I think Chinese women are beautiful. I love blond women and brunette women, and the other night I had a drink at the Fairmont with a black woman who stepped right out of H. Rider Haggard. Do you remember the Zulu queen? What was her name?"

"Freddie, that's enough. I don't know any Zulu queens, and I don't have the foggiest notion of who H. Rider Haggard is."

"He was. He isn't anymore. Good God, what did they teach you there at Sarah Lawrence?"

"Not much, except that you don't ask personal questions. I

should have learned that simple bit of manners, but since I stepped over the boundaries, I will say one thing more. I want you to find a nice girl and marry her and try to be decently faithful to her. And now I think we should go into the living room."

"That's not Barbara Lavette speaking."

"Rest assured, it is."

IN A PART OF THE NAPA VALLEY where the darkness of night was not diffused with any electric light, Harry Lefkowitz pulled off the road and cut the ignition. May Ling turned to him inquiringly, and he explained that he wanted them to step out of the car and to look at the sky.

"I've seen the sky, Harry."

"I want to look at it with you."

"Then why not roll back the top, and we can sit right here?"

"That never occurred to me. Certainly. I haven't put down the top since I bought it. Let's see if it works." He pressed a button, and the top lifted and came down.

"The toys of the rich," May Ling murmured.

"Not at all. I don't have a Rolls-Royce. My friends tell me that you have to have two, one that you drive when the other is in the shop being fixed."

"I'm sorry, Harry. I say awful things."

"Look at the sky," he whispered.

It was a moonless night, and the stars were as bright as if they had exploded with delight at not having to compete with the moon.

They sat for a while in silence. The air was clean and cold, and May Ling shivered. "Do you ever think, Harry, of how many billions and billions of stars there are? We are so small, so insignificant, tiny bits of matter on a little planet."

"I try not to. My ego is small enough. Every time I go into court to litigate, I shrink with horror, and I ask myself, *Who the hell am I, Harry Lefkowitz from Orchard Street, to stand up in court as if I owned the place and spurt stuff that actually means something to anyone?"*

"No, Harry—you don't!"

"I'm afraid—"

"Harry," she interrupted, "I think you're one of the best men I've ever known. I think what you did with Jones was noble and good. Why don't you ever speak of those things? I don't understand you. And why don't you ask me to marry you?"

"Because if you say no, that'll be the end of it."

"Stop looking at the sky and ask me. Or must I ask you to marry me? I'm thirty-seven years old. Don't you want to marry me? You've never even made a pass at me," she said plaintively.

"Oh, Jesus!" he exclaimed. "Do you really mean that?"

"Try me."

"Yes—tonight."

"Harry, we can't get married tonight. You're a lawyer—you should know that. And it would break Mom's heart if she didn't have a month to prepare a wedding and send out a thousand invitations to Highgate. But it's only ten o'clock, and you can turn the car around and we can drive back to Highgate and whisper to Eloise that we want to stay overnight, and she'll call Mom, and there is a guest house, and you can crawl into bed with me and put your arms around me and tell me that you love me."

Harry couldn't think of anything to say appropriate to the moment. She leaned over and kissed him, and then he turned on the ignition, swung the car around, and drove back to Highgate.

The Unitarian

4

BEFORE OPENING THE LETTER from Philip Carter, Barbara studied the address on the envelope. The even, controlled handwriting brought back the Palmer Method of her childhood, when the children of seven and eight years were taught to sit upright, move their whole right arm, and form their cursive letters so that each word was a flowing example of literacy, the proper way for a young lady to present her thoughts. The problem, in Barbara's case, was that she was left-handed. Her teacher, Miss Hatcher, whom she remembered to this day as Miss Hatchet, was gently and comfortingly cruel, declaring, "There is no such thing, Barbara, as left-handedness. It is all a question of one's mind and one's will, so you will write with your right hand, as all normal children do, and in time you will overcome this handicap."

Barbara, not quite certain at the age of eight that she was left-handed—her mother being of the same mind as Miss Hatcher—obediently performed the task with her right hand, and because her words were practically unreadable, she was always at the bottom of the writing class. She still wrote cursively with her right hand, and her handwriting was still difficult to read, even back to herself. She also sent silent blessings to the spirit of Christopher Sholes, who had invented the first typewriter in 1867, and she was determined someday to write about him and enshrine him as one of the great men of the nineteenth century.

When she opened Philip Carter's letter, handwritten, she experienced the same admiration that the address had awakened. Women still wrote letters by hand; few men did.

"Dear Ms. Lavette," he wrote;

> During the two weeks since I spoke to you here at the church, I have called you several times. I should have left my name on your answering machine, but I was afraid you might be disappointed with our talk and would not call me back. If so, I must apologize, and I hope you will take this letter in good spirit. I would like to have dinner with you some evening, when you are free of other engagements.
>
> I live alone. I am a widower. My wife passed away five years ago, and I must confess to being a very lonely person. I know this letter is rather presumptuous, and if you do not choose to reply to it, I will understand.

It was signed, "Sincerely, Philip Carter." His telephone number was at the bottom of the page.

Barbara read the letter again, certainly the most stilted, old-fashioned letter she had received in years. *What on earth have I gotten myself into?* she wondered. *The man wants to date me. If I read this curious letter right, he's scared to death. Afraid to leave a message because he feels I wouldn't return his call. Yet when we spoke, he appeared to be a perfectly normal person. What do I do, throw it away, ignore it? A Unitarian minister. I still have no real idea of what a Unitarian is. Does he hope to convert me? I'm not convertible to anything.* She thought of the old saw about Unitarians—irritate them too much, and they'll burn a question mark on your front lawn. *This is all ridiculous,* she told herself. *I'm an old, white-haired lady of sixty-nine years, and the last thing in the world I desire is another man in my life. I want to live quietly, write my book—no, no, that's an absolute lie. The last thing in the world I want is to live quietly. Next to the last thing in the world I want to do is to get involved with a minister. And I am not lonely. I am baby-sitting for Sam and Mary Lou tonight . . . They have a perfectly competent maid who gets two nights off a week, but they can't stay home two nights a week. This city teems with high school girls who would be delighted to sit with their brat. No, she isn't a brat. What's happened to me? I never used that word before. But it has to be me, Grandma Barbara. How I hate that! Grandma Barbara. They bury you as soon as you turn sixty.*

She walked through the house, long, stamping strides. *Why do I stay in this ridiculous old shack? Why don't I go to England? I haven't been to England in years. Why don't I go to Australia? I've never been to Australia.*

She picked up the telephone and called Eloise. "Eloise," Barbara said abruptly, "would you go to Australia?"

"What on earth for?"

"With me. Would Adam let you?"

"Adam is not my keeper. Why on earth do you want to go to Australia?"

"I've never been there."

"That's no reason. I've never been to Syria, and I certainly don't want to go there. Barbara, you're babbling. What is wrong with you?"

"I have a letter. I want to read it to you." Then she read the letter to Eloise, and Eloise replied that it was a lovely letter.

"You don't think it's absurd?"

"No. The man wants to have dinner with you. It's a perfectly nice, decent letter. He's the minister at the church you went to, isn't he? He says he's a single, lonely man. Why shouldn't you have dinner with him? . . . Does this have anything to do with your trip to Australia?"

"No. I'm not going to Australia."

"Why? Because I won't go with you? Barbara, dear, I'd love to go somewhere—but Australia?"

"No, no, I'm sorry, darling. I'm not myself."

"Barbara—"

"I'm perfectly all right," Barbara assured her. "This whole thing about Australia is just a crazy notion."

"Barbara, do you want me to drive in and talk to you?"

"No, I'm fine."

Or am I? she asked herself as she put down the telephone. She picked up the letter again. Then she dialed the number of the Unitarian church. A woman's voice answered, and Barbara tried to remember her name—Reba something.

She told Reba-something her name and asked whether she could speak to Philip Carter.

"Give me a moment, Ms. Lavette, he's staining a rostrum." And then Barbara heard her shout, "Phil, I have Barbara Lavette on the telephone!"

A few seconds went by, and then he was on the phone. "Ms. Lavette. You must forgive me for that silly letter. I'm afraid I don't know how to address a woman and ask her to dinner—I've never done it before—I mean, except for my wife. Will you have dinner with me?"

"Certainly. I'm baby-sitting tonight, but tomorrow, if that's clear for you?"

"Friday. Of course. When should I pick you up?"

"Seven?"

"Good. Yes."

"I'm on Green Street. The number—"

"I know the number. Then tomorrow, at seven. Is there any special place you'd like to eat?"

"I'll leave that up to you."

"Wherever you choose."

"Good. Then I'll see you tomorrow."

He sounded like a young boy on his first date, Barbara thought. *Well, it is his first date. Five years without taking a woman to dinner—or to bed, I imagine. Now what have I gotten into?* She went to a mirror and examined herself thoughtfully. Not too many wrinkles, considering her age. She wore her white hair pulled back and clasped at her neck, but wouldn't it look better if she simply combed it out and let the cowlick shape it? She tried that and shook her head. *Too young, much too young, Barbara.* She retreated from the mirror, and then turned around quickly, trying to see herself as a stranger. *Well, I rather like it.* She decided that she would wear it that way tonight and note her son Sam's reaction. Then she reversed the thought. Sam would scowl. She would not be pushed around by Sam. His comment about having her committed had been teasing but utterly thoughtless, and like all surgeons she had ever met, he was dictatorial, convinced that surgeons were the chosen of God. She recalled his irritation when Sally came to him to find someone to do a face-lift. Her husband, Joe, a general practitioner, had bridled at the thought, so she went to Sam, who told her sourly that she was beautiful enough and that she did not need a face-lift; she had found her own surgeon, and fortunately he was a good one. Sam's wife, Mary Lou, was a gentle, submissive Southern girl who was totally willing to wear her hair, or anything else, exactly as Sam desired.

Barbara's hair was cut shoulder length, and unlike most straight hair, it was thick and still lustrous. Once it had been a fine honey color, and Barbara had always delighted in it; but most of its turning white had happened in the six months after Carson's death, and Barbara, deeply depressed, had had no thought of touching up the white streaks. As with all slow changes, she had looked into the mirror one day and realized it: She had gone white. She rather liked it; it set a seal on Carson's departure. He would be the last man in her life; she'd had enough of marriage and men, and now it was over.

Yet she could not help thinking of how good Sally had looked after the face-lift. Sally was only twelve years younger than Barbara, yet when they walked on the Embarcadero, men's heads turned to look at her, not at Barbara.

It was Barbara who made that distinction. Her eyesight was still good—not 20–20, but good enough for walking if not for driving—yet she insisted on wearing her glasses. Sally once whispered to her, via Dorothy Parker, "Men don't make passes at girls who wear glasses," and somewhere in Barbara's mind that must have stuck. She had not worn her glasses when she spoke to Philip Carter.

But she would never have a face-lift. As she said once to Eloise, she had earned every wrinkle, not on the sands of some Hawaiian beach, but under the hot sun of North Africa during World War II; and as for her hair, she would comb it out and wear it that way—let Sam say whatever he would. She sensed the contradictions and the general confusion of her thoughts, and admitted to herself that in spite of her initial reaction to the letter, she was quite excited about tomorrow's evening.

FREDDIE HAD NOT EXACTLY picked up Judith Hope, but on the other hand, he had not exactly been introduced to her. He had gone into the bar at the Fairmont, and every table was taken except one, where a black woman sat alone. She was a good-looking woman, indeed a beautiful woman, and her face was somehow familiar. He stood and tried not to stare at her while he searched his mind. The name came to him, and he walked to her table and said, "Aren't you Judith Hope?"

She looked up at him with a glint of amusement in her eyes. "I don't think we've met."

"No. Quite true. But your picture was on my desk last week, and I took the liberty—"

"Why was my picture on your desk, if I may ask?"

"May I sit down?"

"I'm waiting for someone. He should be here very soon."

"Until he comes?" Freddie asked.

She scrutinized him carefully, head to foot, and he had the feeling that she was stripping him down to his bones. Then she nodded, and he took the chair facing her. "I'm a vintner, Ms. Hope."

"You sell wine?"

"We own a winery, my father and I, out in the Napa Valley." He was struck by the fact that she knew the precise meaning of *vintner*. "We grow the grapes, make the wine, bottle it, and sell it. We're not a very big operation, but we do some advertising." He placed one of his business cards on the table in front of her. "We've never dealt with the Nob Hill Agency; they're too big for us; but they're after our business, and Frank Fellish over there sent me a stack of photos, yours among them. When I saw your photo, an idea struck me. I feel we make the best Cabernet in America, and I thought, *Why not use a beautiful black model and pitch the ad to the black middle class?*"

A long moment passed, and then she said, smiling slightly, "And are you going to?" She didn't drop her eyes to look at his card.

"I'm afraid not. Your price is out of our league."

"You're not here to talk my price down, are you?"

"For heaven's sake, no. I saw you, and I wanted to meet you and talk to you."

"Why?"

"Why not?" Freddie persisted. "I'm not married and looking to cheat on my wife. You're a beautiful and interesting woman."

"Thank you. But you're white and I'm black."

"I happened to notice that," Freddie said. "Does that mean you can't talk to me?"

"Certainly not. I talk to all sorts of people. By the way, what is your name, Mr. Vintner?"

"Frederick Lavette."

She raised a brow at that. "One of the great Lavette family?"

"Not great, but we are a family."

"And that's a virtue these days. And now that we've been introduced, Mr. Lavette...?"

"Would you have dinner with me?"

"Possibly. Where and when?" She slipped his card into her purse, and glanced behind him.

"Thursday, here," Freddie said. "Seven o'clock, in the lobby." He pushed back his chair and turned around. A short, well-dressed black man was approaching their table, and since she said nothing to Freddie to make him stay or to introduce him, he walked on past the small man, who nodded and went on to the table where Judith Hope sat. Freddie caught her eyes again as he left the bar, and at least it appeared to him that she nodded slightly. He recognized the black man as Jerry Delrio, the jazz pianist.

And now it was Thursday, a week later, and Freddie had been waiting for Judith Hope for twenty minutes in the lobby of the Fairmont, and he was ready to give up, afraid that he would never see her again. Then his fears were set at rest as she appeared at the entrance to the hotel, and Freddie realized that he had only seen her seated, never standing. She was at least six feet tall, wearing a white sheath, a loosely woven ruana wrapped around her shoulders, her height enhanced by two-inch heels. As she swept into the lobby, all eyes turned toward her, and Freddie stretched his six-foot, two-inch length as he went to meet her.

She took his hand, smiled her slightly ironic smile, and regretted being late. "You will forgive me, Mr. Vintner?"

"There is nothing to forgive," Freddie said gallantly. "Waiting for you is part of the pleasure of seeing you."

"Very nice."

"I try," Freddie said.

The headwaiter was all smiles. "Mr. Lavette, I have your special table. And Ms. Hope, a pleasure to see you again."

Again, all eyes were on them, and Freddie speculated that by tomorrow, this would be the prime discussion at Highgate as well as in various places in the City. With dinner, Freddie ordered a bottle of Cabernet—"Highgate, you know."

"As if I didn't know." The waiter smiled.

Ms. Hope ordered a small New York steak and a salad.

"I don't drink red wine," she said.

"We have a Highgate Sylvaner," the waiter suggested.

"Sylvaner?"

Freddie waited, watching her keenly.

"I don't think so. I don't like German wines. Too sweet."

Score one for her, Freddie thought, and said gently, "Not German, my dear. Alsatian—that is, in the original. We keep the European names, I don't know why, but this is a Napa Valley vintage, much drier than the Alsatian."

"Let me call the sommelier," the waiter said, not willing to get into a discussion of wine on this level. The sommelier was a grandly stout man, with a red apron and a set of keys dangling from a leather belt.

"I suggested our Sylvaner," Freddie explained, "but the young lady prefers something drier."

"With steak," Ms. Hope said sweetly. "I know it's odd, but I can't tolerate red wine."

"Perfectly natural," Freddie said. "I often feel that way myself." The sommelier frowned at this desecration but smiled quickly and suggested a Chardonnay.

"French, please."

"Of course. We have a Château Lemaire 1977—an excellent vintage." Freddie, who knew the wine list, recalled that a Château Lemaire 1977 was priced at sixty dollars a bottle, but he joined in the approbation, swallowing his distaste for any wine not grown in California. As for Château Lemaire 1977, he considered it dry to the point of sour and a highly overrated wine.

The meal, however, went well. Freddie turned on all of his charm, and bit by bit, he was able to break down the wall of distrust and sarcasm. He learned that she had a degree from Berkeley, a master's in business management; that her father was a dentist in Oakland; and that when she applied for her first job, at a tire factory, they had decided that they preferred her as a symbol for their product.

"They wanted to break into the black trade—blacks buy a lot of used cars and they're a good market for tires. But when I appeared at the Nob Hill Agency—they handle Magnum Tires—my business career was over. That was seven years ago."

"And today you're the highest-priced model in California."

"So they tell me."

"And you don't wear a wedding ring."

"Why should I? I'm not married. Are you, Freddie?"

"No. I'm divorced. But you—you're one of the most beautiful women I've ever seen."

"Well, flattery helps. You don't know much about colored folk, do you, Freddie?"

"No, not very much. But I'm willing to learn."

She leaned back, looking at him thoughtfully. They had each of them consumed most of their bottles of wine. Freddie was not obviously drunk, but he had that alcoholic feeling of being very clever, very charming, very desirable.

"Are you a good learner?"

Freddie shrugged.

"Tell me, child," she said, "do you own this great winery of yours?"

"No. I suppose I will someday. My father, Adam Levy, owns it."

"Oh, are you Jewish?"

"Does that matter?"

"Why should it matter? I'm black, in case you haven't looked at me closely."

"Oh, believe me, I have. No, I'm not Jewish, although I just as soon would be. My father was Thomas Lavette. My mother divorced him and married Adam Levy. I came with the package."

"Thomas Lavette—the Seldon Bank—you certainly don't come of poor people, Frederick Lavette."

He poured the last of the white wine into her glass, then the last of the Cabernet into his, impressed as before with the extent of her knowledge. And she did not appear to be the slightest bit drunk. "You know," Freddie said, "they know me here at the hotel from way back. I can get a room for the night without any trouble."

She smiled, a very thin smile. "You must be a very important person in San Francisco, Freddie. Lean toward me. I want to say something very serious to you."

He leaned over and she leaned toward him until her lips were only inches from his. Then in a low whisper, she said, "Fuck you, too." Then she rose, picking up her purse and her ruana, and strode out of the dining room.

AT ELEVEN O'CLOCK, Freddie called Barbara, and said, "I'm here at the Fairmont, Aunt Barbara, and I'm too crocked to drive home, but I can get the car over to your place, and I have to talk to you. I know it's late, but I'm desperate."

"Freddie, I'm on my way to bed. Can't it wait until tomorrow?"

"I suppose so. I can get a room here."

There was something in his voice so sad and forlorn that Barbara said, "All right, Freddie. And for God's sake, drive carefully."

Ten minutes later Barbara, wrapped in a bathrobe, opened the door for him, told him that she had a pot of coffee brewing, and led him in to the kitchen. He dropped lightly into a chair.

"What happened, Freddie?"

"Aunt Barbara," he said, "what on God's earth is wrong with me?"

"Freddie!"

She poured a cup of coffee for him. "Sugar and cream?"

"No, thank you. What is it? Am I backward, brain damaged, or just stupid?"

"Well, you did graduate with honors from Princeton."

"Don't tease me, Aunt Barbara. You're the only one I can talk to."

"Freddie," she said patiently, "I don't know what's wrong with you or if *anything* is wrong with you. You're a little drunk, and my suggestion is that you go upstairs to the guest room and get a good night's sleep."

"I have to talk."

"Then talk, Freddie. It's late. What did you drink?"

"A whole bottle of Cabernet."

"Don't you have more sense than that?"

"Apparently not. Do you remember when I went down South in the sixties with some of the boys from college and I was beaten half to death? Doesn't that give me points?"

"I'm not likely to forget it," Barbara said.

"I'm not a white chauvinist pig—or am I?"

"Whatever that means. Suppose you tell me what happened tonight?"

He narrated the sequence of events, leaving nothing out. Barbara listened without interrupting and then sat in silence for a minute or so while Freddie sipped the coffee, his eyes cast down, for all the world like a small boy caught with a cigarette.

"Freddie," she finally said, "would you expect a white woman to fall into bed with you on the first date?"

"It happens."

"What is a woman, anyway? Have you ever asked yourself that?...Why do you come to me, Freddie?" There was an angry edge to her voice now. "I'm not your confessor and I'm not a psychiatrist. You do a nasty, degrading thing to a woman and she spits in your face. And she's a black woman. Has it ever occurred to you to think of what it means to be a black woman, or a white woman—or any kind of woman? We've known each other since you were a child. I watched you being baptized at Grace Church. Yes, yes, you went down to Mississippi to register black voters, and you were very brave and it broke my heart to see you in the hospital down there, but what did you learn? I spent my whole life trying to be something that any woman has the right to be, and you were always like a son to me and I always loved you, but you treat women like dirt, not like people."

"I don't treat you like dirt."

"Freddie, would you say what you just told me to a man? Probably, whoever the man, he'd laugh it off and say something like, 'Sonny, it comes with the territory.' At least you have the decency to know that you did something disgusting. That's not much of a plus, but it's something. You're forty-two years old. You almost destroyed May Ling, and you haven't been able to make it with any woman. Yes, they love you. You're tall and handsome and you carry the Lavette name. Freddie, get some help, please. That's all. Now go upstairs and sleep it off. I'll see you in the morning."

He had no retort to what she said, but he took himself upstairs like a whipped dog, and when Barbara came downstairs in the morning, Freddie was gone. He'd left a note on the kitchen table:

Dear Aunt Barbara:

Thank you for your good advice. What I remember
of what you said should have been said to me a long time
ago. I helped myself to last night's coffee and three of your
aspirin. I'll see you soon.

With love,

Freddie

ELOISE WAS KINDER THAN BARBARA. She walked over to the
aging room at the other end of the winery. Freddie's office was in
the old building, which was joined to the new, larger building. He
had refitted it into a suitable office for himself and for Ms. Gomez,
his secretary. Eloise entered his office, came up behind him where
he sat at his desk, and kissed the top of his head.

"Mother," he said. "No one else kisses me on the top of my
head." He stood up to face her, wincing.

"What is it?" she asked.

"I have a frightful headache."

"I suppose so. You know, Adam was going to talk to you. I
said I would."

Sensing what was coming, Freddie said, "Adam is a Puritan.
All the world can't behave like Adam."

"Adam is a good, loving man. He considers you to be his son.
Fran Johnson—well, I called her about the wedding flowers,
and—"

"Go on, Mother."

"And she told me"—it was very hard for Eloise—"she told
me that you were at the Fairmont the other night with a black
prostitute and that you made a scene." Eloise shook her head and
blinked away tears.

"She's a foul-mouthed bitch!" Freddie exclaimed. "Yes, I was
at the Fairmont—with a wonderful woman. Yes, a black woman—
who is as far from a prostitute as you can get. She has a master's

in business administration, and she works as an advertising model in commercials and in stills. She is one of the most successful and sought-after models in California. I did not make a scene. She left the table and walked out because I said something stupid to her and hurt her feelings. That's all it was. I was a bit under—too much wine. It was not a scene."

"I'm sorry, Freddie." She dropped into a chair. "Give me a tissue, Freddie." She wiped her eyes, and he bent over to kiss her. "I'll explain to Adam, and there'll be no more said about this." Then she paused and said very tentatively, "Do you like this woman, Freddie?"

"Precious lot of good if I do. She won't forgive me."

"Women do forgive, Freddie. Otherwise our lives would be impossible."

BARBARA TELEPHONED BIRDIE MACGELSIE. Barbara had never asked Birdie, or for that matter anyone else, what his or her religion was, but Birdie had organized at least half of the protests, marches, and sit-ins in San Francisco over the past twenty years, and Barbara recalled her once saying something about the Unitarians. They had been organizing a delegation to the United Nations—one that Barbara missed, being at that time in El Salvador—and now she decided that it was worth a call.

Birdie, a large, good-natured woman, congratulated Barbara on the way she handled the theft. "What a gesture!" she exclaimed. "I meant to call you."

"Birdie, let me ask you a curious and personal question..."

"Wow! I'm as old as you are, so I'm not pregnant. Angus has taken to sleeping in the guest room, thank God. What else is there?"

"Are you a Unitarian?"

"Well, that does it. I would never have thought of that."

"Are you?"

"Sometimes. Maybe one Sunday in three or four or five. Angus is a totally fallen Catholic. I'm sort of—well, it's hard to describe. Why this curious and personal question?"

"Phil Carter is taking me to dinner tonight. I need some background."

"You're kidding."

"No, God's truth."

"Thank goodness. Do you know how long we've been trying to find you someone? How did this happen?"

"I came in out of the rain one Sunday," Barbara said. "How old is he?"

"What an expression of faith! You came in out of the rain. He's somewhere in his seventies—seventy-three or seventy-four. Madly in love with a wife who died—I think five years ago."

"Well, don't jump to any conclusions."

"I'm way ahead of you. You need someone, Barbara. You can't go on living alone in that house."

"Stop right there," Barbara said. "Thank you for the information, Birdie."

"Stay in touch, Barbara."

"One more thing," Barbara insisted. "You intimated that I am the first in his long vigil of mourning?"

"As far as I know."

Barbara said good-bye and felt abashed that she had derided his letter. Birdie was right in her declaration that Barbara needed someone. She had never before lived any length of time without a man in her life, but her instincts shied away from a minister. As far as she was concerned, a person's life should be involved with facts, and facts were of material substance and not of dreams; when one set about to dream, the facts had to be rejected or destroyed. She remembered only too well the first time she came face-to-face with what she regarded as the plain facts of life. That was in 1934, during the great longshoremen's strike on the docks of San Francisco, when she had become emotionally involved with the strikers' need for food. She had worked in a food kitchen then, and her experience there had been the pivotal turning point of her life. Yet she had to admit to herself that when she and Birdie MacGelsie and a few other women had organized Mothers for Peace during the Vietnam War, the first man to join them was Father Matthew Gibbon, a Jesuit priest, and after him a dozen other clerics. Who else had there been to turn to then? The thought hammered at her mind. She was too easily given to cynicism, which she was well aware of, and when she fell into that trap she disliked herself. She had not lived a cynical life; every step she had taken was out of simple belief in the rightness of a cause. *But, Barbara,* she thought, *how many men have asked you to dinner since Carson died?* She had not fallen into a morass of mourning; she had gone on with her life—but it was a lonely life. At first, every one of her friends had been eager to invite her to dinner, but she had tired of being the lone woman out. Single men of her age were hard to find, and the dinner invitations became fewer. There were days that stretched on endlessly. She walked alone on the Embarcadero; she once took to needlework, and after a day of earnestly trying, she cast it aside in disgust. There was once an entire week when she could not approach her typewriter. Why was she writing a book? There were enough books in the world, and how many women of seventy wrote books? The more she tried to re-create the beginnings of her family, the more she became overwhelmed by the toll that time had taken on them.

Finally she put all thought of the past aside and dressed herself for the evening date. She chose loose brown slacks, a pullover, and a beige cardigan. It was one of those cool summer days, and by nightfall there would be a cold wind from the Pacific. She tied up her hair and then shook her head with annoyance, untied her hair, combed it out again, and let it fall into a cowlick, shoulder length.

I always used to wear it that way—explaining to herself. And then, at precisely seven o'clock, the doorbell sounded. It occurred to her that if he had come five minutes early, he would probably have waited outside until seven.

She opened the door for him, and he greeted her with a shy, self-effacing smile, someone quite different from the confident man who had spoken with her at the church. "I'm very happy to see you," he said. "I felt my letter was a bit foolish. Old-fashioned."

"I like old-fashioned things," Barbara replied. "When one gets to my age, one *is* old-fashioned." Small lies, and why not? "Come in."

He wore gray flannels, a white shirt, a bow tie, and a blue blazer. His shoes were old and comfortable. "You're not ready?" he asked.

"I'm ready enough. I thought we might have a glass of wine and talk a bit—get to know each other a little as people, rather than as a confused parishioner and her adviser." She was trying desperately to put him at his ease.

"Well—" He paused. "I try not to think of myself as an adviser. I mean—well, I'm as confused as the next person."

"Will you have some wine? I don't have any hard liquor."

"Sure, that will be fine."

"I have white in the fridge. I can open a bottle of red if you prefer."

"Oh no. White will be fine."

While she went for the wine, he looked around the modest living room: a grospoint rug on the floor, two armchairs and a couch upholstered in bright printed cloth, a very small upright piano, a Victorian chair tufted in black horsehair, and an old leather chair in the last stage of survival. On the wall, an oil painting of a handsome woman who he guessed was her mother, some prints, and a watercolor of a freighter.

Barbara returned and handed him his glass. "What shall we drink to, Mr. Carter?"

"Philip, please."

"Very well, Philip."

"Our meeting, perhaps?"

"Why not?" Barbara said. "May it be a good meeting."

"I feel that I should tell you about myself." He looked at her inquiringly, as if he expected approval or rejection. "I mean—well, people do know a lot about you—I mean, I've read a couple of your books. The one about prison and what it means—that moved me a great deal—and of course your book about El Salvador. I think it was the best book about the horror that we inflicted on that poor, suffering country."

"Oh no—no." Barbara shook her head. "There are better books, believe me."

"Don't sell yourself short," he said. "Now, where shall we have dinner?"

"You leave it up to me?"

"Yes. You know such things better than I."

"Then we'll go to John's Place, down on the Wharf, because I'm dying to have some fish and chips and crabmeat and beer. Do you like that kind of thing?"

"Very much."

"And we can walk there, and you can tell me more about yourself on the way."

"You're sure? I thought you might want to go to some—well, more elegant place."

"Not a bit. I was hoping you'd agree."

"And you want to walk?"

"Certainly," Barbara said. "That's why I dressed the way I did. Flat heels."

The sun was beginning to set over the Golden Gate as they started down the hill. "Downhill is worst," Barbara observed. "It seemed I could fly down the hill when I was a kid. Now I realize that I have knees."

He smiled. "I know about knees—knees and hips."

"We won't talk about that. We're on a date—my first in heaven knows how many years."

"My first ever, I suppose, and that's odd, isn't it?" He was talking more easily now. After all, he was a man who preached sermons. "I never had what you would call a date with Agatha. She was a nun and I was a priest. We worked together, and one day she said to me, 'I think I'm in love with you,' and that's a frightening thing for a nun to say."

"I suppose so. I never thought much about nuns"—reflecting that nunhood was the last thing she would ever try to unravel. She loved men too well. Holding his arm now, feeling the pressure of it against her breast, she realized how much she had missed this, the hard feel of a man's muscle, the strength of his body. She stumbled once and he steadied her.

They talked about the City and its hills. He had been born in Kansas, one of eight children, the youngest. Most of the others had died. "I am by eight years the youngest," he explained, "a great surprise to my mother, a gift from God, as she put it. I never quite understood that, but I accepted it. I was too young to dispute her or anyone about gifts from God. I was educated by the Jesuits from the word *go*, and I never dreamed that there could be any other future for me. But when they sent me here—well, I knew I was home."

"People feel that way," she agreed. She could not imagine living anywhere else. "They sent me east to a college called Sarah Lawrence. We had family in Boston. My grandmother was from Boston, and this was always an uncouth frontier town to her. I was sent east to learn the manners of civilization. My grandfather Seldon came around the Horn in one of those square-rigged three-masters, like the *Balclutha*—the old museum ship—and being a hard-nosed Yankee, he started a bank with the money he inherited from his father."

How long it was since she had spoken about this to anyone! Suddenly the memories came floating back. Her father, Dan Lavette, was born in a boxcar full of Italian and Irish laborers sent west to build the Atchison spur line into San Francisco. No inheritance there.

Philip told her how he had worked as a carpenter after he left the Church, how much he and Agatha had wanted children, and how each time she had become pregnant, she lost the child.

Their verbal intimacy was explosive, bottled up for silent years, and now suddenly pouring out to each other.

They sat at a bare wooden table at John's Place and ate fresh crab and deep-fried fish and fried potatoes and drank beer, and Barbara, eating with a fine mixture of pleasure and guilt, quoted, " 'When all the rules of sloth and greed go down before the gut...' " *And the hell with it,* she thought. *I am actually enjoying myself. I'm pigging out, and thank God I don't gain weight.*

"And now you're a Unitarian pastor," Barbara said, leading to a question she had been storing up. "How? Or have I no right to ask you that?"

"It came about. I learned to meditate, simple Zen meditation, when I was a Jesuit. I had a good teacher, and that's the great contradiction in the practice—that is, for a Catholic. The Vatican doesn't look kindly on meditation. God becomes ineffable, but both Agatha and I needed a church. You can take a Catholic out of the Church, but how can you take the Church out of a Catholic? I worked four years as a carpenter, first as an apprentice and then as a union man, basic stuff, building tract houses. I'm good with my hands, and my father taught me the art as a kid. Agatha worked on and off as a temporary, typing and office work. I got the job through Angus MacGelsie, a builder who was a member of our church. His wife, Birdie, is a Unitarian, and through her, we came to the Unitarian Society. Well, the rest followed. I had the theological background, and I took some courses, and when the minister left, they offered me the job. We're not a big order—only one church in town."

"It's a small world," Barbara said. "I'm glad we did this tonight. My first reaction to your letter was to say no. I couldn't face the thought of a date with anyone. Now..."

He smiled. "And now?"

"It's been a good evening."

"Perhaps we can do it again?"

"Perhaps."

THE GUESTHOUSE AT HIGHGATE, to which Harry Lefkowitz and May Ling had returned to spend the night, was a small stone building, once a horse barn just large enough to hold two teams, and converted by Freddie into a pleasant home for himself and May Ling. When their child was born, a son whom they named Daniel, Freddie moved out. When May Ling took over her mother's job as Joseph Lavette's assistant at the Napa office, she took herself and her child to Sally's home in Napa. It was said that the local Napa paper had a chart pinned up with the various Lavettes and Levys, who could always be counted on for good copy; and Barbara, now the senior member of the family, had promised herself that one day she would check out this rumor, as a bit of color for her Lavette–Levy history.

Not today; today Sally had pleaded with her to come for lunch and to go over the list of wedding guests, and Barbara would have to be back in San Francisco by six, to address the Democratic Women's Club. Sally was more like a sister than a sister-in-law, turning to Barbara with almost every problem that confronted her. When Barbara entered the house Sally was in a royal rage, shouting into the phone and then slamming it down. May Ling came in from the surgery and said, "Mother, there are patients inside. For God's sake." She saw Barbara and embraced her, and then vanished back into the waiting room.

With a perfunctory kiss on Barbara's cheek, Sally snorted. "That bastard! No time to talk to Sally Lavette. If I were Charlton Heston or Frank Sinatra, he'd slobber all over me!"

"Who, Sally? Who were you talking to?"

"Your president and mine, Mr. Reagan. When I met him at the studio, he did slobber all over me... You're so lovely, Ms. Lavette. Did you hear what happened?" she asked Barbara.

"To the president?"

"No, no. I mean at San Ysidro—just an hour ago. I heard it on the radio. Some lunatic, loaded with rapid-fire weapons, walked into the local McDonald's and killed twenty people and wounded sixteen others, and it's just the worst massacre of its kind that ever took place—can you imagine, thirty-six people shot down by one man. And I thought that if I called Reagan—my goodness, I had dinner with him, I know the man—he could go on the air and make this the end of those awful weapons. Barbara, do you know how many gunshot wounds Joe and I treated when he had his office in the barrio? Do you know what one of those weapons does at close range?" She embraced Barbara. "Oh, God, Barbara—what is happening to us? What is the world coming to?"

"Sally, Sally, whatever it's coming to, we can't do anything about it here and now. We can't help. San Ysidro is a long way from here."

"That doesn't matter. It's all over."

"Sally, calm down and don't eat your heart out over every obscenity. We do what we can. I'll find out about this, and I'll talk about it tonight. I'm speaking in the City—I have to leave here in two hours at the most."

"At least you do something. You talk to people, and they listen to you. I'm locked up here in this damn house, and when May Ling leaves, I'll be in the office again."

"You won't be. Sally, darling, you become concerned with every possible situation whether you can change it or not. Did you really expect Ronald Reagan, coming from a town where every frightened woman owns a gun, and himself the darling of the National Rifle Association, to go on the air and damn guns? No way; it's unthinkable. He just doesn't believe in gun control—or so I've heard. Now pull yourself together. What happened in San Ysidro happened."

"I know. You're right. Let's have lunch."

Lunch was a salad and coffee. Sally was still slender and beautiful, and like every aging film star, she lived with the hope that some producer with a long memory would call her back to work. At lunch she informed Barbara that May Ling desired to be married by a rabbi.

"Well, why not? Harry's Jewish."

"He never mentioned it. I still can't get used to the idea that May Ling is marrying him."

"It's time you did get used to it. And May Ling's Jewish, isn't she?"

"I really don't know how you come to that. My mother, Clair, was not Jewish, and Daddy never set foot in a synagogue. May Ling is one-quarter Jewish. I sometimes think that half of California is part Jewish, and I've heard that a rabbi will not perform an interfaith marriage ceremony. And Harry, from what May Ling says, just doesn't care, as long as she will marry him."

"I have an easy solution," Barbara said, smiling. "I know a Unitarian minister who will gladly marry any two people who love each other."

"What on earth is a Unitarian?"

"Unitarianism is a religion, very open and easygoing. They say it was Thomas Jefferson's religion and Ralph Waldo Emerson's—and do you know, Sally, the man who invented the cable car system in the city was a Unitarian—and this minister is very sweet and very gentle."

"And how do I sell that to May Ling?"

"Why don't you leave that to me?" Barbara said. "Isn't she going to join us?"

"She doesn't want to. She says the wedding is my affair. And here's the list"—pushing a sheaf of paper over to Barbara. "I have three hundred names, including couples counted as two; Harry gave me sixteen couples, which makes thirty-two, and eight more singles, forty in all."

Barbara shook her head. "Sally, did you include the people working at Highgate?"

"Candido will take care of that."

"Sally, you can't invite four hundred people to a wedding— you simply can't."

"I don't have your list. I thought you would bring it with you."

"I have twelve couples and six singles, and I haven't had a chance to ask Sam who he wants to invite. Suppose it rains?"

"It won't rain in August. You know that."

"God knows that. I don't," Barbara said, and added, "It did last year."

"We'll have pavilions."

"Did you discuss this with Eloise?" Barbara wanted to know.

"Eloise?" Sally asked innocently. "I thought I'd leave that to you."

"Did you! Sally, when will you grow up?"

"That's an awful thing to ask me. I'm fifty-eight years old, and I think I'm quite mature."

"Darling, I apologize," Barbara said quickly. "I didn't want to hurt your feelings. Please forgive me."

"Oh, of course. But you and Eloise are so close."

"I love Eloise. She's my dearest friend. But Adam is your brother."

"Adam washed his hands of the whole affair. He says he has enough to do running Highgate."

"Well," Barbara said, "if we can cut the guest list to three hundred, I'll try to sell it to Eloise."

"Bless you."

TWO WEEKS AFTER HIS DINNER with Judith Hope at the Fairmont, Freddie sat down to write a letter. He instructed his secretary, Ms. Gomez, that he was not to be interrupted with any calls or visitors.

"Dear Judith," he wrote. "I am a wretched letter writer, so it has taken me some time to know exactly what I must say to you. To begin, what I did that evening was beneath contempt. I can't apologize, because no apology can cover or make up for my insensitivity and gross stupidity. So if you were to tear up this letter without reading any further I would understand and know that you were right to do so. I could plead for a chance to meet you for the first time all over again, but that isn't possible, is it? And I have been brooding over this part of the letter all week." (He crossed out the last sentence.) "If only it were possible." (He crossed that out.) "The more I think about it, the worse my behavior appears to me." (He was going to cross that out, but after a moment's reflection, he allowed it to stay.)

"In spite of all that happened, I would very much like to see you again—if you can endure to see me. I know this is asking a great deal, and I will not blame you" (He crossed out the last six words.) "and I will understand completely if you ignore this letter. If, however, you should find it in your heart to at least" (He crossed out that sentence.) "In a few weeks we are having a family wedding at Highgate, and if I can bring you to Highgate, it will be a great thing for me. If you care to see me again, you can drop me a note as to where I can pick you up. I will of course send you an invitation." (He felt those should be reversed, but was not sure. He tried again.) "I would not dare to ask you for another date, but we are having a family wedding at Highgate. There will be at least three hundred guests to check on my behavior. I will see that you get an invitation, because I think you may be curious to visit a winery. If I don't hear from you, I will accept that." (He felt he had said that before, but he also felt that it might bear repeating.) "But if you are curious about the winery, you might drop me a note with your home address, so that I can pick you up for the wedding."

He reread what he had written, and in utter despair he started all over. His second attempt was far from satisfying, and he found himself checking words of more than two syllables. Then he threw the dictionary aside and said bitterly, "So much for four years at Princeton."

Ms. Gomez entered his office and said, "It's five o'clock, Mr. Lavette. I'll be going now, unless you want me to stay." She put a sheet of paper on his desk. "You had seven calls. I listed all of them. The one from Mr. Carroll in Oakland he said was urgent and would you please call him back. He'll be in his office until six. Candido wants to see you, but I told him you couldn't be disturbed. Your mother wants to know whether you'll be there for dinner."

"Yes, yes, sure," he muttered.

"For dinner?"

"Yes."

"I'll call her and tell her."

"Yes, that's fine. Sure. Thank you."

She left, and he set about writing the letter.

Highgate

BARBARA CAME HOME at about eleven o'clock in the evening. Her friend Birdie dropped her off in front of her house. Barbara had led a discussion of the Democratic Women's Club and then had sat for another hour with Birdie and some other members of the club, trying to clear her head with two cups of coffee and wishing that she had never met Tony Moretti. It was Tony Moretti, now long dead but at one time the moving force behind the Democratic Party in San Francisco and San Mateo Counties, who had talked her into running for a seat in Congress. Now, years later, she could thank God that she had lost the election, had not become a commuter between Washington and San Francisco, and had not become a part of an organization for which she had little respect and less hope.

But the margin of defeat had been so small that she could not dispel her friends' belief that she was a super-candidate, and that if she ran once more in the same district, she would win. Their argument was that her candidacy would throw the whole Reagan movement in California off base and possibly tilt the state against him—none of which she agreed with. Indeed, her feeling was that the whole idea was nonsensical, that with Reagan sweeping the state, she would lose by a huge margin—and she had come to a point where she hated politics. She said she was thinking of resigning— which was the reason that four of the leading lights of the club had corralled her into Katy's Place for coffee and cake. There she tried to convince them of Tony Moretti's maxim, that in politics one took advantage of what was on the edge of happening and that one did not come out of the woods with some cooked-up notion and attempt to make it happen. "And it can't happen," she said decisively. "Reagan is going to take the state, and nothing we or anyone else can do will stop him."

Now, dropping her off at Green Street, Birdie said, "You might just change your mind."

"Never! Not a chance," Barbara responded.

Birdie drove off, and Barbara, tired and irritated, fumbled for her key, opened the door, walked through the tiny hallway with its night-light, switched on the living room light, and confronted Robert Jones in the flesh. She felt a moment of almost overwhelming fear, and then Jones held up both hands, palms out, and begged her, "Please don't scream, Ms. Lavette."

The fear vanished. "I'm not going to scream," she declared in as close to a snarl as she had ever achieved. "What in hell are you doing here, and how did you get in?"

"I picked the lock."

"Yes, that's your thing! What do you want? Jewelry—but you took it all. Or did you come back for the ring?"

"I came to return the jewels. They're all laid out on your desk. I was leaving as you came in."

"Yes, of course you were!" She snorted.

"Look at your desk," he said hopelessly. "I won't run away. The telephone's working if you want to call the cops."

She strode past him without giving him another glance, swept into her study, flicked on the light, and stared at the jewelry—all

laid out neatly on her desk, just as he had said. She studied the desk
for a very long moment, and then she sighed and walked back into
the living room. He was standing where she had left him.

"You didn't call the cops," he said.

"They wouldn't arrest you for bringing it back."

He shrugged. "Breaking and entering."

"Do you want some coffee?"

He hesitated and then nodded.

"Come into the kitchen and sit down. You look better without
the mask."

"Tools of the trade," he said resignedly. He followed her into
the kitchen, pulled out a chair, and sat quietly while Barbara prepared the coffee.

"Are you hungry?"

He nodded his head.

"Toast and butter and cheese?"

"If it's no trouble, Ms. Lavette."

"I'm hungry, too. No trouble. Tell me, are you still a thief?"

"No. I gave it up. I don't like cops, and sooner or later they
get to you. Anyway, I have a job. Mr. Lefkowitz has a client who
owns an engineering firm. He got them to take me on."

"That was very decent of him," Barbara said.

"He's a decent white man," he admitted.

"Couldn't he be just a decent man?"

He hesitated over that. "I suppose so, if you want it that
way."

"You're a civil engineer?"

"Yes."

"What," she asked, "does a civil engineer do?"

"Public buildings, bridges, roads."

"That should be very rewarding."

"If you do it. I don't. I do some specs, pricing, call manufacturers for prices and compare them, and I'm also a gofer when they need coffee or lunch inside—"

"It's a beginning, isn't it?"

"I guess."

"Why did you bring back the jewelry?"

"I knew you couldn't claim the insurance with all that stuff in the papers."

"I gave the jewelry to you."

"Not really, Ms. Lavette. You gave me a second chance."

She poured the coffee and put out the toast and cheese without replying.

Jones ate hungrily, and Barbara regarded him thoughtfully. He was a handsome man, strong bones in a lean face, dark skin, and a good mouth. His long-fingered hands were deft and smooth in their movements.

"Do you want to smoke?" she asked him.

"If you don't mind?"

"No, I don't mind."

She brought out an ashtray, and he lit a cigarette.

"Are you married?"

He shook his head. "I have a girl. She was spooked by the newspaper stories, but we'll work it out. Can I tell you something, Ms. Lavette?"

"Anything you wish."

"I'd like to repay you sometime. I don't know how, but if you need anything that I can do..." He took out his wallet and gave her a card. "I had them printed up. You can reach me at that number." He bent his head and shrugged. "I don't know what else to say. But like I said, if you need anything..."

"Like picking a lock?" And then she would have given anything to take back the words, but he simply said, "Yes, like picking a lock or anything else."

When he had gone she climbed the stairs to her room, took a hot shower, and crawled into bed. But sleep did not come easily.

A FEW DAYS LATER she drove out to Napa with Philip, so that he could talk to Sally about the wedding. Philip had readily agreed to do the marriage ceremony. Their relationship had progressed no further than a restrained kiss on her cheek, but Barbara sensed his affection and his struggle to hold back. They were both in their seventies, and each of them carried a large backload of life and grief and happiness. Barbara enjoyed the feeling of being with a man who cared for her. Since Carson's death her life had been hollow and empty. She was not the kind of a woman who could settle down to widowhood and allow empty days to slide by, or do charity work in some hospital. There was a small gift shop in the hospital where Sam, her son, was chief surgeon, and he had suggested that if time hung heavily, she might take over the shop.... The pay was nothing, the shop being nonprofit; and Barbara had rejected the notion indignantly. "I am a writer by profession," she replied, "and when I am ready to retire, I will let you know."

Driving to Napa now with Philip, she told him of her encounter with Robert Jones. "Why did it leave me so empty, Philip? Why couldn't I have at least a bit of satisfaction at getting the jewelry back? What is wrong in all this?"

Barbara expected him to brush aside her question with a few reassuring words, but after a minute or two of silence, he asked her whether he could tell her a story.

She shrugged. "If you wish—of course."

"It's an old Sufi story—the Sufis are a small mystical sect of Islam, not like the fundamentalists—something else. It concerns a smuggler, Abdul Hassan by name. For thirty years, he practiced his trade—the most famous smuggler in the Middle East. Every month, month after month, he would come across the border with ten donkeys, each loaded with wood. Each time, the guards searched him head to foot, went through his clothes, unloaded the wood, even split the larger pieces, but they could never find what he was smuggling. Yet they knew he was a smuggler. He made no secret of it. As the years passed he became rich, built himself a fine house, took care of his many children; and after thirty years he announced that he had retired and that he would smuggle no more. When he made this announcement the customs inspectors decided that they would send a small deputation to visit Abdul Hassan and to ask him, please, for the sake of their profession, to explain what he smuggled and how he did it.

"He greeted the customs men pleasantly, gave them Turkish coffee and halvah, and smiled in answer to their question. 'Gentlemen,' he said, 'it is really very obvious what I smuggled. I smuggled donkeys.' "

"That's it?" Barbara asked.

"Yes, the whole story."

They drove on in silence while Barbara brooded over the story. Finally she said, "I resented him bringing back the jewelry."

"The cynics say that no good deed goes unpunished."

"What did I miss?" Barbara asked with some asperity.

"A black man who earns what—what could they pay him? Nine, ten thousand a year? The edge of the poverty level. What's inside of him? You gave him fifteen years of his life. He could easily think that he deserved it, that it's no crime to steal from a rich white woman. To him, it's the difference between wealth and poverty."

"Do you really think it's no crime for a black man to steal from a wealthy white woman—as you put it?"

"I'm not talking about us. I'm talking about him. There is a point to that Sufi story. It's so easy to miss the obvious—especially when we're clever. We're both very clever, Barbara. I mean no put-down. I have so much respect for you. But forget for a moment that he's black. He's a good man, and we're surrounded by so much rot that plain decency becomes difficult to accept."

They drove on, and they were almost at Napa when he said, "You're angry with me, aren't you?"

"No, I've been thinking."

"Do you want to talk about it?"

"Well, yes. I *was* provoked. I wanted sympathy, and instead you told me something about myself. That's always cruel."

"I didn't intend to be cruel."

"No, I'm sure you didn't. I'm a writer. I know the addiction to stories. I suppose for a minister it's even worse."

"It is," Philip admitted. "I wasn't going to speak about personal things, and I know we've only been together a few times, but I'm very fond of you and..."

"And what?"

"Another time," he said uneasily. "We're almost there."

How will I ever know this man? Barbara wondered. At one moment he was a sage, and the next moment a high school boy at the senior prom. Well, he had been a Catholic priest and had left the Church and married a nun. That must have been hard. *Let it be. Whatever will come will come.* She certainly wasn't in love with him—and could she ever be, with him or with anyone else? The story still annoyed her. He could have told her what he felt she had missed without the parable, but then he was a priest and a minister, or had been a priest, and at least the story was interesting and provoking.

Both Sally and May Ling were waiting for them, and Sally had properly prepared coffee and tea and small sandwiches. Sally had looked up Unitarianism in the encyclopedia; May Ling had not. Sally made an excuse for Barbara to join her in the kitchen, and then Sally whispered, "Let me get this straight, Barbara. Is he your boyfriend? Is something cooking?"

"For heaven's sake," Barbara said, "we're both old. I do not have boyfriends."

"Well, don't get huffy. I mean, do you like him?"

"Yes, I do. I like him. That's all."

"All right. It makes a difference."

They returned to the dining room. The cottage was small and unassuming; the surgery, which Joe had built onto the original house, was almost as large, with its waiting room, two examining rooms, operating room for emergencies, and small laboratory. The simplicity of the cottage struck Philip as rather odd, considering all he had heard of the Lavettes and their wealth.

As he was apparently answering a question May Ling had asked him, Barbara and Sally entered the room quietly and sat at the table.

"...yes, we're a religion, if you choose to use the word. We also welcome people who have no religion or mystical belief, and we don't try to force any belief on them. In your case, I would be performing a marriage ceremony—as I would for any woman and man who love each other and who ask me to marry them. It places no religious obligation upon you."

"But are you Christians?" May Ling asked.

"Some of us are. Some are Jewish. Some are Muslims. Some are Catholics, some are Protestants."

"Do you mind my asking all these questions? I feel so foolish, not knowing anything about your people."

Philip shook his head. "No, not at all. Please ask anything you wish."

"Daddy's father was Italian and Daddy's mother was Chinese. Her name was May Ling, and I was named after her, but I was brought up with no religion except to respect what other people believe. Mother's father was Jewish, but her mother was a Protestant. So you can see how confused it all is. The man I'm going to marry, Harry Lefkowitz, is Jewish. He has no wish except to be married, and he suggested Judge Horton, an old friend of his; but I don't want to be married by a judge—it's just something I feel about judges and law."

"Would Mr. Lefkowitz resent being married by a Unitarian minister?" Philip asked.

"Oh no, not at all. He left it entirely up to Mother and me. But I would like to be able to tell him something more about Unitarians."

"Of course," Philip agreed. "What shall I tell you? Our church is on Franklin Street, just off Geary, a brown stone building with a bit of a stubby bell tower—"

"Yes, I've passed it so many times."

"—and it's quite old for San Francisco, almost a hundred years. We're a reasonably old faith for America. Thomas Jefferson was a Unitarian, and he decided that in a hundred years, all America would be Unitarian. I'm afraid he was very wrong, but we don't proselytize much. Thoreau was Unitarian, and so was Ralph Waldo Emerson. To bring it closer to home, the man who invented and built our cable car system was a Unitarian."

"Do you believe in Jesus Christ?" Sally put in.

"We don't preach a belief—only the inherent worth and dignity of every human being, a deep respect for religious pluralism, and a conviction that this pluralism enriches our faith. Of course, I believe that Jesus was a great prophet and a great spiritual leader, but you must remember that I was trained as a Jesuit priest and my belief is my own."

"And would your sanctuary be large enough for three or four hundred people?"

"I think so, Ms. Lavette." He smiled.

May Ling responded to his smile. "Mother believes in large weddings. I was married and divorced. Does that matter?"

"No. Of course not."

"Then I think I would be pleased and honored if you would marry Harry and me. You will like Harry."

"I'm sure I will."

"And I can't think of anything you said that he might disagree with."

When Barbara and Philip got into her car to leave, Barbara sighed and said, "Well, thank goodness that's off my mind."

"What are you, my dear?" Philip wondered. "Are you the Mother Superior, so to speak, of the entire Lavette–Levy tribe?"

"Mother Hen would be a better title. War and death have taken a terrible toll on us. We are not a long-lived family. Even Adam, with his white beard and his attitude of being something out of the Old Testament, is eight years younger than I, and his wife, Eloise, my dearest friend, is four years older than Adam. That leaves me, skin and bones, as the senior member of the family."

"You're hardly skin and bones."

"I'll be seventy in November, and thank you—and that gives me a delightful idea. What do you have planned for the rest of today?"

"Nothing. I took the whole day off for this trip."

"Have you ever been through the Napa Valley?"

"Once. I came here with Agatha."

"Good. I'm going to turn right here, and that will put us on the Silverado Trail, which is the best way into the Valley—not spoiled by tourist places like Oakville or Rutherford—and we'll end up at Highgate and they'll give us dinner and we can spend the night in their guesthouse, and you can learn how wine is made."

"I couldn't do that," he protested. "I can't just turn up and ask to spend the night with a woman. For heaven's sake, Barbara, I'm a minister."

"Are you really?" She had turned the car and was now driving north on Route 121. "And Unitarians don't allow their ministers to do such vile things? You never mentioned that to May Ling."

"Barbara, what will they think?"

"They'll think more things than we have ever done, I can assure you of that. Philip, how old are you?"

"You know well enough how old I am."

"You're seventy-three. I'm sixty-nine. They will be happy to see you. They know all about you. They will give us separate rooms. What on earth are you afraid of?"

It took him a while to answer. "I have no clothes," he finally said, rather lamely. "A shirt and trousers and a sweater. You can't come to dinner that way. I don't even have a razor."

Laughing, she said, "Oh, you are wonderful, Philip my dear. You don't have a razor. And you don't have pajamas, do you?"

"No."

"Philip, don't look down. Look up. If God wanted a model for paradise, he couldn't do better than the Napa Valley."

She realized that he had surrendered, nor had it taken much persuasion. They were in the Valley now, none of the craggy rocks and deep gorges of the coastal range, but gentle undulating hills that folded lovingly into each other, and into an old road lined with live oaks and rosebushes and ponderosa pine and hemlock and Pacific madrone and the ever-present alders. Every half mile or so a little road twisted into the gentle hills to mark a winery, and on every side of these old roads were fields covered with vines in lines so straight that they might have been drawn on a map, with a burst of green leaves and fruit at the top of each thick stick. The blue sky and the gentle breeze barely moved the leaves.

Barbara enjoyed being his tour guide. "There's Chimney Rock—and right behind it, Stag's Leap—you've seen those in the stores. And there—I think that's Sinskey's place, and over on the left is Pine Ridge. You won't see Mondavi or Krug or some of the other big ones—they're on the other side of the Valley on Route 29, but this road is far lovelier. And that's Pine Ridge—they make a fine white—"

"How do you know so much about this place?"

"Philip, I've been up and down this road a hundred times—no, five hundred times. Of course, there are wines just as good from Sonoma and Sonoma Mountain, but somehow Napa catches people's fancy. And in a few minutes we'll be at Highgate—we used to spell it H-i-g-a-t-e, but Freddie didn't like it spelled that way because people began to pronounce it 'higgate,' and he convinced Adam to change it..." She turned off the main road onto a hard oiled-dirt road that led into a cross valley, and then through two tall stone posts that had once supported a heavy iron gate, replaced now by a wooden ranch gate that was almost always open. Ahead of them, on either side, the vine lines stretched away, folding into the low hummocks; and close by and clumped together were seven stone buildings, some large, some small. Barbara drove into an asphalt parking area where there was an assortment of cars, trucks, and farm machines.

"Well, here we are," she announced, "and no pajamas. Do you feel abducted, Philip?"

"*Kidnapped* would be a better word," he said ruefully.

"Philip, Philip, you're here to see the bride's grandmother and grandfather. Kidnapped, indeed!"

"We could drive back to San Francisco after dinner."

"Philip!"

"Well—I suppose—you could find whatever I need?"

"Even a razor, Philip."

IN THE KITCHEN WITH ELOISE, helping Cathrena decide what to serve for dinner and setting the table, Barbara told Eloise that they would be staying over and that they would occupy two rooms. Adam had taken Philip in hand and was instructing him in the process of turning grapes into wine.

"Two rooms. Will you please tell me what is going on, Barbara?"

"He's a minister."

"You and a minister. I don't believe it."

"It's not me and a minister, Ellie. May Ling has agreed to

his marrying them. He's a Unitarian. Let me tell you about Unitarians—"

"I know about Unitarians, Barbara, and I know you. I'm very happy that Sally has agreed to something. Did he know you were bringing him here?"

"Well, not exactly," Barbara admitted.

"You mean you kidnapped him?"

"Well, no, not exactly. I took the liberty of inviting him here. He was somewhat upset. He's a widower, and I don't think he's even looked at another woman since his wife died. That was five years ago. Don't you think he's quite good-looking?"

"Barbara, for heaven's sake, will you tell me what's going on?"

"Ellie, I'm not entirely sure what's going on. Do I look old—I mean really old? You haven't changed a bit, but—"

"No, I haven't changed, Barbara. I weighed one hundred and ten when I married Adam, and now I'm one hundred and seventy, and I dye my hair—"

"You haven't a wrinkle on your face."

"Neither would you if you were as fat as I am."

"I have more wrinkles than I can count. My wrinkles have wrinkles."

"You have bones. I don't have a bone in my body."

"I don't believe what we're saying!" Barbara exclaimed. "Cathrena, do you hear us?"

"I don't hear foolishness," Cathrena said. "You are both beautiful women."

Barbara sighed. "I hate to live alone."

"It's unhealthy, *señora*," Cathrena said. "Nobody should live alone. A man needs a woman, a woman needs a man."

"The trouble is," Barbara said, "that he needs pajamas and a razor. That was his excuse for not staying overnight. I suppose he also felt dreadful about wearing his socks two days in a row. He was raised in parochial schools, seminaries, and that kind of thing.

He was a Jesuit priest and his wife was a nun. They left the Church and married. He's the sweetest, most thoughtful man I ever knew, and he thinks you don't hold hands in public. He kisses me on the cheek."

"You do have a good eye for men," Eloise admitted.

"Jesuits," Cathrena said. "I tell you something, *señora*. They are very smart. He gives up his soul for a woman. That's a man."

"There you are," Eloise said. "Do you love him?"

"It's hard to decide. I read somewhere that women over seventy don't fall in love."

"Who tells you that?" Cathrena asked indignantly.

"My publisher," Barbara said lamely.

Eloise said, "Let's get out of here and find them before Adam has him drunk. He does drink wine?"

"Oh yes."

"Then we'd better find them. There's nothing Adam likes better than opinions. He'll have Philip tasting every vintage we have. And heaven help him if he doesn't like Cabernet."

TO FREDDIE'S SURPRISE, the letter to Judith Hope elicited an almost immediate reply: on a small sheet of white letterhead, these few words: "I would be pleased to have you pick me up on the 22nd, at eight o'clock, at the above address. We are invited to a party. As for forgiveness, we shall see." It was addressed to Mr. Frederick Lavette, to the address on the card he had given her. It was signed simply "Judith Hope."

He read and reread the few words. "We are invited" puzzled him. Who knew about the incident? How much had she told? What kind of a party? Nothing about whether he might cor the possibility that he would not be able to come—just a queenly command. *We are invited.*

He was all smiles and charm when he entered the dining room and was introduced to Philip Carter. Barbara, who had witnessed his depression of two weeks ago, was pleased. Freddie's chameleon-like changes of mood could not be counted on, and she wanted this dinner to go nicely. He praised Cathrena's chicken in *mole, pollo con chocolate,* assuring her that it was as good as anything he had ever eaten in Mexico City, and he held forth on the wine, a Navarra of sorts that was an experiment of Freddie's with which Adam was not too pleased—indeed, a wine too heavy for the taste of most of them, but which Cathrena had praised as a companion to the bitter chocolate sauce. On a visit to Spain years before, Freddie had spent a week at a winery on the south slope of the Pyrenees and had returned with a packet of seeds that he had nursed in the greenhouse. They never made more than a few hundred bottles—a wasteful process, according to Adam—and most of those went to the wine merchants in New York who sold them to Spanish and Portuguese tourists at thirty dollars a bottle. Adam ordered his own Cabernet and advised Philip against the heavy Spanish wine. Barbara felt that Philip ought to have a glass of both. "Each has its quality," she told him.

Eloise smiled knowingly at Barbara.

Seated next to Barbara, Philip leaned over and whispered, "Don't they ever talk about anything but wine?"

"Of course—politics and books and art. Except that Adam is so furious at Reagan that Ellie is trying to keep the conversation local," Barbara whispered back.

"What on earth are you whispering about?" Freddie wanted to know.

"Freddie!" his mother said, and to Philip, "Please forgive him. He has no manners. Have you been to the Valley before, Mr. Carter?"

"Please—Philip."

Reynold Couer, a young Frenchman, was trying desperately to follow the conversation and sipping warily at the Navarra. He was a guest of Freddie's who had come to California on what he called an investigatory visit. Barbara, whose French was excellent, the result of living there for more than a year, explained that the dark sauce on the chicken was chocolate without sweetening.

"It's a famous old sauce of the Aztec people"—and the language breakthrough led to a conversation in French that all joined in except for Adam, who had no French to speak of. Eloise promptly invited Couer to stay for the wedding, but he made his apologies. Freddie explained that he was flying to New York the next day to visit the wineries in the Genesee Valley. Adam managed to follow that, and in English snorted his contempt for New York–grown wine, and that led to a discussion of the new Australian wine that had just made its appearance in California. "Their white is all right, but their red..." And thus it went on and on.

Outside after dinner, in the cool night air, Barbara apologized to Philip. "At least," she said, "it made young Reynold feel at home."

"They're wonderfully warm people," Philip admitted, "but I felt out of it."

"But wine does play a large part in religion, doesn't it?"

"I suppose so. But Unitarians don't have communion. I mean, we do drink wine. We have nothing against it, you understand."

"Of course, Philip. It's a beautiful night, isn't it?"

"Just perfect."

"Even with all the boring wine talk?"

"Even with all the wine talk—absolutely. And it gave me a chance to use my French."

"And your French is excellent. Where did you learn?"

"School, college—but you speak it like a native."

She took his arm. "Do you want to know my whole history, Philip?" The sound of a piano came from the house behind them. "That's Freddie. He's so gifted, and it all dribbles away. That's the Italian Concerto; I've heard him play it a dozen times. He calls it his meditation. Do you want to go inside and listen?"

"I'd rather be out here with you."

The winding brick paths from house to house were lit. At the bunkhouse, a group of winery workers sat and smoked and talked softly in Spanish.

"Do you meditate?" she asked him.

"Yes. I began when I was a priest."

"Do you believe in God?"

It took so long for him to answer that Barbara thought that he had not heard her question, or if he had heard it, had chosen not to answer. But then Philip said, "Most of the time, yes. I don't have an unshaken faith."

"I have no religion," she said. "When I go into Grace Church for a funeral or a wedding, the place smells dry and musty and old and forbidding. I smell the money my grandfather put into its building. He was a wicked old man who was determined to buy his place in heaven. My first lover died in the Spanish Civil War. My first husband was killed in Israel in 1948. A man I loved was murdered in El Salvador. We've had our own holocaust, and I can understand what the great Holocaust meant. The only time I felt a sense of something you call religion was when I walked out of the rain into your church."

His reply was unexpected. "I think you're deeply religious," he said.

"Oh no, Philip." She shivered. "It's getting cold. I'm tired."

"So am I."

She peered at her watch in the dim light. "It's after ten. Shall we turn in?"

"If you wish. Don't we have to go inside first and tell them?"

"No. I'm family, and they know you're with me. The rooms are made up, and you'll find a razor and pajamas and a robe in yours, and Eloise provided clean socks and underwear."

"You're teasing me. You make me feel like a stodgy, impossible old man."

Smiling, Barbara agreed. "Yes, you're rather impossible."

"I try. I did agree to come here and spend the night."

"And be bored to death with wine talk."

"Oh no, no, absolutely not," he protested. "As a matter of fact, it was enlightening. I know absolutely nothing about wine. At Saint Mary's, when I was assistant pastor, I was responsible for the wine for communion. I used to buy Manischewitz, a sort of interfaith gesture on my part."

"Good heavens, no!"

"Why not? It's very sweet and everyone liked it."

"I'm sure they did. But please, please never mention this to Adam."

"Why? He's half Jewish. I should think he would appreciate it as a gesture. And once or twice I bought an old Israeli wine—I believe it's called Malaga. I felt that a wine out of Israeli grapes would enhance the Eucharist."

"Oh, my dear, bless you."

"You're teasing me again," Philip said, frowning.

"I am, and I promise never to tease you again unless I must. Let's not talk about wine."

In the guesthouse, the two rooms Eloise had prepared opened off the entry hall. The small stone cottage was plain and unadorned. Each guest room was furnished more or less alike—a double bed, wicker furniture, prints on the wall, a rag rug, and an adjoining bath. Before he went into his room, Philip grasped her by her shoulders and said, "I would like to kiss you."

She made no reply, and he kissed her on the lips.

"Good night, dear Barbara." He opened the door to his room. "I'm glad I came here with you. It was good."

She smiled. "Good night, Philip."

In her room, Barbara asked herself, *How, oh how do I pick them? There must be a reason. It's my fate, my destiny. Philip would say it's my karma, whatever karma is. I should have known when he sent me that letter. Well, Barbara, faint heart never won fair love.*

She stripped down, put on a shower cap and showered, and then rubbed her hair with a towel, combed it out, and brushed it. Eloise had laid out toothbrush, toothpaste, brush, comb, and an assortment of small perfume bottles—with a warning that Barbara was to take the room to the right. She chose a perfume at random and used a few tiny drops; she was not crazy about perfume. There was a freshly washed cotton nightgown on the bed, and for a few minutes she studied it thoughtfully. Putting it on, she looked at herself in the mirror. "Oh, what the hell!" she said, and pulled it off and wrapped herself in the cotton flannel robe that hung in the bathroom. Then she slipped out of the robe and regarded herself in the mirror. *Not bad,* she thought. Her breasts were small and firm, her hips and legs not too different from what they were twenty years ago. Sighing, she pulled on the cotton nightgown, which fell to her knees and was hardly fitted, but rather tentlike, to cover Eloise's abundant bosom. She nodded and shrugged. *Even Everest is climbed in stages, and to seduce a man who refuses to seduce you is not easy*—and then the thought of seduction in terms of herself and Philip Carter made her burst out laughing. Then she pulled herself together, donned the robe over her nightgown, left her room, knocked at the door of Philip's room, and entered. Clad in a pair of Adam's pajamas, he was sitting up in bed and reading, his reading glasses perched halfway down his nose.

"I thought I'd peek in and see whether everything is well. You're very handsome in pajamas. What are you reading?"

"*Guide to California Wines.*" He held up the book for her to see.

"Well, that is a surprise."

"Found it on the bookshelf. There are also two books by Zane Grey, *Finnegans Wake,* and *Just So Stories.* A nice balance."

"That's Eloise." Barbara seated herself at the foot of his bed. "Do you like reading aloud?"

"That's part of my discipline. Yes, I rather enjoy it."

"Then read to me," Barbara said. "I don't have my reading glasses. They're in the car."

"About wine?"

"Yes. Why not? Though I'd have thought you'd choose *Finnegans Wake*."

"I don't like it."

"Neither do I. Let's hear about wine."

"If you insist." And picking up the book, he said, "I chose Cabernet, since that's Adam's favorite"; and reading, " 'The finest Cabernet Sauvignons are produced from considerably more than the legal minimum of fifty-one percent of grapes of that name, as the wine will not stand much blending without loss of character. The best have a deep ruby color, an expansive bouquet, and a remarkable flavor, easy to recognize and appreciate. When young they possess a dryness and aromatic pungency that smooth out with age to a rich mellowness. A common mistake is to serve them at a temperature cooler than the average room. At room temperature their inherent tartness will dissolve—' "

"Philip," she interrupted, "take off your glasses."

He raised a brow. "I can't read without them."

"I know. I don't want you to read."

"I thought you did?"

"No, Philip, I didn't come in here to have you read to me. I came in here because I think I love you and I've decided to seduce you. I am well aware that women of my age don't seduce anyone much, but what the hell! Being nearly seventy doesn't seem to stop me from loving a man, and I have the crazy notion that you are very fond of me."

"I am," he said.

"Good. Now put down the book and take off your glasses, and turn off that light."

Like a small boy caught in some egregious act, he followed her instructions, saying lamely, "Barbara, I don't wear the pajama bottoms."

"That's nice"—slipping out of her robe and crawling under the covers next to him.

JUDITH HOPE LIVED IN A SMALL WHITE HOUSE in Pacific Heights, and when she opened the door for Freddie, he realized that the entire first floor was a single room, backed by a curling iron staircase to a balcony. The windows were doors, floor to ceiling, and the room, paved in white vinyl blocks, was flooded with sunlight. The furniture was Mexican, the fine laminated wood and wicker that can be found in Guadalajara and nowhere else. She was dressed and waiting for him, and she nodded, smiled slightly, and held out her hand. She wore a long white pleated skirt, a white silk shirt, and a pale gray cape, buckled at her throat.

"Welcome, Mr. Vintner. You're right on time."

"I try," Freddie said. "You look absolutely beautiful. If I am permitted to call you Judith, might you call me Fred?" He had rehearsed. He had been rehearsing things he would say all the distance from Napa.

"My friends call me Judy. How about Freddie, and that will be a pact of peace between us."

"Thank you, Judy." His hand on her arm was a light touch, since she wore a cape. When they were in his car, he asked her where they were going.

"Russian Hill—it's an apartment house. I'll direct you."

Sitting next to her, he sorted out the conversation he had rehearsed:

"Why did you agree to see me again?" he began.

"Were you surprised?"

"Yes, I was," he admitted.

"Well, Freddie, I was touched by your letter, and I'm free, black, and well over twenty-one. I don't have a boyfriend at this moment—and by the way, are you married?"

"I told you I was not."

"So you did, but you told me other things, too."

"I was divorced. I have a child, a little boy of four. He lives with his mother."

"I see," she said. "Well, in answer to your question—you're very good-looking, you're tall enough, and you dress well. Perhaps you're also intelligent. We'll see."

"I hope so," he said, with a sense of futility.

"And I haven't ever dated a white man before. Consider it an experiment."

He had been put down gently but deftly, and now he decided that his sins were forgiven. He would not try to match her wit or irony, but neither would he be subdued by it.

"Who are your friends—I mean, the people to whose home we're going?"

"That's Larry and Jane Cutler. It's their apartment. There'll be eight or ten couples—two doctors, the Browns; she was a nurse but when he began to make some money, she went on to medical school. Jerry Delrio—you met him that first night at the Fairmont—the jazz pianist, and his wife, Dotty, and the Gershons and Kier Dumas—and I suppose others that I've not met. You'll see."

He considered telling her the story of Barbara and the black man who had broken into her apartment, but he thought better of it. And then they were there, in front of an elegant apartment house on Russian Hill, with a doorman who took Freddie's car and the ten-dollar bill that he pressed into his hand; and then up the elevator and into a crowded living room with a broad picture window that overlooked San Francisco Bay and the sky, bathed in the colors of the sunset; and men and women were kissing and embracing Judith Hope, well-dressed men and women to whom he was being introduced—and Freddie realized that he was the only white man in the room, and that this was the first time in his life that he had ever been in a room as the only white man present.

A woman put a drink into his hand. "It's gin and tonic—but you can have Scotch, if you prefer, or white wine."

"No, thank you. This is fine."

He stood awkwardly alone for a long moment, and then a man came to him and said, "Did I hear Judy call you Frederick Lavette?"

"Yes."

"Excuse me, I don't want to pry, but are you any relation to the Barbara Lavette I read about—oh, maybe five or six weeks back—the woman who said she wasn't robbed of a hundred grand in jewelry?"

Freddie hesitated, then nodded. "She's my aunt."

"I'll be damned! How did Judy find you?"

"Judy," someone called out, "come over here!"

Freddie shrugged uneasily. Another man joined them, and then a couple, and in a few minutes Freddie was the center of a circle of people.

"Come on, she really gave him the jewelry?"

"Did they know each other?" a woman wanted to know.

"No," he replied, and tried to explain. "The way she put it, she was buying the fifteen years he would have served. She knows what prison is. She was in prison once."

"Come on!"

Judith Hope had never made the connection, and as she joined the circle around Freddie she stared at him as if she had never seen him before.

Taken wholly aback by the look on Judith's face, he had a sudden rush of panic. "Here I am babbling away—I shouldn't be speaking about this. If a cop took down what I'm saying—"

"Freddie," Judith said, "there are no cops here."

Larry Cutler, their host, was an attorney and knew Harry Lefkowitz, and he filled in pieces of the story. Freddie had another gin and tonic, and the talk turned to the first case of Robert Jones and the term he had served for punching the armed guard. Bit by bit, Freddie forgot his white skin, and when dinner was served, he ate hungrily of the fresh roast and fixings. He was just a little drunk, relaxed, and he accepted the plate of food that Judith chose for him with a whisper of gratitude.

When he dropped Judith off at her house, well past midnight, after she opened the door, she leaned toward him and kissed him—and then swirled away and closed the door behind her. He drove back to Highgate, lost in a maze of interesting thought. Fortunately, there was almost no traffic at that hour.

HARRY LEFKOWITZ WAS INVOLVED in the closing of an important case, and May Ling had agreed to meet him in San Francisco for lunch at his office so that they could talk to Philip Carter. Harry was perfectly willing to leave all wedding arrangements to Sally and May Ling, but Philip felt that he should at least have a talk with Harry before the ceremony. May Ling planned to do some shopping while in town, and she arrived early, with her four-year-old son, Danny. She had hoped to leave him with Sally, but Sally complained that she could not cover for May Ling in the surgery and take care of Danny at the same time.

At Harry's office, his secretary, Alice Goldman, a fat, good-natured woman of fifty or so, said that she would gladly look after Danny for the next hour, but Danny refused vociferously, and May Ling decided that the best choice was to take him with her. After an hour of shopping, May Ling returned to the office with a tired and irritated little boy, explaining to Harry and Philip, who were already there, that this was not his usual behavior and that Market Street and Macy's had gotten the best of him.

He was a handsome little boy, part Chinese, part Jewish, and part Anglo, straight brown hair and large brown eyes. Harry had put out a sumptuous spread—chicken salad, a pâté, a green salad, small rolls, and ice cream—but Danny would have none of it until finally, with his mother's urging, he settled for the ice cream.

Harry shared the boy's uneasiness. He had pondered the question of adoption, and while he felt that Freddie would not stand in the way of such a course, his feeling—not unusual in a Jew—was that with his natural father being a Lavette, the child would have more opportunities with that name than with the name of Lefkowitz. Harry had raised this question once with May Ling, and it evoked the only anger he had ever seen her display. "You are Lefkowitz and I shall be Lefkowitz, and if Freddie agrees that you adopt Danny, he will be Lefkowitz and proud of it. My father was Jewish, Harry, and so am I. I don't want you to forget that." Harry realized that this was not strictly true, since under Jewish practice the descent is through the mother, and Sally's mother was not Jewish; but Harry had been in no mood to argue the matter.

Harry had intended to look up *Unitarian* in the encyclopedia, but time and the closing of his case prevented this, and very uneasily he broached the question of cults to Philip, who took it with good nature. "No, Mr. Lefkowitz—we are older than the United States and we exist all over the world. We are a very simple and straight-forward religion. I brought some material that we publish, which you may read when you find time." He put the material on the table and selected a single pamphlet. "This is our marriage booklet. It has dozens of suggestions, and you may choose any of them or any combination of them—or May Ling and you may decide to write your own ceremony. We have no liturgy that we press on anyone."

"That's hard to believe," Harry said. "If you're trained as a lawyer, you live on liturgy. It becomes our religion."

"From what I hear, that's hardly the case with you."

"Thank you," Harry said, looking at his watch. "I only wish it were so. I'm defending a man who may or may not have stolen five million dollars from his stockholders, and I'm ashamed to admit that I don't actually know whether he's guilty or not. Our liturgy is very complicated, Dr. Carter."

"Well, there is one rule in our church. No one is permitted, without correction, to call me Dr. Carter."

"I'll remember that, Philip."

THAT EVENING BARBARA DINED with Philip at her home. More and more often she had been inviting him to partake of her own cooking, since he insisted on getting the check when they dined out. She was a good cook. Her time in France had been at least in part an investigation into French cooking, and she had an assortment of French cookbooks on her kitchen shelf. He ate what she cooked with delight and gusto, and complained gently that for the first time in his adult life he was gaining weight, which she dismissed as nonsense. "You're thin as a rail. It's just that for the first time in years you're enjoying what you eat, instead of what they serve you in those dreadful restaurants you patronize."

"They're not all dreadful."

"Most are. Chinese food is very salty, and the doctor said you should cut down on salt. Oh, what's the use? You don't listen to anything I say."

"I certainly do," he protested. "And I'm healthy as an ox."

"However healthy that may be . . . Tell me about today. What happened?"

"It went nicely. May Ling is a lovely, gentle woman."

"And Harry Lefkowitz?"

"He puzzles me. I mentioned him to Bob Doyle, who's a member of our church and a U.S. Attorney. He says Lefkowitz is one of the sharpest lawyers in town, and the others hate to go up against him because he ties them into knots and wins most of his cases. On the other hand, Doyle says that Lefkowitz's office does more pro bono work than any large firm in town. I don't like to judge people—especially when I know so little about them."

"Saint *and* sinner?" Barbara asked.

"Perhaps."

"I thought you didn't have sin in your discipline?"

"Do you mean we don't admit to sin, acknowledge sin?"

"I suppose."

"Of course there's sin—just look around the world we live in. The difference is that we don't deal with sin against God or the rules they make up concerning sin against God. We deal with sin against men and women, and that's an entirely different matter."

She nodded, rose, and went into the kitchen for dessert and coffee. She returned with the coffeepot in one hand and a big platter in the other, which Philip took from her as its weight began to tell.

"What on earth is this?" he asked her.

"It's a superb Australian dessert called a pavlova. She was dancing in Sydney, I believe, and they were so delighted with her that they named this dessert after her. It's all egg white, sugar, and flavor—not a drop of cholesterol, and it rips the fat off you."

He had two helpings of the pavlova and praised it, and when she started to clear the table, he said, "No—please, Barbara. Sit down. I'll help you clear later. There's something I have to say now."

"Now? How about in the living room, and I'll pour some brandy?"

"No. Here, right now, before the telephone rings. Your friends always call when they think you've finished dinner."

"What an odd thought! All right, my dear Philip, here, now." She leaned over the table and put her chin on her palms.

"I want to marry you," Philip said flatly.

"Do you? That's very flattering. But why?"

"Because I love you."

"Thank you, dear Philip. But you don't have to marry me to love me. Is that the result of seeing Harry and May Ling? May Ling is thirty-seven, and Harry is somewhere around fifty, and it's quite intelligent for them to marry. You and I—"

"I know how old we are. That makes no difference. I want very much to marry you, for us to be man and wife."

"But why marriage, Philip? This isn't the largest house in the world, but I have three bedrooms and a bathroom upstairs, and a good many closets, and you could move in—and believe me, I have thought about it—and you could be perfectly comfortable here. You have stayed over here, let me see, four times at least. We could turn the extra bedroom into a study; one of the bedrooms, as you have seen, has a large window with a view of the Bay...I've been married twice, Philip. Don't you think that's enough?"

"What has that to do with this?"

"Oh, a great deal. I'm not much good at marriage."

"Barbara," he said, "we can't live together."

"Why not?"

"Because I'm a minister of a church."

"What!" Barbara exclaimed. "After all you've told me, after all your sermons about equality and the rights of women and the freedom of choice, you tell me that we can't live together! They would fire you because you're living with me? Then it's all a lie, isn't it? How can you say that you love me?"

"I do love you." He had never seen this part of her. "And they wouldn't fire me. They wouldn't care—but I would. Do you know, I never kissed a woman after my wife died; never been with a woman. Do you think I'd be in bed with you if I didn't adore you? I was a priest. You can take a man out of the Church, but you can't take the Church out of the man."

"So you keep telling me. Thank God I never had a church inside of me."

"Why are we doing this? For heaven's sake, Barbara, marry me. We have no obligations to anyone."

She burst into laughter, rose, and went around the table; stood behind him and put her hands on his cheeks. "Poor Philip, poor Philip. And I'm to blame. I seduced you, deliberately and wantonly."

"No, you didn't. I was praying to God that you would come into my room. I didn't have enough courage to go into yours. Like President Carter, I lusted in my heart."

"Poor, dear Philip," she said. "My darling Eloise will have a nervous breakdown before May Ling's marriage is over, and you want to wish another one on her."

"No, we'll be married in the church—with no fuss and no toll on Eloise."

"And who will marry us?"

"I'm not the only Unitarian minister. Are you saying you'll do it, you'll marry me?"

"I suppose so. That's not very romantic, is it, Philip? But I hate sleeping alone, and when I wake up in the middle of the night and reach out and touch you, I feel safe and I can sleep again. We'll wait until the big wedding is over—but don't tell anyone, especially Eloise. Then we'll do it quietly and slip away somewhere for our honeymoon."

"Thank you," he whispered. "God bless you, Barbara."

"And do you suppose that church you carry around inside of you will allow us to sleep together tonight?"

"I think it could be arranged."

The Wedding

6

EARLY IN THE MORNING five days after Barbara's discussion with Philip, Eloise telephoned, a note of panic in her voice. "Barbara," she said, "what are you doing today?"

"What I do every day, working on this damn book."

"I need you. I am going out of my mind."

"Ellie, calm down. What is happening?"

"The wedding. Please come down today."

"We have two weeks before the wedding, and I must work."

"Why must you work?" Eloise asked plaintively. "You don't have a boss. Your pay won't be docked—and it's not only the wedding, which would be enough, but Freddie."

"What's happened to Freddie?"

"I can't talk about it over the phone. Please."

"All right, Ellie. I'll drive down. I don't know why, but I will."

Actually, Barbara was not displeased. It was a beautiful summer day, cool and sunny, and the wind from the Pacific was sweeping gently over the City. Barbara had been sitting at her typewriter for an hour, writing nothing and trying to decide whether a walk on the Embarcadero might refresh her mind or at least relieve the guilt she felt whenever she stayed indoors on a day like this. The memoir she was writing was the most difficult task she had ever attempted, heartbreaking when she wrote of the dead, puzzling and embarrassing when she turned to herself, and facing her with knife-edge decisions when she wrote of the living. She had started out to tell everything, and having no reservations in talking about sex, she did not hold back in the first hundred pages. Her publisher read the pages and decided that while sex usually did not hurt sales, she should remember that she was an icon. To this, she replied furiously that she was not an icon and that she had never sought to be one and that she had no intentions of being one; nevertheless, his warning gave her pause and made the work even more difficult. She'd been rereading the page she had written the night before:

> I don't brood about death or fear it, but the deaths of the men I have loved were so senseless, so futile. I tell myself that if Marcel had died fighting for the Spanish Republic, I might have felt different. But he was a newspaperman; he took no sides, except the side of love and life and beauty. He was as gentle as Bernie was hard and intractable—

She stopped there and fiercely crossed out the sentences that followed, and then she crossed out the words *hard* and *intractable*. That was not Bernie. Why was it so difficult to explain a man she had married and taken to her bed and to her heart? Bernie was not hard, he was gentle as a lamb; yet his profession was war. He had fought in Spain, in Africa during World War II, in Europe; and then when war broke out in Israel in 1948, he had taken a flight of C54s to Czechoslovakia and bought arms and died in Israel. It was death that she could not forgive—and that made no sense . . .

Let it wait, she said to herself. *I'll think about it, and then— who knows—then I may begin to understand. It's just too hard to write about people you loved, easier to write about strangers.*

The drive to Highgate would give her time to think. She had

called Eloise and told her that she would be there in an hour and would stay for lunch but not for dinner and not overnight.

A distraught Eloise was waiting at the parking lot when Barbara pulled in. She embraced Barbara and led her to a table on the terrace, where coffee and sandwiches were set out.

"You must be starved," Eloise said. "You never eat breakfast. You should. It's the most important meal of the day."

"Ellie, did you drag me out here to lecture me on nutrition?"

"Oh no, no. I'm in trouble, Barbara, and Adam won't listen to any of it. Sally is his sister, so you'd think he'd show some interest in it, but no. He has this damn winery"—her use of the word *damn* was an indication of her distress—"and nothing else matters. When I mention Freddie, he simply turns off."

"Let's leave Freddie for later and talk about the wedding."

"Very well—and I don't blame Adam. Do you know what Sally has done? She has invited over four hundred guests, and that doesn't include Candido and his family, and Cathrena and her family, and three of the process supervisors and their kids—and, good heavens, where am I to put four hundred and fifty people?"

"You ordered a tent?"

"There are no tents big enough."

"Then use two large pavilions open at the ends. Put them together."

"The worst is yet to come. Sally forgot about the growers in the Valley. All right, they're not overnighters, but we have at least sixty people whom we must lodge. Where can I put them? I can't scatter them around in the villages."

"Why not?" Barbara asked. "Take Saint Helena and Rutherford and Oakville and Yountville and Napa—all within short driving distance. Reserve the rooms. We'll make maps for each group. I'll help you."

"Oh, Barbara, would you? I'd be so grateful. But we're up to seventeen thousand dollars already—everything's so expensive."

"Do you mean to tell me that you and Adam are paying for this?"

"Well, Sally says she can't afford—"

"Oh, come off that, Ellie. Joe has a good practice, and they do have money. What about Harry?"

"He offered to pay for everything, but I'd die first."

"Yes, I suppose you would." Then she added, "I can take half of it."

"Never!" Eloise declared.

"Then I'll speak to Sally. It's her daughter. As a matter of fact, I'll talk to Joe."

"Joe doesn't live in this world."

"Then I'll drag him back into it. He is my brother," Barbara said.

"And there's no way we can cook for such a mob, so I made a deal with a caterer. Twenty-five dollars a plate—without wine. Sally says she wants our best Cabernet, and she wants to buy ten cases of white wine. Adam hit the ceiling. He was already grumbling about giving away his best red. You know how he is."

"I do. I also remember the sweet boy you married."

"He grew up," Eloise said ruefully. "Oh, sometimes I hate this place and the whole ideology of wine. We're already over seventeen thousand without the wine."

"Darling, we'll work it out. I have more money than I know what to do with, and Joe is my brother and May Ling is my niece, and let me whisper something else to you: There'll be another wedding—oh, a month or two from now, and it won't cost twenty cents."

"Barbara, tell me! Philip?"

"Yes."

"And he proposed it?"

"Yes."

"Don't just keep saying 'yes.' How old is he?"

"Seventy-three."

"I mean, how did it happen? Why don't you just live to-gether?"

"He regards sexual intercourse as a sacrament. Oh, don't ask me to explain, Ellie. I'm old and lonely. He's old and lonely. And we both live in a world that's damn strange."

"And where will you be married?"

"In his church. Just a simple ceremony with a few members of the family."

"And we'll have a big party here," Eloise said cheerfully.

"Have you lost your mind? It will be at least a year before you recover from this one. No, we'll go away. He's lived like a monk and hasn't gone anywhere. I think we'll go to England and perhaps to France."

"And to Australia?"

"Australia? Why Australia?"

"Barbara, you're wonderful. And thank you. If it weren't for Freddie, I could relax a bit."

"Yes. What's the problem with Freddie?"

"He's in love."

"But Freddie's always in love with someone."

"Yes—but this time he wants to get married. He sounded me out yesterday. 'Mother,' he said, 'how would you feel if I married a black woman?' "

This time Barbara had to catch her breath. "Not the lady from the Fairmont?"

"How do you know about that?"

"I hear things."

"She's a model; according to Freddie, the highest-priced model in the San Francisco area. He showed me a picture of her in a magazine—in *Vogue*. Very good-looking and six feet tall—can you imagine? I'm five-foot-three."

"And how did you react when he told you that?" Barbara asked.

"I didn't react. I just stared at him. He said, 'Mother, are you all right?' I wasn't all right. I told him to let me think about it."

"And what have you thought?"

"I telephoned you and asked you to come out here."

"Were you shocked?"

"Suppose Sam came home and told you he was going to marry a black woman?"

Barbara shrugged. "I don't know. I suppose I'd be a little concerned at first. But it would depend on the woman. Can you deal with it, Ellie?"

"I don't know. I never believed I was prejudiced. Do you think I'm a racist, Barbara?"

"No more than I am, and I don't think I am. Anyway, you know Freddie."

"I thought I did," Eloise said hopelessly. "This time I think he's serious."

"And if he is, would it be so terrible?"

"I don't know. Joshua is dead. I've been thinking about him and that terrible Vietnam War. I shed some tears last night. Freddie's the only one left, he's all we have. For God's sake, Barbara, tell me what I should feel, because I don't know."

"Ellie—Ellie, darling, how can I tell you what you should feel? If we go by Freddie's record, he won't marry this woman, but suppose he does? Julian Huxley said that the world's future lies in miscegenation, or maybe the world's hope. It can be either frightening or exciting. I have lived by Eleanor Roosevelt's maxim that it's better to light just one little candle than to sit and curse the dark. I don't think that what we do in this little corner of the earth matters very much—but just think of the wedding: May Ling, who is part Chinese and part Wasp and part Italian, marrying Harry, who is Jewish. A hundred years ago this would have been unthink-

able, or it would have spurred the vigilantes into action. Now it's
a blessing. In those hundred years a gang of roughneck Irish and
Jews and Italians have built us the most wonderful and beautiful
city on the face of the earth. The point is that anything is possible
if we have the courage to make it possible."

Eloise wiped away her tears. "I'm doing it again. If only I
were like you, Barbara."

"You are. We're as close as two people can be. What has Adam
said to this?"

"I haven't told him yet. Freddie wants to bring her to the
wedding."

"Good. We'll have at least a dozen other black people. Let me
talk to Adam."

Suddenly Eloise's face brightened. "Barbara, I have a wonderful idea." She paused and regarded Barbara thoughtfully. "You are
going to marry Philip?"

"Yes—it would seem so. He asked, 'Will you,' and I answered,
'I will.' I always thought that age would take care of desire, but it
doesn't, and I have no talent for celibacy."

"Now listen, Barbara—listen to me and don't say a word until
I have finished. Here we are talking about May Ling's wedding, and
the money we're going to spend and all the difficulties we're facing,
and all the good people we never see except when there's a wedding
or a funeral—"

"No!" Barbara exclaimed. "I know what you're getting at. No.
Absolutely not."

"Barbara! Will you please let me finish, and think about it?
The people are the same. You told me Philip has practically no
family, and all your ideas about the two pavilions give us the space
we need, and it would make me the happiest woman in the world,
and why should you be married in some somber church when we
could do both weddings here, since all the preparations have to be
made—and, oh, it would make me so happy—so why not?"

"No, no, my dear. I don't even know—I mean, I'm not entirely sure that I want to marry Philip."

"But you said—"

Barbara sighed. "Yes, I said—but, Ellie, it's not even two months since I met Philip. I want to know him better. You don't rush into things at my age, and I've been married twice before, and this will be May Ling's day, as it should be."

"Then you don't know May Ling. It would make her so happy—believe me. She loves you, and everyone you would want to invite to a wedding will be there, and I can't imagine anything more delightful, and if your mother were alive—Barbara, your mother was the closest thing I ever had to a real mother—Barbara, please, please consider it. Think about it. You don't have to decide this minute."

"I would have to talk to Philip. It would mean more guests, at least a few from Philip's church."

"Does that mean you'll agree?"

"No, Ellie. It means I'll talk to Philip."

"I do hope he agrees."

Eloise rose and embraced Barbara, who said she had to get back to the City but would like a word with Freddie before she left. Eloise said he was in his office, and she walked there with Barbara.

"I would prefer you didn't mention our talk about Judith Hope," Eloise said. "He spoke to me in confidence, but I keep nothing from you, Barbara."

"Of course not," Barbara agreed.

FREDDIE WELCOMED HER WITH A BEAR HUG. "Now, what on earth are you doing here at Highgate? What a good surprise!"

"Freddie, do you have fifteen minutes to spare for me?"

"I have all the time in the world to spare for you. Has Mother been talking to you about Judith Hope?"

"No, about the wedding. Freddie, I've never spoken about this, but what did you do with the twelve million your father—my brother Tom—left you in his will?"

Freddie stared at her curiously. He had not changed much since Thomas Lavette's will was read, still tall and slender, his blue eyes as clear as a child's, his blond hair only touched with gray. "Please sit down, Aunt Barbara," he said. "Are you broke and coming to hit me up for a loan?"

"I'm not broke—no."

"The money's invested, some in Highgate, some in other places."

"What about Adam? What is his financial condition?"

"Stranger and stranger," Freddie said. "Adam is land rich and equipment rich. I'm sure you have a reason for asking, but I'm damned if I know what. Highgate is like a great ducal estate, but it's no money machine. We have a good business—but Adam? Adam has no money to speak of; he plows it back into the land."

"That's what I wanted to know," Barbara said. "Freddie, I'm going to put this bluntly. May Ling's wedding is going to cost at least twenty-five thousand dollars."

"You're kidding! That's crazy."

"So are most of the things we do."

Freddie shook his head. "Joe can't afford that. He's the pro bono doctor of the Valley. I know. I take care of what little money they have. If you're thinking of that million my father left him in his will, most of it went into his surgery. Do you know what those machines of modern medicine cost?"

"I have a good idea, yes."

"So how the hell did Sally fall into this?"

"Freddie, where do you live? Sally's not paying for this, your mother is."

"What?"

"Yes. Don't blame Sally entirely. Ellie wanted the wedding

here, and Sally's invited half the population of San Francisco—over four hundred people. Now listen to me, and I'm going to be very blunt with you. You owe this to May Ling. You owe a lot more than this to May Ling. You married one of the finest women I ever knew, and you didn't have the heart to stay with her."

Freddie dropped into the chair behind his desk. The telephone rang and he ignored it. When Ms. Gomez opened the door, he snapped, "No calls—no one!" Then he said to Barbara, almost pleadingly, "You don't think much of me, do you?"

"Freddie, I think the world of you. I love you, you know that. You're like my own son. It's simply that when it comes to people, you have both feet firmly planted in midair."

"You want me to pay for this wedding?"

"If you don't, I will."

"No, you don't have to. I'll pay for it. It'll take a bit of arm-twisting with Mother and Adam, but I'll pay for it."

Driving back to San Francisco, Barbara reviewed her actions and motives, wondering whether she had done something worthy or not. She was not given to interfering in the lives of others. But here she had interfered, and grossly, and it worried her.

She had made arrangements to meet Philip at the church and have dinner with him. It was seven o'clock before she parked her car at Franklin Street and entered the church. For the first time she saw Philip distraught and worried. "Thank God," he said as he embraced her. "I've been calling your home since noon—you did say you would be home working all day?"

"Yes, dear Philip, and it's my fault. Eloise telephoned from Highgate and begged me to drive out. There was no way I could refuse her."

"Is something wrong there?"

"I'll tell you all about it. We'll talk about it at dinner."

"Just let me wash up, and I'll be with you."

They had dinner at a small Italian place on Geary Street, and after they had ordered and Barbara had taken her first sip of wine, she sighed with relief. "Do you know, Philip, I haven't been this content in a long time. Just to know you were waiting for me. But you must never worry about things happening to me."

"But things do happen to you, my dear. You have a penchant for things happening to you. What was it that took you off to Highgate this time?"

She told Philip the story of her day, and he listened attentively. And then she asked him, "Did I do something wrong?"

He shrugged. "There's no question of right or wrong. You did what you had to do, being yourself. As for Freddie, this will help him. He needs every bit of good karma he can amass."

"Karma—karma. For heaven's sake, Philip, what is this karma thing? I've never gotten into this California cult mania."

"It's not a cult thing. In Buddhism it's a belief that what you do in this life controls your destiny. It's a process of creating your own soul and destiny. In reincarnation it determines your next existence."

"Philip, you don't believe in reincarnation—or do you?"

"My beliefs have nothing to do with it. Many people do believe in it. For me, karma is a way of keeping score. You do a decent or charitable thing, and it changes you. Is that so strange? Think of the way you were fifty years ago. Are you the same Barbara Lavette now as you were then?"

Barbara thought about it. The food came, and she burrowed into the pile of pasta and clams on her plate. The wall facing her was covered with a poorly painted mural of maidens in diaphanous dresses dancing in front of an ancient pillared temple; it reminded her of a wall painting she had seen in Pompeii on her honeymoon after she had married Carson—forty years ago, fifty years ago? How many lives had she lived? And why had she told Philip everything about the day except Eloise's suggestion that they be married on the same day?

"I would have to know who Barbara Lavette is, and I'm not sure that I do," she said.

"Oh?"

"I was answering your question, Philip. I don't talk very well when I'm stuffing myself with pasta. You asked me whether I'm the same person I was fifty years ago, and I have to say that I don't really know." It occurred to her that she wouldn't have done very well with Philip half a century ago, when he had been a Jesuit priest.

He nodded.

"The food here is good."

It was difficult to entice Philip into a judgmental statement. She had never loved a "saintly" man, and she had loved many men and fought and scrapped her way through her life. She was Dan Lavette's daughter, and now she found herself becoming irritated at Philip's talk about karma. She didn't do things for self-gain, and she prided herself on doing what she thought was right, regardless of the consequences; and the events of her life had given her a deep suspicion of religion and religious people. A trifle truculently, she asked Philip whether he was religious.

"That's an odd question, Barbara."

"Why?"

"Because I don't know what you mean by 'religious.' "

"Of course you do." Now she was irritated, and she said to herself that she must get off this kick, or it would develop into a real fight. This morning she had crossed out a page of her memoir because she felt she was incapable of understanding people she had loved. *Listen to him,* she told herself.

"Well, put it this way," Philip said, smiling slightly. "You abhor every religious institution—even my own Unitarianism—yet I think you are the most deeply spiritual person I have ever known."

"And how did you come to that conclusion, Philip?"

"Ohhh"—stretching the word—"by knowing you, loving you, being with you, and experiencing you."

" 'Experiencing' me?"

"Exactly. You love people, you're filled with love—you have such a capacity for love. That's what my faith consists of. If Unitarianism means anything, it's that."

"I was all ready for a scrap," Barbara said. "You're beguiling."

"I don't intend to be."

"And you're impossible to fight with."

"Oh no. Just wait and see."

She abandoned what remained of her huge mound of pasta. "I was sitting here and stuffing myself and trying to decide whether I loved you."

"I'm patient."

"Oh, damn it, Philip. I'm an old lady. Do I really want to get married? I've loved and lost so much—what is left?"

"More than I ever dreamed of."

"Do you really love me that much?"

"I won't say I love you more than I've loved any other woman. I loved my wife enough to leave the Church, and she loved me enough to do the same. I thought I was through with love, that it would never happen again. But it has happened, and I want to live with you and be with you the rest of my life—for whatever time we have."

"I wish I could say that, but I do love you, Philip, and I will marry you because it's better to be with you than without you. I'm no good at marriage and I'm no good at living alone." She paused—then decided to change the subject. "I have to tell you about Eloise's proposal. But remember that Eloise is all emotion and romance, even at sixty-six... Everyone I know, more or less, will be at May Ling's wedding, and Eloise suggested that we be married at the same time, and I said I would discuss it with you."

He considered it for a few moments, and then he asked, "How do you feel about it?"

"I don't know. At first I rejected it, but—"

"But what?" Philip asked. And when she did not reply, he said, "I think it's a wonderful idea—if you agree."

"Oh, what the hell," Barbara said. "Why not? It will certainly be a great party. How many guests must you invite?"

"Not many—three or four."

"Then come with me, and we'll work on invitations and scribble in the double marriage. But you can't marry us?"

"No, but my assistant is a minister, and she'll do it happily."

AFTER THE PARTY ON RUSSIAN HILL, Freddie had four dinner dates with Judith Hope and she declined only two others—once when her photography session went well into the night, and a second time when, as she explained, a birthday party was being given for her father. Freddie considered four out of six a very good record indeed, but still he was limited to a sisterly kiss on the lips. It was a totally new experience for him, and he could not recall having dated a woman whom he had not taken to bed on at least the third night. Each time he took her to a very public place, in either the Fairmont or the Mark Hopkins Hotel. This was deliberate on his part; he knew a dozen good small restaurants in San Francisco, but he refused to let her think that he was hiding a relationship with a black woman.

At the fourth dinner she asked him abruptly, apropos of nothing they had been discussing, whether he was straight or a switch-hitter. As used as he was to her frankness, this took him aback.

He stared at her blankly, then pulled himself together and said, "My God, I've never been asked that before. What makes you ask?"

"Because you're so goddamn good-looking."

"Well, thank you," he said frostily.

"Come on, Freddie. This is a new world we live in. This city is high on the AIDS list, and you know that."

"You can't catch it with brotherly kisses or holding hands."

"I know. But I had to ask."

For the next few minutes, he sat silently, staring at his plate. Judith reached across the table and touched his cheek. "Freddie, Freddie, forgive me. I think I'm taken with you, and this is the first time it's ever happened to me with a white man. I'm scared."

"So am I," he mumbled.

"Let's get out of here and go home."

At Judith's door, he paused. She opened the door and then motioned him in and closed the door behind her. Inside, he turned to her, hesitated for a moment, and then took her in his arms and kissed her. It was not a brotherly kiss.

"The bedroom's upstairs," she said, pulling away from him. "There's a guest bathroom straight ahead. You'll find a robe and towels, and you can shower if you want." With that, she started up the stairs without glancing back. Freddie walked to the indicated door. It was large for a guest bathroom, the walls, floor to ceiling, covered with bright tiles. He showered and then wrapped himself in a white robe and, barefoot, climbed the circling iron staircase to the balcony. The door to the bedroom was open: the floor of white tile; the great swan bed, king size, covered with a mauve quilt and a pile of pillows. She was sitting up against the pillows, naked, her small round breasts and her hair, cropped to the shape of her head, giving the impression of a bronze sculpture.

Freddie stared at her, thinking that he had never seen anything quite so beautiful in all his life. He felt awkward and not a little bit afraid, like an adolescent at his first encounter. She looked at him inquiringly. He dropped the robe to the floor and crawled under the covers, his heart pounding madly, and embraced her.

AT ELEVEN O'CLOCK IN THE MORNING—the morning after her dinner with Philip—Barbara's doorbell rang. Philip, who had spent the night with her, had already left for the church, and she couldn't imagine who it would be.

It was her brother Joe, and after she had kissed him and

welcomed him in, she asked what could possibly have brought him here to San Francisco at this hour.

"I had a bad emergency in the middle of the night, something I couldn't handle, and I called Sam, and he said to bring her into the hospital here. It was one of those hopeless, godforsaken pregnancies—I don't want to go into it, but it was a procedure I had never done." He appeared to be totally tired. Three years younger than Barbara, he was older in every other way, a big man gone to weight, bags under his eyes, and his day's beard dark and heavy.

"Coffee?" Barbara asked. "I've never seen you look so tired. Did you have breakfast? Come in the kitchen and sit down. I'll fix you something to eat."

"Sure, thank you. I had some coffee at the hospital, that's all. I'll have to go back there and see her again. If I could lie down for an hour or so?"

"Of course."

He sat in a chair at the kitchen table, watching Barbara pour coffee and put bacon up to render. "Just drop the eggs into the bacon grease. I like it that way, and I don't dare ask Sally for it."

"No, she wants you to keep alive. Like all doctors, you ignore every rule of nutrition."

He nodded. She gave him the coffee. He put two spoons of sugar into it and as much cream as the cup would hold. "Barbara," he said after he had sipped the coffee, "I have to talk to you about something serious."

She had never seen him actually angry. A word like *serious* was as far as he would go.

"Go ahead." She cracked the eggs and dropped them into the bacon grease, thinking that once more would not kill him.

Silent, he sat with his eyes half closed. Barbara felt that he would fall asleep at the table. Then he shook his head, like a shaggy dog freeing itself of water, and she thought of what Philip had said about karma. In a world where few doctors still made house calls,

Joe drove up and down the Napa Valley and often over to the Sonoma Valley to deliver a baby or to put together a broken body. Time had not been good to him. His stomach bulged; his eyes were red from lack of sleep.

"Joe, go ahead and tell me what's on your mind," she said, filling his plate with bacon and eggs and taking toast from the toaster. She had anticipated what he was going to say.

"It's about the wedding." He was hungry, and he ate as he spoke. "I understand that Freddie is paying for the wedding. That hurts me. I can pay for my daughter's wedding. I hear that you put Freddie up to this. You shouldn't have done that."

"Twenty-five thousand dollars plus. Joe, you can't afford that. It's good for Freddie's soul."

"I don't give a damn about Freddie's soul. It's my daughter and my responsibility. I know how Sally blew this all out of proportion—well, Sally is Sally, and let it be. But I'm going to pay for it."

"Don't blame Sally. Eloise wanted it this way. And it's not only May Ling's wedding. It's mine as well, and I don't intend to allow you to pay for anything."

He perked up at this. "What do you mean, your wedding?"

"I mean that it's to be a double wedding. May Ling is marrying Harry, and I'm marrying Philip Carter."

"No. When did that happen?"

"It's been happening."

"Why didn't I know about it?"

"Because it was just decided. Are you going to pay for my wedding, Joe? I can understand how you feel—but this was never Eloise's intention. Joe, let it be. You've been doctoring Eloise and Adam and everyone else at that winery for years and you never send them a bill, and when they send you a check, you return it."

"Barbara, they're family."

"Then let them be family. What happened last night?"

"A third-trimester abortion. The child's brain was outside its skull. God, I hate those things..."

He finished eating. She steered him upstairs to the guest room, pulled off his shoes, and loosened his tie. "One hour," he mumbled. "Then wake me. Call Sally and tell her to cover for me." He fell asleep even as Barbara stood there.

ONE EVENING A FEW DAYS LATER, Freddie drove Judith Hope to her parents' home in Oakland. It came about in this manner:

He had said to her, "I want to meet your parents."

"Why?"

"I'll tell you why. You agreed to come to the wedding at Highgate. You'll meet my mother and father. That's perfectly normal and natural, considering the way I feel about you."

"And how do you feel about me, Freddie?"

"I love you. That's how I feel about you. If you were a white woman, I'd know your family by now. I don't see why it should be any different because you're black."

"Suppose I feel it's different? I'm not a white woman. Suppose I had no father and my mother did day work and she lived in the Oakland ghetto?"

"You would never permit your mother to do day work. I know you well enough to know that. You told me your father is a successful dentist. You told me you go there every week on Friday for dinner. I want you to bring me along and for them to expect me to be with you."

Eventually she gave in, and now they were on their way to Oakland, Freddie bearing a package of four bottles of wine as his dinner gift. The house, a modest white front-hall colonial, was by no means in the ghetto, but on a pleasant hillside; and Judith's mother, a plump woman in her fifties, opened the door and greeted them, kissing her daughter and taking Freddie's hand with a smile. Dr. Hope, behind her, a large, full-bodied man, was unsmiling. He nodded when Judith introduced Freddie and he shook hands with him, murmuring something that Freddie did not get.

They went into the living room, simply furnished with a couch, two armchairs, and a television set. There were photographs and some prints on the walls, and there were more photographs on a small piano. A coffee table was loaded with chips and a dip and a bowl of crudités. Freddie offered his gift of wine without going into its origin. Mrs. Hope asked what he would have, and since she was pouring white wine, he agreed that he would have that, although he had no taste for white wine and had brought Cabernet with him. Judith suggested that he might like red wine, but he shook his head firmly.

Dr. Hope, his voice deep and throaty, asked where they had met, and lying smoothly, Judith said they had been introduced by Art Brown at the Fairmont. Dr. Hope said he had never been to the Fairmont, and Judith reminded him that she had taken him and her mother to the Fairmont on her mother's fiftieth birthday. He grumbled that it was different, Judith being a celebrity. Freddie, trying to measure Dr. Hope by his denial that he had ever been to the Fairmont, against Judith's declaration that he had been there, decided that, like his daughter's, Dr. Hope's thinking took two paths. Being at the Fairmont meant walking in with his wife, both black, whereas Judith lived with one foot in another world.

Mrs. Hope said, "Five minutes. I can't have you late to the table," and disappeared into the kitchen.

"She's doing chicken with dumplings," Judith explained. "She's a wonderful cook. When she puts the dumplings into the boiling water, they have to be out and on the table to the minute."

"Mrs. Hope's from South Carolina," Dr. Hope said, as if that were the final word on her cooking.

The food was delicious, tiny carrots and greens to go with the chicken. Dr. Hope opened a bottle of the Cabernet that Freddie had given them and said that he didn't go along with this nonsense that you drank only white wine with chicken. "The chicken doesn't know the difference, and in my world, wine is red." He had finally opened up and was talking directly to Freddie.

"I couldn't agree with you more," Freddie said. "I thought the Chardonnay you served before was delicious, but for me, wine is red wine—especially a Cabernet."

Judith watched Freddie and her father with interest. So far she had said little, except to reply to her mother's questions about the food. "Mama, your food is delicious, the very best in the whole Bay Area. You always ask me, and I always tell you that."

"But you eat in all those fancy foreign restaurants."

"None of them can hold a candle to your cooking."

Judith had become something Freddie had never seen before. The glamorous model was gone. Dressed in a pleated blue skirt and a white pullover, this was a child with Mama and Papa, behaving very properly. She had removed the bright fingernail polish that was a part of her usual costume and she wore no makeup. Her only jewelry was a small gold cross on a thin gold chain around her neck.

After dinner they returned to the living room, and Judith helped her mother bring in a tray with coffee and cookies. Dr. Hope opened a box of cigars, took one for himself, and offered the box to Freddie, who didn't smoke cigars, though he was tempted to take one just to enhance the relationship. As the better part of valor, he refused.

"Not a smoker," Dr. Hope rumbled. "Good thing. No good for the teeth. No good at all."

"I have a matter of great importance to me," Freddie said, "that I would like to discuss with you, Dr. Hope, and with Mrs. Hope, of course. It concerns your daughter, Judith—"

Judith was suddenly alert and waiting.

"—and my feelings for her. I would like to ask for her hand in marriage and your permission to do so."

Judith sprang to her feet and shouted, "How dare you! How dare you come here with that idiotic speech without telling me! We're leaving—right now!"

"Sit down, girl!" her father snapped. "Just sit down and keep a still tongue in your mouth. You're not going anywhere. Just sit down and behave."

To Freddie's amazement Judith sat down, looking daggers at him.

"What this young man has done is perfectly proper. Proper, and I respect it. We live in a time when these small amenities of decency are forgotten. Now he and I are going to talk, and you will sit there and listen. Do you understand?"

"Yes, Papa," she answered succinctly.

Mrs. Hope said nothing, only breathing deeply and trying to appear sympathetic to all sides.

"Now, son," Dr. Hope said to Freddie, "how old are you?"

"Forty-two."

"Old enough to know your own mind. I gather you've been married before?"

"Yes. I'm divorced," Freddie said.

"Any children?"

"A little boy. He's four years old. His mother has custody, but I see him frequently."

"Was that a court decision?"

"No, sir, it was my decision. His mother's a wonderful woman—it just didn't work."

"Yes, I can respect that. I don't hold with this business of divorce; Mrs. Hope and I have been married thirty-nine years. But I suppose there are times when it's necessary. Now, what do you do for a living?"

"I manage a winery in the Napa Valley. It's called Highgate. The wine I brought you tonight is our product. We specialize in

Cabernet Sauvignon, and we like to think that our Cabernet is the best produced in America. We're not the biggest winery, but we do a substantial business."

"You don't own this winery, or do you?"

"No, sir. I have a share of the stock, but the winery is owned by my father, Adam Levy. He adopted me when he married my mother. My biological father was Thomas Lavette. I still use the name Lavette."

"You mean Thomas Lavette the banker?" Dr. Hope asked.

"Yes, sir. He died five years ago."

"And what is your religion, young man? I ask that personal question because your request is a personal one."

"I'm Episcopalian, sir. I was baptized in Grace Cathedral"— not mentioning that he had not set foot in the church or taken communion since his father's death.

"We're Baptists, but I don't hold any man's religion against him. You understand that if my daughter should agree to your proposal, the ceremony would be held in a Baptist Church. You have no objection to that?"

"No, sir," Freddie said, "absolutely none."

Dr. Hope looked at his wife, who smiled and nodded and said, "I think he's a very nice young man."

"Well, Frederick," Dr. Hope said, "I believe it's up to my daughter, and I'm sure you will discuss it later. She's a woman of sound judgment, and she knows her own mind. And now I suggest we pour some of that wine you make and drink to the happiness of both of you."

Judith listened to all of this in stony silence, and when the wine was poured she barely touched it to her lips. When they rose to leave she kissed her father and mother, and when her mother asked her to please wear the warm wrap that had been her Christmas present and not walk around half naked just because it was summer, she said, "Yes, Mama, I will. I really don't walk around half naked."

In Freddie's car, driving to San Francisco, she stated her feelings in two words: "You bastard!"

"That was pretty harsh."

"You miserable, revolting bastard! You planned this whole thing. Don't try to deny it. What a cheap, low-down trick!"

"Why, Judith? Because you let me know how much you love and respect them? I want to be your husband. I want that more than I ever wanted anything in my life, and I knew that if the doctor and his wife were against your marrying a white man, my case would be damn well lost. So there it is. Will you marry me?"

"No. Not now. Never."

"Why? I love you. I think you're the most wonderful woman I have ever known. I haven't looked at another woman since I met you. I can't live without you."

"Freddie, stop it. I'm black, you're white. Finished."

"Never is a long time—and you know, I may be a bit flaky, but I noticed from the beginning that you are black and I am white. It makes no difference to me; does it matter to you? There's no prejudice in my family. They will open their arms and embrace you. My mother's the most open-minded gentle woman in the world, and my father will love you. Furthermore, I'm two inches taller than you are, and unless you decide to marry a basketball player, you'll have a hard time finding someone who'll top your height."

She was laughing now. "Watch your driving, and don't try to kiss me while you're driving. My father warned me never to let a man touch me while he was driving. Freddie, I do love you. I can't imagine why, but I do. Marriage is something else. I don't know whether I'll ever marry anyone."

"I'm patient. I can wait."

"My dear Freddie, we live in a world that's divided into two parts, and they're as separate as Europe and America. I've watched people try to cross into the other part, and I've never known it to work."

"I can show you twenty marriages that I know of, white on white, that don't work, either. My father divorced my mother for a woman he later came to hate. My mother married my stepfather, who is Jewish, and that's the best marriage I've ever known. Some work, some don't work. We have sex going for us, and I swear to God, I'll make it all work."

"Love isn't something you can pick apart and analyze. I can appreciate the respect you showed my parents, and I think I may even be falling in love with you. But I won't marry you."

"All right. We'll let that rest for the moment. But you'll still come to May Ling's wedding?"

"Not if I'm the showpiece nigger."

"I hate that word," Freddie snapped. "I don't like it from your lips any better than you would like it from mine."

"I'm sorry. You know what I mean."

"Well, you won't be. Judge Horton is coming, and he's black. I invited the Cutlers, Larry and Jane. There's Sam's scrub nurse at the hospital—she's black—and there'll be others."

"You win. Now let's go home and curl up in bed."

Since her relationship with Philip Carter began, Barbara had taken to going to the Unitarian church each Sunday morning, after which she and Philip would spend the rest of the day together. On this Sunday his sermon was titled "The War Against the Women." He spoke of the agelong struggle of women for equality, for the vote, for the right to be treated as persons instead of property. He spoke of the end of the eternal war against women, and he called Walter Mondale's choice of Geraldine Ferraro a cause for celebration.

Barbara had always been an easy cry. She felt the tears in her eyes as Philip continued, "This is not a part of my sermon—or perhaps it is, since I think of you as an extended family, and the joining together of two souls is very much a sermon. I've asked a woman, who has been sitting among you for some weeks now, to be my wife. Her name is Barbara Lavette, and she has been kind enough to agree. We will be married soon."

Barbara was terrified that he would ask her to stand, and grateful that he didn't. The congregation broke into applause, and when finally they filed out, her anonymity disappeared. Birdie MacGelsie threw her arms around her and kissed her, and then when Philip did the same, the congregation pressed to meet her and offer congratulations.

Finally the entry had emptied out and they were free to go. As they walked down Franklin Street, Barbara said, "Now you've done it. I can't back out, can I?"

"Do you want to?"

"I don't think so, Philip. I'm not only getting used to you, but I'm becoming very fond of you. Who is going to marry us?"

"Reba Guthri, our assistant minister. You met her back at the church, a small woman with close-cropped gray hair. She's the one who told you how beautiful you are."

"You want me to remember her? There were at least two hundred people there. And, Philip, under that Jesuit incorruptibility of yours, there's a very deceitful person. No one ever said I look beautiful."

"My word of honor."

"All right, I accept, even if I don't believe it. My mother always told me that if someone says a nice thing, never deny it. Just say 'thank you.' So thank you."

AS THE DAYS PASSED, Barbara began to wonder how she had ever allowed herself to be drawn into what she began to think of as the Mad Hatter's wedding. Philip came to her with the suggestion that they be married twice, once at the church and again at Highgate.

"Otherwise," he said, "I'll have to invite twelve people, and I don't see any way out of that."

"I only agreed to marry you once," Barbara said, and Philip argued that this was no laughing matter. "Then I'll give you twelve invitations," Barbara said. "Stop worrying."

"I think about Freddie," he argued. "How, in all conscience, can I do this to Freddie?"

"Freddie's rich. He's loaded with Lavette money, which he did nothing to earn. You yourself said this would be good for his immortal soul. Invite your twelve people. Once is enough. I simply do not intend to be married twice."

Then Eloise called, crying that she had lost the caterer. "He decided that he can't handle four hundred people."

Four hundred and twelve, Barbara thought.

"And I still don't have the final list. Why can't people understand that when they get a wedding invitation, they are under an obligation to reply to it? I told him that I must have at least one hundred portions of cold poached salmon for those who won't eat chicken, and he said that was impossible. He's terrified of being stuck with all that salmon, and it brings the cost up. He was up to fifty dollars each. That's up to twenty thousand for just the food and serving. Oh, Barbara, how did I ever get into this?"

"My mother once got into the same thing," Barbara said. "So she booked a room in the hospital and sent a note to everyone that she had pneumonia. She got at least fifty bouquets of flowers and saved a lot of money."

"Barbara, how can you laugh at it? You have to find me a caterer. You're there in the City, and I have no idea of what goes on in San Francisco."

"Eloise, darling, when we give a party it's always for a good cause and everyone brings her own pot of food. We don't use caterers."

"Barbara, you know I can't do that. Why are you teasing me?"

"I think I can find you a Chinese caterer at half the price."

"Barbara!"

"I'll find one, Ellie. How about crab instead of salmon? The advantage with crab is that they can hold them in a refrigerated truck and cook them after the orders are in. That means the live crabs won't be spoiled if the orders go short. And I'll keep it under fifty dollars if it's humanly possible."

"Oh, thank you, my dear, bless you. How is Philip?"

"Brace yourself for a shock."

"Oh, God—is the wedding off?"

"Oh no, it's on. I think I'm falling in love with him. But he says he must invite twelve people to the wedding."

A long sigh in reply. "Oh, well, what will be will be."

Barbara was thumbing through the Yellow Pages when Harry Lefkowitz called and asked whether he could sit down with her and Philip for a half hour or so. He had a problem.

And who doesn't? Barbara thought.

"Perhaps you and Philip could come to my office someday soon at one o'clock. I'll have lunch for you. I don't know who to turn to with this, and Barbara, believe me, I would be immensely grateful."

"Tomorrow, Harry?"

"Yes, tomorrow would be fine."

She put it to Philip, who agreed reluctantly. "The thing is, Barbara, that I'm not a father confessor."

"I don't think Harry goes in for confession. He's Jewish, and if they need confession, they go to a shrink."

"Then why me?"

"Because you're a levelheaded, wise, and compassionate man."

"Yes, and flattery will get you everywhere. When?"

"Tomorrow at one. He'll give us lunch. It seems he likes to eat at his office in the Transamerica Building. And by the way, you may not be the father confessor, but I seem to have taken on the role of mother confessor. Eloise just lost her caterer, and I'm to find her another one." She went back to the Yellow Pages.

The Absolute Caterers were high on the list, located on Detroit Street. She dialed their number, mentioned her problem to the woman who answered, and was switched to Mr. Sam Cohen. He had a cheerful voice, and he asked her what he could do for her.

"My name is Barbara Lavette."

"Ah-ha!" which indicated that he recognized the name. "And what can I do for you, Ms. Lavette?"

"Do you cater as far away as the Napa Valley?"

"Once a month, at least. Are you talking about Highgate?"

"Yes, and I'm talking about four hundred people, plus. Can you handle anything like that?"

"Four hundred people? It's a lead-pipe cinch. No problem. I just did three hundred for the Republican Women's Committee. You want a reference? Call Mrs. Thatcher—not in England but here in San Francisco. That's a joke, forgive me. Mrs. Elbert Thatcher. Where did you get our name?"

"I got you out of the Yellow Pages."

"You should know how many times I've talked to my brother, Jerry, about expanding our ad in the Yellow Pages. Where do you live, Ms. Lavette?"

"I'm on Green Street." He had a sense of humor, which Barbara liked.

"You'll give me the number and I'll come over for a talk. With a big proposition like this, we always have a talk with the customer. I'll bring a lemon meringue pie, just a token. You're free today?"

"Between four and five, yes."

She gave him her address and put down the telephone. *Just like that,* she said to herself. *Now we'll pray that Mr. Cohen can deliver.*

Mr. Cohen was a large, stout man who bore a pie as if it were a treasure, and he arrived at exactly five minutes after four. "We'll sit in the kitchen, yes? You'll give me a cup of coffee and a pie knife, and you'll taste something. Like a picture is worth a hundred words, a taste is worth a hundred claims of good cooking."

Barbara contributed the coffee and agreed that she had never tasted anything as good in the way of pie.

"And the thing is, it doesn't melt on the plate on a hot day. The reception will be outside, yes?"

"Under pavilions."

"And you have chairs and tables and dishes?"

"No dishes, no. Chairs and tables and the pavilions."

"No problem," Mr. Cohen declared. "We'll supply them. And the food—hot or cold?"

"Cold, if you can manage that."

"No problem. We have two large refrigerated trucks, and we bring ice; if you need water, we bring water."

"There's a good spring," Barbara said; "all the water you need."

"Then there's no problem. Tell me, Ms. Lavette, and forgive me for a personal question. Are you Dan Lavette's daughter?"

"Yes, I am. Did you know my dad?"

"No. But my father, may he rest in peace, catered his wedding to your mother."

"Wonderful!" Barbara exclaimed. "That makes us practically family."

"And now the food."

Barbara went into her thinking on crabs and chicken, but Mr. Cohen shook his head. "You'll forgive me, Ms. Lavette, but cold chicken is always a problem, unless it's chicken salad, which I don't think you want."

"Why is chicken such a problem?"

"Because you don't know. The white meat can become hard and tasteless. Let me make a suggestion. I deal with a farm in

Petaluma, and they can supply me with little rock Cornish hens, small birds so delicate they melt in your mouth. We cook them and mold them in a special aspic, my own invention. Delicious! Tomorrow I send you one, if you want. You serve a whole hen on each plate."

"But that must be terribly expensive."

"Wait with the expense until we finish. Now, about the crabs—yes, Bay crabs are the most delicious seafood in the world, but these crabs, you got to keep them alive and cook them as you serve them, and what I'm left with, I don't know what to do with. You can't keep them alive for too long. Now, salmon—that's something else. I can buy the best salmon at a very good price. We divide them into proper portions, poach them, and set them in aspic molds. Beautiful. You serve them with sliced, slightly marinated cucumbers and a German potato salad—something fit for a king, believe me. And what's not used will stay. I always have a call for poached salmon and we have good refrigeration in our trucks. And I bring you a sample of everything. You're not buying a pig in a poke."

"And what do you suggest to go with the Cornish hens?"

"Rice and little sweet peas. But with both dishes, first a salad. And then for dessert? You'll have a wedding cake—or I can give you the lemon pie. And, of course, coffee and tea. Do you want wine?"

"No, we'll take care of that."

"Now, the wedding cake. We bake it, our own rum fruitcake. For this occasion, you need at least forty pounds. We age our cake for at least a month, so we always have it ready. Or maybe fifty pounds. I'll have to do the arithmetic. We decorate it and slice it for you on the occasion. We top it with a small bridegroom and bride."

"Two of them," Barbara said. "Not only is my niece being married, but I am as well."

"Congratulations. Who is the lucky man, if I may ask?"

"Philip Carter. He's the minister at the Unitarian church."

"Of course, a good man. I do a little for them sometimes. Mostly they do it themselves...Two brides, two grooms. I'll take care of that. And we bring a crew of twenty for such a crowd. Now if you'll let me sit here for half an hour, I'll work out the price. A lot of older people?"

"I'd guess half are past fifty."

"They'll go for the salmon. I can tell you from experience, it will divide evenly, but we'll have extras of everything. I'll bring wineglasses, of course."

"And you can give me a price now?"

"Of course. What will the timing be?"

"The ceremony will be at eleven."

"Then we'll be there by ten. Lunch at twelve. My crew will help you move the chairs. Nice men, nice waitresses."

In her study, Barbara sat and waited. Her husband's name— her first husband's—had been Cohen. She was lost in thoughts of the past. Once, when they stood at Coit Tower, Bernie had said to her, "Look at it, the most beautiful city on the face of the earth, built by a pack of mongrels."

Mr. Cohen exuded confidence, but then a good salesman always exuded confidence. Philip would now and then refer to guardian angels, and she once asked him flatly, "Philip, do you really believe in guardian angels?" "The trouble is," he replied, "that I'm never sure what I believe in." Had this been a guardian angel or the Yellow Pages?

Her thoughts were interrupted by Mr. Cohen's voice, and she went into the kitchen. Mr. Cohen sat with a sheet of paper covered with numbers and scribbles. "Ms. Lavette," he said, "before I give you a price, let me make a suggestion. We have been in this business since before the earthquake, and I never had a customer who complained about our poached salmon. Let me bring you four hundred servings of poached salmon. The price is the same."

"I love cold poached salmon—but there are people who won't eat fish. Can I take a chance?"

"Believe me, take a chance. For them, I'll have a reserve of Cornish hens."

"All right."

"So we have that, and salad and bridal cake, and the dishes, and twenty in help, and when we leave, you won't believe we were ever there. I'll give you a flat price, and if it should be four hundred and twenty guests, the price is the same. Did I say coffee and tea? Absolutely. The price is sixteen thousand dollars, even. I know that Highgate specializes in Cabernet, so if you wish, I'll throw in twenty cases of an excellent Chardonnay for only a thousand dollars more, and what you don't use, I take back and refund the money. That's a rock-bottom price for a good white wine. I always buy Highgate when I want a Cabernet, and I know how Mr. Levy feels about Chardonnay."

"That's great. Poor Eloise was worried so about the wine. Everyone who knows Adam will drink red, but I imagine a good many will want white. Seventeen thousand—"

"You can check with other caterers."

"We already have. You have a deal, Mr. Cohen."

"Just give me the date, and I'll send the contracts out tomorrow. I'll need a five-thousand-dollar advance."

Barbara couldn't wait to call Eloise, and when she told her the details, Eloise sighed with relief. "But do you trust him?"

"If I'm any judge of character, yes. Call Glen Ellen or Mondavi—I'm sure they've used him. And tell Freddie I'm paying the five thousand deposit. He has enough with everything else. And, Eloise, if I'm not wrong, you don't have to lift a finger. They'll even move the chairs and tables."

THE LUNCH AT HARRY'S OFFICE the following day was another matter entirely. When Eloise objected to Barbara's paying for any of the cost, Barbara won easily. Eloise was never a good contender, and Barbara showed up for the lunch still glowing with her successful arrangements. The glow spread only to Philip, who always glowed when he saw her. Harry was glum and apologetic. "I don't know how I had the nerve to drag you over here. I charge three hundred an hour for stupidities not worth listening to, but I'm desperate. You don't mind talking while we eat?"

He had put out a platter of corned beef and pastrami, Jewish rye bread, and a bottle of wine.

"Of course we'll talk while we eat," Barbara said.

"It goes the other way in business meetings, but this isn't a business meeting. It's about Danny."

"Danny?" Barbara asked, puzzled.

"Small Danny. May Ling's four-year-old son. I never had children of my own when I was married. It broke my wife's heart, but she had a condition that prevented conception. I always wanted children, and when Freddie agreed to my adoption of Danny, I was delighted. May Ling wants to have another child, and I can't tell you how happy that would make me. But Danny hates me."

"Oh, come on," Philip said. "Four-year-old children don't hate."

"I've tried everything," Harry said. "Toys, the circus, ice-cream sodas. Every time I try to take his hand for a street crossing, he pulls it away and says—" Harry shook his head.

"Go on," Barbara said.

"I don't want to offend you."

"We can't be offended, Harry," Philip said gently. "We're here to help—in any way we can."

Harry sighed and said, "He pulls his hand away and says, 'Fuck off, you creep.' "

A long moment of silence, and then Philip asked, "Those words?"

"Exactly."

"Have you discussed this with May Ling?" Barbara asked.

"How could I? The child is the center of her life. How could I repeat those words to her?"

"He's in nursery school?" Philip asked.

"Yes. And he watches television."

Philip nodded. "It's 1984," he said. "I can offer one thing, Harry. Children of that age don't hate. Not in the sense that we understand hatred."

"Then what is it?"

Philip looked at Barbara inquiringly, and she said, "Go ahead, Philip. You're better at this than I am."

"All right. I can offer two guesses, anger and fear. The anger because he thinks you're taking his beloved mother away from him, as well as his father. He can't understand divorce, and I wouldn't try too hard to explain it. Does he know that you intend to move him to San Francisco?"

"I imagine he does."

"Then that's the fear part—to be separated from the house he knows and the children he knows."

"He's not happy here in San Francisco."

"Those words he uses are meaningless. He picked up the phrase somewhere—it's everywhere today. Does he ever say it in front of his mother?"

"No, not that I know of."

"At least he knows that it's forbidden."

"Then, for heaven's sake, what do I do?"

"The first thing I'd do is discuss it with May Ling. Then don't press too hard. Listen to what May Ling says; that's important. I would suggest that both of you take him to Highgate as much as you can. Let May Ling, if she agrees, stay with him at Highgate until the wedding. He can see Freddie whenever he wants to, and let him see you and Freddie together as friends. That should change things and help with his fears. May Ling, I think, should explain about the phrase as much as she can. It's amazing how much a four-year-old can understand. Give it time."

They went on with their lunch and talked more about the problem, and when they left, Harry was a less troubled man. Outside, Barbara said to Philip, "You're very wise about some things."

"Not all things, believe me."

"I didn't say 'all things.' I don't want to boost your ego out of sight, now that I'm beginning to love you. But you never had children."

"No, we never did. We wanted them desperately, but it was no use. We could have adopted children, but we felt that childlessness was our punishment, and we accepted it."

"Oh, come on, Philip. You're a Unitarian minister."

"So I am. Not a very good one, but still I am. Does that mean I shed my belief in God?"

They were at the garage now. Barbara handed over her tab for the car, and while they waited, she studied Philip thoughtfully. He was a handsome man, she decided, in spite of the sharp Irish nose—the Kennedy nose, she called it—and his lined sunken cheeks. He walked with no stoop, and his hands were untouched by the brown spots of age. Did she love him, or was she simply grateful that she would not have to spend the last years of her life alone? Love was to be felt for children and men—and most men remained children until they were worn and old. He was not worn and old, and she felt a great tenderness for him. She often thought of his wife, the nun who had left the Church for the love of a man, and she wondered whether she could have done that, whether she was capable of that kind of love. She was firm in her beliefs; all her life she had fought against oppression and human degradation— spitting into the wind, she called it, a phrase that she got from her father. Two nights ago she had spoken to a group of women, a newly formed group of Bay women in support of Geraldine Ferraro, trying to convince them that the choice of Ms. Ferraro for vice-presidential candidate was the most important event in the feminist struggle, pleading with them to understand what this choice meant, and wondering why there were so many faces unmoved and unchanged.

Philip had said that he was not sure what he believed. Barbara knew what she believed.

When the car emerged from the garage, Philip reached into his pocket to pay the fee. Barbara did not protest. She had decided that, meager though his funds were, she must allow him to pay for their restaurant meals and whatever other expenses they incurred. A decent man was a decent man, but still a man. As for going abroad for their honeymoon, as they planned, she would deal with that when the time came.

In the car, she said to Philip, "Why have you never asked me whether I believe in God?"

"That's a deeply personal question. I don't ask people whether they believe in God."

"I'm not people. I'm going to be your wife."

"For which I thank God. You see, Barbara, the Buddhists have a saying: If you see the Buddha, kill him. That's not to be taken literally, but to Buddhists the Buddha was a man—no different than other men, only wiser—and if you think you see the Buddha, you are a victim of illusion, because God—or what we call God—is ineffable. I believe that all human beings believe in their own definition of God, and for me it is not definable."

"And for most of us here in America, the definition is money," Barbara murmured.

"If you want to be cynical. I don't think you're cynical."

"I don't know," Barbara said. "My father, who was careful never to set foot in a church except when he went to a funeral, believed in decency, and that was enough for him. I was baptized in Grace Church, and every time I took communion after that, until

I was sixteen, I could only think of the musty smell. When I was doing the story in El Salvador, where I saw men and women and children murdered by the death squads the CIA had set up and trained and armed, the same death squads that had murdered Jesuit priests and nuns and a Catholic bishop on the altar of his own church, I said to myself that God is for others but not for me. I've lived my life very well believing in the decency of most people and the indecency of the few."

"Then that's your worship," Philip said after a moment. "I would not try to convince you otherwise."

"But you still think I believe in God?"

"It doesn't matter what I think. I'm absolutely content with you just as you are."

THE WEDDING FINALLY CAME ABOUT—not in a month, as Sally had planned, but early in September. The day was cool and clean, a day made to order for a festival in the Valley. Barbara, who almost never wore white, had only one white pleated skirt and two white dresses, one of them being her wedding dress from her marriage to Carson Devron. It was a lovely and expensive dress, and it still fit as well as the day she first wore it; but it brought too many memories with it, and she could not bring herself to wear it. She tried the pleated white skirt, but it was silk and to wear it with a blouse was simply wrong, and anyway, it was too short. The other white dress was of cotton, made in India, and she had bought it a decade ago for forty dollars; the cotton was fine and full, and the skirt was double, and the simplicity of it pleased her. Certainly she had no desire to distract from May Ling's beautiful bride's dress. She decided for the India cotton, rejecting any thought of buying another wedding dress that she would wear only once. Even if she could not predict the future, she was absolutely certain that she would never marry again; and Philip, seeing her in the white cotton, decided that she and the dress were absolutely wonderful. Philip wore a white jacket and a black bow tie, as did most of the men who were present. The female guests, sheltered under broad white hats, presented a dazzling display of color.

The parking lot was overwhelmed, and cars were parked for a quarter of a mile up and down the Silverado Road. It was the beginning of harvest time, and the vines were loaded with ripening grapes. The two pavilions, striped in pink, stood on the spacious lawn—two full acres that Eloise had successfully fought for and prevented from being plowed up for vines. A forty-by-forty dance floor had been put down, and Candido's gift to the bride was a seven-piece Mexican band. Instead of flowers each table had a centerpiece of ripe, luscious grapes. Mr. Cohen and his crew and his two trucks had arrived at ten, and by the time the guests began to appear, 420 chairs had been spaced on the dance floor, with an aisle in the center for bride and groom. The chairs overflowed onto the lawn, which Eloise did not mind at all. May Ling and Sally, who was in lemon yellow and white and very much the former film star, were properly secluded in the main house, but Barbara, who had no intention of playing the bride's game in this, her third marriage, was part of the reception team; and for the first time she met Judith Hope.

Afterward, when Freddie asked what she had thought on meeting Judith, Barbara replied that Judith was magnificent—and that this description was not an exaggeration. Wearing flat, silver-embroidered shoes and wrapped in a pale pink sheath, under a broad white straw hat, she stood a trifle more than six feet, escorted by Freddie in a white dinner jacket, his blond hair making a dramatic contrast to hers. Eloise, wearing her best light blue, felt dwarfed, speechless for a moment, but then pulled herself together and said, "Welcome to Highgate, my dear," and then went up on her toes to kiss her, an arrangement that Judith thoughtfully helped by bending and embracing Eloise.

Freddie was relieved. It went better than he expected. Adam, in a jovial mood, stood tall enough to kiss Judith's cheek, while Eloise was thinking that Judith was wearing the same perfume Freddie always gave *her* at Christmas, and which he must have bought for her.

"And this," Freddie said, "is my aunt Barbara, who writes books and gets involved in wars and revolutions, and who runs Gloria Steinem a close second in the women's movement—"

"Freddie," Judith said, "I know very well who your aunt is, and I'm delighted to meet her."

"And I've heard a great deal about you, Judith, and I'm glad to finally meet you"; and with that, Barbara kissed Judith and embraced her. Philip, standing beside Barbara, nodded in agreement and gave his hand to Judith, and said words to the effect of how good it was for all of them to be here on this happy occasion.

Birdie MacGelsie couldn't wait to get Barbara away from the receiving group. "This is more important," she declared. "Who is she, and where did Freddie find her?"

"I believe he found her in the Fairmont Hotel. Her name's Judith Hope."

"Well, what is she? Come on."

"She's a woman. Isn't that obvious?"

"Barbara, don't play games with me. I've known you too long. She's gorgeous. Is she in films?"

"She's a model, Birdie. I can't stand here talking. I'm a hostess here. Poor Eloise is overwhelmed."

"I should think so. Is Freddie going to marry her? Is this for real?"

"You'll have to ask Freddie."

"I must meet her. Hello, Philip," she said belatedly. "Congratulations."

But it wasn't easy. Judge Horton had already staked out his ground, as a companion in color, and others moved in around Judith and Freddie.

Barbara sighed and turned back to the arriving guests, and Philip wondered whether they shouldn't seek the same seclusion that was granted to May Ling.

"Absolutely not. You have a dozen people from the church whom Eloise does not know, and there are others, and I will not leave her to this alone."

"She is beautiful," Philip said softly. It was the first time she had heard him comment on another woman's appearance, and he was not talking about Eloise.

"I'm glad you noticed," Barbara said shortly.

Now the guests were flooding in, and Eloise, caught in that trap of amnesia that more than ten guests always brought upon her, was struggling with names. Abner Berman appeared with his ex-wife, Reda, who explained quickly to Barbara, "I couldn't miss a double wedding, not even if it meant coming with Dracula." And Abner grinned and shook his head and kissed Barbara and whispered, "What could I do? The dragon lady's the dragon lady." Carla, Candido's daughter and now president of the Bay Area Chicano Union, turned up with her new husband and asked, "Where is the Black Beauty? No, I'm not going to make a scene. This is my husband, Diego. Freddie's safe," she assured Barbara. Barbara's son, Sam, and his wife, Mary Lou (in a blazing designer dress), and their child, Jean, who immediately dashed away, kissed and hugged her; then Jean joined Danny and half a dozen other children whom Eloise and Barbara had not even counted on. Sam had to whisper, "Mother, marriage is a terrible habit." And Father Gibbon, in full regalia, who turned out to be a former classmate of Philip's, shook hands with Philip and insisted, "We must talk, Phil. We must."

Consuela Gomez, Freddie's secretary, sat at a small folding table, checking off the list of names, and she had reached a point of utter confusion. She pleaded with Barbara for a moment of attention and then said hopelessly, "They don't even stop for me. Ms.

Lavette, I have checked off two hundred names, and there must be twice that many here."

"They feel at home," Barbara said. "Forget the list." She turned to Philip and begged him, "Take over, darling, please. I must talk to Mr. Cohen." Adam, smiling benignly, his white beard giving him the appearance of an Old Testament patriarch, told Barbara not to worry. He and Eloise had everything in hand. Eloise had taken refuge in a continuous smile and had surrendered on the problem of names, and Adam simply smiled and nodded.

Barbara raced over to the trucks and found Mr. Cohen sitting on a folding chair, drinking a cup of coffee, and calmly smoking a cigar. "Do you see those kids?" she asked. "We should have put 'no children' on the invitations, but how could we?"

"On a Sunday," Mr. Cohen said sagely, "baby-sitters are hard to find. We haven't been in this business almost a hundred years for nothing. I always bring twenty folding chairs like the one I'm sitting on. I always bring a box of frankfurters and frankfurter rolls. They won't eat salmon, anyway. We'll make the kids a picnic on the side. They'll sit on the grass and be happy, and meanwhile, my guess is that you got four hundred people at least and maybe more. So I have the folding chairs for an emergency. Please don't worry. It's ten minutes to eleven. Who is first, you or your niece?"

"We're first, then my niece. Ours is a very simple ceremony."

"All right. Now, you bring the minister or rabbi or whoever is doing it up to the lectern—"

"She's a woman."

"So she's a woman. I got an open mind. When I see her there, I got a steam whistle on my big truck and I give three short blasts. That will stop the talking and moving around and then she can tell them on the microphone to take their seats. I see half of them are already seated. When the ceremony is over, Mr. Levy tells me, wine will be served at that long table. Three of my girls will serve the wine. The name cards are already on the tables, where Ms. Sally placed them. Extra guests, extra chairs. We squeeze them in. Ms. Gomez, Mr. Lavette's secretary, is going to help. So you go ahead now, and don't worry."

Philip and Barbara had chosen their marriage ceremony from those published in the church pamphlets, as had May Ling and Harry. When Philip told Reba Guthri, his assistant minister, what his and Barbara's choice was, she was somewhat perturbed. "The Wine Ceremony is rarely used, Philip, and you are the minister."

"It's Barbara's choice," he explained. "The Highgate winery is the single thread that runs through her whole life. It has tied the two families, the Levys and the Lavettes, together for three generations. They're somewhat like the old farm families used to be, yet different. I didn't object, because in the Catholic Church, where I was trained, wine is venerated. So I can understand what she feels."

Reba Guthri, a stocky woman of fifty or so with iron gray bobbed hair, was already at the rostrum, poring over some papers with Philip. Barbara told her about her talk with Mr. Cohen and took Philip's arm. "You're the groom this time, so let's get back and get ready to march up the aisle." She hurried Philip through the crowd, and they had barely gotten into place when the steam blasts sounded. As Mr. Cohen had said, there was a moment of silence, and Reba Guthri suggested that the guests be seated.

"As you know," Ms. Guthri announced, "there are two weddings to be celebrated here today. I am Reba Guthri, Philip Carter's assistant minister, and I shall perform the marriage of Barbara Lavette and Philip Carter. As soon as you are all seated, we will begin."

Barbara had given Candido's Mexican band severe instructions. During the ceremonies, only the guitars, two regular and one bass; no conga drums, no trumpet. Her bridal march was to be a moody Spanish love song called "Always." To be sure that her instructions were understood, she delivered them in impeccable Castilian— which surprised the musicians. Now the soft Spanish music began, and Barbara and Philip walked down the aisle, Barbara hatless in her white cotton ankle-length dress, her straight white hair shoulder length and loose, and Philip in his white dinner jacket. She had rejected any thought of a bouquet or bridesmaids or anyone to give her away. She was senior in the family, and in two months she would be seventy; and Eloise, sitting with Adam, was already in tears, whispering to Adam, "How beautiful she is."

Reba Guthri was holding a silver chalice of wine, and when Philip and Barbara stopped in front of her, she said, "Barbara and Philip, will you take each other as man and wife, to live together in the covenant of marriage? Will you love each other and comfort each other in sickness and health, forsake all others, and be faithful to each other as long as you shall live?"

Both answered, "I will."

Then, holding up the chalice of wine, Reba Guthri said, "The years of our lives are a cup of wine poured out for us to drink. The grapes, when pressed, give forth the good juices of the wine. So, too, under the winepress of time, our lives give forth their labor and honor and love. Many days you will sit at the same table and eat and drink together. So drink now, and may the cup of your lives be sweet and full to running over. From this time forth may you find life's joys double-gladdening, its bitterness sweetened, and all things hallowed by true companionship and love."

Reba handed the chalice to Barbara, who drank and then handed it to Philip, who drank and gave the cup back to Reba. Then he took Barbara in his arms and kissed her, and the audience applauded, and the trumpeter in the Mexican band, unable to contain himself, sounded a wild fanfare.

Adam was overwhelmed. There were tears in his eyes as he embraced Barbara, and then she took her seat between Eloise and Freddie, who was whispering to Judith that there could have been three weddings. Judith said to Barbara, "It was so beautiful—just so beautiful." Philip, who kissed Reba and thanked her, called out, "Please keep your seats. You will have time to greet and kiss the bride after we are finished. By now I am sure you all know who I am. I am the minister at the First Unitarian Church, and I shall now celebrate the marriage of May Ling Lavette to Harry Lefkowitz."

The band struck up the Wedding March, and May Ling, tall and slender and lovely in her wedding gown, on the arm of her father, Dr. Joseph Lavette, walked down the aisle, and following her, Harry and Sally.

IT WAS OVER. At long last, the weddings were over. Freddie had written out a check and had handed it to Mr. Cohen. The salmon had been a great success, and the children had gobbled down the frankfurters and rolls. The wedding guests had gone, and Mr. Cohen's crew had picked up the last bit of rubbish, and Mr. Cohen's two catering trucks had departed, and the sun was dipping to the gentle slopes of the Valley; and Barbara was as forlorn and depressed as ever she had been in all her life. Philip, who had not slept the night before, had gone to their room for a nap; and alone Barbara was walking slowly through the vines, heavy with ripe grapes, on the path that led up the hillside to the little clearing where long ago—or so it seemed—she would sit with Eloise and talk about everything and nothing.

Where was the joy that a bride was supposed to have? But she was not a bride; she was an old woman who asked herself why on God's earth she had allowed this to happen. She felt trapped and filled with hopelessness, and as she reviewed the last few months, she felt like someone caught in a hopeless morass. She recalled an incident years ago when a mouse had appeared in the big kitchen, and with a broom Cathrena chased the terrified little creature trying so desperately to flee from the giant foe.

Barbara was sick and tired of people telling her that she was still beautiful. She had never taken proper care of her skin, scorning the endless advertisements and persuasions for this or that cream that took twenty years off one's age and miraculously made one young and beautiful overnight, and her face was covered with a network of fine wrinkles. Eloise had urged her to use a rinse that would turn her hair ash-blond, to which she replied that she had never been an ash-blond and had no intention of becoming one now.

Last month her son, Sam, out of his omnipotence as physician and surgeon, had told her that she must begin to take Premarin, and that he would give her the proper prescription; otherwise, he warned her, she would develop that bowed, hunched look that so many older women have. She resented this, even as she resented all of Sam's warnings and commentary about her health, and she threw the prescription away—her own small assertion of independence. Was it all about independence? Then why was she lonely? Did she love Philip, and what was love? Where did it come from? She remembered her first love, Marcel, the newspaperman she had met when she was living in Paris, who had left to cover the Spanish Civil War and whose thighbone had been shattered by shrapnel; and she remembered the passion she had felt for him, the feeling that he was a part of her, the joy in their sex, her screams of pure rapture when she had an orgasm, and his pleas of "Quiet, quiet, my beloved, or the landlord will cast us out of here as depraved creatures," and she remembered the utter desolation that had overcome her when he died.

She would never forget the day he died in the hospital in Toulouse. The world ended and hope passed out of her life. And this brought to mind the thought of how she would react if Philip died. She would weep, but she would also be free; and that thought turned her against herself and filled her mind with contempt for herself, as she felt herself to be utterly heartless.

She had reached the clearing and she sat down on one of the benches in front of the open fireplace, arguing with herself that she loved Philip, that Philip was the best man she had ever known, that there wasn't a bone of hate or anger or resentment anywhere in his body—"And that's the whole damn trouble!" she said angrily. "I don't want a man to love me in spite of what I am. I want a man to love me because of what I am." And after that small outburst, she felt somewhat better, and decided that she would tell Sam that she had lost the prescription for Premarin, and that she would begin to take it as he had suggested; and she took comfort in the fact that she would not be alone anymore. She recalled that on the nights when she had a dinner date with Philip, she would wait for the doorbell to ring and be anxious if he was delayed and came late. She told herself that she did love him; he was sweet and kind and gentle, and she remembered how delicious it was to have a warm body next to her at night, and when she woke at night to feel him there beside her and roll over and press her body to his; and he never resented being awakened at four in the morning by her embrace—and you don't do that with someone you don't love. Her thoughts wandered, and she shivered with the increasing chill of the night.

Suddenly Philip appeared, carrying a woolen serape, which he folded over her shoulders. He had changed into blue jeans and a sweater, and he told her that Eloise had suggested that he would find her here. "I looked everywhere else, and for a moment I thought you had fled. But your car was still here, so I decided that you were hiding. Not that I blame you."

"I didn't mean to hide, Philip. I wanted to be alone and think."

"About our marriage being a great mistake?"

She stared at him in bewilderment.

"It's a very common post-wedding feeling," he said.

"Is that how you feel?"

"No, but I'm not Barbara Lavette. I'm the luckiest man in California, and that makes me nervous."

She smiled. "Philip Carter nervous? That will be the day. I

never told you how good you were with May Ling and Harry. It was an absolutely beautiful ceremony."

"Thank you, my dear. It's getting cold and in a little while it will be dark, and I have no confidence in being able to make my way down that path in the dark. Eloise told me that there will be supper in the kitchen—she and Adam, whom I have come to like enormously, and May Ling and Harry, and Freddie and that incredible woman of his, and you and me—if you can ever forgive me for leaving you and falling asleep. I only meant to lie down for a few minutes. Eloise promised to wake me, and she let me sleep for an hour."

"I think I can forgive you, Philip."

"Yes, bless you. Harry and May Ling are leaving for Paris tomorrow. Danny will stay here until school begins next week, and then he'll be with Sally. You see, I've integrated myself with the family. Now all I have to do is to prove to you that our marriage is going to be a very happy one."

Barbara rose and threw her arms around him, and he kissed her gently.

"No!" she said. "Don't kiss me like that! Open your mouth and kiss me as if you want to crawl inside of me."

He did, and then they walked down the path to join the others in the kitchen.

IT WAS A STRANGE DINNER that evening at Highgate, and Barbara was both the observer and the observed, intimately entwined yet apart from it, thinking that it was some sixty-five years ago that Jake Levy, newly discharged from the service, and Clair Harvey, his bride, had driven down the Silverado Trail and bought Highgate for a song from a bitter old Irishman who spent his days cursing the Volstead Act and staying drunk. Sixty-five years—what a long, long time! Her father, Dan Lavette, had brought her there for the first time at age eight—Jake was his partner's son—and Jake kept a saddle horse. Dan had swung her up in front of him, and up the path to the hilltop they went, until the whole Napa Valley was spread out before them.

And now, after all the rejoicing, the family was strangely silent around a dinner table that always bubbled with sound. The toasts were over. They were confronting America's agony, a black woman who sat among them. Barbara asked herself, *If I were Judith, what would I be thinking?*

Adam was carving a leg of lamb. Dinner was late. It was nine o'clock—but Barbara had only pecked at her lunch, and a glass of wine had given her a strange, heady feeling. Freddie filled her glass again, and she rose, glass in hand.

"Am I permitted another toast?" Barbara asked. "I will make it short because I am hungry. Somewhere in the Bible—which I must confess I have not read in more years than a duck has feathers—it speaks of the stranger within your gates. But there are no strangers here. When you break bread at this table, you are part of our family. Judith, I toast you and welcome you. I am the senior member of this gathering, and I thank whatever gods may be that I have lived long enough to welcome a beautiful black woman into our hearts."

They drank and both Eloise and Judith wept. Freddie had never seen Judith weep before. He went around the table, embraced her, and kissed her. Barbara's eyes were wet, and she said to herself, *What a sloppy, sentimental toast that was.* She wouldn't dare put it in her book, yet it had worked, and everyone was talking and eating, and Adam even explained to Judith that this was not their best vintage, that their best vintage had disappeared into the bellies of the wedding guests.

The Wind and the Sea

FREDDIE HAD A TWENTY-FIVE FOOT CATBOAT that he'd named *Thrush*, and that he anchored at a marina in Sausalito in Marin County. It was a wooden boat with a tiny cabin forward, an outboard motor of ninety horsepower, and no wheel but an old-fashioned tiller—a very simple boat, built by his grandfather, Dan Lavette, more than forty years ago. All this he explained to Judith while driving out to Sausalito. The boat had been kept in perfect condition, hardly ever used by Dan Lavette, and had come to him as a birthday present from his grandmother, Jean. Now, on the Saturday a week after the wedding, he'd asked Judith to go sailing with him.

"This is the worst time for me to try to get away from the winery," he said, "now when the crop is being harvested. Everything goes frantic, but Adam insists on Saturday as a day of rest, thank God. The *Thrush* is no yacht. They used to call them mosquito boats, and I guess they were the first small pleasure boats to be used on the Bay. But any idiot can sail a catboat. They're beautiful, responsive little craft."

"Not this idiot, Freddie. I've never been sailing. The men I've dated have had no boats—not a black thing."

"Can you swim?"

"Can a fish swim?" Her laugh was like a soft, musical ripple. "I was captain of the swimming team in high school and again in college. I won first place in the West Coast Women's Trials. They wanted me for the Olympics, but I couldn't face a year of spending four hours a day in a swimming pool. My breasts are already small enough, and they were beginning to disappear under a pair of over-sized pectorals. Forgive me for boasting, but you touched a nerve. Truth is, it's my height that gives me the advantage."

He glanced at her. She wore a sweatshirt and blue jeans, her feet in sneakers, and Freddie felt, as he often had, that she was the most beautiful woman he had ever seen.

"—which is why I've always kept my woolly hair cropped close. Good for swimming, and the photographers love it. But swimming—oh, Lord, Freddie, how could you live without it? I'm in the pool every day, right behind my house, twenty minutes. It's the only exercise I take—I hate exercise. I read a book by a Welsh woman—I forget her name—who claimed, and with a lot of good proof, that the evolution that created man took place on the sea-shore, that women were constructed so that they could nurse their babies in the surf out of harm's way, and that the only place where there was enough protein for the taking was on the seashore. You know, the only animals that have a brain the size of man's are the amphibious mammals, the sea otter, the orca, the whale, and the dolphin. I wrote a long piece for *Natural History* about it, and they pooh-poohed it, the way they discard any new idea offered by a woman. But swimming—yes, I can swim."

Freddie, listening with a bit of awe, admitted that he had never thought of that. Each time he was with her, he discovered a new side of her. "Who wrote that book?" he asked her.

"I'll find it in the library, and I'll get it for you," she promised.

The marina man took them out to the boat. Freddie unhooked it from the buoy and began to haul up the sail. "Take the tiller until I get the sail. Just straight on, just hold it straight and steady. The wind's from the west, so I'll rope her on a slight tack until we face Alcatraz, and then we'll head for the Golden Gate." He crawled into the tiny cabin while Judith, thrilled with an utterly new sensation, held the tiller. Freddie checked his radio and then came back with two life jackets, one of which he tossed to Judith.

"Put it on," he said.

"No way. It's too hot."

"It'll cool off. Put it on or we go back. I'm the captain, remember? Law of the sea. It gives me the power of life and death."

"Bullshit," she said succinctly.

Freddie slipped on the sleeveless life vest, and tied it. "Seriously," he told her, "you must wear it." He dropped on the seat next to her. "The Bay is treacherous. I've seen boats flipped in a sudden squall. I'll hold the tiller, and if you're hot, you can take off the sweatshirt and wear the life vest."

"All right, Freddie...I never want to have a real fight with you. I was stopped one night by a mugger with a knife—yes, a black man. We don't discriminate. I grabbed his wrist and flipped him over and broke his arm." She smiled soothingly and leaned over and kissed him. Then she peeled off the sweatshirt and put on the life vest. "Let me hold the tiller, please. I love it. And tell me what tacking is. I hear about it all the time."

"All right. We're tacking now. The wind is coming from the west. We're sailing southwest, obliquely to the wind. That's why I have the boom, the wooden pole that holds the bottom of the sail, roped and almost over our heads. It creates a suction and the boat moves off the direction of the wind. Now we're in the Bay, and there's Alcatraz, and to reach the Golden Gate, we're going on what we call a broad reach. In other words, we're sailing against the wind."

"It sounds impossible."

"If it were, Judy, we'd be in an awful fix. But look at the other boats, how they're zigzagging. We'll do the same thing. Now, here's the tiller." He loosened the sheet and told her to keep her head down. With one hand on the tiller, moving it slightly, he pulled in the boom. "Now we're reaching. Watch the island, and you'll see that we're moving against the wind."

"We are, we are! I love it!" she cried, throwing her arms around Freddie.

"Watch it!" he cried. "The tiller's alive when you're on this tack."

"Let me steer, Freddie, by myself."

"All right, but keep her into the wind. Watch the sail. Don't let her get away from you."

"We can't turn over?" she asked, alarmed for a moment.

"No, don't worry. Just keep her into the wind."

The Bay was alive with boats, some of them running before the brisk west wind, others on the same tack as the *Thrush*. Freddie, hanging on to a rope, leaned back for balance, watching Judith, impressed with the facility with which she managed the tiller. Then he sat down beside her. "Let me take the tiller. We're coming about. Keep your head down." The sail flapped idly for a moment and then filled out as they took the other tack.

Judith appeared to be ecstatic. "Freddie, I want a boat—I want to sail for the rest of my life."

"You have a boat. You're sitting in it." Her excitement communicated itself to him. He pointed to a large oiler making its way ponderously through the Bay. "That piece of junk is going to make us wallow. Just be easy. You're not getting squeamish?"

"Me, squeamish? Freddie, I was born for this." And then she suddenly said, "Freddie, I love you. What right have you to that fuckin' golden hair? You're so goddamn handsome, and you know it—why aren't you black or brown or something?"

"We'll make it with the kids. They'll come out brown or something."

"I'll never marry you and I'll never have kids! Am I crazy enough to bring kids into this lousy white world?"

"It's a damn nice world right at this moment."

She burst into laughter as the boat pitched and tilted in the wake of the oiler. "Right on!" she shouted.

"Keep it this way," Freddie said.

She threw her head back and in her deep, throaty voice, sang:

I sing because I'm happy,
I sing because I am free.
The Lord has his eye on every sparrow,
So he must have his eye on me!

On the next tack, a sightseeing boat passed them, its rail lined with tourists whose eyes were fixed on the black woman and white man in the little catboat. As they pitched in the wake of the sightseeing boat, Judith stuck out her tongue at the tourists.

In sudden exuberance, she pulled at the laces of her life jacket, dropped it off, and sat half naked, letting the spray wash her body. The tourist boat had passed by. She spread her arms.

"Put the damn jacket on!" Freddie yelled. "Have you gone nuts?" Yet he could not help admiring the beauty of her body, the breasts so firm and taut, her torso like a bronze sculpture.

"Put it on!" he yelled again.

"Freddie, have you ever made out in a catboat?"

"We're close-hauled. If I let go of the rudder, we'll go over. Please, Judy, put the damn jacket on."

There was a note in his voice that had not been there before. Like a small girl caught in some egregious act, she put on the vest, tied it, and said, "You're sulking, Freddie. You're really angry at me."

"Absolutely. You can swim to shore. I can't."

"Freddie, beloved, I'd never let you drown. I love you."

"Not that I can't swim," he said. "Only, no one ever asked me to join an Olympic team...I'm not really angry."

At the Golden Gate he swung the boat around and they ran before the wind, Judith cuddled against him. "This is glorious, Freddie. Can we do it again?"

"And again and again."

"And I'll never take off the vest. I promise." She opened a picnic basket, and they munched sandwiches and drank beer while Freddie cradled the tiller under his arm.

"Tell me about your aunt Barbara. She fascinates me."

"Yes, she's something."

"How old is she?"

"She'll be seventy in November."

"I don't believe it. She moves like a young woman." Judith was looking at the City now, the streets climbing the hills like lines drawn on an enormous map, the white buildings piled one on another. "The most beautiful city in the world. It's a miracle. She's like the City, she's something else entirely."

"Who is?"

"Barbara. She was in prison once. That's what unites us. We're a people of the prisons."

"Who? What are you talking about?"

"The blacks. Me. My people. Freddie, do you ever use that pretty head of yours for anything but your fancy sailor cap?"

"There you go."

"I apologize."

"I graduated Princeton *summa cum laude*."

"Freddie, darling, you're brilliant about everything that doesn't matter."

"Thank you."

"Now, about Barbara. Why did she go to prison?"

"Well, it's a bit complicated. She was involved in the Spanish

Civil War in 1938, and she was part of a group that established a hospital in Toulouse for wounded and sick Spanish Republicans and their families. She raised a lot of money from people like my grandfather and others she knew, and then she was subpoenaed by the House Un-American Committee and told to give them the names of the contributors, and she refused. Contempt of Congress. They put her in jail for six months."

"For being decent and honorable?"

"Decent and honorable don't pay off."

"How did she get that way? Her family was so rich."

"It's not being rich that corrupts me and makes me different from my aunt Barbara, it's having a father who left me more money than I ever needed—not Adam, who adopted me, but my biological father—what a disgusting term—Thomas Lavette; and whenever my aunt Barbara has one of her numberless causes, marches, or campaigns, she comes to me and gets enough money to ease my conscience."

Back at Sausalito Freddie tied up his boat while Judith furled and knotted the sail. The rubber dinghy took them to shore and, both of them starved now, they drove back to San Francisco and to Gino's, a small Italian restaurant. "My grandfather Dan Lavette used to eat here," Freddie told her. "Now Gino's son runs the place. They make their own pasta, and it's the best. When I'm filled with life and energy, the way I am now, I always want pasta. It's genetic. I'm one-quarter Italian, you know."

The younger Gino embraced Freddie. "Where have you been? I haven't seen you in months." He stared admiringly at Judith and then stared questioningly at Freddie.

"I kidnapped him," Judith said.

Bewildered, Gino led them to a table. "A bottle of Highgate red?" he asked.

"Absolutely. And linguine with clams and garlic and olive oil."

"I'll have the same," Judith agreed.

Each plate was enough for a family of three, and they ate and drank and ordered another bottle of wine and stuffed themselves with bread and pasta, and Judith declared that it was the best of everything; the best bread, the best wine.

"I feel human with you," Freddie said. "I'm born again. I'm not a good Christian, so how about a born-again pagan? Will you have me?"

"I might."

"Will you marry me?"

"Maybe. I'm ready to think about it."

"Me, not the boat."

She smiled. "I'm ready to think about it, Freddie. Of course, the boat comes with you. I'm a bit drunk, so when I sober up I may change my mind. Your face is red as a beet. You're blushing."

"I'm sunburnt. I don't blush. My God, this is the first time you even bent a little. Judy, I loved you the first time I saw you."

"Did you? You thought I was a classy hooker, and all you cared about was getting me into bed."

"Is that so terrible?"

"Freddie, you're drunk, and how are you going to get us home?"

"Very carefully."

"You know, sweet man," she said, "I'm glad you took it to my mama and papa that night. Otherwise, if I simply told them I was in love with a white man, my papa might have put me over his knee and walloped me. You've lived an easy life, Freddie. Now the hard part begins."

"Not so easy. I was at Princeton during the big civil rights drive of the sixties. A bunch of us went down to Mississippi to register black voters. A gang of rednecks caught us. They killed one of the kids and whipped and beat me half to death. I ended up in a hospital in Mississippi."

"Freddie—Freddie, why didn't you ever tell me this?"

"Why should I? It was nothing to boast about. I'm here. I'm alive, and I'm all right."

She had tears in her eyes. "Yes, you're here. Take me home, Freddie. I want to hold you in my arms. I want to make love."

A FEW DAYS AFTER THAT SATURDAY, Barbara received a letter from May Ling. "My dear Aunt Barbara," it began, "We're here in Paris..." Ruefully, Barbara reflected that she had agreed to put off their own journey until October, due to tasks Philip faced at the church. But at least May Ling was in Paris.

> ...and it's wonderful. Oh, if I could only speak French the way you do! My Spanish is good, but two years of high school French aren't enough to talk to a waiter; Harry says that we'll go on to Madrid and Barcelona, where I will at least have the power of speech. Harry speaks French like a native, and he appears to know everyone in Paris. Of course that's an exaggeration, but he has an office here and we've been to dinner three times at the homes of French people he knows. His firm has a small apartment on the Quai d'Orsay.
>
> Harry was always so shy. I know I'm shy, but with me he was even worse, and he's like another person I never knew. He worships me, Barbara, and I don't know how to be worshiped. We had lunch yesterday at Le Moulin du Village—I had to ask Harry how to spell it—and I felt that I was in the most romantic place in the world, and the proprietor and the waiters made such a fuss over me. They thought I was from Java or some such place, and everyone has been wonderful to me, and when they see I don't understand their French, they say very flattering things that Harry translates later with great glee. I tell him I don't believe a word of it.
>
> Wasn't the wedding simply wonderful? I will never forget it as long as I live, and when Daddy told me that

Freddie paid for most of it, I sat down and cried. I never understood Freddie, and I guess he never understood me. Mother was very sweet to Harry the day we left. Harry said to her that he had no object in life more important than to make me happy, and Danny actually kissed him and Mother wept. But she's quite happy, because Daddy has a new nurse, and that frees Mother, who met a producer at the wedding—I don't remember his name, but I guess you invited him—and he knew about Mother's career, and he has a small role for her in his new picture, and I do hope she's not disappointed, but she was so happy.

Harry is the sweetest, most caring man, and I can't believe that he's the terror of prosecutors, as they make him out to be.

We also went up in the Eiffel Tower. I'll write again soon, probably from Spain. How's Philip—I don't mean as a husband, but how is he?

Love,
May Ling

"THANK GOD FOR SATURDAY, and you don't have to work," Judith said. "I wait all week for Saturday. I'm a born-again Baptist. Are you a Jew, Freddie?"

"I'm not a Jew. I'm nothing. You know that. I'm a heathen who worships a black goddess."

"You shouldn't say that. It's blasphemy."

"So be it. Adam decided to stop being Jewish today and declared it a workday. The harvest waits for no man's religion. If he could, he'd have my mother out there picking grapes. I told him I was going sailing, and he threw a fit. Don't think I don't sacrifice for you."

She sat in the stern, the tiller under her arm, her head thrown back in sheer ecstasy—"Tell Adam that I passed up a job today for this. When the harvest's over, it's going to be every Saturday and Sunday. But after church on Sunday."

"You go to church?"

"You know I do."

"And you meant what you said about blasphemy?"

"Absolutely. I don't want to be worshiped. That's bullshit, and you know it is. I'm a God-fearing Baptist, and don't you ever forget that—and those four children you've scheduled for me are going to be baptized Baptists, not Episcopalian Catholics."

"Whatever you say. And that means you're going to marry me?"

"That way I get the boat."

"It's a deal," Freddie said. "What did you think of the wedding?"

"I loved it. But you met my father. Either I get married in his church or I'm not married at all, and you'd better make it soon. I think I missed my period."

"No. You're kidding?" he said incredulously.

"Maybe I am, maybe not. I've been late before, but not when I've been sleeping with someone every night."

"Hallelujah!" Freddie exclaimed, leaping back to embrace her.

"Freddie, you'll swamp us!" She clung to the tiller as he embraced her and kissed her.

JUDITH HAD A PHOTOGRAPHY SESSION with Frank Halter, perhaps the best known of all fashion photographers, at ten o'clock in the morning. She called Obie Johnson, a cabdriver, to pick her up at nine. Judith liked to arrive early for photography sessions. She was meticulous about her work and had the reputation in the industry of being one of the easiest models to work with.

Judith did not own a car. The thought of driving in San Francisco daunted her, and she had two cabdrivers, both of them black, who were utterly devoted to her, and whom she would call a day in advance with her schedule. On this morning she wore the swimsuit she would be modeling under a sport skirt and pullover. She preferred to dress at home whenever it was possible. Simone Casis, her maid, a black woman, would come to her house from eight to twelve, dust, make the bed, and help her to dress if the costume was complicated. This morning it was a simple matter, and Simone walked to the door with her, carrying a cashmere sweater. The morning was chilly, and she was trying to convince Judith to take the sweater.

Outside, Obie Johnson, a burly black man, was standing beside his parked cab. He adored Judith and considered himself her bodyguard as well as her driver. Judith took the sweater from Simone and leaped into the cab, telling Obie, "I'm late, Obie, and Frank Halter gets snotty when I'm late."

"Nobody gets snotty with you, Ms. Hope. Not when I'm driving."

"Then take off."

Obie was a better-than-good driver, but he adored Judith. He took a shortcut on Taylor, broke half a dozen traffic rules, and then swung left down Russian Hill toward the Embarcadero; and what happened was something that happens all too often in San Francisco. A truck cut him off, and for all that he stood on his brakes, he could not stop—and broadsided the truck.

FREDDIE WAS IN HIS OFFICE at Highgate when Ms. Gomez opened the door and said, "Mr. Lavette, there's a San Francisco police inspector on the phone. He wants to talk to you."

"Oh, what have I done now?"

Ms. Gomez put the call through. Freddie picked up the phone and said, "Frederick Lavette."

"Do you know a Judith Hope? This is Inspector Morrison."

"Yes, of course."

"I'm sorry to tell you this. She's been hurt."

Freddie's throat choked up. He tried to speak, but the words would not come. Then he gasped, "How bad? Is she alive? What happened?"

"They've taken her to Mercy Hospital. That's all I can tell you now."

Freddie put down the phone and left his office, telling Ms. Gomez, "I'll probably be gone all day. Judith's been hurt. They've taken her to Mercy Hospital."

"That's your cousin Sam's hospital. Do you want me to call them?"

Freddie hesitated. "No, I'm going there."

He was not a reckless driver, but now he broke all records between Highgate and San Francisco, the pain inside of him as great as if the hurt had been to him instead of Judith. He was not a person who prayed, but now he pleaded to a God he had never given much thought to, begging, "Please, please, let her be alive. I'll care for her, I'll be with her every minute of my life. Don't let her die. She's too good, too beautiful. I love her. I love her the way I've never been able to love another human being. Don't take her away."

DR. SAM LAVETTE COHEN, the son of Barbara's first marriage, had called Highgate a few minutes after Freddie left, and now he was waiting as Freddie drove into the parking lot at Mercy Hospital, where Sam was chief of surgery. He blocked Freddie's impulsive rush toward the entrance.

"How is she? Where is she?"

"She's in the operating room, and she'll be all right. She'll live, and she has one of the best teams in the City working on her. I'd be there now, but I wasn't on duty when she came in. So pull yourself together, Freddie. I told you she's not critical."

"For God's sake, what happened?"

"She was in a car crash. She was riding in a cab. The driver was killed. Now I'm going to take you upstairs, and I want you to sit down and stay calm."

"When can I see her?" Freddie begged.

"When she comes out of the operating room, she'll go into intensive care. I'm going to change and join the team. I know what you're feeling, but the only thing you can do is to stay calm and wait. I'll try to get you to her when she comes out."

"But what happened? How badly was she injured?"

"Later. Now, I don't know. I only know that she'll live."

A FRANTIC ELOISE CALLED BARBARA and told her that according to Ms. Gomez, Judith Hope had been injured, and that she had called Mercy Hospital and tried to reach Sam, but he was not to be found, and the hospital would release no information.

"But what happened?" Barbara asked. "How was she hurt?"

"That's it. I don't know and I can't find out, and according to Ms. Gomez, Freddie was terribly disturbed and took off like a gust of wind. Barbara, I've never seen anything like this in Freddie. Oh yes, there have been other women, but he is absolutely insane about Judith Hope. He talked with Adam and me last night. He is determined to marry her, and he wanted our agreement, which of course we gave. Adam feels that a few kids running around the place would be wonderful, and I agreed, because I can't think of a better place for a child to grow up than Highgate. Freddie said that at first she wouldn't even talk about children, but now that she agreed to marry him, she wants at least four kids—" Eloise had a tendency to go on and on with the telephone, and Barbara had to cut her short and promise that she would drive over to Mercy Hospital, and that she would call Eloise as soon as she found out what had happened to Judith.

Barbara called Mercy Hospital, but they would give her no information about Judith, and Sam could not be reached. She left a message for Sam that she would be at the hospital in half an hour.

It took longer than that. She was on her way out when the telephone rang. It was Philip. He told Barbara that he'd had his radio turned on, driving to the church, and he'd heard that Judith Hope had been hurt and that she had been taken to Mercy Hospital.

"Philip, is she alive?"

"I don't know. You know how they announce it—a breaking story and 'keep tuned for further information.' So I just don't know."

"Eloise called, but she couldn't get any information. Freddie took off for the hospital, and he must be there by now. I'm on my way."

"Should I meet you there?"

"If you can. You might help."

"Yes, I'll meet you there," Philip said.

Philip was already at the hospital when Barbara parked her car and walked to the front entrance. There were two policemen at the entrance, and several reporters and a TV truck. The policemen were keeping the reporters out, allowing only patients, family, and doctors to enter. Barbara said that her son, Sam Cohen, was chief of surgery, and this was a family emergency; Philip showed his credentials as a minister, and after a short argument, they were allowed to enter. The woman at the admitting desk knew Barbara and told her that she would find Dr. Cohen on the fifth floor. "I'll call for him to meet you at the nurses' station."

Sam, in a green operating gown, was waiting for Barbara and Philip. He explained quickly that he had only moments to talk. He had a patient who was being prepared for surgery, and he had to be in the operating room immediately. "Judith's going to make it," he told them in his dry medical manner. "She has serious lacerations on her face and neck and damage to the shoulders and a hairline fracture of the skull. They did the best they could. She'll be out of critical in a few hours, I think."

"What does that mean—'the best they could'?" Barbara wanted to know.

"The best they could. Her face was injured."

"What does that mean?"

"Mother, I have to go," Sam said shortly. "Freddie's in the waiting room on this floor."

"Is he always like that?" Philip wondered as Sam hurried away.

"More or less. They say grandchildren and grandparents love each other because they have a common enemy. Oh, God knows, Philip! He can be very sweet when he wants to."

They found Freddie slumped on a chair in the waiting room. He rose and embraced Barbara, his face a pattern of gloom.

"Did you see Judith?" Barbara asked.

"Briefly. Yes, I saw her. Her head is swathed in bandages."

"Sam says she'll be all right, that the injuries are not life threatening."

"Yes—so the surgeons told me. They also told me that her face was badly injured. What will that do to her, Aunt Barbara? Her beauty is her life."

"What happened to the driver?" Philip asked him.

"He's dead. They say it was a horrible crash. If she had been sitting in the front seat, she would be dead, too."

"Her beauty isn't her life, Freddie," Barbara said softly. "As much as anything, you are her life."

Dr. Hope and Mrs. Hope came into the waiting room then. Philip went to them and assured them that their daughter would recover. Dr. Hope asked about Obie, the driver, and Mrs. Hope burst into tears and went to Freddie, who took her in his arms.

"I want to see my daughter," Dr. Hope said firmly.

"She's in the recovery room," Freddie said. "I'll take you and Mrs. Hope there. I think they'll allow us to see her, but the anesthesia hasn't worn off yet. She's bandaged. She can't speak."

FINALLY FREDDIE LEFT THE HOSPITAL with Barbara and Philip. Barbara persuaded him to come with her to Green Street. When they reached Green Street, Barbara asked him whether he had lunch, and he replied that he couldn't eat. He seemed to be utterly exhausted. They talked for a while, and Freddie told them of the days on the catboat. Glancing at his watch, he said with surprise that it was only three o'clock. "Today has been like forever. I'm tired," he said apologetically.

Barbara asked Philip to take him upstairs and have him lie down in the guest room. Freddie nodded, and Philip went up the stairs with him.

There was a message from Eloise on Barbara's answering machine, and Barbara called her at Highgate. "Is he all right?" Eloise wanted to know.

"Perfectly all right. Totally miserable and consumed with worry, but otherwise all right. And Judith escaped—miraculously, I hear. The poor dear is injured but she'll be all right."

"I was so afraid," Eloise said. "If anything happened to Freddie, I couldn't go on. My heart goes out to that poor woman and the driver, but if anything happened to Freddie, I would just want to lie down and die. Can I talk to him? It's selfish, I know— I should be thinking of Judith—but you know how I feel about Freddie."

"He's exhausted. Philip took him up to the guest room, and maybe he'll sleep for a while. Philip was good with him. I think he helped him a little."

"Then don't disturb him. I've been listening to the radio. This has started a tremendous wave of protest about the traffic laws. Cars come thundering down those hill streets as if they were racetracks.

I never realized how much Judith was loved and admired. How is Freddie? I've never seen him like this with any other woman."

"Eloise, nothing happened to Freddie."

"Will you drive him home?"

"All right," Barbara agreed reluctantly.

"Thank you, dear—tonight?"

"Before sunset."

"I want to hold him in my arms," Eloise said.

"If he's asleep, I'll let him sleep for an hour. Then I'll bundle him into my car and drive him down to the Valley."

But Freddie shrugged off his mother's sentimentality and made it plain to Barbara that he would not return to Highgate. "I'm not a child. For heaven's sake, Aunt Barbara, I'm a middle-aged man, and the only thing that makes life worth living is lying in Mercy Hospital with her life on a thread. I'm staying here in town. If you can't put me up, I'll go to a hotel."

"Freddie, of course I can put you up. But at least call her. Try to understand your mother. It's only eight years since your brother came back from Vietnam and took his own life. Can't you imagine what that did to her?"

"I'm well. I'm fit. Nothing happened to me."

"Please call her."

"All right. I'll call her."

"And it's harvest time," Barbara said gently. "Can't you explain to Adam what you are feeling? You know what happens to him at harvest time."

"No way. If I talk to Adam, I may say something I will regret forever. They can harvest the damn grapes without me, and anyway most of it is over. And now I'm going back to the hospital."

Philip had listened silently to this exchange. After Freddie left, Barbara turned to Philip hopelessly. "Say something!"

"What shall I say, Barbara? Until I met you, I never actually knew what family is. I love this family. I love you. I watch Freddie and your brother Joe, and Adam and May Ling and Eloise, and now Harry and Judith and all the others whose names I still don't have at the tip of my tongue, and of course your son, Sam, and that lovely wife of his—what is her name?"

"Mary Lou—and what has that got to do with anything?"

"You asked me to say something."

"So I did," Barbara said shortly.

"Well, I'm trying."

"Oh, Philip, why do I get so snippy with you?" Barbara went to him and kissed him. "Forgive me. Go ahead."

"All I meant was that I'm beginning to understand how it works, and I feel pity for people like myself who have been alone. When I was a little boy, I would be given a hank of wool to hold while my mother took it off my hands strand by strand and rolled it into a ball. It's all there, but different."

Which is that? Barbara asked herself. *The Zen Buddhist or the priest?* But she said nothing.

"Freddie has grown up. He must get out of that tangled ball of wool. Some of us grow up at twelve and some at forty. Leave him alone, and tell Eloise to leave him alone. This is his mountain to climb."

"Philip, I don't understand."

"Try."

"You mean her face?" Barbara whispered.

"Yes, and according to what Sam said, it was badly smashed and torn."

"Poor Judith. Poor Freddie."

"I think you'd better call Eloise," Philip said.

OUT OF INTENSIVE CARE, Judith was in a hospital room when Freddie returned. Still under the effect of the anesthesia, she lay with her eyes closed as evening fell. Her head was covered with bandages, except for her eyes and an area around her nostrils and mouth. Mrs. Hope sat quietly in the darkened room. Freddie bent to kiss her cheek, and then he asked in a whisper whether Judith had recovered consciousness.

"She opened her eyes. I think she saw me. Then she closed her eyes again."

"She said nothing?"

"Only was Obie all right. I told her he was dead. Maybe I shouldn't have."

Freddie told her he would be back in a few minutes, and then he went out to the nurses' station and spoke to the nurse in charge.

The nurse was a tall, stout woman, and when Freddie explained that he and Judith were to be married, she regarded him dubiously.

"When can I speak to her?" Freddie asked. "I mean, when will she understand me?"

"She's very heavily sedated and she'll sleep through the night. She's a very strong woman, and all her vital signs are good. She should be able to talk tomorrow, but it will be a strain for her."

"Can you tell me anything about her injuries?"

"You'll have to ask her doctor," the nurse said.

"Dr. Sam Cohen is my cousin," he said lamely, thinking that this might penetrate her professional wall.

"Then you should ask him."

"Is he in the hospital?"

"Not now." She looked at a chart on the wall. "He's scheduled to operate at nine A.M."

He thanked her and returned to the room and told Mrs. Hope what he had learned. "It's important that all her vital signs are good and they haven't kept her in intensive care. That means they feel she's out of danger."

"Thank God," Mrs. Hope whispered.

"She's heavily sedated, and the nurse says she'll sleep through the night. I'll have a private nurse here in the morning, and there's nothing either of us can do now."

"I can pray for her," Mrs. Hope said in a gentle reprimand.

"And I will. Can I drive you home?"

"I thought I might stay here the night. Dr. Hope will be here at nine to pick me up, but I thought I would stay. There were a lot of people in the corridor about an hour ago, but the nurse would not let them into the room. There were some reporters and a man—I think his name was Frank Halter. He's a photographer, and he was very upset—" She paused to wipe away her tears.

"I don't think they'll let you stay all night. I'll stay until Dr. Hope comes, and I'll be here in the morning."

THINKING THAT AT LEAST Barbara and Philip could provide a clean shirt and a toothbrush, Freddie returned to Green Street that evening. He telephoned Sam from Barbara's study and asked whether Sam could arrange for a private nurse. When Sam agreed, Freddie said, "Now, please, Sam, tell me about her condition." Freddie sat at Barbara's desk, staring at a picture of a freighter that flew the leopard flag of the Levy–Lavette Line. The ship was called the *Clair,* named for old Jake's wife, Clair Harvey.

"Her condition is good," Sam said with a note of irritation that always entered his voice when he was asked a medical question by a relative.

"What does 'good' mean? For God's sake, be more specific."

"Just take it easy, Freddie," Sam said more gently. "I know you care for this woman. As I told you, there's a very faint hairline fracture of the skull."

"Well, that's serious, isn't it?"

"No, I don't think so. There's no sign of brain trauma, and it will heal quickly. It doesn't incapacitate her. There's a slight fracture of the cheekbone and some damage to her face. Her nose was broken and there are lacerations. There's no sign of damage to the spine and her limbs respond properly. I'm trying to put this simply. She had a team of the best surgeons we have working on her. We'll remove the bandages from her face in a week or so and begin taking out the stitches. We had to use more than thirty stitches."

"Oh, my God—"

"No. Don't go bonkers over that. At the worst, she'll be a candidate for plastic surgery."

Freddie's hand was shaking as he put down the phone. For a long moment he sat and stared at the picture of the freighter, the odd thought crossing his mind that a ship always merited the feminine pronoun—quite naturally, since it carried life in its hold. Judith was pregnant. Had she lost the child? Why hadn't he asked Sam that? He started to call him back, and then hesitated and put down the phone. That was between Judith and himself. Would the doctor know?

He joined Barbara and Philip in the living room. They were listening to music on the radio, and Philip switched it off as he entered.

"Did you reach Sam?" Barbara asked him.

"Yes. I hate to call doctors at home. They're touchy about it."

"Freddie, you're mumbling," Barbara said.

"Am I?" Then he raised his voice and said, "She is pregnant."

"Judith?"

"Yes, Judith. I forgot to ask Sam about that—and I'm afraid to call him back," he added hopelessly.

Tenderly Barbara said, "I think you should tell us what Sam said."

He told them, almost word for word, and added, "Do you know what it means? Her face is cut up and smashed. She had the most beautiful face in the world, and now it's gone. A broken nose. Thirty stitches. Barbara, she was so beautiful."

"She still is," Philip said.

Freddie appeared about to say something and then swallowed his words. For a few moments they sat in silence. Then Freddie asked, "What was on the radio when I came in?"

"Something by Mozart."

"Would you turn it on?"

Philip switched on the radio, modulating the sound. "Suppose," Barbara said, "your face had been smashed up like that, Freddie? Would she still love you? Accept you?"

"No, don't lay that on me," Freddie responded, almost angrily. "You know the answer."

Barbara shrugged. "Why don't you say that men and women are different?"

"That's not fair," Philip put in. "That's simply not fair, Barbara."

"I'll leave it to Freddie," Barbara said. "Tell me, Freddie, am I being unfair?"

Staring at the floor, Freddie did not answer. They waited, and finally Freddie said, "No, you're not being unfair. You're talking about love, which I suppose is the most overused word in this country. I think I love her—but—well, we'll see, won't we? I'm very tired. I think I'll go to bed."

ELOISE HAD NEVER SEEN ADAM QUITE SO ANGRY. "Doesn't he know that we're pressing the grapes! The Chardonnay was his own damn foolish notion! Doesn't he have any sense of responsibility? I sent a wire to him at the hospital, where he seems to have taken up residence!"

"Adam Levy," Eloise said coldly and firmly, "have you become so old and mean with that white beard of yours that you've forgotten what it means to be in love? Don't you dare talk to me about pressing grapes! You were pressing grapes before Freddie was born. He's at the hospital because the woman he loves needs him more than you do. The truth is that you don't need him at all.

You have Candido and you have me. He's with the woman he loves."

"That's another thing—"

"Don't you dare say it! One word about her being black, and I will never forgive you! Never!"

"I wasn't going to say anything about her being black," he pleaded. "We just received two truckloads of white grapes. I said I would think about it, and he went ahead and ordered them, and he isn't here. And he bought them from Delfuzio, who makes the lousiest wine in the Valley. I don't do business with Delfuzio. Freddie knows that, and the driver wouldn't budge until I paid him cash. You know how low we are on cash after the harvest. What is it with you—do you think I'm a racist?"

"I'm not sure. I'm learning a lot about racism."

"Have I ever said anything—one word?"

She softened and kissed him.

"And haven't I given him every Saturday off so he could go sailing in that damn boat of his?"

"You're Jewish. You give everyone Saturday off."

"Not in the harvest season."

"He'll be back the day after tomorrow."

"How do you know?"

"I spoke to him. They're taking the bandages off today," Eloise said gently. "So let's go out and look at those grapes, and we'll talk about Chardonnay. Everyone else drinks it, you know."

EACH DAY FOR A WEEK, Freddie had shown up at the hospital and had spent most of the day with Judith. She had closed herself off. She would have no visitors. After the third day, she whispered to Freddie to tell her mother and father not to come. She would see them at home. She accepted Barbara twice, but grudgingly. As the room filled up with flowers and plants, her annoyance increased and she told Freddie to get rid of them. He loaded his car with them and took them to Judith's home, where Simone, Judith's housekeeper, begged for a chance to visit her. He said that he would speak to Judith, but Judith refused. Photographers, advertising people, friends, and reporters lined up outside her door, and it was Freddie's job to refuse them entry—and no easy job it was.

She said once, speaking slowly and with difficulty, "Why don't you go away, Freddie, and leave me alone? It's over. I'm six feet of nigger woman without a face."

She was out of bed, as she had been after the second day, and staring at her bandaged face in a mirror. They had changed the bandages twice, but always when she was safely in bed, and now, as Freddie stared at her splendid figure, he said, "I've never been much of a face man. It's your gorgeous ass and tits that turn me on."

A vase of flowers had just arrived, and she picked it up and threw it at him. He dodged it, and after the crash a nurse came running into the room. Freddie explained that he had dropped the vase, and Judith was laughing, the first time he had seen her smile or laugh. "You're a nasty, unfeeling son of a bitch, and it hurts me to laugh."

"No pain, no gain."

"Get out of here. I never want to see you again."

But he stayed.

Each day Freddie appeared with an armful of newspapers and magazines, endured the barrage of her anger and annoyance, read to her, told her stories, and sat beside her while she slept. Barbara had persuaded him to remain at her Green Street house. One night he went to see a play with Barbara and Philip, and another night he went off to see a film by himself. When he spoke of switching to a hotel, reminding Barbara of Benjamin Franklin's statement that fish and guests begin to stink after three days, Barbara and Philip talked him out of it. "We want to know you, Freddie. Philip does, anyway."

But it was himself that Freddie wanted to know. Seven days after the accident he spoke to Sam and told him what he had in mind.

"I don't see why not," Sam said. "Only be careful."

He turned up at the hospital at eight o'clock in the morning, and Judith said to him, "Get out of here! I don't want you here! They're taking off my bandages today."

"I know."

"So get out of here. I told you I don't want you here."

"Yes. But I'm not going."

"I have rights here," she said. "I can tell them to throw you out."

"No, you can't. I fixed it with Sam. I have some rights, too. I've invested in you."

"What did you ever invest?"

"Love. Time. Dreams."

Judith stared at him and said nothing. A nurse's aide entered with Judith's breakfast, and she ate hungrily. Then Sam and another doctor came into the room, along with a nurse, who removed the tray stand.

"Lie back, Judith," Sam said.

"Get him out of here."

"I can't," Sam said. "Lie back and don't be difficult, and don't move. We'll take out most of the stitches."

"Damn you, Freddie," she said.

Freddie stood across the room, watching while the bandages were removed and the stitches were snipped out, to be replaced with strips of tape. Her nose received a new plastic bandage. Her face was marred, but still it was her face.

"The scars will fade," Sam said. "I'm going to discharge you today. You're healthy, and very lucky. Come back next week, and we'll see about your nose." Then he and the other doctor left the room, the nurse following them.

Judith climbed out of bed and stared at herself in the mirror. "Yich," she said.

"You're very beautiful," Freddie said, "and I like those strips of tape."

"Why don't you get out of here!"

"In due time." He opened his briefcase; took out a pair of blue jeans, a sweatshirt, and a pair of sneakers.

"They're yours," he told her. "I got them from Simone. Put them on."

"Why?"

"Because we're going sailing."

"You're crazy! You're absolutely crazy! I'm sick. I'm in a hospital."

"You're no sicker than I am."

"I can't go sailing," she whimpered. "I'm through with you. You're through with me."

"Like hell I am. And you *can* go sailing. I spoke to Sam about it. So get dressed and let's get out of here. I never want to see the inside of a hospital again."

THE SOFT WIND BLEW, and the tack took them across the Bay, past Alcatraz. Sitting with the tiller, she stretched her long length, with one arm reaching toward the cloud-flecked sky.

"Oh, Freddie!" she said.

"Stay on the course. We're close-hauled. When I tell you to come about, do it neatly. Both hands."

"Yes, sir. How long can we sail?"

"How's your head? No headache?"

"None."

"Forever."

"That's what I want, Freddie. Forever."

The Holy Land

BARBARA FOUND IT DIFFICULT to believe that in his seventy-three years, Philip had never been out of the country, except for an excursion trip to Mexico and a drive with his wife Agatha to Vancouver. During the war he had been a chaplain, assigned to a camp near Augusta, Georgia, and then to Fort Totten on Long Island. As he explained, he and Agatha had never had much money, and they were saving for a long trip. His wife died, and after that, he had no desire to travel. But over five years had passed, and he was as delighted as a small boy to go to Europe with Barbara. His family had originated in the English Midlands, a farm family, and had emigrated during one of the anti-Catholic fervors that shook England in the seventeenth century. He knew the name of the town, and he had always planned to go there one day.

Barbara, who had lived and worked in France and spoke French like a native, had been to England several times. She had no desire to go to France; there were too many heartbreaking memories that she would not awaken. She and Philip pored over a map of England and found Thornby in the county of Northamptonshire.

Her mother's family, the Seldons, had originated in England, but she had no idea of where and when, and she agreed with Philip that it might be fun to try to track down the name.... Her father's family came from a small town in the north of Italy, a few miles from Milan.

She loved Italy, although she had been there only once, during the honeymoon after her marriage to Carson Devron. Pompeii and the Bay of Naples had cast a spell on her, and she wanted to return and spend a few days on the Isle of Ischia and to visit Pompeii once again. She thought it would be pleasant to fly from England to Switzerland, where she had never been, and to take a train from Switzerland through Italy, stopping at Rome and going on to Naples and Ischia. Then on to Israel, either from Greece or from Italy. She assured Philip that if they flew with El Al, the Israeli airline, there would be no worry about terrorists.

She had no great desire to go to Israel, where she had been before—and where her son, Sam, had taken his medical training and her first husband, Bernie Cohen, was buried—but Israel was a lifelong dream of Philip's. He wanted to see Jerusalem and walk in the steps of Jesus and feel for something that had always been deep in him. He wanted to see with his own eyes the Mount of Olives, the location of the Holy Sepulcher, and Calvary. Barbara was still unable to untangle Philip's beliefs and disbeliefs, but with each day that they were married and lived together, she had come to love and respect him increasingly. If his desire to go to Israel was this deep—well, she would go along with him. The church had given him a bundle of vacation time that he had never used, and Ms. Guthri would take over his pulpit for six weeks. The congregation's delight in the fact that he had finally found someone was such that they were ready to agree to anything he asked for.

The disagreement between Philip and Barbara concerning their trip was, strangely enough, about the cost of the excursion.

"Let us be practical," Barbara said. "This is 1984. Women are beginning to be looked upon as human beings, and there are even voices that say we are the equal of the male sex."

"Superior, if you ask me."

"That's a fine statement, true or not. But the plain fact of the matter is, my darling Philip, that you are very poor and I am reasonably wealthy. If we are joined together in the holy bonds of matrimony, then we are joined together in everything else. I have a huge inheritance from my grandfather—"

"You put that in a foundation. I know all about that."

"I kept some. I've earned money. My brother Tom left me two million in federal bonds, which I have never touched, and I've earned more than enough money to keep this house, in spite of your insistence that you pay your share. I'm not a fool about money. It means little to me—the fortune or misfortune of having rich parents—but I acknowledge it."

"Barbara, I'm well paid—"

"Oh yes. I know how well paid you are."

"Barbara, I'm not poor," Philip argued. "All the years Agatha and I were married, we saved money for a trip we never took. Since her death I've lived like a monk, and I've squirreled away over twenty-five thousand dollars."

Barbara refrained from commenting on that.

"Well, how much will this trip cost?"

"I'm afraid to tell you. I've been laying it out with a travel agent. I'm an old woman, Philip; I can't be satisfied with youth hostels and cheap hotels, and good hotels are expensive. I love you, and I have the right to give you gifts. You drive a car that's twelve years old and has a hundred and thirty thousand miles on the odometer."

He sighed and admitted that he'd never won an argument with her. "Suppose we compromise. I'll pay for the airline tickets, and you can pay for everything else."

"Do you mean that? You won't be reaching into your pocket every time we want a cup of coffee?"

"I can afford a cup of coffee," Philip said.

"Will you stick to that?" Barbara asked. "If you do, I can live with it. But everything else goes on my American Express card. And the travel tickets won't be cheap. We fly over the pole, nonstop, to Heathrow."

"The North Pole?"

"Oh, I love you, Philip. Yes, the North Pole. But we'll be warm and comfortable, and you won't see a thing. We'll be in Israel for my birthday in November, and I don't want any silly jewelry. I want you."

THERE WAS ONE MORE DINNER at Highgate before Barbara and Philip left. The harvest had been good and the winemaking had begun. Adam predicted a superb Cabernet that would make 1984 a year to be coveted and remembered, and the white grapes were even putting forth Chardonnay that satisfied him.

The whole family was there, including Harry and May Ling, who had just returned from France. Sam, Barbara's son, and Sally's son, young Dan, himself a resident at Mercy Hospital, were seated next to Joe Lavette at the far end of the big table, so that they might confine their talk about illness and intrusive surgery to each other; while Mary Lou, Sam's wife, sat with May Ling and chattered away about Paris. Soon enough the national election would take place, and Barbara and Philip had already filled out their absentee ballots. Adam was intent on explaining to Harry why each harvest was different, and why the wine of one year tasted a bit different from the wine of another year, even though they came from the same vines. Harry and May Ling had spent a weekend at the château-winery of a client of his Paris office, and he used his newly acquired knowledge of French winemaking to sustain the conversation with Adam, whose first appraisal of anyone was at least partly based on their knowledge of wine. May Ling, with Freddie on one side of her and Mary Lou on the other, appeared to be a changed woman. She had kissed Freddie and embraced him tenderly. With Mary Lou she talked about the shops in Paris and how she had argued to stop Harry from buying her things.

As for Freddie and Judith, they had eyes only for each other. Judith's nose, after a second operation, was still taped, but except for the thin lines of the scars, her face was much the same. She wore no makeup tonight, but she had experimented privately with a concealing foundation, and she already had four photography dates for the time when the bandages would come off her nose. After two dinners with her family, Freddie felt at ease and at home with the Hopes, and the date for the wedding had been set.

Here, at Highgate, Adam had gone out of his way to initiate Judith into the secrets of winemaking, and for this dinner, he had opened six bottles of the prized Rothschild Mouton Cadet, from a case presented to Clair Harvey, Jake's wife, years ago in Paris.

"This toast and this wine is in honor of the new member of the family," he announced. "May she know the joy of the grape and the love of our hearts."

Eloise was overwhelmed. Adam was not given to sentimentality, and the toast was so unexpected that she began to weep, recalling her harsh characterization of him as a racist. As for Judith, her eyes filled with tears. But later that evening Adam spoke privately with Freddie, asking him what his opinion was of the Mouton Cadet.

"Good."

"Not great?"

"Good. Not great. How great can a wine be when you get past the bullshit?"

"Do you think we could do it?"

"Maybe."

"Let's work on it."

"Nothing I'd like better," Freddie said.

AFTER THE DINNER Sally took Barbara aside and said to her, using the term she used to address Barbara, "Bobby, dear, we must talk. Let's walk outside, just the two of us."

Barbara told Philip, deep in conversation with Freddie and Judith, that she was going to take a walk with Sally and would join him later. It was a chilly night, and both women wore sweaters; they wandered along the curving paths among the stone buildings. After a few minutes of silence, Barbara asked Sally what was bothering her.

"The part was nothing. It was nothing, four words. I'm too old even for the character parts."

"You're only fifty-eight, Sally, and you're lovely."

"They want forty-year-olds for grandma parts, or old women with white hair. I don't mean you, Bobby. You know what I mean. Oh, it isn't that. Why am I always so discontent? I've been going to church in Napa, but it does nothing for me. Joe hired a nurse. At least when I was his nurse, I would talk to him occasionally. Now I hardly see him. I sit and contemplate my navel. I wish I could find someone to have an affair with. At least it would break up the day."

"You're kidding?"

"No, I'm not kidding. I thought of divorcing Joe, but I could never explain to him why I was doing it, and I do love him—sort of—and he loves me."

"You really want my advice?" Barbara asked her.

"Certainly I do. Why do you think I dragged you away?"

"OK," Barbara said. "Get a job."

"Doing what?"

"You're a superb actress. Start a playhouse. God knows, we need one here in the Valley; culturally, this place is barren. We all use Highgate and the family as a refuge, but Sam and his wife are in San Francisco, and so is your son, and May Ling and Harry will be living there. Get the local church behind you. They're always looking for ways to get people inside the not-so-pearly gates. Pull in some of your Hollywood friends, and you can sell tickets up and down the Valley and over in Sonoma, too."

"Bobby, do you think I could do it?"

"You can do anything you want to, Sally, and don't tell me you haven't dreamed of directing a play."

"Do you know any actor who doesn't go to bed with that dream every night? Bobby, will you help me?"

"When I come back—yes, surely. But it's a long drive from the City...You start it tomorrow. Don't put it off, and when I come back, I'll write you a play. I've always wanted to try it."

Sally threw her arms around Barbara. "What a neat idea. I will, I will, if it kills me."

"It certainly won't kill you," Barbara said.

RAPTUROUS WAS THE ONLY WORD Barbara could think of to describe Philip's arrival in London and his first stroll through the city. On the plane she had said to him, "It's odd to think of a man your age who has never been to Europe," to which he replied, "Most of the people in this country have never been to London or anyplace in Europe, and here I am, Philip Carter, floating over the North Pole in a 747 the size of a cruise ship."

"Not really the size of a cruise ship. We haven't come to that yet. But, Philip," she teased him, "don't you think that if God wanted us to fly, he never would have given us the railroads?"

"Absolutely," he agreed, and she admitted that this was a new Philip. "When Agatha and I left the Church, I felt that I had escaped, that we had been in a prison and somehow we had broken out. You see, I loved her madly for two years before we dared to admit it to ourselves and to each other; and after that for quite a while we looked over our shoulders, so to speak, like criminals always in danger of being caught by the cops. When she passed away, I had the same feeling, that they had captured one of us and taken their revenge on me."

"And who were 'they'?" Barbara could not help asking.

"Ah. That's the question, isn't it?"

But after customs at Heathrow and the cab ride to Brown's Hotel, Barbara had the feeling that he would never look over his shoulder again. His face lit up as they rolled into Albemarle Street, and he smiled with pleasure as they walked into the old hotel. She had explained to him that the reason she chose Brown's was because it was, in her opinion and in Freddie's—an inveterate traveler— not only the best hotel in London, but also the most English. His eyes rolled over the entryway, delighting in everything. At the desk, for the first time in many years, he signed, "Mr. and Mrs. Philip Carter." The room was large and comfortable, with an alcove as a tiny sitting room and a huge king-sized bed. It was eleven o'clock, London time, but they were not sleepy. Barbara asked Philip whether he wanted dinner. He shook his head. They had both eaten well on the plane.

"Then as a final step in the process of liberation, I would suggest that we go down to the bar and have a small nightcap."

He was enchanted with everything. "They likely won't have your Highgate Cabernet," he said.

"I am not wedded to Highgate, I am wedded to you, and when Adam is not watching, I prefer a Chardonnay. Anyway, I was thinking of a brandy."

"Do you mind if I have a glass of their ale?"

"Mind? Why should I mind?" she wondered.

"I'm a neophyte. My England has existed only in the books I have read, but it's very real. Though not as real as it appears to be. I never read that they shine every bit of brass and that the floor squeaks. How old is this place?"

"I don't really know—perhaps a hundred and fifty years."

"And they don't tear it down and build a high-rise in its place?"

"Heaven forbid!"

They went down to the bar. They made a handsome couple, Philip tall and slender, and Barbara with her shock of white hair, still in sweater and skirt. People smiled and said good evening as they walked to the bar. The handful of people in the bar were at tables. Barbara and Philip sat at the bar and ordered their drinks. Soon it was a half hour to midnight.

Back in their room again, they found that the maid had turned back their bed.

"Take out what you need," Barbara said. "We'll unpack tomorrow." She found a robe and went into the bathroom to change. When she came out, Philip was sitting on the bed in his underwear.

"I couldn't find my pajamas," he said.

"Since when do we sleep in pajamas, Philip?"

"Well, we're in a strange place. Suppose the maid walks in?"

"Philip, darling, we are not in a strange place. We are in London, which is the most civilized city in the world, and maids do not just walk in, and I'm not going to bed with a man in pajamas. I never knew a lack of pajamas to inhibit you in San Francisco or at Highgate."

"It's different here."

"It is no different here, and I suggest we go to bed. And in the morning, we'll find your pajamas, wrinkle them, and lay them out on the bed, so that the maid is impressed with the fact that you're a proper clergyman."

"You're laughing at me."

"Yes, I am. Now take off your damn underwear and let's get to bed."

BARBARA FELT LIKE A TOUR GUIDE, alternately delighted and provoked. She recalled taking her son, Sam, to the Cemetery of Heavenly Rest in Los Angeles when he was twelve or so. It was a place she had never been to before and would never have visited, dead or alive; but she went because Sam demanded it, having read about it; and in the end she was pleased that she had seen the weird, incredible place. Philip also had prepared a list of places he wanted to see. The list was long and would have required a month's stay in England, yet she decided that she would do her best. The flight from Los Angeles had befuddled their time sense: nine hours' difference—or was it eight? Neither of them could get it quite right.

Awake at six, they unpacked their luggage. Barbara wore a pleated skirt, a blouse, and a sweater, and convinced Philip that a pair of comfortable old trousers would not offend Londoners. "A good sweater," she said. "You don't know what the weather will be in October, and we're lucky to have a sunny day to begin."

In the dining room for breakfast, Philip looked at the menu and blanched. "Do you see what they charge for breakfast in this place? At home—"

"Philip, we are not at home," she said sternly. "The prices are in your menu, not on mine. That's an English custom. They relish odd forms of courtesy here. Do you remember our agreement?"

"Agreement? But these prices, when you translate them into dollars—"

"We made an agreement. You pay for the plane tickets. I pay for everything else. We sealed it with a handshake and a kiss. Several kisses, if I recall correctly. I took you for my husband as a man of honor, and you've always told me that honor rates very high with the Unitarians. For better or worse, you were foolish enough to marry a wealthy old woman, and I should be very upset at you if you keep raising this issue."

"I'll have coffee, that's all."

"You will not. You'll eat a very hearty breakfast—you always lecture me on it being the most important meal of the day."

"You're not angry. You're teasing me again, aren't you?"

"Yes, my dear, serious Philip. I am teasing you."

He sighed and nodded.

"And if ever there was a man who should shun macho, it is you, Philip."

They ate a hearty breakfast and then left the hotel. Feeling that they were proper tourists, they wandered down Old Bond Street, peering in the shop windows, and then down Piccadilly and through Green Park to Buckingham Palace, where they arrived in time for the changing of the guard. Philip admired Green Park, chortled over the clean beauty of the place. They found the Queen's Guard among a small group of tourists gazing with admiration, and Barbara felt compelled to say that they did not guard the queen at all, leaving that to the police. Then she felt quite wretched and made a promise to herself that she would tease Philip no more, for all that he took it so good-humoredly and hung upon every word she said with utter devotion. No man had ever loved her in so total and uncriticizing a manner, and it was strange that this should have come to her so late in life; yet she could not help recalling a time some years ago, on a previous trip to London, when she sat on the balcony of the House of Commons, surrounded by a group of Labor members who deplored the whole spectacle of the changing of the guard as worthless and costly, a show for tourists and nothing else. But standing here with Philip, she thought of how much less the guard cost than one of Broadway's bad musicals, and what a delight it was for those who watched. Time, she realized, had tempered her judgments.

They then walked north through Hyde Park, where the magnificent old oaks were turning color, and paused to admire the swan boats on the Serpentine and revel in their memories of Barrie's *Peter Pan*. They put off the multiplicity of museums; Philip was not a museum person, and he was delighted with the faces they saw, black men, women in colorful saris, men in turbans—all the modes and colors of the crumbling empire upon which, once, the sun never used to set. Tired, their legs reminding them of their age, they lunched on fried chunks of fish and chips in a small pub. It was delicious, and Barbara had to know what kind of fish it was. The waiter informed her that it was rock salmon, which the Yankees called catfish. Then they returned to the hotel for, as Barbara explained, a lie-down. She dozed off in Philip's arms, thinking of how ridiculous was all she had ever read and heard about love and sex among the old.

That evening they went to the theater and saw one of those improbable British farces in which there are at least four doors on stage and an actor is exiting one door as another enters by a different door, just missing the first, and the confusion mounts until there is apparently no way of untangling it. They enjoyed it hugely, and Barbara told Philip that she had never been in London without an almost identical play running somewhere. He replied that he wanted to see *The Mouse Trap*, Agatha Christie's play that had been running almost forever. Barbara agreed for the following night, though she had seen it before.

The next day they went to Westminster Abbey. Philip went from stone to stone, commenting that everyone in British history was buried here. A priest in vestments paused beside them and informed them that the service would start in a few minutes, and if they wished to, they could come and receive communion. Barbara whispered to Philip, "I haven't received communion in half a century."

"Why not?" Philip asked.

" 'Whatever Gods may be'?"

"That's a proper Unitarian attitude."

"It's the wine-and-wafer thing that gets to me. I can't drink from a cup that forty people I don't know have already put to their lips."

"You don't have to," Philip assured her. "Just dip the wafer into the wine. It's quite satisfactory and reasonably sterile."

"A fine Episcopalian you are."

"You're the Episcopalian. I'm a Unitarian minister trying to convert you."

"Fat chance," Barbara said.

But the service was pleasant and simple, and Barbara found herself enjoying it, in spite of her disdain. She dipped the wafer in the great silver cup of wine, and the priest smiled at her, which acknowledged her sanitary doubts. Philip did the same as Barbara. The service lasted only twenty minutes or so, and once outside, Philip told her a story that his Zen Buddhist teacher had related to him.

"He happened to be Jewish," Philip said. "You know, you can be Jewish Zen or Catholic Zen. It's less a religion than a belief that every human being has the Buddhist nature within him and that God is ineffable. Well, my teacher—Bill was his name—was in New York at the time, and he was caught in a cloudburst, and there was a small old church and he popped in to get out of the rain—just as you did, which accounts for our being here. Except that it was a Catholic Church and they were just giving the Eucharist, and being a Zen Buddhist, to whom all religions are the same, he received communion, drinking the wine. I suppose he was indifferent to sanitation. And then Bill walked out, the rain having stopped, and he told me that every person he saw upon leaving the church had a sort of halo around his or her head."

"That's a nice story," Barbara said. "Do you believe it?"

"I've told you, my dear, that I never know what I believe or what I disbelieve."

"Do I have a halo about my head?"

"You always have a halo around your head."

"That's a crock," Barbara said. "But thank you."

They spent four days in London, and then Barbara decided that they had walked at least fifty miles and that it was time to seek out Philip's ancestors. She decided to keep the room at Brown's until they returned to London. It was a hundred and sixty dollars a day, off-season. Philip weighed the thought of a protest, remembered the agreement, and remained silent. Barbara congratulated him. They took the smallest piece of their luggage, and since they had yet to ride on the Underground, they took it to King's Cross Station, which the concierge at the hotel informed them was the proper place from which to depart for Northampton. Philip, who recalled stories of the Underground used as a bomb shelter in the firebombing of London during World War II, was thrilled to take even so short a journey in that manner. He was easily thrilled, easily pleased, and Barbara had begun to cherish the very fact that he had survived to the age of seventy-three.

At King's Cross Station, Philip asked the ticket seller whether one could buy a ticket to Thornby.

"Thornby? Well, sir, you're Americans, aren't you. Maybe you got the wrong line. I never heard of a Thornby on this line."

"It's near Northampton."

"Ah, well, that's something else, isn't it? I can sell you tickets to Northampton for you and the lady, and when you arrive, there's sure to be a cab. The driver will know every town in the neighborhood. A good many towns in the neighborhood of Northampton."

It was off the rush hour, and the train car was half-empty. "Anyway," Barbara consoled him, "it's a nice clean car, and I've never been to the Midlands, and if we can't find Thornby, we'll simply consider this a side trip. I never understood why you were so interested in your ancestors. On my part, I couldn't care less. I had always hoped that I would dig up a pirate or something romantic, but I think the Seldons were all bank clerks, or maybe people like Bob Cratchit. My grandfather Lavette, who died before I was born, was a fisherman—I guess from a long line of fishermen."

"Oh, I don't know. I never thought about it until we decided to go to England. I suppose there are thousands of Carters in America. When Jimmy Carter was elected president, I thought he might be a relative. Foolish of me."

"Not so foolish. You have the name Thornby, and there was probably only one family of Carters in a small town."

The cabdriver at Northampton knew where Thornby was, a good twenty minutes' drive over narrow country roads. "Not much of a place. You got kin there?"

"No, we just want to see the place."

"Nothing much to see, an old church and a few houses. You do better at Brickworth. Old Saxon church there with real Roman tiles in the floor. Most American tourists who come here, they want to see Brickworth." He pronounced it *Brikwo*, and Thornby as *Thirnee*. Barbara asked him for the spelling of Brickworth before they took off. Then she whispered to Philip that the price was outrageous but that she wanted the cab to wait, after the driver had informed Philip that the trip would be twenty pounds and waiting time fifteen pounds.

"Absolutely not," Philip whispered back.

"We made an agreement"—and said to the driver, "We want you to wait for us—unless you think we can find a cab in Thornby."

"Cab in Thornby? Hardly."

"Then you'll wait."

Thornby was as small as the driver had indicated. He tried to be helpful by pointing out what had once been the manor house, and then appeared to be at a loss as to what else to tell them. Barbara suggested the church.

The cab waited at the gate to the churchyard while Barbara and Philip wandered through the old cemetery. The names on the stones were difficult to decipher, and those that went back more than a hundred years were the most difficult. An old bearded man, shears in hand, came around the church and asked whether he might help them.

"I'm the gardener," he explained. "I do the church every other week, cut back the shrubs and vines. They tend to eat up the old place."

"Where could we find the minister?" Philip asked after explaining about why they were there.

"Ain't no vicar no more. There's a rector, lives in Brickworth. Serves four churches. Not here today."

"Ever hear of a family named Carter?" Philip asked.

"Can't say I have."

"Or have you seen the name on any of these stones?"

"Don't know. My eyes are bad. I don't try to read the stones. Some names inside where they buried people under the floor. These graves—they've been used for three, four, maybe five bodies, on top of one another."

It appeared to Barbara that Philip had a sudden sense of revulsion. He thanked the old man, took Barbara's arm, and led her back to the cab, and she didn't question his decision. The countryside was lovely, gently rolling hills, farms, grazing sheep. Philip was silent, lost in his own thoughts. When Barbara asked whether he wanted to stay at some local inn, he shook his head, said that he preferred to return to the hotel. He spoke little on the trip back to London.

They had a late dinner that night in the hotel dining room. Philip was still listless and only nibbled at his food.

"Do you want to talk about it?" Barbara asked him.

"About what?"

"Your depression."

"I'm not depressed, Barbara. I've been thinking."

"I've noticed."

"What do you believe, Barbara?"

"We've been through that before. I believe in many things."

"We're not young. Do you ever think about dying?"

"Not very much. It's just something that happens. You close your eyes and you sleep."

" 'Only the sleep eternal in the eternal night.' "

"I detest Swinburne. What a ghoul he must have been! I like Stevenson better. Do you remember? 'Under the wide and starry sky,/Dig the grave and let me lie./Glad did I live and gladly die,/And I laid me down with a will.' He had consumption. He faced death every day. As all of us do," she added after a pause. "And it doesn't matter."

"Do you really believe that?"

"Sort of. Years ago I was really depressed, so I went to a psychiatrist. It helped somewhat, but I crawled out of the depression myself. Here I am. I'm Barbara Lavette, for better or worse. That's all I am. In the enormous scheme of things, I'm of no great importance." She thought about it for a long moment. "Don't misunderstand me, Philip. I'm a total pacifist. I believe that the taking of a human life, under any circumstances, is unforgivable. I believe that the dance of death that the human race performs with their demented wars is obscene."

"Then you do have faith."

"Philip, darling, I don't know what faith is. If it's religion, I have no religion. My first husband, Bernie Cohen, Sam's father, was not the way one thinks of Jews. He was six feet tall with blue eyes, and an ardent Zionist. He joined the Abraham Lincoln Brigade and fought in Spain against Franco—as he put it, to learn to be a soldier—so you see, I have changed. He carried my lover, Marcel, off the field, badly wounded, during the awful Battle of the Ebro. Marcel died when his leg was amputated at the thigh. Gangrene. I was living in Paris then, and Bernie came to see me and tell me of Marcel's courage. I fell in love with Bernie. He enlisted and fought through the North African campaign, and after the war, we were married. Not the best marriage, believe me. In 1948 he directed the ferrying of six old Constellations from California to New Jersey, where he picked up two suitcases packed with two million dollars in cash, flew them to Czechoslovakia, bought guns, and flew those to Tel Aviv. He died in Israel, killed by the Arabs. What should I have faith in, Philip—all the ghosts that mark my life?" She reached over and took his hand. "Perhaps I have faith in love. I love you very much, Philip, and we are the only two people left in the dining room, and the head waiter is watching us, and he's pleading with his eyes for us to leave, and I've talked enough."

"At the price we're paying, let him plead. A little humility will do him good."

Later, in bed, Barbara put her arms around Philip, and said to him, "The last thing I want to do to you, dear Philip, is to shatter your faith. I don't know what came over you in that old graveyard, and perhaps someday you will be able to explain it to me. I know I say things that hurt you, and you have no way of fighting back."

"No, no, you've never said anything that hurt me."

"We won't argue. Here is my thought: I know that deep down you agreed to this trip because of your feeling about what must be to you the Holy Land. Believe me, I can imagine the struggle inside of you that brought you from the Catholic Church to a Unitarian pulpit—and the struggle that let you marry me. I didn't know, when we married, whether I actually loved you. Part of my uncertainty was the misery of those two years alone. I cannot live alone, Philip. I've come to love you a great deal. We'll go abroad many times in the years that are left to us, but right now, I want to go to Israel. We can shuffle our tickets and reservations tomorrow, and leave tomorrow or the following day."

"You would? And give up Switzerland and Italy?"

"They'll be there. We can go on from Israel if we decide to. We can do anything we want to. But right now, something pains you."

"It's not pain—it's bewilderment. I had thought of not going on to Jerusalem at all."

"All the more reason to go there now."

"You're a very wise woman," he whispered.

ELOISE REMARKED TO ADAM that Freddie had changed a great deal since Judith's accident. "I've noticed," Adam agreed.

"He works too hard."

"He has to work," Adam said. "It's his way of coping."

"He's only forty-three, and his hair is turning white."

"It happens. He's been through a hard time."

"I want grandchildren desperately, Adam. I think Judith's pregnant. If she is, I'm happy for her."

"Give him time," Adam assured her. "It's not just having kids. He still has some mountains to climb."

Harry Lefkowitz had also noticed the change from the man he had known in Freddie before Judith's injury. Harry had driven out to Highgate with an interesting proposition, which derived from his utter fascination with the wine business. He and May Ling had taken a large apartment in San Francisco, and apparently their relationship had some hurdles to overcome.

"Freddie," he said, after a few formalities, "the Hawthorn Winery, about a mile down the road—do you know the place?"

Freddie nodded. "Yes, I know the place very well. They put out a good Chardonnay. It's all right, but it should be better—it's not their grapes but the way they use them. Old Greenberg isn't really interested in winemaking. I think he bought the place because he wanted a winter home for him and his wife, and the wine keeps him occupied. His wife passed away a year ago, and he just put the winery up for sale. The price is too high."

"I've been looking into it, Freddie. May Ling is less than happy in the City. She grew up in a small town, and I think San Francisco frightens her a bit. I decided that I can buy the winery—it has a good house and we can improve it—well, if I buy the winery, I'm jumping into the water without knowing how to swim. I love my business; I'm not going to retire from law. My partners will keep the office, and I'll have the office there and do a very occasional case; but more or less, I want to retire, be with May Ling—I might as well tell you, she's pregnant again—and make wine. And your son will be much happier back in the Valley."

"Wonderful about her being pregnant, but before I break out the brandy and cigars, let's talk about it. Greenberg has about a hundred acres, half of it in vines. The land needs taking care of, work and fertilizer. The untilled acreage is a problem—woodsy. The aging plant needs a good many new casks, and the bottling plant is in fair shape, but not great. He has no sales team to speak of, and with this harvest, I hear he's selling half of his grapes. I would have bought some myself if Adam wasn't so set against Chardonnay. Greenberg also has a lot of unsold bottled stock. And, as I said, his price is too high."

"I know that. He wants five million."

"And you'd have to put three hundred thousand more into it to get it into proper shape. And, Harry, I know you and love you, but making good wine is a fine art. You can't just plunge in."

"I'm not plunging in. I think I know exactly what I'm doing. I want to be with May Ling, and if I remain as I am, it's twelve hours of work a day. Now, here's my plan, and please listen. I know Greenberg's lawyer, and no one's made an offer on the place. The lawyer knows it's overpriced, and I think I can get it for four million. We'll get a mortgage for two million. You put in a million and I'll put in a million, and the ownership will be either Highgate and myself or you and me, whatever you wish. You buy everything we need to make it a first-rate modern winery, and I'll pay for it. That will be my share. Your share will be teaching me, and if you want me to, I'll take a course in vintnership at U.C. I'm a damn good businessman and a good manager, and I have enough money to sit out a few bad seasons."

"You'll have them. It's no way to get rich."

"Does that mean you're with me?"

"Suppose I really go through the place with Adam, and he decides it will take four hundred thousand of new equipment?"

"Whatever it takes."

"Good. It certainly sounds promising. We need more white wine, and we have the sales force and the distribution and the name. You would call it Highgate?"

"Absolutely. I'd be honored."

"You'll be putting in more than we will."

"Not really. You've got the know-how and the distribution. It would take me years to match that. The only question is, Freddie, can we make a good vintage with their grapes?"

"I can almost guarantee that, but I can't guarantee anything else. It'll be a tough argument with Adam, but I think I can convince him. He hasn't any money to speak of. I'd put up the money, and we'd have to work out some stock-sharing plan, and maybe I'd finally have the right to drink a glass of white wine at his table. Are you sure you can get it for four million?"

"Pretty sure."

"Let's take a run down there this afternoon. I'll talk to Adam tonight. Will May Ling agree? Are you sure?"

"She'll be the happiest woman in San Francisco. So get out the cigars and the brandy. We'll drink to a beautiful little baby."

IT WAS FIVE DAYS BEFORE the tickets could be manipulated and they could book passage to Tel Aviv on El Al. Barbara suggested a trip to Cornwall or to the Lake Country, but Philip wanted only to stay in London. "We've barely seen it," he argued. "I'm not a scenery man," he explained. "I get more simple pleasure out of walking along one of the avenues here and watching the faces than I would out of seeing the Alps. A mountain's a mountain and we're ridden with them in California. But this city is a history of civilization."

Basically they were two very different people. Yet they were good companions, and hand in hand, they explored all of London within walking distance of Brown's Hotel, and returned to the hotel in time for tea—reputed to be the very best tea in London—and then dinner and bed, where he was as loving and kind as any man she had ever known.

It was a new experience for her. Her first two marriages had been far from ideal; she had never been with a man as quietly solid as Philip, a man who could cling to what he believed and accept what she believed, a man who had no other desire in life than to be with her. They were both strong and healthy and wore their age easily and casually. Barbara would remember those days in London with great joy. They explored Harrods, which was the only one of the many great department stores Philip was interested in, recalling for her the old saw about the man who went into Harrods and asked whether they had elephants in stock. And the clerk, not batting an eyelash, asked calmly, "Which kind, sir, African or Indian?" But when Barbara whispered to Philip to ask the same question of the clerk he flatly refused; and she said, with mock bitterness, "We'll never know, will we? That's the trouble with apocrypha— no one puts them to the test."

On Charing Cross Road they found an old and remarkable bookshop where they spent a pleasant hour. Barbara bought a book of Elizabeth Barrett Browning's poems and Philip a selection of Charles Lamb's letters. That night, in bed, Philip said to her, "I must read something to you. This is from a letter that Lamb wrote to William Wordsworth in 1801, when San Francisco was not yet in existence. Wordsworth had invited Lamb to spend a week or so in the country with him. Lamb wrote back:

> Separate from the pleasure of your company, I don't much care if I never see a mountain in my life. I have passed all my days in London, until I have formed as many and intense

local attachments as any of you mountaineers can have done with dead Nature. The lighted shops of the Strand and Fleet Street; the innumerable trades, tradesmen, and customers, coaches, waggons, playhouses; all the bustle and wickedness round about Covent Garden; the very women of the Town; the watchmen, drunken scenes, rattles; life awake, if you awake, at all hours of the night; the impossibility of being dull in Fleet Street; the crowds, the very dirt and mud, the sun shining upon houses and pavements, the print shops, the old bookstalls, parsons cheapening books, coffee-houses, steams of soups from kitchens, the pantomimes—London itself a pantomime and a masquerade—all these things work themselves into my mind, and feed me, without a power of satiating me.

"Well, my dear—there's a soul who felt about London much as I do, and that was almost two hundred years ago."

Feeling not sixty-nine but enchanted with something all her youth had never quite given her, Barbara read from Elizabeth Barrett Browning in response:

In my old griefs, and with my childhood's faith,
I love thee with a love I seemed to lose
With my lost saints—I love thee with the breath,
Smiles, tears, of all my life—and if God choose,
I shall but love thee better after death.

AT HEATHROW AIRPORT two days later, an Israeli security man studied them carefully and then examined their passports.

"Americans?"

"Yes," Philip replied, "of course."

"Nothing is of course," the security man said. "Why are you going to Israel? Business?"

"No, we're tourists."

"About your luggage, did you pack it?"

"Oh yes," Barbara said. "We packed it this morning."

"Was it ever out of your sight? Did you leave it in your room when you had breakfast?"

"I'm afraid we did," Philip admitted.

"I'm very sorry," the security man said, "but I shall have to go through all your luggage."

Barbara sighed and said, "Yes, I can understand."

Up and down the long counter, other travelers were enduring the same thing.

"Only a few minutes," the security man said.

They had three suitcases, two large ones and one small piece. He went through them expertly without removing the contents. Other security men were emptying luggage, taking apart every piece. Following their glance, the security man said, "We have a profile. You can go through now. We'll be boarding in about thirty minutes."

As they moved away, Barbara remarked that the security men spoke English with a British accent.

"Because they're Brits," Philip said.

"But they're Jewish, aren't they?"

"There must be three, four hundred thousand Jews in England. Does that surprise you?"

"I never thought about it," Barbara said. "Philip, I never asked you. Do you speak Hebrew?"

"Of course I do. I was a Jesuit priest. Altogether, I had seven years of Hebrew—which simply means I can talk to God, via the Old Testament, but whether I can talk to Israelis or understand what they say remains to be seen. For example, I don't know how to say 'airplane' or 'auto' or 'radio' or a hundred other things in Hebrew, but I should be able to pick it up. We'll see."

"I should think 'airplane' would be 'airplane.'"

When they finally boarded the big 747, Philip screwed up his courage and said to the attendant, "We have seats forty-one and forty-two" in what he felt was passable Hebrew.

The flight attendant looked at him strangely, glanced at the boarding passes, and then nodded and said in English, "Yes, sir. This way." Seated, Philip mumbled to Barbara, "I don't think that the seats of the mighty are quite the same thing."

"You'll get the hang of it," she said consolingly.

The last one to board, as the plane prepared for takeoff, was a tall man who walked down the aisle, scrutinizing each passenger carefully and coldly. Philip whispered to Barbara, "Notice the way his jacket bulges. I think he has a gun there."

"I have heard that one of the reasons El Al planes are never hijacked is that they have a guard on board, with orders to kill any hijacker instantly," Barbara whispered back.

"Oh no."

"I think oh yes, Philip—but I wouldn't worry, not after the way they went through the luggage." After the plane took off, Barbara dozed and then awakened rather abruptly. "Philip," she whispered, leaning close to him, "there's nothing I love better than to have you caress my thighs, but not here and not with two people who look as Waspish as you and me. We don't want to give the wrong impression."

"I hardly knew I was doing it," he whispered back.

"Naturally. There's nothing as wild as a fallen clergyman."

"Barbara!"

"Darling Philip, I'm teasing. It's the worst part of my nature, and it's so tempting. Will you ever forgive me?"

He kissed her.

"That's better. Kisses are like wine—and that reminds me. Freddie wants us to taste every kind of Israeli wine. It's become a large export business, I hear."

"And we'll roll through the land drunk."

"Why not?" And then she added, "No—as a matter of fact,

Philip, there is little drinking here—some wine, coffee, and tea. Mostly the tourists drink. There is good food and plenty of it, but the Jews here are as different from those we know at home as night is from day. I know that at least twenty percent of your congregation are people who were once Jewish, but they are not enough different from us to be recognized as Jewish. I certainly can't tell the difference."

"What is the difference?"

"Well, for one thing, almost half of the Israelis are native born. They're called Sabras, which is the name of a prickly pear—you've eaten it in Mexico, I'm sure, tough on the outside, sweet and soft on the inside. And then, thank God, most of them speak English, at least some English. I'm told that Hebrew is an extremely logical language."

"Oh, it is. It surely is. I was amazed at how quickly we learned it in school. But I'm listening to some of the people around us. I catch one word in three."

A middle-aged man, sitting on the other side of Philip and obviously listening to their conversation, tapped Philip's arm and, speaking in heavily accented English, said, "You're a rabbi? No. No, you're not Jewish. So where did you learn Hebrew? I apologize for asking. You're a diplomat? No, not in tourist class; they ride first class." His apology for asking was no apology at all. Obviously, on an Israeli plane, he felt secure in interrupting a conversation by total strangers, something Philip and Barbara were to encounter again and again. An independent, self-willed, and generous people, the Israelis cared little for the texts of polite social intercourse. If one heard a question directed elsewhere and one had an answer, one answered.

"No, we're not Jewish," Philip said. "My name is Philip Carter. I'm a Unitarian minister. This is my wife, Barbara. She's an author."

"Ah-ha, so you learned Hebrew in the seminary?"

"Yes, in the seminary."

"Let me introduce myself. This is a long trip—not to Israel, but possibly they stop in Geneva, which you don't know with El Al. I'm Chaim Hertzog. I'm a chicken salesman for a *moshav*, which is something like a *kibbutz*, only it's different because everyone in a *moshav* is an independent farmer, and sometimes they work a collective. Our collective is chickens. We produce half a million chickens a year and freeze them. So I'm in London, selling chickens."

"That's fascinating," Barbara said.

"Not fascinating, but a good living," Mr. Hertzog corrected her. "Now, about Hebrew. We call what you learn in the seminary, synagogue Hebrew: very good for talking to God, not so good in Tel Aviv or in Jerusalem. After a few days, you listen carefully, you can talk Tel Aviv Hebrew—maybe not the best, but a little."

"Do you live in Tel Aviv?" Barbara asked him. "We're booked into the Samuel."

"A very fine place. Very fine. No, I live at a *moshav*, Moshav Akiba. My family grows oranges—that's personal, the chickens are collective—we have twenty-one trees, real California seedless oranges. You'd be surprised how many oranges you can get from twenty-one trees. My wife, Sara, she takes care of the trees with my two sons when they're not in service in the army, and thank God I travel."

"We're from California," Philip said.

"Wonderful! I never been there, but someday, maybe—who knows? Chickens are a worldwide commodity."

As Mr. Hertzog had predicted, the giant 747 made a stop, not at Geneva but at Bonn, to take on passengers and cargo. While the plane stood on the parking strip, a Jeep with a mounted machine gun circled it. The man Philip had pointed out, with the cold eyes and the bulging jacket, spoke to Hertzog in Hebrew, and then Hertzog explained to Philip and Barbara that these were extra security measures, following a bombing in Frankfurt; and Barbara reflected on the miracles of time and change, that the land where she had almost been put to death as an anti-Nazi forty-five years ago should now be protecting a Jewish airplane being loaded with German cargo.

The cargo, Mr. Hertzog explained, was typewriters fitted with Hebrew type. "Germans make very good typewriters," he said, somewhat apologetically. "They make good machines. I know the guard. His name is Shmuel," referring to the man with the bulging jacket. "He's very competent."

The landing at the Tel Aviv airport was smooth and easy, and Philip and Barbara were delighted by the colorful October sunset. A Mercedes taxicab—the Mercedes were a part of German reparations, and seen everywhere—took them to their hotel. It was the season of the Jewish High Holidays, and while Barbara would have preferred to stay at the Sheraton Tel Aviv, where they were originally booked, she could not change their reservation there and had switched to the Samuel. She was surprised at the elegance of the place, and after they had registered they were shown to a well-furnished suite with broad windows that faced the Mediterranean.

"Well, here we are," Philip said, "in the Holy Land. How many times I've thought of this!"

"We think of it differently," Barbara mused, almost sadly. "Here is where my first husband died. Sam went to medical school here; he even thought of making his life here. He was a medic in the Six Day War—fell in love here, spoke Hebrew like a native— and then gave it all up and returned to San Francisco and married Mary Lou."

"Are you happy or unhappy to be here?" he asked her.

"I don't know," she answered slowly. "But wherever I am, I'm happy to be with you."

When he crawled into bed later and moved close to Barbara and touched her face, he felt tears. He refrained from any words as to why she wept, and for that, Barbara was grateful. She was in no mood to exchange thoughts or words of any kind with him. If she could have her own way and if she were willing to bring total chaos into their relationship, she would get out of bed and pack her bag and take a cab to the airport and take the first plane out—to anywhere—and why she felt this way at this moment, she could not for the life of her understand. Her whole life had been threaded through with Jews. Her first husband, her father's partner, the people at Highgate, Sally; her lawyer, Sam Goldberg, who had cherished her and who left her the house on Green Street in his will; Boyd Kimmelman, who had taken Sam Goldberg's place in her life after Goldberg died and who worshiped her ... And why had it been that way? She had read somewhere that Mark Twain had said that Jews were like anyone else, only more so. Was she also like anyone else, only more so? If there were any real barrier between Philip and herself, it was the fact that he knew who he was and she did not know who she was. When he suggested teaching her to meditate with him, and she asked him why and what it would do for her, he had replied that among other things, she would know what and who she was. "I know who I am," she had replied indignantly. But the truth of the matter, as she had begun to realize, was that she didn't know.

Finally she slept, and Philip knew this when her breathing became easy and regular. A three-quarter moon was hanging outside the window. Philip watched it for a little while and then closed his eyes and slept.

In the morning they awakened together and looked at each other, and Barbara rolled over into his arms. "Make love to me, old priest, and try to remember all I taught you."

"Now? I'm starving."

"Now. Earn your food."

They made love, and then they stood at the window, with the sea and the broad white beaches spread out beneath them, and at the edge of the horizon, a freighter sailing north. "Here it began," Philip murmured. "The Philistines landed on these beaches with their longboats; Gaza to the south, and in the north, Tyre."

"And we should dress and eat," Barbara said. "We have three days here before we go to Jerusalem."

"Why don't we go to Jerusalem today?"

"Because we have no room in Jerusalem for today. I had to switch things to get you out of your depression, and we're just past Yom Kippur, which is the Day of Atonement. It's like trying to get a room at the Mark Hopkins for Memorial Day weekend. In three days, we have a room at the King David Hotel, which is where to be if you're an American tourist in Jerusalem. The advice of Mr. Hertzog is to take off here in any direction with a guidebook in your hand. There are more museums and theaters here than you can shake a stick at, so let's go and eat and buy a guidebook."

Breakfast was overwhelming; the food was laid out on a long table—cereal, milk, cream, herring in sour cream, scrambled eggs, French toast, bagels, five kinds of cheese, fruit, green onions, cucumber, and sliced tomatoes, and coffee and tea and hot chocolate.

They ate well and went out into the cool sunshine, guidebook in hand. For a while they wandered aimlessly. If ever there were a city in constant eruption, this was it: cars honking their horns, buses, people in motion, houses being dismantled, houses under construction, business streets that suddenly became delightful residential areas, a tiny old cemetery tucked between office buildings, tourists speaking half a dozen different languages, neon signs advertising in Hebrew, street peddlers selling quick food—Oriental versions of what at home Barbara would have called junk food. Compared to this explosion of energy, London was quiescent, old, and settled into grateful accomplishment. Finally, having done at least three miles, their wandering brought them to Dizengoff Street's comparative repose, the string of restaurants and cafes making a not-too-successful attempt to imitate the Left Bank of Paris, small tables and chairs set

out on the sidewalk. In a way, these outdoor tables, in the benign
fall climate of Tel Aviv, were a sort of social center of the expanding
city.

It was past the lunch hour, so most of the tables were unoc-
cupied. At one shop a soldier on leave, his rifle slung over his
shoulder, sat with his girlfriend, a pretty redhead. At another table
two black men, obviously Americans, drank beer and ate flat bread
dipped into a sticky concoction; and at a table in the other direction
three old white-bearded men drank tea from glasses and were engaged in a vociferous argument in Hebrew, to which Philip listened
intently, proudly able to inform Barbara that he could understand
enough to know that they were talking about excavations in an old
Jewish cemetery.

"Not that I understand much of it, but I do get the thread
when they slow down, words like *sacrilege* and *God's commandment*.
It's absolutely remarkable. Give me another week—they use a word
that I think means 'clutching,' probably an excavator. Trouble is
they talk so fast; but the little fellow with the blue eyes, he's given
to judgments and he speaks very slowly. Now he's looking at us.
Tayar, I think that's the word for tourist."

"You're delicious," Barbara said. "A Jesuit priest who speaks
Hebrew. If I lived a lifetime here, I'd never learn."

"It's a beautiful, logical language."

"Not when they shout at each other." A waiter came out, and
Barbara pointed to the soldier. "Beer for both of us, and that stuff
they're eating."

"Pita and hummus."

They drank the beer, broke up the pita bread and dipped it
into the hummus, and washed it down with more cold beer. "*Cold*
beer," Philip said, "thank goodness."

"Very American," Barbara agreed. "When I was in Egypt during the war, the GIs stationed there moved heaven and earth to get

into Israel, which was not yet Israel, but the only place in the area where they could find ice-cream sodas."

"Tell me," Philip asked her, "what is or who is Dizengoff? I've heard of Herzl and Ben-Gurion and Yigal Alon, but Dizengoff? You know, we have a Hanukkah celebration at the church every year, along with our Christmas festival, and we do a lot about Israel. But Dizengoff?"

"He settled and I suppose originated Tel Aviv. From what the guidebook says, it was all sand dunes before Mier Dizengoff came here with some sixty families and began a city. Now there's more than a million people."

"More than San Francisco," Philip said with some awe.

"Just about, with parks and concrete sidewalks and asphalt streets, and museums and theaters and all the rest."

At that moment a bus pulled up to the curb opposite where the soldier and his girlfriend were sitting. He hastily kissed her and then turned to the open door of the bus—and as he set foot on the step there was a tremendous crash and an explosion that flung the soldier off his feet and shattered the windows of the bus and of two cafés. The force of the blast rocked Barbara and Philip but left them unharmed. And the bus burst into flames.

Afterward, as she recollected it, it seemed to Barbara that Philip acted instantaneously, but he told her that he took a moment to see that she was unharmed. Then he leaped toward the bus. The driver, unconscious, was hanging half out of the open door. Philip, with strength she had never known he had, lifted the driver out of the bus and laid him down on the sidewalk. Then Philip plunged into the bus, and as Barbara got to her feet and ran toward the burning vehicle—the redheaded girl meanwhile bloody and scream-ing in terror—Philip emerged with a small, whimpering, blood-covered child in his arms. He handed the child to Barbara, who had no voice, but took the child and laid her down on the sidewalk, and in that time Philip emerged with a second child in his arms and his own hair aflame. Barbara tore off the light sweater she was wearing and smothered the flames on Philip's head as he carefully bore the little boy of ten or so away from the bus, shouting to Barbara, "Take the other one! It could explode! Get the child!"

She picked up the child, a little girl, and followed Philip away from the bus to where the three old men had been arguing, and she laid the child down on the table. Philip laid the little boy on the sidewalk. The three old men had not moved; they were staring mutely frozen in place, apparently unable to comprehend what had happened. Then Philip ran back to the bus and started toward its door, as if to enter it again; but the waiter, who had come out of the café, and Barbara held him back, Barbara finding enough voice to plead, "No, you can't go in there, you can't! You'll die! It's all on fire!"

All of this happened in a matter of seconds, and hardly a minute had gone by since the explosion. Suddenly the whole world was alive with screams and shouts, and soldiers on leave pushing people back from the burning bus, and the distant wail of police cars and fire engines.

"There are children in there!" Philip yelled.

A soldier on leave joined them, helping to hold Philip back. "Fire engines coming—firemen." The street traffic had halted, and a man came running from his car, shouting in Hebrew that he was a doctor. "Let him through!" someone yelled in English. The soldier hanging on to Philip said, "Mister, two men bleeding on the sidewalk. We take them away, the bus shouldn't explode. Now help me."

Philip and the soldier picked up the bus driver, in spite of the doctor's protests, and carried him up the street to where the two children lay sobbing. Barbara took the unconscious soldier's feet while the waiter picked him up by the armpits, and they carried him after the bus driver. The doctor, a small man with brass-rimmed glasses and a bald head, was already stanching the blood of the driver's wounds. He snapped a command at the soldier, who went to the wounded soldier and felt his pulse. The redheaded girl was kneeling by his side. The child Barbara had put on the table saw blood running from her nose onto her dress and began to scream. Barbara lifted her in her arms and tried to soothe her.

And then, suddenly, their role was over. A fire engine went into action and began flooding the bus with water, and an ambulance arrived with people to tend to the two men and the two children, and Barbara fell into the arms of a bloody, blackened Philip, half of whose hair had burned away, and began to whimper, like a small child.

Another ambulance arrived, and a man in a white coat said to them, "Come with us. We take you to the hospital."

Meekly Barbara and Philip followed them.

AT BREAKFAST AT HIGHGATE, Eloise, opening the folded copy of the *San Francisco Chronicle* that had arrived that morning, went white, and her hands began to shake. Freddie took the paper from her and read aloud to Eloise and Adam: "Headline, 'San Francisco Couple Hailed as Heroes in Israel.'" He asked Eloise, "Did you know they were in Israel? Weren't they supposed to be in Greece or somewhere?"

"Will you read it?" Adam growled.

Special to the *Chronicle*. The Reverend Philip Carter, minister of the First Unitarian Church in San Francisco, and Mrs. Carter, the former Barbara Lavette, recently married and on their honeymoon, were saluted by Yitzhak Shamir, prime minister of Israel, for exceptional courage in the face of danger.

At two P.M. today, Israeli time, a bus exploded in Dizengoff Circle. The bus was starting its run, and the only passengers were two men and a woman with three children.

Apparently a terrorist's bomb in the briefcase of one of the men exploded prematurely, and the bus burst into flames, killing the terrorist, the other man, the woman, Rebecca Kahn, and one of her three children. A soldier attempting to board the bus at the moment of the blast was severely injured but is in stable condition at Tel Aviv Hospital, as is the bus driver.

At great personal danger, Reverend Carter dragged the driver to safety and then entered the burning bus and carried two of Mrs. Kahn's children to safety. As he bore the second child to safety, his hair caught fire. His wife, who had stood by the open door of the bus to receive the children, managed to smother his burning hair with her sweater. The Reverend Carter attempted to enter the bus a third time but was restrained by a soldier on leave. Then he and his wife carried the two children and the two wounded men out of harm's way. Dr. Leon Phagel, a passing motorist, gave immediate medical aid to the two men, who are expected to recover. The two children carried by the Reverend Carter to safety were uninjured, but suffering from shock. . . .

Freddie paused. The story went on with the reaction in Israel to the suicide bombing, and the measures to be taken against terrorist groups.

"I would never have thought it," Adam said. "He's such a mild-mannered man. Thank God they're all right."

"Poor Philip," Eloise said. "I can't imagine what happens when hair burns."

"It'll grow back," Freddie assured her. "There's a sidebar about Barbara. Shall I read it?"

"Please."

Mrs. Philip Carter, formerly Barbara Lavette, is the scion of one of the oldest and most respected San Francisco families. Her great-grandfather Thomas Seldon Sr., was the founder of the Seldon Bank. After his death her grandfather Thomas Seldon Jr., continued as head of the bank. Her father, Daniel Lavette, is still remembered as one of the most colorful figures of the post-earthquake era, and Ms. Lavette has had a memorable career as a novelist and a screenwriter. Twice widowed, she married the Reverend Philip Carter this past September. She was a candidate for Congress in the forty-eighth Congressional District and has been active in Democratic politics and in many liberal causes over the past twenty-five years. She is a close associate of Mayor Dianne Feinstein, whose comment on her actions in Israel was that she would expect nothing less from Barbara Lavette.

"Pretty neat, don't you think?" Freddie said.

Eloise shook her head. "Wherever she goes..." She had tears in her eyes.

"Why don't you call her in Tel Aviv?" Adam suggested. "You'll feel better after you speak to her."

"I don't know where she's staying," Eloise complained. "She called me from England last week to tell me that she was rearranging their schedule to go directly to Israel because Philip was deeply depressed. She was supposed to stay at the Sheraton, but she couldn't get a room when they altered their plans."

"Then she'll either call or write," Freddie said. "Come on, Mother. There's nothing to worry about. Aunt Barbara has a charmed life. Nothing is going to happen to her."

BUT A GREAT DEAL WAS HAPPENING to Philip and Barbara. After the blisters on Philip's head were treated, with the burned hair cut away in half a dozen places, he asked Barbara what he looked like, and she shook her head hopelessly.

"Philip, dear," she said, "you're a brave wild man, and I don't care what you look like."

"God giveth and God taketh away," he said. "I felt very comfortable in England with all that hair. And I'm not brave. I didn't know what I was doing. If I'd had time to think about it, I wouldn't have dared to go near that bus."

"Two beautiful children are alive. The bus driver is alive. The soldier is alive. You saved their lives. It's a wonderful thing. Allow yourself to have it. Now let's go back to the hotel and rest."

· "And pray for those poor people who died."

But there was no time for rest or prayer. Word had gotten out that they were staying at the Samuel, and when they stepped out of the taxicab they were surrounded by reporters from the local newspapers and the *Jerusalem Post*, the *New York Times*, the *Los Angeles Times*, and the *Washington Post;* London newspapers, German newspapers, Reuters, the Associated Press; photographers, television cameras, as well as Tel Aviv natives and tourists. The most insistent question was, "What made you act, Reverend?"

Philip disliked being called Reverend. He shook his head hopelessly.

Barbara felt that with the bandages and the tufts of singed hair sticking out here and there, he looked like something out of a carnival. "He acted," Barbara replied, "because he's a decent human being."

Philip managed to say, "I did what I had to do."

And Barbara pleaded that they were exhausted and that they had to rest. And finally they were allowed to go to their room, where a dozen telephone messages awaited them.

They decided to have dinner in their room, since they were afraid to set foot in a crowded dining room. Evidently the waiter in the café had given the entire story to the press, and among the messages was one from Prime Minister Shamir and another from the mayor of Jerusalem, Teddy Kollek, asking them to be his guests at the VIP guesthouse in Jerusalem for a week, where an apartment would be provided facing the Old City. Would they call and confirm?

Philip took some painkillers that they had given him at the hospital, and Barbara began to cry; and when Philip asked her why she told him, "Because I haven't wept all day. So please allow me to cry."

Dinner was brought to their room, and the waiter who wheeled in the cart informed them, in very bad English, that it was his brother-in-law's cousin, Chaim, who was working in the café and gave the whole story to the press, and who clung to Philip to keep him from entering the bus a third time, and please, God forgive him for asking, could he have their autographs? Philip dumbly signed a page from the waiter's receipt book, and Barbara wiped away her tears and signed it as well.

When he had left, Philip said, "Do you know, my dear—" It was hard for him to speak. A burn on his cheek hurt when he spoke. "Do you know, my dear," he whispered, "I've never been asked for my autograph before."

She didn't know whether he was pleased or upset. "What has happened to us?" she said woefully. "We come here to walk in the steps of Jesus, which you've been practicing for years, and the world explodes."

"Not the world," he whispered. "Just a bus."

She took the warmers off the dinner dishes. There was beef stew and peas and potatoes. They sat staring wanly at the food.

"You should eat something," she told him.

The phone rang again, as it had at least five times since they entered the room. This time it was the manager of the hotel, who wanted to know whether there was anything he could do for them.

"If you could have the operator take our messages for the rest of the day, it would be helpful," Barbara said. "We're very tired."

"Absolutely. Absolutely."

Philip took a piece of the stewed meat and chewed painfully. "It's very good," he said.

Barbara shook her head. They had ordered a bottle of wine, and now she opened it and poured a glass for each of them. "I think I'm going to get drunk," she said. "Have you ever seen me drunk, Philip?"

"No, not really."

She raised her glass. "To what?"

"Shalom."

"Good enough." She took a mouthful of meat and agreed with Philip. "Very good, but a bit strange. The wine, on the other hand—well, it's wine... You do look odd, Philip dear. How do you feel?"

"Not bad, except when I lie down on the bed. That hurts. I'll have to sleep in a chair. They sent us a bottle of champagne, compliments of the house. Did you notice, they didn't send us a dinner check? Ouch," he muttered.

"You don't have to talk, darling," Barbara told him. "Just sit quietly and bask in glory. I think you're wonderful—absolutely wonderful."

"Oh, come on. You're embarrassing me."

Barbara burst out laughing. "Oh no! Why am I laughing? An awful thing happened and I almost lost a brand-new husband. What time do you think it is at Highgate? It's either yesterday or tomorrow."

"I think it's tomorrow," Philip said vaguely, "or maybe this morning."

She poured herself another glass of wine and filled Philip's. She was never much of a drinker, and the wine on an empty stomach was having an effect. "Last night," she said, "which was at least a month ago, I was in the depths of despair. I wanted to pack up and get out of here. Today, for some reason I don't quite understand, I feel wonderful. Not totally wonderful—guilty-wonderful, because I think of that poor woman and her child trapped in that bus. Still, I feel wonderful. Do you think that's terrible, Philip?"

"I know the feeling. You saved a human life. In the Talmud, it says that he who saves a human life saves the whole universe."

"You saved the children, not I."

Philip stood up, walked around the table, turned Barbara's face up to his, and kissed her. "I love you, beautiful lady," he whispered. "My hair was on fire. You smothered it. You didn't have to think. You just tore off your sweater and smothered the flames."

Barbara shrugged. "You must eat something, Philip . . . It was an old sweater, not even wool, cotton knit. Now sit down and eat."

He sat down and raised his wineglass.

"How do you know all this Talmud stuff?"

"The seminary. I sometimes think Jesuits know more about the Jews than Jews do . . . Those painkillers work. I can almost talk without any pain. Here's a toast:

How odd of God to choose the Jews,
But not so odd as those who choose
A Jewish God and hate the Jews."

"Oh? And where did you get that?"
"Same place."

THE NEXT MORNING Barbara called Eloise. It was the previous evening in California. "We're both safe and well. Philip looks somewhat like a Fiji Islander, but they assured us at the hospital that his hair will grow back," Barbara told her. "We're going back to the hospital today, and I think they'll take the bandages off. He wasn't badly burned—just a few blisters."

"I'm so glad you're safe. It was all over the papers today. Barbara, can you possibly stay out of trouble until you return?"

"I'll try," Barbara agreed. "Will you call Sam and reassure him? Tell him that we're not insane and that we don't go looking for trouble. And call Philip's people at the church."

"Barbara, I miss you so," Eloise said plaintively. "When are you coming home?"

"I don't know. Teddy Kollek—he's the mayor of Jerusalem—invited us to stay for a week at a guesthouse that the city maintains for VIPs. Philip is so excited about staying in a place where he can look out and see Old Jerusalem that he can hardly wait to get there. But tonight, if Philip is well enough—"

"I'm well enough," Philip said in the background.

"—we're to have dinner with the mayor of Tel Aviv . . . Yes, Philip is absolutely wonderful, considering his age. And be sure to tell Adam that Israeli white wine is interesting, but that's the best I can say of it."

"Freddie wants to speak to you."

"All right. Put him on."

"Aunt Barbara—you're all right?"

"We're fine, Freddie."

"Will you do me a favor?"

"Freddie, you know I will."

"I sold ten cases of Zinfandel—you know, the stuff we still produce for the synagogue and church trade—to a dealer in Jerusalem. His name is Kurt Levinson. He's on Saladin Street. If you could ask him how it's taking?"

"Freddie!"

"All right. Don't get angry. I'm only asking."

"Freddie, I love you. Good-bye."

"What was that all about?"

"Freddie sold some wine to a dealer in Jerusalem. He wants to know whether it's selling."

"Well, that's Freddie," Philip said. "You shouldn't be annoyed."

"Doesn't anything ever annoy you, Philip?"

"Yes, these cursed blisters on my head."

At the hospital a Dr. Levinson, who had been at medical school in Israel with Barbara's son, Sam, removed the bandages and talked to Barbara about her son. When he heard that Sam was chief of surgery at Mercy Hospital, he complained enviously about living in a country with a surplus of physicians. "I'm going to put something on the blisters that will tend to dry them. Don't worry if some of them break... We have too many doctors here. We need laborers and farmworkers, not a doctor for every ten people."

"Ten people?" Barbara exclaimed.

"Well, maybe every three hundred. Who counts? How is my English?"

"Very good. What shall I do if a blister breaks?"

"Just pat it gently with a clean tissue. I'll give you some codeine pills and a salve. But use the salve sparingly. I'll take you to a room, and I want you to wait there until I find the hospital barber, and I'll send him up."

"You have a hospital barber?"

"He's a volunteer. He's very good." The doctor, a fat, round-cheeked man, grinned. "Bet you don't have one at that Mercy Hospital of yours."

"I never asked," Barbara said.

The barber, a man in his late sixties, told them that his name was Cosmo Santina. "I was with the GIs in North Africa. I'm from Brooklyn. My pop was Italian, my mother was Jewish. That makes me a Jew by Israeli law. We got a furlough in Israel before they closed the gates. I went AWOL. I like it here. Tel Aviv was just a village then. I get out of one army and they put me in another—in 1948. So I been through it all, and I had the best barbershop in Tel Aviv. My pop taught me the trade. Don't worry," he said to Philip. "Just sit down and relax. My son runs the shop now, but I'm better than he is. You won't feel a thing."

"Thank you. That's very reassuring," Philip said.

"I like that." Santina nodded and said to Barbara, "Your husband's a gentleman. You live here in Tel Aviv, you appreciate a gentleman. Don't get me wrong. We Israelis are the best people in the world—but gentlemen, that's something else. Not you, Reverend—I hear that before you jumped into that bus, which was a very fine thing, believe me, you had a head of hair like the Brits, nice and full. I can't give that back to you, but I'll give you a nice short cut. And even under the blisters, it'll grow back. Meanwhile, I give you a yarmulke. We got plenty of yarmulkes here at the hospital."

Back at the hotel Barbara studied Philip thoughtfully. "I kind of like it," she decided. "You're almost bald. They say bald men are very passionate. It's true, it looks a bit like a boiled beet, but they assure me that will pass. Does it hurt very much?"

"No, not too much. With the yarmulke, I'm either Jewish or a cardinal. There's a man in our congregation at home who always wears a yarmulke."

"You don't make him take it off, do you?"

"Heavens, no."

"We had a call from Teddy Kollek's secretary. She says that an apartment has been reserved for us at the"—she pronounced it carefully—"Mishkenot Sha'ananim. We are welcome to stay as long as we please. As guests of the City of Jerusalem."

Philip shook his head despairingly. "Barbara, I am so embarrassed I could just crawl away and hide. I did nothing that any decent human being wouldn't do, and if I had only been a bit quicker, that poor woman and her child wouldn't have died—and instead of blaming me for their deaths, the Israelis are making me a national celebrity. I am so ashamed."

"Of what? Are you completely crazy, Philip? If you had gone back into that flaming bus, there would have been three dead. The bus driver is going to recover and so is the soldier, and there's no way in the world that you could have gone back into the bus. You struggled like a demon when we held you back. I feel so wonderful—why are you depressed?"

"It could be my hair. At heart, I'm very vain."

"You're not vain. You're *meshuga*. That's a Jewish word for 'crazy.' "

Their argument was interrupted by the telephone. The husband of the woman who had died in the bus was downstairs in the lobby, and the hotel manager asked if they would see him. "Yes, of course," Barbara replied.

He entered the room slowly, a big, sunburnt man with heavy sloping shoulders that reminded Barbara of her first husband, Bernie Cohen. He held out his hand to Philip, who took it and winced under the crushing grip of the man. "My name—Enoch Shelek. I have not much English to say much—"

"Speak Hebrew slowly," Philip said in Hebrew. "I have some Hebrew."

He nodded, and speaking very slowly, he said, "You gave me the gift of life, two of my beautiful children. My wife perished, may she rest in peace, and this morning we buried her and my baby son. But you gave me two lives, my son's and my daughter's. God sent you from faraway to stop the hand of the Malakh Ha-Mavet. I don't know how to thank you. I'm a small farmer, but all that I have is yours."

Barbara didn't know how much of what he said was understandable to Philip, but she saw tears welling up in Philip's eyes, and then he went to the man and embraced him—and for a long moment, both of them were locked in that embrace. Then Philip let go and wiped his eyes, wincing, for the lashes were gone and his lids still inflamed. Then Shelek offered his hand to Barbara and said something in Hebrew. And then he turned to the door and left.

Philip dropped into a chair and closed his eyes. For a few minutes he and Barbara remained silent.

Then Barbara asked, "Did you understand what he said?"

"Mostly, I think. Gratitude—and something about the Malakh Ha-Mavet, who is the Angel of Death in Jewish folklore, and the two children who were saved. Before he left, when he took your hand, he blessed you and all our children. I understood that, very biblical, and somewhat ironic. We have so much, Barbara, that I should not lament the fact that we have no children."

"We have children," Barbara said. "All the children in the family. Children don't belong to anyone."

That evening they dined with the mayor of Tel Aviv, a tall, handsome man; his wife; and a professor, Zvi Harana by name, chairman of history at the local university; and his wife. The professor was a stout, bearded man, his wife a plump pudding of a woman who reminded Barbara of Eloise. The mayor's wife was a talkative, pretty woman who wore an elegant evening gown as companion to her husband's dinner jacket. This surprised Barbara, in a land where the necktie was almost unknown—the first dinner jacket and black tie she had encountered. They were all warm and congratulatory toward Philip and Barbara, and they all spoke English with facility; and then the talk turned to the Carters' stay in Israel and where they should go and what they should see. There were also numerous questions about Unitarianism, and the mayor's wife wondered how it was different from Judaism.

"Well," Philip explained, "we have no given rituals or doctrines. We don't ask that anyone should accept any concept of God as against another. We read from the Old Testament and the New Testament, and we honor Jesus as a great prophet. We believe in the ineffable nature of God—"

"Please," Mrs. Harana interrupted, "I don't know what that word means—*ineffable*."

"Unknowable, Hannah," her husband said. "But that is very Jewish, Dr. Carter. In fact, our Bible specifies the unknowability of God."

"In fact," the mayor put in, "in one of the most provoking verses in the Bible, I believe it's Exodus 3:14, Moses asks God for his name, and God replies, 'I AM THAT I AM.' And again, in the next verse, God is the great I AM."

Philip nodded. "In seminary, we discussed that for hours. I was a Catholic priest before I left that Church and became a Unitarian."

"A Jesuit?" the Professor asked.

"Yes, a Jesuit. I fell in love with a nun, my first wife. We left the Church together. She died five years ago."

"May I say that I believe such an act took singular spiritual courage?"

"Perhaps. I don't really know what 'courage' means. Love, yes—but courage?"

"I won't argue the point," the professor said.

"Do you have any Unitarian congregation here?" Philip asked.

The mayor shrugged. "I really don't know. We have total freedom of religion and at least a few of every sect I have ever heard of—but Unitarians..."

Barbara listened with a degree of awe. Their conversation was of matters she had never given any thought to, and later that evening, back at the hotel, she mentioned to Philip that it was odd to hear a group of highly educated people discuss God as a matter of reality.

"They are Israelis," Philip said. "After all, the Old Testament was written in their language."

"But I always thought that most Israelis were irreligious."

"Perhaps, but not in the sense of your use of the term. Jews, I have learned, are very complicated. Even when they become Unitarians, and we have a good many of them, they remain Jewish. As for the Israelis—well, I haven't met enough of them to dare to generalize, but with them, the Bible is not simply a religious tome. It's their history."

"I never thought of it that way," Barbara said. "I haven't opened a Bible since Sunday school. Shall I read it, Philip?"

"You might try it. But remember I made a promise to you, and to myself, for that matter, never to try to convert you to anything."

"You're against conversion, aren't you?"

"Somewhat. I think people should find their own way."

The next day was Saturday, the day they had decided to check out of the Samuel for the trip to Jerusalem, but when Barbara presented herself at the desk to pay their bill, the woman she spoke to said that there was no bill. "The manager's instructions," she said; and when Barbara went into the manager's office, indignant and determined to pay her bill, the manager was equally indignant. "How could I face any of my employees if word got around that we had charged you?"

"But that is one thing and what my husband did is another."

"You are going to stay at the Mishkenot in Jerusalem. Do you think Teddy Kollek will charge you? You're our guest. Please say no more about it."

Barbara nodded. "Thank you."

"No, thank *you*."

Barbara had an understandable aversion to buses, and she wondered whether cabs would be available on the Sabbath. They were, a line of them outside the hotel, and she and Philip seated themselves in a large four-door Mercedes driven by a man who introduced himself as Ezra Cohen. His English was heavily accented but adequate. "Jerusalem?" he said. "Where in Jerusalem?"

"The Mishkenot Sha'ananim," Philip said.

"Seventy kilometers." Then he turned from his driver's seat and studied them carefully. "You're the man," he said to Philip. "You went into the bus for the kids, right?"

Philip sighed, and Barbara replied, "Yes, Mr. Cohen. I'm his wife."

"For anyone else, it's fifty dollars. You, I don't charge."

"Of course you will charge us."

"Three reasons I shouldn't, Mrs. Carter. First reason, I wasn't going to work today. It's Shabbat. My wife says to me, 'All of a sudden you're religious? You don't go to shul, even on Rosh Hashanah. You smoke on Shabbat. So don't tell me you will lie in bed all day.'" And turning to Philip, "You don't mind I take a cigarette?"

"No, I don't mind."

"Second reason," Mr. Cohen continued, starting to drive, "I got my sister in Jerusalem, I haven't seen her in months. Third reason, I tell my wife I met Mr. and Mrs. Carter, she's so impressed she don't make me crazy for maybe two days."

Barbara relaxed and whispered to Philip, "You can't win an argument with them. They love to argue."

"And they're like family. Everyone knows everyone else, or so it seems. I think it's wonderful. I never really had family, it was only Agatha and myself. That's why Highgate is so pleasant for me."

"I think the church was your family, Philip."

"Yes and no."

A few miles from Tel Aviv, they saw on their left a wide green meadow, planted in wheat, that stretched away to the north. Years and years ago, more years than she cared to remember, Barbara had seen that meadow; and recalling it, she said to Philip, "That's where King Saul fought the Philistines—right there in that meadow."

"And beat them," the driver put in. "Gave them a licking they never forgot."

"I'm sure," Philip agreed, staring, fascinated. "You can't imagine what this means to me."

"I think I can," Barbara said.

The road wound on, curving through terraced hillsides covered with forests of evergreen. "I read," Philip remarked, "that when the

Jews first declared independence, all these hills were bare. They planted all these trees since then."

"Millions," the driver agreed, "millions of trees. The terraces were built in the time of the Maccabees, but the tree planting—each day more." The air was clean and saturated with the sweet smell of the pines, and as they drove on toward Jerusalem, the climate changed, becoming brisk and cool.

Expecting the walled Jerusalem of the illustrations he had seen, Philip was amazed at the city that appeared, new high-rise apartment houses, tree-lined streets, smart shops, and rows of well-built homes. They finally approached the King David Hotel, swung around, and were at the Mishkenot, a high wall and a pair of large glass doors facing the street. Barbara and Philip said good-bye to Ezra, their driver, who had given them the titles and subtitles of every village they had passed; they thanked him and persuaded him to accept a twenty-dollar bill.

"Enjoy," he told them. "It's a beautiful city."

A young woman rose from behind her desk in the lobby, which was a broad, comfortable room, and told them that her name was Sarah, that she was the day attendant, and that they should call on her for anything they required. She had been expecting them, and since they must be tired, she would take them to their apartment immediately. Sarah spoke a British-accented English as if she had been born to it—she was native to Israel, they learned—an accent they were to hear frequently.

A young man carried their luggage. The apartment, a duplex with a large living room and a kitchen on the first floor and two bedrooms above, had walls of stone, and the floor, too, was stone. As Barbara closed the door behind Sarah, she heard Philip exclaim, "Barbara! Barbara, come look!"

He was standing at a glass door that opened onto a balcony; and joining him Barbara saw, below and across a valley, the

Old City of Jerusalem—crenellated walls, towers and pinnacles of churches, and the glistening Dome of the Rock, all of it there as if it had been painted in a large panorama, the walls golden in the light of the setting sun.

"I hadn't dreamed," Philip whispered.

"You were so disappointed in the New City."

"Yes, I thought the old place was gone—but there it is across the valley, so close we could almost reach out and touch it. I can see Jesus riding up to that gate. It's all there, Barbara."

"Yes, and you're a Jesuit again," she said, putting an arm around him. "I'm glad we came here, Philip. Don't mind if I tease you. I know how important this is to you."

"That valley between us and the city—what do you suppose it's called?"

"I have a map here. Somewhere." She went to look for the map, and Philip opened the door and stepped out onto the balcony.

The air was cold and sharp, like San Francisco on a winter evening—a place on the other side of the world—and this was the navel of the world; and all the old memories and practices returned, and tears welled into his eyes at the thought that he was here, truly here—something that Barbara would never completely understand. She was of the earth, wholly, completely, and there was a core inside of her that needed no support other than her mind and her body. But wasn't that the basis of his love for her, this strength that she gave him?

"I think it's called Meve Shaoaam, or perhaps that's some other place. Philip, it's cold out here. I never thought it could be so cold in Jerusalem."

The valley was deep black now, but the sun still reflected the minarets and church towers of Old Jerusalem.

"Come inside," she said.

"It's not real. I can't believe I'm standing here."

"You'll believe it if you get a chill. You're still doped up with the painkillers and the other stuff they gave you. Come and we'll have dinner, old man. I'm starved."

When they asked Sarah where they might find some dinner, she suggested a French restaurant; and when Barbara raised a brow, Sarah attested to the fact that it was a wonderful restaurant, opened some years ago by French Jews. "You see, Mrs. Carter, we have everything here. If your taste turns to Italian food, we have an Italian Jewish restaurant down near the old railroad station, but you'd never find it by yourselves. Tomorrow Mr. Kollek is sending a guide and a touring car for you, and it will be at your disposal."

Barbara shook her head in disbelief, and Philip asked, "Can't we just walk from here to the Old City?"

"Yes, if you're good walkers. But I think you would do better to take the car to the city gate and walk from there. The Old City is a maze, and if you've never been there, you'll want the guide. He knows the Old City, and he's a charming young man, an Egyptian Jew fluent in Arabic."

"That would be wonderful," Barbara decided. "At what time?"

"He'll be here at nine A.M.—or whenever you're ready. His name is Abdul Carim."

"Aren't we an awful burden to you?" Philip asked.

"No, not at all. This house is maintained by the government for visitors of distinction."

" 'Visitors of distinction,' " Barbara repeated as they walked down the street to the French restaurant. "Here I am, fortunate enough to be married to a man who is a valid hero, crazy enough to jump into a burning bus and become a national symbol. I know that pride is a sin to your way of thinking, but you married a sinful woman, and I'm very proud of you. So from now on, please, let it happen, pride or not."

"Heaven knows what will happen. Don't forget, my hair is gone, and my skull is smeared over with white paste—"

"Pride again. Do I ever protest the white paste when I go to bed with you?"

"I try to blot it off each night."

"And then you make love to me like a seventeen-year-old—that's prideful and sinful...I know. I said I would stop teasing you. Please forgive me."

The food in the French restaurant was very good, and they were seated by a window where they could see the lights of the Old City. The champagne that was brought to them as a gift of the house was valid French brut.

"How do they know?" Barbara wondered.

"I'm sure Sarah called them. There's something very familial about this country," Philip said. "Everyone appears to be related. My dear Barbara, let me explain something to you. I went to a Catholic primary school, a Catholic high school, and then a Jesuit seminary. In all this education we were given to feel that the world of Jesus had disappeared with his crucifixion. Well, not really in that sense, but Jerusalem was a religious symbol, not an actual place where one could go. Remember that then, in the thirties, there was no country called Israel, just a handful of Jews trying to scrape a living out of the desert. What happened was a miracle, but I can't adjust to the fact that tomorrow I will walk in the steps of Jesus, in the streets where he walked. It doesn't matter that I am a Unitarian minister and have been a Unitarian minister for years. So you, with all your rationalism and distaste for the symbols of religion—you must somehow put up with me."

Barbara took his hand. "My dear, sweet Philip," she said. "I never put up with you. It's the reverse—you put up with me, with my teasing, my nonsense, and my irascibility. I'll be seventy in two weeks. How many widows of seventy could find a man like you?"

"Now you're really embarrassing me."

"I know. But I have to embarrass you to reach you. And we've hardly touched the champagne. What shall we drink to?"

"Shalom?"

"Why not?"

THEIR GUIDE, WHOM THEY MET at nine o'clock, was a dark, handsome young man who explained that his name was not really Abdul but Eliazer, but he had been given the nickname of Abdul because his Arabic was so good; he said it should be, since he had lived in Cairo until the age of twelve. His English was also excellent. Sarah had told him of their interest in the Old City, "And since you are both Christians, I think we should enter the walls by Saint Stephen's Gate. Also, better parking outside for the car." He went on to tell them that while there were eight gates in the walls, the Saint Stephen's Gate was preferred by most Christians. "It leads directly into the Via Dolorosa, and there, if you wish, we can follow the stations of the cross. But only if you desire. We call it the Lions' Gate because our troops entered there when we captured Jerusalem." Then he added, "If I talk too much, just tell me to shut up."

"We won't tell you to shut up," Philip said. "We're grateful for all you can tell us."

"Afterward, we can explore the city. It's a marvelous place, like a museum two thousand years old. Have you had breakfast?"

"We had coffee and buns. That's plenty," Barbara said.

They parked outside Saint Stephen's Gate and followed their guide through the wall. Abdul explained that the Church of Saint Anne had been built by the Crusaders, and that Barbara and Philip could come back and examine it on another day, but that now they would follow the path of the cross.

"But that's up to you," he added. "It is also said that the mother and father of Mary are buried under the church, but I think they invented that for the tourists."

"Leave it for the time being," Philip agreed. "Go ahead with the stations of the cross."

They walked on and stopped at the yard of an old Arab school. "It was here," Abdul said, "that Pontius Pilate met Jesus. He questioned him and then told the crowd, '*Ecce homo*' ... That's called the Chapel of the Flagellation. The clothes of Jesus were torn off, and he was whipped and crowned with a wreath of thorns. The Romans must have known of this in advance, because they had the wreath and the purple robe all ready. The scholars disagree about that, but scholars always disagree. Then he was given a cross to drag to his own crucifixion. So we have here the first and second stations of the cross. Only, it was not exactly a cross, as we know it today, but a plank of wood on a square pole, shaped like a T. Again, I'm quoting the scholars."

Barbara was watching Philip, who stood at the spot as if mesmerized. Abdul did not urge them on, and after a minute or so, Barbara took Philip's arm and gently moved him forward. Tourists were passing by, some with guides, others simply strolling down the Via Dolorosa. At a small chapel Abdul said, "Here is the third station. He falls here." Philip nodded. "And here, at the fourth station——," Abdul said, and Philip murmured, "He falls again. In three of the gospels, Simon of Cyrene takes the cross and carries it the rest of the way. According to John, Jesus carries it the rest of the way. But how could he, a piece of wood large enough to hang a man by his hands? And here his face is wiped by Veronica. This *is* the sixth station, isn't it?"

Abdul merely nodded. To Barbara, this was all strange and somewhat troublesome. If she had ever been told in Sunday school what the stations of the cross were, she had long ago forgotten. Sensing her feelings, Philip kissed her and whispered, "Don't be alarmed, my dear. Tomorrow I'll be a Unitarian again. Right now this is an emotional experience I can't shake off."

"The stations are marked," Abdul said. "I don't think I have to explain them." He and Barbara let Philip walk ahead of them as they entered the Church of the Holy Sepulcher, Abdul telling her softly, "The last four stations of the cross are inside this church. I think Mr. Carter knows that. The church was built on the Hill of Golgotha, but I suppose most of the hill was leveled before they built the church. The Old City was much smaller then, and two thousand years ago, this spot was outside the walls. These present walls are only four hundred years old, but the tourists like to think that they are the original walls of the old Jewish city. These little chapels belong to the Greek Orthodox, the Armenian Christians, the Roman Catholics, and others. Protestants are not allowed to hold services here."

Philip had disappeared in the crowd of tourists gathered around the final stage of the cross, where Jesus was buried and then resurrected. The church itself was dimly lit, gloomy, dirty, and in poor repair—this, the holiest spot in the Christian world, fallen into decay and disrepair, airless and unwelcoming. The smell of the place was rank and disturbing, and Barbara said to Abdul, "We'll wait for my husband outside." She shivered.

Outside she said to Abdul angrily, "Everything in Israel is so glistening, clean, and impressive—and this! This means nothing to me, but to my husband and others it's the center of mankind, and you allow it to rot and decay. You boast of the freedom of religion in your country and you turn this into a slum!"

"Don't blame us," Abdul pleaded. "We have no authority here, and no right to touch anything here. It's the Christian sector of the city, and it's governed by the Catholics and the Greek Orthodox and by other Christian churches here. We've begged them to let us reconstruct. We've offered them money to do it themselves. We make this area available to people of every faith. We guard it and keep it safe. But we have no authority to touch any relic or chapel or church."

Barbara listened and said she was sorry. In any case, why take out her feelings on Abdul? . . . What had provoked her so? Why did all this make her skin creep? Did she want Philip to scorn this strange display of what had happened two thousand years ago, or was she hardening the rift that had always existed between her and Philip? And if so, she told herself, it must stop. Somehow she must understand without condemnation. Somehow she must accept religion as a thing millions of people required, and without which they could not live, though she had lived without it and lived well—or so she felt when she reflected upon it—and most of the people she knew and loved lived without it, and they lived well and kindly. She had been drawn to the Unitarians, after the first retreat from the rain that led her there, because they appeared to be a group of people who simply felt that gathering together to celebrate life and compassion was sufficient—and yet under that celebration, when she thought deeply, was a need for something more than themselves and each other. Now, she told herself firmly, she must be neither provoked nor impatient with her husband. She would let him take the lead, whether to talk about it or not to talk about it.

Through all of her cogitation, Abdul remained silent, thinking perhaps of his own experiences with those who had come down the Via Dolorosa to the Church of the Holy Sepulcher. He had guided people of every religion down the street, Jews and Christians and Muslims and Buddhists, but this woman was difficult to understand. He had been told that the man was a Unitarian minister, but what a Unitarian was, he had not the faintest notion. As for the woman—well, she was a Christian. He had given up any attempt to understand Christians.

After about fifteen minutes, Philip emerged from the church and announced, "I'm hungry. Where can we eat?"

Abdul suggested an Arab restaurant. "Have you ever eaten Arab food?"

"No, but isn't it dangerous?"

"To go to an Arab restaurant? Oh no. They're very hospitable people. Many of them are angry with us, but when you break bread with them, they are very pleasant. If you can still enjoy walking, we'll go through the Arab part to our parking place. It's very interesting."

The Arab marketplace reminded Barbara of the Italian market in the North Beach area of San Francisco when she was a child. The stands were filled with fresh vegetables, corn and squash and beans and tomatoes and potatoes and cabbage, and stands of fresh-baked pita bread. "The old bread," Abdul explained. "It's why our matzo is round, not like the square matzo we export to the States. They flattened the pita and let it bake in the sun...You do know what matzo is?"

"I should think so," Philip said. "The winery where my wife's family lives began its business by selling sacramental wine to the San Francisco synagogues and churches." Then he bought one of the pitas and broke it up, and they ate the fresh bread as they walked. They passed a butcher's stand, chickens and cuts of lamb. "Was that during what your country called Prohibition?" Abdul asked.

"The sacramental wine?" Barbara asked him. "Yes, they had to make that legal. This bread is absolutely delicious." She was tired when finally they reached Saint Stephen's Gate and the car. Abdul drove down the Jericho Road and then turned onto the Port Said Road. Sunshine had warmed the day. Abdul parked the car and led them to an old Arab structure where a balcony was set with tables. Abdul knew the proprietor, and they bowed and exchanged greetings in Arabic.

Barbara and Philip dropped into their seats gratefully, and Abdul went on speaking to the proprietor in Arabic. Finally those two shook hands, and the proprietor left them. They had the balcony to themselves, and Barbara wondered why the other tables were empty. "It's a bit early for Arabs, and few of the tourists come here. He's in an anti-Israel phase now, and he's pleased that I brought Christians here."

"How does he know we're Christians?" Philip asked.

"How does he know I'm Egyptian? My Arabic and the way I look...We tell a story about a religious Jew who goes to Tokyo.

He goes to the synagogue and meets the rabbi, who is also Japanese. The rabbi looks at him suspiciously and says to him, 'You don't look Jewish.' Hassan here doesn't believe I'm Jewish."

A waiter entered the balcony, bearing a tray of pita bread and cakes and a pitcher of iced tea. "They don't serve wine," Abdul said. "It's against their religion, so they only drink it at home."

The table and the tableware were clean, but there were no menus. "They don't have menus here," Abdul explained. "You tell him what you want and it's brought out. I didn't ask what you wanted because I didn't think Arab food was familiar to you. But if there is something special, I'll be happy to tell him."

"Oh no, not at all," Philip said. "I'd much rather see what you ordered."

"Just lunch," Abdul said.

The waiter returned a minute or so later, bearing a great tray that he set down on the next table. There were eight bowls on the tray, and as he set them down in front of them, Abdul listed the contents, "Chopped eggplant and herbs, chopped lamb, peppers and stuff, cucumbers and radish, hummus—and these two I don't know, but very good. Try it all. And this, I think, is some sort of cabbage. You can either put it on your plate or pick it up with pita bread. Yes, I thought so, pine nuts and olives in this one. For dessert, we'll have halvah and honey cakes and Turkish coffee."

They ate everything in the eight bowls, and Barbara, who recalled eating in an Arab restaurant in New York, admitted that it had been nothing like this. Abdul suggested that they return some evening for dinner, when they would be served lamb on a spit— "melts in your mouth"—and rice such as they never tasted. Abdul said that they still had time, if their legs held out, to visit the original wall of Herod's Temple and a new archaeological site that was being excavated nearby. After which he would drive them back to the Mishkenot, where they could rest before dinner. Barbara would just as soon have gone back to her bedroom at the Mishkenot, but Philip

was still filled with enthusiasm, and since his face no longer pained
him as much as it had, he was eager to go on with his exploration
of the Old City. Once, Abdul told them, there had been nothing
but wooden shacks and garbage in front of what was then called
the Wailing Wall, but that was all cleared away after the Israelis
took Jerusalem, and today there was a great plaza in its stead.
Barbara, determined to remain placid and willing, agreed; and off
they went to Herod's wall.

The space before the Wall was governed by Orthodox Jews,
as Abdul informed them with some annoyance, and he gave Philip
a yarmulke to cover his head and warned Barbara to cover her bare
arms with her sweater, telling them that men and women were separated at the great Wall, and must leave their prayers, if they desired
to pray, in separate places. The prayers were to be written on bits
of paper, curled up, and left in the crevices between the stones,
where, so it was said, God received them gratefully. Barbara con-
tained herself, and Philip said he would just as soon whisper his
prayers; and Abdul apologized for such foolishness but reminded
them that religion was religion.

They were impressed with the height and strength of the two-
thousand-year-old wall but found the archaeological dig more fascinating. Half a dozen young men and women were carefully excavating
what might have been an old tomb or place of worship. They were blue
eyed and blond, and when Barbara asked who they were, she was told
by Abdul that they were archaeology students from Sweden.

"They're not Jewish, are they?"

"They could be Swedish Christians, but these happen to be
Jewish. They're from Sweden, so they look like Swedes."

BACK AT THE MISHKENOT FINALLY, Barbara dropped onto her
bed, with a sigh of satisfaction. She was silent for quite a while, her
eyes closed, and Philip thought she was asleep. But then she opened
her eyes and stared at Philip.

"Why not talk about it?" Philip asked.

"To what end?"

"I love you. We're man and wife, and I hope we'll be man and wife for the rest of our lives."

"I hope so, too. But a good part of it is not to hurt each other."

"Good heavens, did I hurt you?"

"No, no, dear Philip, but if I tell you my reactions, I'll hurt you terribly."

"You couldn't do anything to hurt me."

"Ah, well, Philip, that may or may not be so. I wish we hadn't gone to that museum they call the Old City. If I were the prime minister of this land, I'd tear it all down and build a park. For two thousand years, we Christians have murdered millions of Jews—six million in the Holocaust, and God only knows how many millions before that—"

"I'm afraid they'd lynch anyone who even dared to suggest that they tear it down."

"Yes, I suppose so. It's probably the greatest sideshow on earth. And did you notice the Israeli soldiers who guard the Via Dolorosa every step of the way—not against the Christians but against the possibility that the Arabs might interfere with Christian worship. Why don't the Jews hate us?"

"Because they're Jews."

"What does that say? Explain it to me," Barbara demanded.

"I can't. That's why I became a Unitarian."

"Were you a Unitarian today?"

Philip smiled, reached for her hand, took it, and kissed the palm. "I suppose I'm many things," he said gently. "We're all many things. The Buddhists say that when we become one thing, then we are enlightened. I know that this speck of cosmic dust we call the earth is one of billions of stars and planets in a limitless universe, and now the physicists are saying that all we see is an illusion, a momentary play of forces. And I know all the crimes and horrors of Christianity through the ages—perhaps better than you do. The Jesuits trained me well, and they don't look for loopholes in the truth. Perhaps the Via Dolorosa and the Church of the Holy Sepulcher are inventions, but I felt something mysterious and heartrending—perhaps a vibration from the people who were there, perhaps something in myself—but I felt it. You didn't feel it. We are different. I love you for what you are, compassionate and merciful. In my mind, you are the best Christian I have ever known."

"I'm not a Christian," Barbara said bluntly. "I had not taken communion since I was a child. What happened in Westminster was for you."

"Then I love you for whatever you are."

She broke into laughter. "Philip, my darling, how can I argue with you? And all that white gook has come off your head, so you had better go into the bathroom and smear yourself up again. How are the blisters?"

"They're coming along nicely."

"Well, that's something positive. Sarah told me that Teddy Kollek left a message that he is taking us to dinner tonight at eight o'clock, and it's after five right now. I want to have a nap, as befits an old lady."

Mr. Kollek took them to a Jewish restaurant in West Jerusalem, the New City, where they were welcomed like visiting dignitaries. They were overwhelmed with food and wine. Kollek had read one of Barbara's books that had been translated into Hebrew, the most personal of her books, which told of her journey to El Salvador and her experience there with the guerrilla movement, and he appeared delighted to meet them. He enthralled them with the history of Jerusalem, its captures by the Babylonians, the Egyptians, the Greeks, the Arabs, the Turks, the Crusaders, and finally the British and the Arab Legion. "But now it's ours, and you must see every part of it." Barbara had the feeling that he *was* Jerusalem, that there was no separation between himself and the city. The peace in Jerusalem was his peace; every house built, every shop opened, was his house and his shop. Mostly he spoke of the New City of west Jerusalem, the housing, the growth into a great metropolis. The only bit of annoyance he displayed was his anger at the architectural critic of the *New York Times*, who had dared to complain about the towering high-rise apartment houses. "But we have so little land. If we don't go up, we take away farmland."

He mentioned that some members of the Knesset, the Israeli Parliament, then in session, had asked whether Philip would appear there and say a few words, but Philip begged off, pleading that he had done nothing worthy of mention. Kollek agreed that if it caused him pain, he could avoid it, and Barbara found herself liking this plainspoken burly man more and more. He embraced the city, and he told them that now that they had seen the Old City he would tell Abdul where to take them. "There are two places here you must visit. One is Yad Vaskow, our memorial to the six million who died in the Holocaust. The other is our museum and sculpture garden."

"The memorial hill," Philip said. "Yes, I have read about it."

"You speak Hebrew?"

"A little. I can understand it when it's spoken slowly."

"Nobody in Israel speaks slowly," Kollek said. "Everyone is in a hurry in Israel. Everything must be done yesterday. But I will give Abdul a dressing-down. Too much for the first day."

"No, he's delightful," Barbara said.

"Yes, but take your time. Stay as long as you wish. You must go to the Galilee and see Lake Kineret, and perhaps to the Negev, where you will see what we have done to the desert. You are a writer," he said to Barbara. "You must see the miracle we have worked, and then you will be able to write about it in a different way."

FOR THE NEXT NINE DAYS Barbara and Philip, with Abdul at the wheel, roamed through Israel. They saw all that Teddy Kollek had suggested and more. They drove to the Lebanon border in the north and to the Negev and the Dead Sea in the south, and for the first time Barbara had a sense of what Bernie, her first husband, had given his life for.

"This is not a honeymoon," she finally told Philip. "It's a lesson in something, but I'm not sure exactly what . . . I'm three days away from my birthday, and I want to go home."

"When?"

"Tomorrow—if we can get seats."

The following day they left Israel on a flight to Geneva, the only passage they could get on short notice. They remained in Geneva for a single day, so that they might see at least one city in Switzerland. Then they flew to Kennedy Airport in New York, remained overnight, and then went on to San Francisco.

On the flight to San Francisco, Barbara said to Philip, "I was seventy yesterday, or is it today, or is today yesterday? I think it was yesterday. I'm very tired. I don't want to ever go anywhere again—except perhaps to Highgate. I gave Abdul fifty dollars. Do you think that was enough?"

"I gave him fifty dollars," Philip confessed.

"Then it's enough. He's a canny Egyptian."

"Well, we did get to the Holy Land. I got that out of my system."

"Thank goodness. And it rained all the time we were in New York."

"So it did."

"Do you still love me, Philip?"

"That was never in question. Do you still love me?"

"Even with no hair. But I'm glad you got rid of that white gook you had to smear on. You look almost human."

"Thank you," he said.

"Well, it's nice to be married to an old man. You don't worry about his appearance."

"Thank you again," Philip said.

The Sermon

INSIDE THE HOUSE ON GREEN STREET, their luggage still piled in the living room, the two of them drinking coffee in the kitchen, Barbara said, "I'm still uncertain whether it's tomorrow or yesterday. As for the mail, we could hardly get the door open, there was such a pile of it. When am I going to answer all those letters? I don't dare roll back the answering machine. Also, we have to learn to be unimportant. We no longer have a small country at our disposal, willing to pay all our bills. You got the short end of it, my dear. You paid the fare, I went along for the ride."

"We're not unimportant, Barbara. Every human being—"

"Philip."

He paused.

"Philip," Barbara said sternly, "I love you because you're kind and brave and loving, and because you're my husband. I will always love you. You had begun to say that every human being is important. I will not be married to a saintly man. You are a human being. You're not obligated to be personally responsible for every other human being. That's God's job. Leave a little bit for God. Every human being is not important in *our* scheme of things. Every human being may be born equal, but some are more equal than others. Millions and millions die of hunger and war—"

"Barbara, you're angry with me."

"Oh no, no. How could I be angry with you?"

"Yes, I was going to say that every human being is important. I believe that."

She went to him and kissed him. "Why do you put up with me?"

"Very simple. You put up with me."

"I'm going to call Eloise now. Can you get the bags upstairs by yourself?"

"Absolutely. No problem at all."

He took the bags up to the second floor, and Barbara called Eloise, who exploded with delight and excitement. "Barbara, you're back! I'm so delighted. You don't know how I've missed you—and we missed your birthday, but all your presents are piled up here, and it's only a few days to Thanksgiving, and so we will celebrate then—and so much has happened in the few weeks you were gone. I won't try to go into it over the phone, but you must drive down tomorrow."

"Eloise, darling, that's impossible. We've just walked through the door. There's a mountain of mail, parcels and letters and newspapers and all the junk mail, and somehow I must go through it and try to answer some of it. Philip has the church, and he must get to his office and try to catch up. But I promise you, we will be there at least a day before Thanksgiving, so we'll have time to talk and tell you everything."

"And how is the wonderful Philip? Was he badly burned? We couldn't find out through the newspaper accounts, and your postcards were brief to a point of utter frustration."

"Oh, Philip is fine. He has practically no hair, but there is a nice fuzz coming in, and the blisters are healed. Bald men are interesting, don't you think?"

"Barbara, how can you joke about something like that?"

"My dear Eloise, without a sense of humor, no one could survive being married to Philip. No, he's upstairs and can't hear me. We'll speak again soon. I trust the family is well?"

"We're all good. Bless you for coming home alive."

Philip came down the stairs, and Barbara told him that Eloise had blessed her for coming home alive. "A sort of paradox—how else did she expect us to come home?"

"She's a dear soul. I started to unpack, but I don't know where things go—I mean your things—and what should be washed. If you'll direct me, I'll finish."

"Philip, for heaven's sake, go to your office. I'll unpack. I have the whole day ahead of me, and tomorrow and the next day. Don't worry. Just go off to the church, and I'll know where to find you."

He embraced her, kissed her, and left; and Barbara slumped into a chair and wept.

What is wrong with me? she asked herself. *Why on God's earth am I so unhappy? My first husband was the ultimate macho who spent most of his life as a soldier and who died in some bleak desert spot in Israel, and I am a pacifist who has fought against war all her life, and I could love him so much—but would I have loved him if he had lived? Why couldn't I live with Carson? Why did I have to divorce him? Why do I love men so, and find it so difficult to live with them? Why in hell am I so confused? I married the best man I have ever known—why can't I be happy with him?*

It lasted only a few minutes, and then she shook her head, wiped away the tears, and told herself that she would love Philip, that she would learn to love him and be kind and thoughtful to him and never allow him to know what she felt at this moment. *Only this moment. It comes and it goes. We had good days in England and*

Israel, and now I have work to do. I'm seventy years old, and I can
still wear the dresses I bought twenty-five years ago, and Teddy Kollek
told Philip that he thought I was beautiful, and even if he says that to
half the women he meets, it's not bad at seventy. I have been on the
side of decent people all my life, and I think I can say as Blake said,
"I will not cease from mental fight,/Nor shall my sword sleep in my
hand,/Till we have built Jerusalem"—no, not the Jerusalem I saw—
but a place where Philip's belief in the importance of every human being
is real—oh, for heaven's sake, Barbara, you are an absolute manic-
depressive case history, and a moment ago you were in tears, and your
only hope is the fact that they say that if you know you are crazy,
you're not crazy at all—the catch-22 that Heller wrote about so
beautifully.

And then, in her study, she saw her unfinished manuscript lying
neatly in a wooden box on her desk. It was irresistible, and, filled
with remorse, like a mother who has abandoned and put her child
out of her mind, she greedily read the last two pages. There she
was in North Africa, talking to Italian prisoners of war; and now
something one of them had said flashed into her mind. She put paper
into the typewriter and began to write, and ran onto a second page;
and she was lost to Green Street and the telephone messages and
the unpacking—when the telephone rang.

It was Birdie MacGelsie, calling to welcome her home and tell
her she was scheduled to speak before the Women's Democratic
Committee the week before Christmas, and wasn't Philip wonderful?

"Absolutely wonderful, yes." The spell of North Africa and
the Italian prisoners was broken. Almost sadly, Barbara covered her
typewriter.

Then Barbara ran the tape on her answering machine, made
notes on the twenty-three calls the tape held before it gave out, and
went upstairs to unpack.

———

THE DAY BEFORE THANKSGIVING Eloise walked with Barbara to the rear of the bottling plant at Highgate. There in an enclosure with a shed at one end were two large white turkeys and six small ones. "The large hen," she explained, "is Murtle. The enormous cock—and well named—is Turtle. The kids know the names of the small ones. I can't tell one from another."

"Do you mean," Barbara asked, unable to keep a note of horror out of her voice, "that we're going to eat that beautiful bird tomorrow? Eloise, I don't believe it."

"Of course not. Do you think I'm a barbarian? I brought you here because this has become a moral question at Highgate. Adam bought the breeding pair about a year ago. He decided that we might just as well raise our own turkeys. The six small ones are their children. Do you remember Adam, when I first met him at your mother's gallery? He was the sweetest, gentlest young man I had ever met. But when Sally and I said that we couldn't dream of killing and cooking that beautiful, stupid bird, he really lost his temper. He almost never loses his temper. After forty years of marriage, he's turned into an irascible, bearded creature out of the Old Testament. He considers himself a farmer. Can you imagine, with this enormous institution that Highgate has become, he considers himself a farmer!"

Barbara, watching the birds with fascination, smiled and said, "Did you know, Ellie, that Benjamin Franklin suggested making the turkey the national bird of America? He argued that the woods abounded with them, that they made good eating, and that they were altogether noble. The bald eagle, on the other hand, was a killer of small creatures and very bad eating."

"I think he had a point," Eloise agreed.

"And how did you resolve it?"

"Well, when May Ling and Freddie joined in and said they wouldn't touch a bite of Turtle, and May Ling is pregnant, and

Adam is so pleased about having another kid on the place—well, Adam relented and became human again."

"So it's no turkey for Thanksgiving?"

"Of course not. I went down to Napa and bought one of those frozen twenty-pound monsters that are all breast. It's been defrosting for a week, and it will be perfect for tomorrow night."

Barbara stared at Eloise. "Hold on, Ellie. Don't you think there's something wrong in your reasoning?"

"Not at all. What would Thanksgiving be without a turkey? It's the best of all holidays, and Clair, who never knew where the next meal was coming from when she was a kid, used to say that it was a perfectly Christian thing to do to worship food for one day a year, and can you imagine how disappointed everyone would be if we didn't have a turkey?" And then, after a moment, Eloise added, "You're always so reasonable, Barbara, but nothing in this world makes real sense. Adam lost his brother in World War Two, and then when that madness in Vietnam destroyed our son Joshua, Adam and I could have gone out of our minds. But we didn't. We worked it through, and we still had Freddie—and I must tell you about Freddie. Are you cold?"

"No, not at all." Both women were wearing heavy sweaters, Eloise a tightly knit red sweater with a hood, and Barbara a hand-knit Irish sweater. "But it does get cold here in the afternoon."

"Let's walk up the hill to our old place. We'll have a good talk, and we can have a fire. I have matches with me, and there's always plenty of wood there."

"You really want to build a fire, Ellie? We haven't had one up there in years."

"Just a small one. Philip is somewhere with Adam, giving him a history of Israel, I'm sure. Adam is becoming very Jewish, patriarch-style. I argue with him that his mother was Presbyterian, so by Jewish law, he's not Jewish at all."

"Why not let him be Jewish if he wants to?"

"I'm almost hesitant to tell you, but I'm going to church this Christmas. Chalk it up to age. I want Adam to come with me."

"That's the least he could do," Barbara said.

"Do you ever go to church, Barbara?"

"Well, I do go to hear Philip preach. That's where I met him, you know. But real church, Grace Cathedral—no, only for funerals. I'm not a church person. You know, Sam's daughter was never baptized. He's also decided to be Jewish, same process as Adam. And Mary Lou is pregnant again. She's younger than May Ling, but not much. They do wait to the last minute."

"That's wonderful. I love family, and the more the better. And Sally's Daniel is going with someone. I haven't met her yet, but— well, just perk up your ears. She's Chinese."

"Oh no! That's great."

"She's coming to dinner tomorrow. And Freddie—no, I'm saving that."

They didn't build a fire after all; Barbara was tired by the climb more than it had ever tired her before, and they would have to come down before sunset. Even with Eloise's guidance, Barbara did not trust herself to come down the hillside in the darkness. They sat together on the bench, leaning against each other for warmth. "Now, about Freddie?" Barbara said.

"There are two parts to it," Eloise began, "and it's incredible that so much has happened since you left. Well, maybe there are three parts to it. Harry has given up lawyering, and he and May Ling, together with Freddie and Adam, have purchased the Hawthorn Winery down the road. May Ling was unhappy in San Francisco, and they've given up their apartment there. Harry is converted to wine—totally."

"Oh no—no, I don't believe it."

"Then you won't believe the rest of it. Adam has agreed to have them specialize in Chardonnay. Well, the market for white wine is growing and Adam has to be realistic—although there's some word out of France that red wine is life prolonging—nothing much yet, but Freddie has been corresponding with a French vintner who's trying to get some scientists to investigate it statistically."

"Harry and May Ling here in the Valley—"

"And the little boy is happy—now that he has his own Highgate."

"Do they have a house on the place?"

"A lovely house," Eloise said. "We'll drop over there tomorrow, if we can find time. But let me get on to the second part of the Freddie story. He's become part of the faculty at Berkeley. They invited him to give a weekly seminar on winemaking during the next semester. He's as excited as a kid about it. Tuesday nights. He's going to drive in every Tuesday next year, and the first person to sign up for the course was Harry. I think his relationship with Harry is remarkable, considering that Freddie was once married to May Ling."

"Freddie is civilized," Barbara agreed. "He's been around the course and he's paid his dues. He put his life on the line when he went down South for the registration drive, and he almost lost it. I love Freddie."

"And he's kept Highgate going. Adam is no businessman. He grows grapes and makes wine, but if it weren't for Freddie this place would collapse. And I'm glad that he teamed up with Harry. Harry's very smart. But let me tell you the rest of it. You won't believe it—but just listen. Judith is pregnant."

"I knew that. But I thought she had lost the baby in the accident."

"Yes, which is exactly what Judith and Freddie thought, and if you can believe it, neither of them spoke to the doctor about it, and they just went mooning along like a couple of idiot children, and she missed her second period. Then, finally, she had herself examined, and there she was, healthy and pregnant and into the second trimester, and she told her mother about it, and her mother told her father, and the wedding is to take place next week in a Baptist church in Oakland. I would have written to you, but I didn't know when you were leaving Israel, and this was not something I could tell you over the phone. Would you have believed it, Barbara—you and May Ling and now Freddie and Judith."

"How did her father react?" Barbara wondered aloud.

"From all I hear, he was in a royal rage but then quieted down and finally took it with good grace. Judith was terrified. Freddie is happy as a clam. He's babbling about building a house on that stone outcropping on the hillside. So if it goes through, we'll have another child here. Anyway, Judith will be here tomorrow with her father and mother, so I'll have two of the girls in the kitchen to help Cathrena. I don't know how I'm going to survive it, but I will. And there I've been talking all afternoon, and I haven't even asked you about Philip and your trip."

What should she say? Barbara asked herself. That she had married a good man who was driving her up the wall? Or that she hadn't the vaguest notion who she, Barbara Lavette Carter, was; or that she was content and unhappy, selfish and unselfish, bewildered and unable to live with Philip or to live without him? Would Eloise understand—or would Eloise listen in total confusion? One thing she had come to realize—she could never leave Philip. She accepted that. Philip should have married someone like Eloise, but he had fallen in love with Barbara and married her.

"Philip . . . ," Barbara said, and then she hesitated and paused for a long moment. "Philip is a dear, saintly man—it's not a bit easy for an old warhorse like me to be married to a saintly man, but I'm working it out."

FOR PHILIP THE PROBLEM WAS even more inscrutable. He was a sensitive man, and he had been quite sincere when he said to Barbara that she was one of the most religious persons he had ever known;

but a religion without faith, without any belief other than a compassion for human beings, or for that matter for all living things—he had watched her delight in the three dogs that had the range of Highgate—such was beyond his understanding. Being Philip, he looked at his own faith, examined it as he never had before, and refused in any way to blame Barbara. He was deeply moved when he learned that in his absence, when news of his experience at the bus appeared in the press, his congregation had prayed for his recovery, not yet knowing the seriousness of his burns, and had lit candles. There was nothing in the doctrine of Unitarianism—if indeed it could be named a doctrine—that called for faith or a belief in the mystery of man's being. His own faith was deep inside him, so deep that he had never actually questioned it.

Having lived for so long without family of any kind, without even his wife, Agatha, he had taken to Barbara's extended and marvelously mixed family with delight. It was like the consummation of impossible dreams, and he adored Barbara and even bore the guilt of realizing that this was a new kind of love, in his mind almost pagan in the sexual passion he felt for her and in his willingness to learn newly how to make love to a woman.

He had always felt that the sermon he delivered Christmas Eve was the most important sermon of the year—a feeling he kept to himself. He would make notes and begin to lay it out starting around Thanksgiving Day. He had none of Barbara's facility in writing. When he read her *Notes of a War Correspondent* and was informed that she had written much of it on an old portable typewriter at the place where the things she wrote of were happening, he had reacted with awe. Himself, he struggled with each word—started and threw everything away, and started again and again. Finally he realized that he could not write about his own experience in Israel without first understanding Barbara's experience.

Lying in bed that night, propped up on one elbow and watching Barbara as she brushed her hair, Philip said to her, "Barbara, if ever you should tire of me and no longer wish to live with me, I shall expect you to tell me so. No fuss and no bother."

"Now, what on earth brought that on?"

Philip shook his head. "I simply wanted you to know."

"Suppose I didn't want to know?"

"Yes, I should have thought of that."

She crawled into bed and put her arms around him. "I suppose it's your hair. You were very vain about your hair, Philip dear, but I'm quite used to this. Kiss me. I don't think that when a man and a woman make love, they should talk about it, even old folks like us. I do love you very much, but if you ever again apologize for loving me—well, you've seen me angry."

"Yes, I have," he admitted.

"Now make love to me. No more talking. No more apologies."

They made love, and after that, content and fulfilled, Barbara fell asleep. Philip remained awake, and asleep she moved close to him, throwing an arm around him. He dared not move for fear of waking her, and in time he slept, their bodies intertwined.

IN THE MORNING AT BREAKFAST, Freddie warned them to eat lightly. "I've been rereading Ring Lardner's story 'Thanksgiving.' Do you suppose I should read it to the guests before dinner?" he asked his mother.

"Don't you dare!" Eloise said. "I hate that story."

"Very piggish," Barbara agreed, and to Philip's blank look added, "It's about overeating. Sometimes I like Ring Lardner, sometimes I don't. I think he's brilliant, and he wrote with a knife. His brilliance is forgotten today. That's the fate of so many good writers. But such a savage commentary on Thanksgiving—well, I don't know."

"I hear you're going down to Harry's place today."

"I was going," Eloise said, "but I can't. I have to stay with Cathrena. Do you know how many we have for dinner tonight? At least eighteen, not counting the children. I'm going to feed them first. Freddie, are you sure Judith is bringing her mother and father?"

"Yes, and for heaven's sake, embrace them, kiss them. This isn't easy for them. Maybe it's the hardest thing they ever faced."

"Your mother knows that, Freddie," Barbara said sharply.

"How old is Jean?" Adam asked, anxious to change the subject.

"Four—or five. Which is it, Barbara?"

Jean was Sam's little girl. "I'm ashamed to say I'm not sure, perhaps four and a half. I'm a rotten grandmother."

Freddie said apologetically, "It's just that I'm nervous. Judith isn't bulging much yet, but—well, weddings are terribly serious to the Hopes. They're very religious and very straitlaced, and I haven't seen them since Judith told them."

"It will be all right," Eloise assured him. This is not the first time it's happened."

"Let's not anticipate." Barbara smiled. "Just go with the flow."

"I'll walk them down to Hawthorn," Freddie said. He turned to Adam. "Harry sent over four cases of Greenberg's Chardonnay. He's loaded with it. I've been trying to find a buyer in Los Angeles. They'll drink anything with 'Chardonnay' on the label."

"We won't serve it tonight. I won't give it to guests," Adam said firmly.

"It's not bad at all," Eloise said. "You two remind me of Hemingway and all his nonsense about noble wines. Why shouldn't we serve it? I will not offend Harry."

"It's not Harry's vintage. It's Greenberg's."

"Well," Freddie said, "Dr. Hope likes red wine."

"That does it!" Adam declared. "I will not have the father of Judith Hope drinking Greenberg's lousy Chardonnay. Sell the rest of it out in L.A. for whatever you can get."

"Pop," Freddie said, his tone gentle and conciliatory, "I have the solution. We have a case of Cohen's Chardonnay left over from the wedding. It's very good. I also have some lovely dry Chablis that I've been experimenting with. I'll put some Hawthorn labels on it, and Harry will be delighted. We'll all of us here drink the Cabernet."

"Good heavens!" Eloise exclaimed. "You talk like we're a family of drunks. How much wine do we need?"

"A lot," Freddie said. "We give six white and six red to Candido for Thanksgiving. He knows more about wine than any of us."

"Watch Adam," Barbara whispered to Philip, who was listening in amazement. "He admits to no one knowing more about wine than he does."

Adam's face tightened, but he said nothing. Eloise said soothingly, "Dr. Hope will drink your best Cabernet. In fact, this might be the time to open a bottle or two of the Rothschild, if you have any left. This is a joyous occasion. Enough talk. Now, Freddie, take Barbara and Philip down to Hawthorn. It's a cold morning, so wrap up. The walk will do you all good."

The stroll down the old Silverado Trail on this fine November morning was a treat in itself. The sky was steel blue, the air sweet and clean. The road was unspoiled, much as it had been fifty years ago, except for blacktopping; no towns, no stands, just the old oaks and hemlocks and an occasional ponderosa pine. As they walked, Philip observed that wine was a sort of religion in this place.

"Not religion," Freddie said. "It's a way of life. The big places, like Gallo, have tried to turn it into a science, but the really great wines are the result of the vintners' experience and instinct. Take Sauterne, for example. You can make a dozen different Sauternes, from a sweet dessert wine to a dry table wine that is as good as anything California produces. We make some Sauterne at Highgate, and we label it table wine. We blend in some Thompson grapes, which are usually considered to be table grapes, and it's been enormously successful."

"Then why don't you serve it tonight?" Barbara wondered.

"We sold it all, every last bit of it. It's a point of honor not to go into wine that has been sold or promised, and anyway, it's not dry enough for Adam's taste. And while it's very good, Pop is a sort of château freak. Don't get me wrong, I love Adam—but we fight like cats and dogs. When I insisted on calling this simply dry table wine, he gave in, but not very willingly. There's no such thing as a super-great wine or noble wine, not even the Imperial Tokay, of which we produce a few gallons out of seeds from the emperor Franz Joseph's winery. Mother, who knows more about wine than she would admit to, read a book by Hemingway in which he talks about a noble wine, and Mother was ready to scream. She agrees with Adam that Highgate Cabernet is as good as any claret wine, and when I go to France I taste them all. Some are different, but I don't know that any are much better than ours. Joyce Ansel, who is the head of the department at the university and rates very high as an expert in viticulture, agrees with me. Of course, it depends on the year and the crop. There are great years and there are indifferent years. And the claret grapes that we depend on for the Cabernet also vary. But we're a business, and either we sell the wine or we go out of business."

Philip, who had listened to Freddie's discourse with fascination, mentioned the wine auctions where a single bottle fetches anywhere from a thousand to five thousand dollars, for the great names like Rothschild.

Freddie laughed. "They're buying a pig in a poke, and nobody knows what's in a bottle until it's opened. It's great publicity for the wine business, but there's no such thing as one wine being a thousand dollars better than another. When you come down to it, wine is wine, and if it's good, it's good, and if it's bad, it's bad.

Why don't you ask Adam about it tonight? I'd love to hear what he says."

"I don't dare," Philip said. "When it comes to the rites of wine, I'm just an onlooker."

"How is Judith taking tonight?" Barbara asked. "Is she nervous?"

Freddie shrugged. "You haven't seen her yet? She's absolutely beautiful. When she covers the scars, you'd never know. Her nose is different—well, you'll see her. She'll be here by noon. I told her what a crowd we're having, and in spite of my assuring her that we have adequate help, she wants to help Mother. Maybe that's not so crazy. Do you remember Steve Cassala?"

"Of course I do." And she explained to Philip, "Steve's father, Tony Cassala, financed my father and his partner, Mark Levy, in the shipping business. It's a long story and I won't go into it, but during the big earthquake the regular banks were burned or had their vaults locked by the heat. Tony Cassala used to lend money to and hold it for the Italian fishermen who didn't trust the big banks. So when the old banks burned, he became a banker—and grew into a very large one. But, Freddie, I invited Steve to the wedding. He and his wife, Joanna, never showed up. I thought perhaps he had died."

"Almost, but not quite. He's in better shape, and she's in good health. He's eighty-nine, but she's a good deal younger. She's coming with him and her sister, Rosa, and Rosa's husband, Frank Massetti."

"Your poor mother," Philip said.

"Don't pity her, Phil. She loves it."

Barbara, for all her good spirits, felt strangely tired, more tired than she had ever been after a walk of only a mile.

They were at Hawthorn now—signs of construction everywhere, piles of lumber and stone, a concrete mixer; the main house being enlarged, the bottling plant being reconstructed. "If it were not a holiday, there'd be a dozen trucks here. Harry is plunging in on this," Freddie told them.

Small Danny ran out to meet them, followed by May Ling and Harry, who appointed himself tour guide. Evidently the move to the Valley had overcome Danny's objections to his new father, although he ran to Freddie for hugs and kisses. Harry, totally enthralled with his new life, appointed himself guide, explaining that while some of the crop had already been sold, most of it would be turned into wine. He pointed out the mechanical crusher, which, he noted, would be replaced; it was too old. Only the juice of the grapes would be used, since this would be white wine. He explained, in spite of Freddie's presence, that for Chardonnay, the skins were discarded. "Fermentation begins," he said knowingly, "when wine yeast comes in contact with must—and of course, since the yeast is on the skins, we have to add yeast." Freddie remained silent as the lecture on winemaking went on and on—which Barbara regarded as a considerable improvement in Freddie's tolerance, since he had overseen the whole process of renewing the equipment.

Barbara slipped away, leaving Philip to be enlightened, and joined May Ling in the house, which was in utter disorder due to the presence of paint cans, wallpaper, and wood. "I have never been so happy," May Ling told her. "Oh, Barbara, San Francisco may be the most beautiful city in the world, and I'm sure it is, but I can't live in a city. I grew up in the Valley, and I want to spend the rest of my life here. I'm pregnant, and Daddy says that I'm doing fine and that I'm still young and strong, and that if I want another baby, I can have one. I'm only thirty-seven, and Daddy comes by every few days. I think he's the best doctor in the world. And Harry's an angel. Can you imagine giving up a practice like his to make wine? They wanted him back on some special case, but he simply won't leave the place. He says he has enough money."

"You're happy," Barbara said. "That's the main thing. I've never seen you so pleased before."

"When I tell Harry that it won't hurt a bit if he goes into the City for a day or two, he comes back with the story of his grandfather who would never dream of going back to Europe for fear that they wouldn't let him back here again. I think he has this strange feeling that if he goes into the City, they won't let him back into the Valley."

"He'll get over that. But Judith—in every case I've ever heard of where a woman goes through that kind of trauma, she loses the child."

"Except when she doesn't."

"Yes," Barbara agreed, "except when she doesn't."

"You see, she took it for granted that the pregnancy was over—never told the doctors about it. That woman's wonderful," Eloise said. "The newest thing in advertising is the pregnant woman. The unmentionable has become big business, in childbearing clothes, and now Frank Halter—he's the number-one fashion photographer in the City—can't wait for her to bulge properly. He has a job for *Vanity Fair*, and they want him to do four pages of her. They want one of them to be a nude from the side, and the money they want to pay her is sinful. But she talked it over with her father, and he put his foot down, and the magazine agreed that she could wear something diaphanous—but she says that Halter is getting impatient because she isn't bulging enough."

"Give her time. She'll bulge."

"She's so tall and strong—you know, she's six feet."

"She could be seven feet," Barbara assured her, "but you can't do it without bulging. Is the child all right?"

"As far as they can tell at this time."

"And the wedding's next week. It seems that I can't go away for a few days without the world turning topsy-turvy. How is Adam taking all this?"

May Ling smiled. "He's an old dear. He wanted to have another mammoth party here after the wedding, but Freddie and Judith

wouldn't hear about it. We're having only family at the wedding—
it's a small church. Adam has done a complete about-face. Well,
everyone thinks it's wonderful, and Adam feels he's a pathfinder
into a new world, as if this were the first interracial marriage that
ever took place. Do you know, Bobby darling, my only fear is that
they won't be content to live on a farm and will go back to the
City."

"Highgate is hardly a farm, and the City's only an hour away.
She hasn't given up her house, has she?"

"No. She has a pool there, I'm told, and believe it or not,
Adam talks about building a pool here."

"I'll believe that," Barbara said, "when I see it."

"But, darling, I never even asked you how you are? And poor
Philip, with that short thatch of new hair."

"I'm all right," Barbara replied. "I seem to have gotten so
tired during the trip, and it's so hard to shake it off. But Philip's
made of steel. He never complained about his burns. It's that damn
Christian lust for flagellation; the more it hurts, the more he smiles
and bears it."

"And how goes the marriage?" May Ling asked.

"*Comme ci, comme ça*—marriages are made not in heaven but
by ordinary mortals. Sometimes I adore him, sometimes he drives
me up the wall."

"But he's so decent and kind."

"That's it."

"I'll never understand," May Ling said.

"No, darling. Don't even try to understand. The very fact that
this family can live so close without shredding each other to pieces
is a miracle of sorts—you and Freddie, for example."

May Ling shook her head. "I never will understand Freddie.
Never mind. I must show you the kitchen." She led Barbara through
the half-deconstructed house and into a big square room. "The
kitchen was the size of a snuffbox, Barbara. So I tore down the wall

between the kitchen and what was the dining room, and now I have a room twenty-two feet square. Harry was all for it. I think he believes that every winery must have a kitchen the size of Highgate's. I threw out everything that was in there. We're going to do it all in Mexican tiles. Next week I'm going into San Francisco to pick out the kitchen stuff. Will you come with me?"

"I'd love to go with you. I'm sure you know by now that I will grasp any opportunity not to write. Writing is like a man you adore and hate at the same time. Very perplexing. All my books until now were out of some part of my own experience—but now I'm trying to write about the family. Very frustrating. Sarah and Mark, Jake and Clair Harvey, my brother Tom, my father and mother, all the agonies and pleasures and deaths, three wars—it's impossible. But I'm not that good at shopping anymore. After half an hour, all I want is to sit down and rest."

"Then we will."

"Try to find a chair in some of those stores! And won't Sally be hurt? I mean, if you don't consult her."

"Then let her be hurt," May Ling said in a rare display of independence.

Barbara looked at her approvingly. Tall, slender, her skin a pale brown, her eyes almost black, the one-quarter Chinese so marked and beguiling—this was a new May Ling, happy and assured.

"No, I don't mean that," May Ling said quickly. "I love Mother, but this is my life and my place. I will have a lovely room for her and Dad whenever they want to come. But it's my house."

Barbara threw her arms around her and kissed her.

IF THERE WERE A STAR or at least a focal point for that Thanksgiving Day at Highgate, it was without question Judith. As she had promised, she turned up shortly after noon. Barbara was in the kitchen with Eloise and Cathrena, helping to set the big table, which had been extended three feet by a wooden frame that Candido had hurriedly knocked together. Eloise had found two identical table-cloths that would cover the length of it. Eloise was consulting with Barbara about the place cards when Freddie appeared with Judith. A fire was already burning in the big fireplace, and by dinnertime it would be a bed of hot coals with a single large log glowing above the coals. The room was warm with the smell of good food—the enormous turkey in the oven, the cranberries turning into sauce on the stove, the great pot of sweet potatoes simmering, the vegetables being cut, five pies getting their crusts, dough rolled out for dinner rolls, and Cathrena scolding one of her helpers for cutting the dinner rolls too small.

It was at this point of both confusion and activity that Freddie appeared with Judith. Barbara's first reaction was that Judith had lost weight, the strong bones of her face more prominent, and that there was something different about her nose, a certain sharpness; yet she was the same Judith, easy and graceful. She wore blue jeans and a blue work shirt, but she explained to Eloise that she had "fancy clothes," as she put it, in her car and would change before dinner. "I'm here to help, Mrs. Levy," Judith said. "These jeans, they're a badge of work willingness."

"First of all, call me Ellie. Everyone else does. Secondly, Barbara and I are trying to work out the table, and then we'll set it. Can you make twist rolls?"

"Absolutely."

"Then take over from Rosa, who can't. That will release Cathrena for other things. Adam, my husband, insists on twist rolls; and then we'll have a large challah—that's the Jewish festival bread—and Cathrena will give you the measurements."

"You'll want eggs in that, won't you?"

"Oh yes, probably six eggs for the large loaf. Cathrena knows—I'm not sure. But how do you know that?"

"Jewish friends, Jewish bakeries—one right down the street from where my mom lives."

"Your folks will find their way here, won't they?"

"Oh yes, they'll be here." She rolled up her sleeves and went to work quickly, expertly, as if she had been making bread all her life. "We've been to the Valley so many times. They know just where Highgate is. I love to make bread," she assured Eloise. "I've done it before."

AN HOUR LATER, HAVING FINISHED the seating and setting the table, Eloise and Barbara betook themselves to the living room with mugs of coffee, and Eloise lit one of her infrequent cigarettes. The living room at Highgate was a bit larger than the kitchen—twenty-two feet by thirty feet—with a large fireplace that backed the kitchen fireplace and fed into the same stone chimney, encircled by three sofas: two seven-foot couches and one eight-foot couch. There was a grand piano that both Eloise and Freddie played, a television set in one corner, bookshelves on either side of the fireplace, a long table backing the big couch, an eighteen-foot grospoint Portuguese rug with a pattern of pink roses, and armchairs scattered about. The ceiling was beamed, and above a wooden wainscoting, the walls were painted stark white. On the walls were paintings from Jean Lavette's gallery, given to Eloise and Adam as wedding gifts: one a Renoir and another a Picasso; plus a large painting of a Levy–Lavette freighter and a painting of Adam's brother, Joshua, who had died in World War II. There were also groups of family photographs and a glass breakfront containing medals and awards won by Highgate wines.

Barbara loved the room, its comfortable old-fashioned look and its fireplace—lit that morning and now full of glowing embers, as in the kitchen.

After they had collapsed onto a sofa and Eloise had lit her

cigarette, Barbara said, "Well, what do you think?" It was obvious
to whom she referred.

"I think I'm in awe of her. I suppose it's my own fault that
I've known so few black people. To be perfectly honest, it is my
pleasure to embrace her as a prospective daughter-in-law and take
her to my heart. I almost accused Adam of being a racist, and I was
very angry with him for no good reason at all. Do you think I'm
a racist?"

"No more than we all are. Give it time. There are thousands
of people who are racist about Chicanos, but we've lived with them
all our lives. The important thing is that Freddie loves her."

"He adores her."

"Yes, he does," Barbara agreed.

"I can see that part of it," Eloise acknowledged. "I often ask
myself whether I'm not the major reason Freddie has never married
successfully. He's a brilliant businessman and manager, and if truth
be told, we would have failed long ago were it not for Freddie.
We can't produce enough of his dry Sauterne—and if it were up
to Adam, we'd have no white wine at all—and his partnership with
Harry is exactly what we needed, a Chardonnay that we'll sell like
hotcakes. But so long as I'm around—well, he's forty-three in
January."

Barbara smiled. "Darling," she said, "don't go psychological
on this."

"Barbara, would you call me a martinet?"

"As far in the other direction as one can get."

"But for years I ran this house and the guesthouse. I can't let
her walk all over me."

"What on earth makes you think she would? That performance
in the kitchen was introductory, for our benefit. They'll have their
own home. And believe me, she's not interested in housekeeping.
You'll probably never see her in the kitchen."

"Do you really think so?"

"Of course," Barbara assured her, reflecting that the appearance in the Highgate household of a woman as young and good-looking and robust as Judith could not help but shrink Eloise's self-image. How little the young knew about the old—and especially of that inner self in women like Eloise that retains its image and sense of youth. Barbara understood that completely. There had been a day when she and Philip were walking on the Embarcadero and a sight-seeing boat was about to pull away from the dock, and on impulse they bought the last two tickets and leaped onto the boat just as it was beginning to pole off, and they stood at the rail laughing like a couple of kids—to the curious looks of chronological youngsters on the deck.... She still brushed her hair as her mother had taught her to, twenty strokes at night, twenty strokes in the morning, and she would still stare at her mirror and deny the wrinkles. When her son, Sam, informed her that they had a new substance that when injected into a wrinkle would make it disappear, she indignantly assured him that she had earned every wrinkle and meant to keep them—her usual defense to Birdie MacGelsie, who had had a face-lift and urged Barbara to do the same. No, she, Barbara Lavette Carter, would never have a face-lift; yet she brooded over the notion.

ACTUALLY, THE THANKSGIVING DINNER worked out beautifully. Eloise seated Dr. Hope at the far end of the table, at Adam's left, with Freddie at Adam's right, and with Harry next to Freddie, so that the wine discussion might be localized. She instructed Rosa carefully in the pouring of the wine—the tall glasses for the white wine, the round ones for the red—"and keep them two-thirds full, and never, never mix them"—all of this in Spanish, to make certain Rosa understood. The Cassalas, in their late eighties or early nineties, were seated near Barbara on one side of the table, and near Philip on the other, both of them having volunteered their services for the two very old women and the two very old men. Barbara spoke of the old days, of the time of Mark Levy and Dan Lavette, of the run on the Cassala bank, of how Stephan had talked his father into financing the first shipping venture, of how Dan Lavette had courted the beautiful and wealthy Jean Seldon, of all the fascinating people who were dead and gone, and of how Admiral Emory Scott Land came from Washington and talked Dan Lavette into building liberty ships. For a few hours, these old people became young again, and Philip listened with fascination to Barbara as these two very old couples adjusted their hearing aids and resurrected the history of the Levys, the Lavettes, and the Cassalas.

The other guests and the children were spaced down the table, three physicians and their wives and the two children, both of whom Barbara and Eloise had decided must be a part of the company. Eloise sat at the near end of the table, the stove end, with Mrs. Hope on her right and Judith on her left. Two silver seven-branched candelabra lit the table; and a great log burned in the fireplace over the still-glowing bed of coals; and the turkey, carved by Adam, stood like a mound of worthy exuberance. The challah was not sliced, but broken by hand.

Philip suggested that they join hands for the blessing. "We are thankful for the goodness and love around this table, and for all the good memories." Eloise wept, thinking of her son who had lived to see none of this; and old Adam dried his tears and offered a toast: "*Shalom,*" to peace.

Judith chose red wine. She tasted from her goblet, smiled at Adam, and then drank more deeply. "What is it?" she asked reverentially.

"Highgate 1973," Adam replied.

"It's magnificent."

"The best year we ever had. We tried, but we never could do it again."

"What do you suppose does it, Adam?" Dr. Hope asked. "Is it a condition of the soil, or the weather, or something mysterious that you can't influence? And did you save enough for yourself?"

"We can save only so much. When we have a great year, we have to sell the wine. It's not just the money, but a year like 1973 is the best advertising in the world. To answer your question, Doctor, I simply don't know. Yes, the weather, the days of sun— well, God only knows. We have had two successive years of fine wine, but not like 1973."

"I feel honored," Dr. Hope said.

"We're honored by your daughter's entrance into the family, and by you and your good wife."

Freddie listened in amazement. This was not the Adam he knew, and this was perhaps the longest speech he had ever heard Adam make.

"How many bottles are left?" Adam asked Freddie.

"About two cases. I tried to save more. But we have a few outlets where they really know wine, and they pleaded, and we had to satisfy them. I'm saving one case for our wedding—if you will permit me, Pop?"

"I couldn't think of a better use for it."

"Did you ever think of putting some up for auction?" Harry asked.

"You can't get one of those prices for an American wine," Freddie reflected. "We worship the French. Yet I took a few bottles to France some years ago, and I could have sold them a thousand cases if we'd had it."

"It could happen again—although with the blight..." Adam shrugged.

"Still, it *could* happen again," Freddie said. "We make the best Cabernet in California. We also make a Pinot Noir that is not to be sneezed at. We use more than fifty-one percent of the Sauvignons in the blending. We keep a careful record of the blending and the aging casks. There are wineries that mix casks without a second thought. We keep careful records. We have records going back forty

years. We use eight percent more than the legal minimum of the
Sauvignons, but sometimes we vary that and vary the blending
grapes. We never mix casks."

"I'm new to all this, Dr. Hope," Harry said. "I bought a
winery down the road, the Hawthorn place. I'm learning how much
taste means. I'm sure it's a foolish question, but can you teach taste,
Adam?"

"Not foolish at all, Harry," Adam replied, in his element now.
"It's paramount. Taste is the only measure we have when it comes
to wine. But can we teach taste? Well, not really, but you can teach
people to recognize differences. When it comes to taste in clothes
or behavior, you can copy the taste of those you respect. Many of
the big wineries have professional tasters, either under contract or
intermittently—but then the winemaker must cast his hopes on the
taste of others. If you like wine, your taste will sharpen."

"We won't call Harry's white wine Chardonnay," Freddie said.
"Harry and I and Adam agree that it should be called Highgate
White Table Wine, and we're reaching toward a sort of dry Sauterne
Semillon—I've long been fighting a losing battle against the French
names. I think our wines are distinct, and we've done some blend-
ings, and Adam came on some that are very good, even though he
has a bias against white wine."

"For heaven's sake," Barbara cried out, "here's this poor man
at our Thanksgiving table for the first time, and you're boring him
to death with wine talk."

"Oh no, not boring at all," Dr. Hope protested. "This is a
wonderful new world."

"You're not boring Dad," Judith called out. "He's asked me
a thousand questions about this wine business, so please tell it all."

Freddie whispered to Harry, "I've had some labels printed
up, and I'll show them to you later—white paper, classy printing.
How about a price of a hundred and ten dollars a case, which is

rather high for a table wine, but we think the Highgate name will carry it?"

Barbara and Philip—having, along with the aged Cassalas, finished their genealogical recollections and turned to the turkey and trimmings—were now listening to the discussion at the end of the table. Philip, locked into a wine family, was fortunately endlessly fascinated by the lore of wine, and he wondered whether the Greeks and the Jews, the great wine producers of antiquity, had engaged in the same discussions. Certainly the methods had not changed a great deal.

Eloise attempted to apologize to Mrs. Hope for the wine talk, but Mrs. Hope said, "Thank goodness, because he won't talk about dentistry. You know, so many poor people can't afford any real dentistry at all, and they go to dentists who simply pull teeth— even if the cavity is tiny, they just pull the tooth and charge five dollars, which is sinful, and Dr. Hope doesn't do that. If a tooth has to be filled, he fills it, and if some poor patient can't pay, he charges the same five dollars or nothing at all, because he's a good decent Christian. But if he talks about dentistry among the poor, he gets so upset that it just spoils the evening, so I'm very happy that they're talking about wine."

"But you haven't touched your wine."

"Oh, I'm not a drinker. I tasted it though."

Barbara caught Eloise's gaze, and Eloise nodded slightly in the silent language that existed between them. All in all, the meal was a great success. The log in the grate burned down happily. Periodically Adam arose to carve more turkey, and the great beast shrank to its bony skeleton. Contrary to Eloise's expectations, the children ate the turkey with enthusiasm, forgetting all moral questions that might have arisen with Murtle and Turtle, and the hamburger went uneaten. There was enough turkey, but no more than enough. Later, in the living room, Philip, at Barbara's urging, led the hymn of

Thanksgiving, with Freddie at the piano. Barbara counted her blessings and tried to keep the tears back.

THE WEDDING AT THE small Mount Zion Baptist Church in Oakland made Barbara feel that she might have preferred to be married in this manner than with all the poshness and poached salmon and pavilions at Highgate. There were pews for two hundred people at best, and every seat was taken, as well as folding chairs crowded into every inch of available space. Not only were the Levys and Lavettes represented in total, but there were at least a dozen photographers who had worked with Judith, and agency people, and magazine people. At least a third of the congregation was white. In the lower room of the church, where a party would be held after the wedding, Judith stood with her bridesmaids, all of them in pale lavender, while the bride wore white. Barbara went downstairs with Freddie's belated bouquet of orchids, and Judith seized her and drew her to one side.

"Tell me the truth," she pleaded to Barbara. "I bulge, don't I?"

"Not a bit. Absolutely not a bit."

"You wouldn't lie to me?" Judith whispered.

The wedding gown had layers of tulle across the front as well as a veil of beautiful Chantilly lace, and Barbara whispered that even if she did bulge—and she didn't—no one would notice.

"How's Freddie taking it?"

"Nervous as a cat."

"Hang on to him, Barbara. Don't let him run away."

"He adores you."

Upstairs, in the vestibule of the church, Freddie stood with Sam, his best man, both of them in full-dress regalia; and with Dr. Hope, who would give away the bride. "When does this start?" Sam wanted to know. "I'm operating in two hours."

"You will be at the hospital in two hours," Barbara assured him. "Don't be impossible, Sam."

"Oh no," Dr. Hope put in. "He's right. If he has an operation in two hours, we must get started."

"When they're ready, we'll start," Barbara said firmly.

Eloise came bustling into the vestibule, and hearing Barbara, she said, "The choir's ready. Freddie, you look absolutely beautiful." She was in a marvelous array of blue silk that matched her eyes. "I am so excited."

The tones of the choir could be heard now. Dr. Hope turned to one of the ushers and suggested that he go downstairs and tell the ladies to start up the stairs. Sam relaxed, and Barbara, escorted by Sam, took her place in the church, leaving Eloise to enter on Freddie's arm.

Inside, the choir—ten men and ten women, the men in full dress and the women in white—were singing:

Blessed are they who come before thee,
Blessed are they who shall be joined...

It all went beautifully, and in short order Freddie and Judith stood side by side, both of them towering over Reverend Baker, who said firmly, "If there be anyone here who knows of any reason why these two, Frederick Lavette and Judith Hope, should not be bound together in holy matrimony, let him speak now or forever hold his peace."

Since no one spoke—quieting a sudden fear that took hold of Freddie—the Reverend Baker went on to say, "Holy matrimony is a blessed state, ordained by our Lord Jesus Christ, the joining of two souls for eternity. Do you, Frederick Lavette, recognize this state, and do you take this woman, Judith Hope, to be your lawfully wedded wife, to cherish and protect, for richer and for poorer, in sickness and in health, so long as you shall live?"

Freddie nodded, and Judith poked him and whispered, "Say 'Yes.' "

"Oh—yes," Freddie said. "Yes absolutely."

"And do you, Judith Hope," Reverend Baker went on, "take this man, Frederick Lavette, to be your lawfully wedded husband, to cherish and care for, for richer and for poorer, in sickness and in health, so long as you shall live?"

"I do," Judith answered.

Sam hunted for the ring, which he had stowed in his vest pocket, and handed it to Freddie, who appeared surprised to see it. "Don't drop it," Sam hissed.

"Repeat after me," the reverend said. "With this ring I do thee wed, in the name of the Father, the Son, and the Holy Ghost."

Freddie repeated the words and then put the ring on Judith's finger, and then he threw his arms around her and kissed her. The choir burst into a joyful chorus of "Oh Happy Day!"

There was the throwing of the bouquet and kissing of the bride and groom, and then a very good catered dinner in the big room below the church. Then, at seven o'clock, Judith and Freddie changed clothes, took their already packed luggage, kissed Dr. and Mrs. Hope, Eloise and Adam and Barbara and Sally and May Ling, and rushed off to the airport to catch a plane for Paris.

As Philip said to Barbara, raising a glass of wine, "Altogether, a wonderful wedding."

"I feel proud of Freddie," Barbara agreed. "He did nobly, all things considered."

BARBARA FELT A NEW SORT OF COMPASSION for Philip as she watched him slave over his Christmas Eve sermon. It appeared to her like tearing out pieces of his own flesh. She had seen him slave over other sermons, and none of them came easily, but now he filled his wastebasket with torn sheets of paper again and again. The process of writing had come naturally to her; she had written stories

as a child, novels and screenplays as an adult, and newspaper columns. She wrote what she saw and what she felt, and whatever she
wrote was an outcry against injustice and oppression; it was the way
she saw the world, the way she had always seen the world. But
Philip struggled with each word, and when it came to some three
days before Christmas, he finally admitted that he had what he
wanted—or as close to what he wanted as he was likely to come.
For the two Sundays before Christmas, he begged his assistant minister to do the sermons for him.

"Is it anything we can talk about?" Barbara asked him.

"No. It's something I've been struggling with. I have to fight
it through."

Barbara asked him whether he wanted her to read it. She had
read all of his sermons since they were going together, and very
occasionally, she would make some small suggestion. She felt that
the sermons were his, and she had no right to change them in any
significant way; but this time he shook his head and said, "No, my
dear. In this one I speak about you, and I want you to hear it as
the congregation hears it—if you will allow me to speak about you
and don't consider it an infringement on our privacy."

Good heavens, she wondered, *does he want me to object—after
which he would have to rewrite it again, now, three days before he must
deliver it? Does he think I'm that cruel—or is it simply Philip?* She
decided that it was simply Philip, and she replied, "My dear, dear
Philip, nothing you could say about me could hurt me. I've never
known you to hurt anyone, much less me."

He smiled and kissed her. "Anyway, for better or worse, it's
done, and I want to clear my head. We haven't walked in days.
Let's walk down to the Embarcadero and breathe some good sea
air and eat some crab."

She was all for it, and they bundled into sweaters and walked
down to the Bay. It was not a long walk, nothing that Barbara
would normally have thought twice about, but when they arrived

at their favorite fish place and sat down at a table, Barbara was relieved. "I don't know why I'm so tired. Do you suppose I'm catching something?"

He reached out and touched her forehead. "Cool and lovely. No, you've just been working so hard." A few minutes later he said, "Perhaps you ought to see a doctor?"

She laughed. "Philip, my son's a doctor, my brother's a doctor, and my nephew Dan is a doctor. We saw them all just this past Thanksgiving, and none of them said I looked sick. Anyway, in spite of the family penchant for it, I'm not fond of doctors. I don't dare tell them I don't feel well. They'd have me in the hospital in minutes."

But after dinner, with darkness falling, she said, "Philip, I can't face a walk back up the hill. Let's call a taxi."

Philip called a taxi, and Barbara thought about the fact that she had never suggested anything to which he objected. His utter devotion to her had often amazed her, and tonight, when they got into bed, she felt a new kind of deep love and concern for him. He put his arms around her, and she folded her body into his and treasured the feel of his strength, the hardness of his muscles. She gave herself to him, not only physically but with all her body and soul, a kind of melding she had never before experienced, telling herself that this was new, different from the passion of youth, literally a different phase of existence.

"If anything should happen to you—," he whispered.

"Nothing will happen to me, dear man. I promise you."

BARBARA HAD NOT BEEN TO a Christmas Eve service—not at the Unitarian church, indeed not at any church—since her childhood. Her memories of Grace Cathedral were less than clear, and she wondered how the service would proceed tonight. She was there early, fortunately, since after she had taken her usual seat, on the aisle and halfway down, every seat was filled and there were people standing behind the last row—whites, Asians, and blacks. There were also more children than she had ever seen there before.

Reba Guthri made the opening statement after the organ had played "O Come, All Ye Faithful," and then there were Christmas carols and some responsive readings and the offering. Then the choir sang while Philip sat with his papers in his hands. Then Philip stood up and went to the podium and began without looking at what he had written. Barbara suspected that he had written and rewritten it so many times that he knew the words by heart. He began to speak, but not nervously. Whatever his difficulties were with writing, he spoke well, simply and directly:

"As most of you know, I was once a Jesuit priest. The woman I came to marry had been a nun. We both left the Church, yet the years I had been trained as a priest remained with me. It could not have been otherwise. Five years ago, my wife, Agatha, passed away. For the five years after that, I was a lonely man, and then I met Barbara Lavette. I thought I had lost the will to love another woman, but love is very deep in our nature, and this past September, Barbara and I were married. I not only loved her—as I still do—but I felt that she was one of the most deeply ethical persons, one of the most selfless persons, I had ever known. Yet, as she told me, until she began to attend this church, she had set foot in a church only for funerals and baptisms, and neither did she join this church. She is here tonight, and I speak of her with her explicit permission.

"Together we went first to England and then to Israel and Jerusalem, on what we are pleased to call a honeymoon. For me it was something else, a search. I am not widely traveled, and all my life I dreamed of going to Jerusalem, seeing it with my own eyes and walking through the fourteen stations of the cross to the spot where Jesus was crucified. We were graciously treated by the city of Jerusalem and given an apartment overlooking the old walled city. I am sure you know the reason for this treatment, having read of it in the press, so I will not go into that; nor is it pertinent to this sermon.

"The day after we arrived in Jerusalem, so great was my eagerness that we went directly to the gate of the old walled city that opens to the Via Dolorosa. We walked through the fourteen stations of the cross, and there were placards marking them—'Here Pilate questioned Jesus . . . Here his clothes were ripped off . . . Here he was given a cross to carry to his own crucifixion . . . Here he fell and Simon of Cyrene took up the cross'—except, in the Gospel of John, Jesus carries the cross the rest of the way—and finally we came to the Church of the Holy Sepulcher, wherein the last four stations of the cross are placed. And here, supposedly, under this church, perhaps leveled by now, was the place where Jesus was crucified and the cave where he was buried and rose. But this Church of the Holy Sepulcher, supposedly the holiest place in the Christian world, is owned and governed by the Catholic Church, the Greek Church, the Armenian Church—everyone except the Protestants, who are not allowed to hold services there. It is a dank, dreary, gloomy, and foul-smelling place, poorly lit by candles and crowded with tourists. My wife, Barbara, walked out of it almost immediately.

"I remained in the Church of the Holy Sepulcher. I was deeply moved at that moment. Barbara was not—and there began a wedge that drove us apart. Remember that Israel has no rights in that church; the Israelis cannot touch anything or change anything. It belongs entirely to the sects that have chapels there.

"Why was Barbara so repelled? Why does everything that has to do with church or religion repel her? She was born and baptized a Christian; where is her faith? For three months I have struggled with this, and I think that now I understand it.

"You may ask, 'Is this a sermon for Christmas Eve?' I think it is. Two thousand years ago a Jewish child was born, and we celebrate his birth. He lived a life of love and compassion, and because he lived that life and preached that life, and because he preached love and forgiveness, he was crucified. My wife has lived a life of love and compassion. She put her life at risk again and again. She went into Nazi Germany as a spy and almost died there. She went to prison for six months for her belief, for her refusal to implicate others at a time of madness. She went down to El Salvador, where priests and nuns were being murdered; and in the great waterfront strike of the thirties, she used whatever money she had to feed the strikers. There was no time in her life when she separated herself from the struggle for social justice.

"Then I must ask you: Who is the better Christian?—myself, who never put his life at stake, or this woman I am married to? Who is closer to the child born two thousand years ago: myself, with what I call my faith, or my wife, who is indifferent to faith but wholly engrossed in womankind and mankind? She was not thrilled by the stations of the cross. Where was the placard that said, 'Here his pain began'? Where was the placard that said, 'Here his pain was beyond human comprehension'? Where was the placard that asked one to think of the suffering that a crucified man must endure? Where was the placard that said, 'Remember that in this century Christians murdered each other until seventy-five million of them were dead—dead at the hand of Christians'? Where was the placard that said, 'Here died the Prince of Peace, so come in peace and go in peace, and never again raise a hand against your fellowman'?

"No, my wife said none of these things to me. Her mind doesn't work that way. She does not worship things—stones, crosses, dark churches called houses of God. Her faith is in the human race, in love and forgiveness and compassion; and that is the faith we teach here in this church. We celebrate tonight the birth of a man who influenced nearly the entire human race, and who died pleading with God to forgive his murderers for putting him to death in this terrible manner.

"After I have finished this long sermon, we will light candles and we will sing a hymn to the child whose birth we celebrate. But the candles we light are not only for him—he would not have it so—we light the candles to celebrate the life of every human being who has taken part in the age-old struggle for peace and justice— for they walk in his steps. He does not live in dark places; he lives in our hearts, in the sunlight and fresh air, in the laughter of every child born. No one owns him. No one can say, 'Here you shall pray as we tell you to pray.' He is in every child delivered through a woman's pain; and to paraphrase William Blake, here, one day, we shall build Jerusalem in our own good and pleasant land. I thank you, and may God bless you all on this Christmas Eve."

People wiped their eyes and others murmured "Amen" very softly, and Barbara bent her head to hide her tears. Then there was the candle lighting, and then they sang "The First Noel." And finally the service was over and a hundred or so women kissed Philip and Barbara, and a hundred or so men shook hands with Philip; and then he had to speak to this one and that one; and finally, well after midnight, Philip and Barbara were able to leave the church and, arm in arm, walk to where their car was parked.

"I saw you crying," Philip said. "I didn't mean to make anyone cry."

"I'm an easy cry."

"I didn't deliver my sermon at all," Philip said. "I don't know what happened to me. I worked for weeks on that thing, and I had twelve pages, and I never looked at them."

"Twelve pages would have been too long. The sermon was splendid. I never heard you deliver a better sermon. You're not a writer but a fine orator."

"It wasn't much of a sermon. I feel it was confused."

"No one else feels that way."

"You're sure?"

"I'm sure."

"Are we invited to Highgate for Christmas dinner?"

"Of course, if you can stand to hear Adam read about Scrooge and the spirits. I've heard that damn *Christmas Carol* at least twenty times, but if you don't listen with the kids, he'll never forgive you. Otherwise I'll cook something up and we can watch television."

"No, I can stand *A Christmas Carol* again."

"You're putting down my cooking. It's the first time you ever put down anything about me. You're improving, Philip dear."

"Oh no, not at all. You're a wonderful cook."

"But Cathrena's better."

"Different."

"Oh, the hell with cooking. Let's go home and have sex."

They were at the car now. Philip looked at her for a long moment, then shrugged and went around the car to open the door for her.

"The trouble with being a gentleman," Barbara said, "is that you question my ability to open a car door. In England, where they breed gentlemen as thick as flies, a lackey opens the car door for men and women, which is more equality than you're ready to engage in. Trouble is, we're too cheap to employ lackeys."

Philip sighed. "You're impossible."

"I think you're wonderful—just to say that. It's the humanization of Philip, twice in one evening: first my cooking, and now I'm impossible. Soon you'll be a perfectly normal husband."

"I didn't mean it that way."

"Why not? Of course I'm impossible. I've always been impossible, in spite of all your salutary praise. At least I don't lie."

"Do I, Barbara?" He was serious now.

"What about the bus?"

"What bus?"

"The bus in Israel, where you sacrificed your beautiful gray hair."

"I didn't even know what I was doing. How could I speak about that?"

"You knew very well what you were doing. You put your life on the line."

"I will not argue about that. It's of no importance, and a sensible omission is not a lie."

"Why not argue? People who love each other argue and scream at each other and claw at each other."

"Nonsense. Now get into the car and we'll go home and do what you suggested."

"Say it, Philip. For God's sake, say it out loud: 'An old man and an old lady are going to crawl into bed naked and make love and fuck each other with the kind of passion kids can't even dream about.' I dare you to say it!"

Philip burst out laughing, helped Barbara into the car, and then went around to the driver's door. As he drove off, saying, "Thank goodness we're alone. I never used that word in my life," Barbara joined his laughter.

"I don't believe you." Then she added, "Only four letters, an easy Anglo-Saxon word. Try it sometime."

"Maybe—who knows?"

"You are the strangest man I ever knew," Barbara said, "but I've learned to love you a great deal. Bless you, Philip. You've given me more than I ever hoped for."

The Journey

10

IT WAS EARLY FEBRUARY when Barbara telephoned her brother, Joe, at Napa and asked whether he could see her at about eleven o'clock. "About what, Barbara?" he asked. "Those are office hours and I'm kind of busy."

"Yes, office hours. I want to talk to you about how rotten I feel."

"Did you talk to Horowitz about it?" Horowitz was her family internist.

"I haven't seen Horowitz in years. I want to talk to you, and I don't want Philip to know, and I don't want Sally to know."

"Well, Philip, yes. And Sally isn't going to be here. She's off to see May Ling. But if you have a fever, you shouldn't be driving all that distance."

"I don't have a fever. I'm just feeling very weak and rotten."

"There's Sam, right there in San Francisco."

"Sam's not a doctor, he's a surgeon, and he's too pricey for me. I can't afford Sam. Joe, that's a joke. I don't want my son examining me."

"Can you leave now?"

"Yes."

"All right, come on down. I'll clear an hour for you. I saw you just two weeks ago, and you appeared to be all right. Tired, but all right. There's a new syndrome going around, a sort of fatigue thing—but nothing too serious. Anyway, I'll be glad to see you, and maybe I can put your worries at rest. Drive carefully."

Curiously, she felt better once she was on the road. It was a clear, cool day, the sky rumpled with small, fluffy clouds—and she had immense trust in her brother Joe. He was three years younger than Barbara, but they were nevertheless close and comfortable with each other. Dan Lavette, her father, had divorced Jean Seldon to marry May Ling, and Barbara had not known Joe during her childhood. The bonding between them was strong, and when Joe married Eloise and Adam's daughter, Sally, the bonding became even stronger.

Barbara thought about all this as she drove down to Napa. She had told Philip that she might drive to Highgate, but she would be back to join him for dinner at the MacGelsies'. Birdie had induced a Hollywood star to join the Unitarian Association, and she wanted him to meet Philip, thinking that it was time they had some publicity. Ordinarily Philip would have declined. He didn't like that sort of publicity, thinking of the headlines when some celebrity turned Catholic. He shared the belief some church members held that one did not proselytize for the Unitarians—although at times he thought wistfully of Thomas Jefferson's prediction that in a hundred years after Jefferson's time, all of America would be Unitarian—but he gave in to Barbara's urging and her conviction that this particular star was a very decent man and that it would be nice to meet him.

Joe's nurse, Hilda Cahn, a stocky middle-aged woman with short gray hair, took her into Joe's office, and Joe embraced Barbara, kissed her, and seated her in a chair facing his desk.

"Now tell me about it," he said.

"Yes—you know, Joe, I've always been a walker. I'd do the whole length of the Embarcadero, and then back up to my house. Now I do one block and I'm tired."

"When did this begin?"

"Almost three months ago, when we were in London. First I put it down to jet lag, but it got worse when we were in Israel, and bit by bit it's been getting worse since we came home."

"Do your legs hurt?"

"No, they're tired, but it feels like exercise-tired, not pain. My stomach's been bad, but I thought that was only indigestion."

He rose and felt her forehead. "You're cool, but I'll take your temperature anyway."

While she sat with the thermometer in her mouth, he put on his stethoscope and listened to her heart.

"Temperature's all right. Barbara, I'm going to take an electrocardiograph and then some X rays. But tell me, is there anything else different in the way you feel? What about your digestion? Anything at all?" He was taking her blood pressure now. "You've always had good low pressure. That hasn't changed much. You're seventy, aren't you?"

"This past November." She thought about his other question. "Heartburn—I never used to have much heartburn. Now I take Tums."

Joe nodded. "That doesn't signify much of anything. Constipation?"

"Not much, no. Years ago Horowitz gave me a bowel softener. He said to use it instead of a laxative. I still do, occasionally."

"All right. First we'll take some X rays, and then Hilda will give you an electrocardiograph. But don't worry until we have something to worry about—and perhaps we won't." Joe then took her into the X ray room and had her stretch out on the table. He took several X rays, and then Hilda gave her an electrocardiograph. Barbara had not had one in years, and it was an odd feeling to lie there in brassiere and briefs with wires latched onto her chest. In the past Joe had advised her to have a physical every six months—advice she had ignored. When the electrocardiograph was done, Hilda suggested that she make herself comfortable in the waiting room while the X rays were developed.

There were no other patients waiting. Evidently Joe had cleared his calendar for her. She picked up a copy of *Time* magazine, but her usual interest in the current lunacies and injustices of mankind had vanished. She was frightened and depressed. Why hadn't she asked Philip to come with her? She wanted his arm around her, the good cheer and unquestioned hope that he always radiated. Philip would have told her not to worry, that whatever it was, they would meet it and overcome it.

Time passed, an eternity of time, and then she finally heard Joe's heavy footsteps. She waited for him to appear. If he was smiling, all would be well; but he was not smiling, and her heart sank.

"Come into my office, Barbara," he said.

She went into Joe's office and sat again in the chair facing his desk. The X rays were on his desk.

"We have a problem," Joe said. "I don't know how much of a problem, but you have a fairly large tumor on your intestines, and another that is smaller. Now, don't think cancer immediately. I know you well enough to know that you want the truth, as well as I can spell out the truth. I'm not an oncologist, so I can't tell you how serious this is, but there's no reason to jump to conclusions. This may or may not be a malignancy. I've already called Bill Calahan, and he and Sam will be waiting for us at Mercy Hospital in two hours. I told Hilda to switch everything to Dr. Clement here in Napa. He covers for me."

Barbara was silent.

"My dear, take a deep breath. Please don't be frightened."

She was frightened, terribly frightened. She took several deep breaths and then, in a whisper, said, "Why must I go to the hospital?"

"Because they will know what to do. I called Philip at the church. He'll meet us at the hospital."

"Joe," she asked, "am I going to die? Tell me the truth."

"I can't because I don't know. At this moment you're alive, and your heart is good and your color is good."

"I don't want to go to the hospital. I want to go home," she said, like a child pleading.

"Barbara dear," he said gently, "you're my sister and my patient. You must go with me to the hospital. Then we'll know. You do want to know, don't you? There's no alternative."

She was silent for a few moments, her eyes wet; then she nodded. "I'll drive there myself."

"No, I can't let you do that. You've just had a terrible blow. I've canceled everything for today. I'll take you."

"All right, Joe. We'll go in my car," she said softly. "I'm better now that I heard the worst. I'll ask you only one more thing—do I have a chance?"

"Of course you do. I don't even know what these tumors are."

"My mother died of cancer."

"That means nothing."

"If I'm in the hospital, Eloise and Sally will want to come. One of them can drive you back. Or you can drive back in my car. I can do without it for a while."

"Don't worry about the car."

Driving back to San Francisco, Barbara confronted what might well mean her death. She had faced death before, both in Nazi Germany and in El Salvador, but those were moments of high excitement, not unlike Philip's plunge into the burning bus. This was different. She recalled Philip telling her once that part of his opposition to the death penalty was the injunction in Deuteronomy where Moses is told that he must die and never cross over to the Promised Land. *Why,* she wondered, *should anyone be cursed with a knowledge of approaching death? But I am being foolish,* she told herself. *Millions of people die and know that they are dying, and I certainly don't know that I am dying.*

She said to Joe, "Don't ever lie to me, Joe. If I am going to die, tell me so. I don't want that monstrous chemotherapy. I've watched too many people suffer through it. And I don't want to die in a hospital. Can you promise me that?"

"You're not dying."

"All right. I don't really feel that I'm dying. I feel quite well now that I'm over that dumb scene I made. What shall I tell Philip? He loves me so. Do you know, Joe, I was never entirely sure that I loved him—oh, I did love him, but not the way he loved me. Then—oh, just about Christmastime, I fell madly in love with him, absolutely madly, which is very strange to happen with a man you're already married to."

"Not so strange," Joe said.

"And then this."

She was mostly silent for the rest of the drive. At the hospital Philip was waiting for her in the parking lot, and he threw his arms around her and kissed her. Joe went ahead to register her, and Philip and Barbara followed more slowly.

"What did Joe tell you?" Barbara asked.

"Not much. He said there shouldn't be any delay. You'll stay here overnight, and they may operate in the morning."

"He didn't tell me that. Why don't doctors tell me the truth?"

"I suppose he told me all he knew. Joe said he just doesn't know enough to make any sort of diagnosis. Sam and a doctor, Bill Calahan, a specialist in oncology, will meet with you a little later. We'll do this together, darling, and we'll fight it through."

The hospital room was pleasant enough, with a bright shaft of afternoon sunlight cutting through the windows. Philip helped her to undress and she put on the white hospital gown that a nurse brought her.

"Is it all right if I just sit in a chair?" she asked the nurse.

"Of course. If the doctor wants you in bed, he'll tell you."

"I thought Sam would be here," Barbara said to Philip.

"Probably he's with Joe and the oncologist. He'll be here."

"Why have I always been at odds with Sam, Philip?"

"You don't want to discuss that now, do you? I'm sure he's thinking about nothing but you at this moment."

"Dear, dear Philip, who cannot think ill of anyone. Will you stay with me?"

"All night, if they let me."

"I love you very much, and I need you."

"I'll be here."

AT THAT SAME TIME, in Sam's office, four physicians were discussing Barbara's case. They were Sam and Joe; Dr. Calahan, the oncologist; and Dr. David Friedman, whom Sam considered to be the best abdominal surgeon in the hospital. It was possible that Sam considered himself the best, but the thought of operating on his mother himself was inconceivable to him. The four X rays that Joe had taken in Napa were posted on a large viewing light and were being examined by the physicians. Sam felt that Barbara should be X rayed again here in the hospital, and he pointed to two dubious areas.

Calahan did not agree with him. "I know what I see and I know what to expect. You're right, Sam, those two areas are suspect, but these are good pictures. Joe tells me that she was very troubled with the information, and she's been sedated, and she's probably relaxed and more comfortable now. Why upset her more?"

"I'll want X rays in the morning," Friedman said.

"You must operate immediately?" Joe asked.

"No question. No other way to see how far it has metastasized."

"What do you expect?" Sam asked Calahan.

"The worst, I'm sorry to say."

"Why?"

"Well, those spots Sam pointed to. They would indicate the liver, and if it's most of the liver, there's nothing to be done."

"No hope for chemotherapy?"

Calahan shrugged. "It would probably ease your conscience, Sam."

"Don't give me that shit about my conscience," Sam said angrily. "This is my mother."

"Take it easy, Sam."

"What about chemo?"

"If there's no hope for the liver and if it has metastasized to other parts," Calahan said gently, "then chemotherapy would at best only delay the end a few weeks more—with a good deal of suffering in the interim."

"The point is," Friedman said, "do you want to remove the tumors on the intestines? That would be a severe shock to her system, and it would only bring the end on more rapidly. From what you say, Dr. Calahan, nothing can be done about the liver."

"I'm not saying that. I'm only saying what I suspect."

"Then I want both of you in the operating room with me. I've done a good many of these, but still I'm not an oncologist."

"What are you thinking?" Calahan asked.

"We'll have the biopsies, and if you're right, Dr. Calahan, I'll close her up, send her home in a few days, and let her die in peace."

"Damn it!" Sam said. "She's my mother. You want me to pronounce a death sentence."

"Sam, Sam," Joe said. "She's your mother and she's my sister, but she's also Barbara Lavette. I gave her my word that I would tell her the truth. She'll make the decision. Her mother died of cancer, and she's watched friends die after months of chemo. It's one of the cruelest punishments we can bestow, and perhaps it's worth it for those we save. But if it's hopeless, you must tell her that, and she'll make the decision. Barbara is a strong woman, a great woman. She's lived her life fully and with nobility. She should have the right to die well."

It was a strange speech for Joe to make. Sam had always taken his uncle for a stolid, unemotional man; now Joe put his arm around Sam and said, "I'll be in the operating room with you."

They had never been close, and the difference between them was enormous. Joe, at sixty-eight, was a small-town internist and pediatrician; Sam, just thirty-nine, was a brilliant surgeon, chief of surgery at a prestigious hospital, with an income of over two hundred thousand a year. He was a member of a golf club and of the Redwood Club; he bore his father's name, Cohen, proudly, refusing to be known as Samuel Lavette; and he wore three-piece suits. Even when Joe put on a suit for the first time, he looked rumpled and messy, and he had never learned to knot a tie properly.

Dr. Friedman said to Joe, very respectfully, "Doctor, make her comfortable for tonight. No food, but plenty of water. I have an operation scheduled, but I'll drop in later."

IN HER HOSPITAL ROOM WITH PHILIP, Barbara said to him, "I'm not afraid anymore, darling—well, nervous, yes, and I'm still upset, rushed here out of Joe's office and put into this silly gown. I don't like hospitals. I never did. But I'm not afraid. Everyone dies. We pretend that each of us is an exception—but there are no exceptions. But I'm disappointed. I learned to love you, and I do love you very much—I think more than I ever loved anyone else, even Marcel, who was my first love."

"I know that, baby."

"And the truth is, I can hardly remember him. I've never lived in the past. Did it ever occur to you, Philip dear, that this present moment is all that any of us have, and this is a good moment— even here in this wretched hospital. Oh, I love you so much, and we didn't have enough time."

"You're not going to die."

"Don't deny it, Philip. That won't help. Do you know why Joe and Sam aren't here? Because they're somewhere arguing about what to do with me and how to cut me up and what to take out of me. Joe is a good doctor, as good as any of them, only he's no good at deception. When he examined the X rays, I knew the verdict immediately. I know my body better than any of them do, and the truth is that I've been dying for weeks, only I denied it. I didn't want to leave you, and I don't want to leave you now. That's the worst of it. I'm sure they've decided to take out those tumors and sew me up again and then subject me to that horrible chemo- therapy—"

"Darling," Philip said gently, "we don't know what they've decided. I'm sure they'll be here in a few minutes."

"I don't want to be cut up, Philip. I never had an operation. I think that frightens me more than the cancer. You won't let them do anything I don't want, will you?"

"Of course not. You know that. But we're not physicians."

A few minutes later Joe and Sam entered the room, along with Dr. Calahan. Barbara was still in the armchair, and Sam went to her and kissed her on the lips, something he rarely did. He intro- duced Dr. Calahan.

Barbara smiled and took his hand.

"I've heard a great deal about you, Mrs. Carter," Calahan said. "For years now. It's an honor to meet you."

"Thank you. I'm sure Dr. Lavette told you that I must have the truth about my condition. I don't want anything else, only the full truth. I do have cancer, don't I?"

"I'm afraid so."

"Hold on," Sam said. "We haven't even had a biopsy. We don't know."

"Sam," Barbara said, "don't do that. You must allow Dr. Calahan to answer my questions as well as he can. Joe says he's the best oncologist in the City. I must ask questions and he must give me honest answers."

"But, Mother—"

"No!" Barbara said firmly. "I think we should talk alone, Dr. Calahan."

"For God's sake, Mother, be reasonable."

"I am being reasonable."

Sam nodded. "All right. Ask your questions. I don't know what you hope—"

Joe put his arm around Sam. "Easy, Sam. You don't win an argument with Barbara. You know that, and I wouldn't upset her."

Calahan, uneasy at what was happening, said that after all, he was not part of the family.

Barbara apologized for Sam. "He is my son," she said, smiling, "and he loves me and I love him. But I must get some answers."

Calahan nodded. "I understand."

"Are these growths malignant?"

"Knowing your family history, I would say that they are— out of my experience. As a physician, I cannot say they are, because there has been no biopsy."

"If they are malignant, what are my chances to survive?"

"I can't answer that now."

"Why?"

"Because as a physician, I am not permitted to."

Dr. Friedman came into the room, and Calahan introduced him to Barbara.

"I feel terribly important," Barbara said, smiling. "I have never been a patient in a hospital before, and here I am with my husband and four physicians in my room, and I don't even have enough chairs to ask you to sit down."

"Mother," Sam said, "Dr. Friedman will operate. He's a very fine surgeon, and I have full confidence in him."

Friedman smiled uneasily. He was a small, shy man with glasses, and evidently uncomfortable with praise. "I'll do my best. It's not a difficult operation."

"You intend to remove both growths?"

"Yes."

"I've been asking Dr. Calahan some questions—no, it's all right, Dr. Friedman. By the way, did the blood tests show anything?"

Friedman glanced at Calahan and Sam. Then he said, "They're not totally dependable, Mrs. Carter."

"Oh?"

"There are a number of factors."

What a strange lot of men, Barbara thought, *as hard to get straight answers from as blood from a stone.*

A call came for Sam and he said to Barbara, "I'll be back, Mother." And then he left.

Dr. Friedman said, "I'd like to examine Mrs. Carter. Would you step outside?" The three men stood in the corridor, and Dr. Calahan said to Philip, "I wish I could give you more hope, Mr. Carter, but the liver is heavily involved. From what Dr. Friedman said, I would suspect that the cancer has metastasized widely. I'll want to look at the blood tests, as uncertain as they are."

Philip looked at Joe, and Joe nodded. "I love Barbara. I'd do anything in the world to save her, but if what Dr. Calahan suspects is so, then there's little hope."

"Is there *any* hope?"

"We always hope for a miracle," Dr. Calahan said.

"Then what on earth is the procedure?"

"Dr. Friedman will open her up. While she's on the operating table, we'll do the biopsies and we'll know the extent of the damage."

"Will he remove the tumors?" Philip asked.

"Not if the cancer has metastasized to the extent we suspect, although the decision will be Dr. Friedman's. We'll simply close her."

"And then—how long?"

"A few weeks—perhaps a month. Chemotherapy might delay it for an extra few weeks."

"Will there be much pain?"

"We can control the pain, but we can't control the effects of the chemotherapy. It's not a pleasant experience."

"Which means it's thoroughly devastating, is that what you're saying?"

"More or less."

"If it were your wife in this condition, Dr. Calahan—what would you do?"

"Mr. Carter," he said almost pleadingly, "how can you ask me that question? These are two different women."

"Forgive me," Philip said. "My wife will refuse the operation. She will prefer to die quietly. She knows there is no hope."

"Did she tell you that?" Joe demanded.

"Yes."

"My God," Joe exclaimed, "can't you change her mind?"

"I know her. I can't. But why should I? Why should her last days be a perfect hell? My wife is a splendid woman. Why shouldn't her last days be as painless and rewarding as the rest of her life was?"

At that point Dr. Friedman came out of Barbara's room. The three men waiting for him were silent, and he joined their silence in a long moment. Then he said, "I have to tell you this, Mr. Carter. I found two very small lumps in her left breast. There's no doubt

that the cancer has metastasized. She refuses the operation. Do you
want to examine her, Dr. Calahan?"

"To what end?" Dr. Calahan wondered. "Do you want me
to, Mr. Carter?"

"What would the operation entail?" Philip asked Dr.
Friedman.

Friedman shook his head. "Removal of both breasts as well as
the abdominal opening. No, I agree with her. There's no point in
operating. And you're right about the liver, Dr. Calahan—at least,
so it seems to me."

Calahan nodded, and Joe said, "Take her home, Philip. I'll
give you some prescriptions for the pain. If she's hungry, let her
eat—something simple—eggs, toast, and coffee. I'll go with you if
you wish."

"No, I'd rather be alone with her."

Dr. Calahan gave Philip his card. "You may want a nurse later
on. Just call me and I'll arrange it."

"I'll talk to Sam," Joe said. "He'll want to see her later."

THAT NIGHT, CURLED UP NEXT TO PHILIP in bed, Barbara whispered, "We lost, dear man. We played a hard game, but we lost."

"Nothing is lost. You will always have me, and I'll always
have you. We've bonded. Death can't separate us."

"Don't let them take me back to the hospital, Philip. I want
to be here with you. You won't leave me, will you?"

"Not even for a day or an hour."

"Philip, Philip, you must do the shopping and the cooking.
Don't worry, I'll tell you exactly what to do. The eggs were
delicious."

"You hardly touched them."

"I thought I was hungry, and then I couldn't eat. I'm so tired,
so sleepy. What a long, awful day. At this rate, I don't know how

I'll get up and down the stairs. I'm such a big, bony woman. You can't carry me."

"I certainly can."

She had taken a sleeping pill, and now it began to have its effect. She dozed off in Philip's arms and then awoke with a start. "Philip, is that you?" she murmured. "Am I alive or dead?" He kissed her, and she slept. She slept until noontime the following day, and meanwhile, at nine o'clock in the morning, Eloise and Sally arrived. Eloise, having had a long talk with Joe, carried a suitcase, a chicken, and assorted vegetables. She and Sally, learning that Barbara still slept, sat with Philip in the kitchen and drank the coffee he had prepared.

"Is it true what Joe told me, that Barbara is dying?" Sally began to cry. Her eyes were red from previous weeping, and Eloise told her firmly that tears would not help the situation.

"In the first place, if any of us start, Barbara will catch it. You know how she is about tears. So go into the bathroom, Sally, and use some cold water and dry your eyes." Sally did so obediently.

Eloise repeated Sally's question to Philip.

"Not in that sense," Philip said. "She won't die today or tomorrow. But she hasn't too much time. Evidently the cancer has metastasized very quickly. It may be weeks or a month."

"Joe says she won't take chemotherapy or allow them to operate. Is that wise?"

"It's her decision—and I think that as much as doctors hate to give up, they sort of agree with her. Evidently chemotherapy is pretty awful. Barbara is a strong-willed woman, and she wants to go in peace."

"I brought the suitcase because I hope you will allow me to stay for a while. Barbara and I are very close."

"I know that. But I've been speaking to my assistant at the

church. She understands, and I intend to be with Barbara until the end, whenever that is."

"Of course. I wouldn't expect anything else of you. But I know how simply both of you live, and someone has to cook and someone has to help her wash, and if I didn't do it, you'd have to have a nurse. I won't infringe on your privacy, but I've helped other people who've passed away, and I know how demanding it is. I can be helpful."

"I know you can, and it's very kind of you. We have two guest rooms, so there's plenty of space. Also, I expect a good many visitors, and you could take a great load off my shoulders. There are times when I want to be alone and do my own kind of prayer, and if you are with Barbara, that will help. Joe says that she will probably become somewhat disoriented."

Sally, who had dried her tears, said that she would be driving back to Napa after Barbara awakened. "But wouldn't it be better if you brought her down to Highgate?" Sally asked. "Joe would only be a few miles away, and if you needed a nurse, I've had years of experience. She loves Highgate."

"I know she does."

"I would be very grateful," Eloise said, "and so would Adam. We have a big bedroom and bath in the old house. We never use it. And the family is there in the Valley. It would be a place where we could use a wheelchair—and everyone down there loves her. Freddie and Judith were absolutely stricken, and he'll be here this afternoon."

"It's up to Barbara," Philip said.

"Yes, it must be Barbara's decision."

They talked for a while, and then Eloise asked whether she could go upstairs and be there when Barbara awoke. "If you wouldn't mind, Philip? I'll be quiet as a mouse."

"Yes, go ahead. I have some things I must do."

"I'll wait here," Sally said.

Eloise crept upstairs, went into the bedroom, where the blinds were drawn, and approached the bed. Barbara was still sleeping. Eloise sat in a chair by the bed, clasped her hands in her lap, and prayed silently and tried to hold back her tears.

Eloise sat quietly in prayer for at least half an hour. She heard steps on the stairs; the door opened and Philip looked in, said nothing, and then retreated. A while later Barbara stretched, yawned, and opened her eyes and saw Eloise, and smiled—and then suddenly came awake and cried, "Ellie! I'm not dreaming."

Eloise clasped her in her arms and kissed her.

"What are you doing here so early?" Barbara asked, completely bewildered.

"It's not so early. It's almost noon. I drove here with Sally. She's downstairs."

"I thought I was dreaming."

"No, I'm real."

"Do you know about me?"

"I know that you're alive and we're going to keep you alive." She paused and then said, "Yes, I spoke to Joe last night."

"And he told you the whole thing?"

"Yes."

"You're going to keep me alive, Ellie?"

"Absolutely."

"Oh, I do love you," Barbara said. "What would I do without you?"

"You're not going to do without me. I brought some things with me, in case you want me to stay. But my hope is that you'll come back with us to Highgate. We have that big bedroom on the first floor where Freddie used to sleep. There are no stairs, and you'll have your own entrance. Philip told me that he will be with you."

"Strange. I was so frightened yesterday—it was so sudden. It was an awful day. But now I feel all right. Nothing hurts very much.

I took a sleeping pill and some other stuff, and I feel a little dopey, but I don't feel that I'm dying."

"You're not. We won't let you die."

"Oh, sweetie, I try so hard not to be cynical. Philip doesn't understand cynicism. He wants to be my nurse and lover and cook—where is he, by the way?"

"Downstairs with Sally. He knows how close we are, and he wanted to let us have some time alone. That's why I want you to come down to the winery. You'll be out in the open, with the wind and the sky, and people won't be crowding into this room to see you and say all kinds of stupid things."

"You mean they won't say stupid things at Highgate?"

"Oh, Bobby, that's not what I mean."

"Why do I keep on teasing you? Yes, I'll go down to the Valley. I would have asked you whether you could bear to have a dying woman if you hadn't asked me. Help me dress, and then you'll have to help me pack. But remember, I can be an awful nuisance."

"Let us worry about that."

Dressed in an old skirt and sweater, Barbara said, "Would you go downstairs, Ellie, and tell Philip and Sally that I'll be down in a minute or two? I want to be alone for a moment. I want to shake the cobwebs out of my head."

"Can you do the stairs alone?"

"Ellie, for heaven's sake!"

"I only wanted to make sure. Can I do breakfast—or lunch? I brought a cold roast chicken and some veggies."

"Dear woman—no, thank you. Only coffee and toast. Joe prescribed huge vitamin pills—I don't know why, but doctors feel they must, I suppose."

Eloise left to go downstairs, and Barbara dropped into a chair. It was a deep armchair, and suddenly she felt very weak and wondered whether she would have enough strength to pull herself out of the chair. It seemed to her that she had felt stronger when Eloise helped her in and out of the shower, but how could such a change have come about in a few minutes? She dozed off again and dreamed. In the dream, she had left Philip somewhere in Oakland, and she was in San Francisco trying to get her car. She had left it in a garage that her first husband, Bernie, had owned. But the car was too small for two, and Bernie promised that he would stretch it. There was a hotel nearby, and she went in to find a telephone and call Philip and tell him to wait for her, but the pages were torn out of every phone book, or were simply missing. She then called information, but was told that no numbers were available. Vaguely she could remember a gloomy street in Oakland where she and Philip had decided to live. But when she went back to the car it had disappeared. Then she awakened.

She tried to recollect the dream, and after a minute or two she gave up, forced herself out of the chair, and went downstairs. Philip heard her and started up the stairs to help her, but she shook her head. "I'm quite all right, darling." At the foot of the stairs, he embraced her and she clung to him desperately. "I'm so happy you're here."

Sally was standing behind him. Barbara pulled away from Philip and embraced Sally, whose eyes were tearful and reddened. "Poor dear," Barbara said, "I slept the morning away and let you sit here and wait for me."

"How do you feel?" Philip asked her.

"Fine. Where's the coffee and toast Ellie promised me?"

"In here," Ellie said from the kitchen. "And fresh orange juice."

Barbara found that she was looking at things newly, as if she had never seen them before, thinking that this was a wonderful kitchen—its windows overlooking the Bay; its shining white cabinets; its big gleaming refrigerator that was always almost empty, she was such a poor housewife; and the solid kitchen table of two-inch birch planks. Did she really want to leave this kitchen? Would she ever see the Bay again, with its sprinkling of white sails and the wind blowing through the Golden Gate? But on the other hand, if she didn't go to Highgate, would she ever see the low, rolling green hills, the vine stems laid out like soldiers on parade, the old stone houses, and the sunsets, and the Valley drenched with silver moonlight? Time was her enemy now. What was it Philip had said, that each moment is forever and all that we have and all we can depend on?

And it was nice to have people around who loved her and cared for her. Like the three people sitting at the table while she sipped her coffee and ate buttered toast. "Why am I eating alone?" she demanded as Eloise set the brown-skinned chicken and the bowls of peas and carrots and potatoes on the table. "Please eat, or that fine chicken will go to waste. I really can't stand all this attention. I'm being thoroughly spoiled."

"That will be the day," Eloise said.

"Do you really want me at Highgate, Ellie?"

"Unless you don't want me around. We can't all stay here."

As Eloise spoke the doorbell sounded, and Philip opened the door for Judith, Adam, Freddie, and May Ling, who crowded in to the kitchen. They bore baskets of fruit and wine.

No, Barbara said to herself, *this is becoming impossible. With all the funerals I've attended, I never gave any thought to the importance of dying. Eloise is right; the Valley is more practical.*

THE VALLEY WAS SERENE AND BEAUTIFUL. If tourists were still coming there, they did not come over the Silverado Trail, and winter had made a subtle change in the air. It was an old place, as places on the West Coast are measured, and the thousands of acres of stubby grape stands, denuded now of fruit and leaves, did not spoil the landscape. The fruit would come again and the wine would be made again.

There is something special about a place where wine is made;

and when Philip and Barbara drove down the road early the following morning, Barbara smiled and laid her head against Philip's
shoulder, and asked him why she felt that she was coming home.

"I think you are."

"As much as I've ever had a home, I guess. Sam Goldberg
gave me the house on Green Street, and when I'm gone, it will be
yours, Philip. All my things are there—papers, books, and all the
rest of it. I brought a copy of the manuscript with me, but I doubt
whether I'll be able to work on it. So it will be unfinished—if
anyone cares to publish it. I also brought a book of poems that I
wrote—still in manuscript. I never told you about my poems. I
suppose I was a little ashamed of them. Most novelists are not good
poets. There were exceptions, like Thomas Hardy."

"Can I read some of them?"

"We can read them aloud, if you want to. Some of them. Some
of them should simply not be seen, but I can't throw away things
I've written. Like finishing a book once you've started to read it.
As a little girl, I felt it was sinful not to finish a book I started to
read, no matter how boring."

"Yes, I suffered the same syndrome. We make so many rules
for ourselves."

"Too many. And in the end, what does it amount to, Philip?"

"A great deal, believe me."

"Sound and fury," Barbara said.

"There is no death," Philip replied.

"Ah, dear Philip, if I could only believe you."

She dozed off. It was difficult for Philip to believe that this
was a mortally sick woman with only a few weeks of life left to
her. He was relieved that she had decided to come down to the
Valley; it would be good for her not to be alone, to be surrounded
with people who loved her—and to be surrounded in a normal
manner, not with a parade of people crowding into the house on
Green Street to pay their respects. How much better it is to die

quickly and easily. His thoughts went back to that day in July when she sought him out and asked whether she could speak to him. It was only seven months ago, and so much had happened since then. *It is not often,* he reflected, *that a man and woman in their seventies are given a gift of love—passionate and complete love.* He couldn't anticipate her death; she was too alive, too much of this world, and he thanked the God he believed in that through her he had returned to this world from the morass he had fallen into after Agatha, his first wife, had passed away. He recalled once meeting a Buddhist rashi who said to him that no one was alone, that we breathe the air that others exhale, that we are all of the same substance and flesh, that nothing is ever lost; yet at the same time, his heart went out to Barbara. His silent plea was *Please let her believe.*

Barbara awoke as they were turning into the gates of the winery. As they drove up to the main house, Barbara saw Eloise sitting in an Adirondack chair and waiting for them to arrive. Trying to hold back her tears, and then bursting into tears, she embraced Barbara, who soothed her as she would a child and found herself saying, "Poor Eloise—you mustn't."

Eloise dried her eyes and managed to ask, "Was it a good drive? It's such a fine day."

"I slept most of the way," Barbara said. "Pity Philip. I've turned him into a chauffeur as well as housemaid and cook. And do you know what, Philip? I'm going to let you unpack while Eloise and I go off by ourselves."

"That's proper. You've had enough of me for a while."

Eloise led them away from the main entrance of the stone house to a wing with a separate doorway. "Adam built this part of the house for Josh during Vietnam. It's a nice big room with its own bath and shower. We wanted Freddie to use it, but he had his own room and it was a big emotional thing. Mostly, it's been closed up. I aired it out and we changed some of the furniture and put a new rug in there, and the walls have been repapered."

It was a beautiful room with French doors that opened onto the patio behind the house, and big white-curtained windows. There was a double bed piled with cushions, a television set, two large, comfortable armchairs, two chests of drawers, and a large closet. Barbara smiled in delight and told Eloise she had done miracles since she last saw it. The box in one corner, Eloise explained, was a small refrigerator with cold drinks and some bottles of wine—"White wine," she said in a whisper, noticing Adam entering the room with Freddie behind him, both of them carrying the luggage.

After they greeted Barbara she said that she and Eloise were going off by themselves and that they would appear for lunch. She opened one suitcase and took out a thick Irish sweater. Philip reminded her about her medication.

"When I come back. I'm not going to root around for it."

"Now," Philip said firmly. "I have it right here in my pocket." He brought her a glass of water from the bathroom, and she swallowed the two pills and grimaced.

Then she and Eloise left the room.

"Are you sure you're up to walking?" Eloise asked her.

"I am walking. Philip was right about the Percocet—it quiets me. I can't walk for too long, but I think I have enough strength to get up the hill to our place—if we take it slowly." She opened the door of her car. "Ellie, darling, reach in over the backseat. I have a cane there. I'll hate to walk with a cane, but a little prudence is the better part of valor."

Eloise retrieved the cane, and they walked along slowly to the path that led up the hillside. It was at least two hundred yards to the beginning of the rise, and when they reached that point, Barbara gave up. "I can't, Ellie. It would be stupid for me to try. I'm so disappointed." They turned back and found an old wooden bench against the wall of the aging rooms. It was in full sunshine and out of the breeze. They sat down and rested while Barbara caught her breath.

Eloise, for whom chatter was always easy, could think of nothing to say, and finally Barbara asked her, "Do you believe in God and all that goes with it?"

"My goodness, that's a question, isn't it? Yes and no. Not all that goes with it, but I suppose I do believe. I try hard to get to church sometimes, and I suppose it makes me feel good."

"I read a statistic that ninety percent of Americans believe in God. I don't know why I have to be in the ten percent who don't."

"Barbara, do you think all of this just happened?"

"No, not exactly. I believe in evolution. I've always believed that people were born good and then were spoiled. When I was in India in 1945, I witnessed a famine in which six million people died. They didn't have to die. The British and the rice dealers cornered the market when they believed the Japanese might fight their way into Bengal, and that the Assamese and the Bengalese might go over to them. That shattered my last shreds of belief."

"I remember how horrified I was when you told me about that. And six million Jews died in the Holocaust. It isn't easy to put it together, any more than it was easy to live on when Josh died."

"Philip wants desperately for me to believe," Barbara said. "He reads books on this new microphysics, and he tells me that it's well proven that we live in a world of energies and waves, that nothing truly exists, that it's all an illusion, that we're all a part of the Holy Spirit. I can't buy that. The things that are eating up my insides are very real. He wants me to believe that we'll never be parted, that my spirit will survive, and that we'll be together. And what about Carson and Bernie—and Marcel? Will they be there? I ask him. Oh, Ellie, what a lot of nonsense I'm dumping on you! Forgive me."

"For what, darling? Who else can you dump on? I love you. I think it's wonderfully brave, the way you're taking all this."

"Brave? Oh no, Ellie. I'm not afraid anymore. We all die. They gave me sleeping pills, so I fall asleep easily. I never know whether I'll wake up in the morning. Philip prays for me, but I don't pray. I am what I am, and I can't change that now. But I do have one great disappointment. I had planned for all of us, Philip and me and you and Adam, to go to Paris in April. It was to be an anniversary gift to you and Adam, and I bought tickets and made the reservations. Paris in April is the most wonderful place in all the world, and we would have gone to some of the great château vineyards, and I could just picture Adam tasting a wine and whispering to us that Highgate was just as good—Ellie, you must use the tickets and you must drag Philip along somehow."

"What a precious gift! But to go without you—I couldn't."

"You could and you must. I don't want to talk about that anymore. Tell me, when will the baby come?"

"Judith's or May Ling's? Judith is going into her sixth month. May Ling—that's later. But Judith is still modeling—expectation clothes, they call them. Oh, Bobby, please live, please be here. And I'm weeping again. I must stop. But when I think of it—"

"I am here. Right beside you. And tomorrow we'll try the hill again. I must give those dreadful painkillers a chance to work. It takes an hour or so. I feel better now."

"Thank goodness," Eloise said.

"You know, darling, John Drew—the great actor—was dying, and his friends gathered around him, and one of them said, 'John, how does it feel to die?' and he replied, 'Dying is easy, comedy's hard.' "

"Oh, Barbara, how could you?" Eloise exclaimed. "You have me laughing and crying at the same time. How could you!"

"I'm wicked, but at least I made you laugh."

"We'd better go in for lunch. They'll wonder what became of us."

THE EVENING OF THE FOLLOWING DAY, after he had helped Barbara into bed, Philip opened her manuscript book of poems.

Drowsily, Barbara was speaking of how pleased she was to be here and how kind everyone was. Philip asked her whether he should read. "Or would you rather sleep?"

"One poem."

"Here's one dated 1925."

"Oh no. I was eleven years old."

"I like it."

"Well, at least we're alone."

Philip read,

Helga's baking a cake,
I don't know how to bake,
so I sit and watch her take
eggs and sugar in the cake
she is trying hard to make,
all alone for Mama's sake.
I love Mama, she can't bake.

Barbara smiled sleepily. "I was only eleven. Maybe I was ten."

"It was 1925. You were probably still ten."

"It's not too terrible, is it?"

"I like it. Who was Helga?"

"Our cook. And don't read me another one. In fact, I'm sorry I ever mentioned the poems."

Philip put aside the manuscript, went to Barbara, and kissed her.

"Come to bed," Barbara said. "I want something to hold on to."

He dropped his robe, turned off the light, and climbed into bed next to her, folding her into his arms; and she murmured sleepily, "You have strong arms for a skinny man."

"Too tight?"

"No, as tight as you can hold me."

"I love you, Barbara Lavette."

"Barbara Carter, Mr. Carter, Barbara Carter, Philip Carter..."

She was asleep a moment later, and Philip asked himself what would happen next. Would she live through tomorrow—the next day? He would not allow himself to complain, even to himself, about his own agony. She was the one who faced the long journey from which no one returned. His own suffering was not to be compared with hers. Like most men who are older than their wives, he had expected to die first. That was the proper order of things, and out of his own experience as a minister, he knew that women were better than men at handling such things. How could he handle it? How could he go on—and did he want to go on?

He must have fallen asleep, because during the night she had rolled out of his arms, and now she was awake and nudging him. "Wake up, old man. Everyone here is up at dawn, and now it's ten o'clock in the morning. What will they think of us?"

"How do you feel, baby?"

"I'm afraid the dope is wearing off. Would you bring me some fresh water and another dose? I'm groggy. I guess it's the sleeping pills. You know, I could swig down the whole bottle, and that would be quick and easy."

"Don't you dare think about it."

"Ah, the old priest in you has his dander up." He brought her medicine and water, and she drank it down, but slowly.

"Shall we get you into the shower?" Philip asked. He pulled back the bedclothes, but she had difficulty getting her legs over the side of the bed. He helped her to a standing position and into the bathroom.

"What's next, Philip? A wheelchair? I hate the thought of a wheelchair. But I don't know how I'll ever get to the kitchen."

"Is there much pain?"

She nodded. "It gets worse. I suppose I had some pain during the last few days, but I just ignored it. That's your Barbara."

"We'll try the morphine later if the pain persists. Joe said you can have it whenever you need it. I found a small metal stool for the shower, so you can sit down. I'll help you."

"How did I ever find you? All in a rainstorm, and if it hadn't rained that day—oh, my God, Philip, what would I do without you?"

"I'm right here, always."

Sitting in the shower under the warm water, she sighed and said that she could stay here all day.

"Except that we need breakfast. I'll get you dressed, and then I'll bring it to you."

"One thing before I forget. I want you to call Harry and ask him to please come over today—if he can find the time."

"I'm sure he'll find the time."

"I feel a little better. Let's try for the kitchen. I'll lean on you. I always do."

Harry had been there two days ago, not long after Barbara had arrived at Highgate—but then he had come with May Ling and others and she had not had a chance to talk to him alone. Today he arrived early in the afternoon, and Barbara convinced Philip that she must talk to him alone and that they were not to be interrupted. She was seated in one of the armchairs when Philip opened the door for him, and then Philip left after the greetings had been exchanged.

Barbara asked him whether he had brought a notebook.

"I'm afraid not."

"Would you hand me my briefcase? I have a notebook in there, and everything else I need, including a copy of my will. I had Abner Berman draw it up before we left for Europe—a time when I thought, as I guess everyone does, that I would live forever." She opened the briefcase and handed him a notebook, a pen, and the will. "I'm going to impose on you, Harry," she said.

"You couldn't impose on me, Barbara."

"We'll see. I want a new will, and I want it no later than

tomorrow. It will be very simple. I would like to spell it out now. Have May Ling type it out, and I want no one to know about it until after I am gone. You and May Ling will be my witnesses. Can you do that?"

"Of course."

"Can you take notes while I speak?"

"I made a poor living with shorthand while in law school. It comes in very handy."

"We'll start with the house on Green Street. There's no mortgage. I want Philip to have the house."

"There'll be a tax."

"I know. Aside from the house and all it contains—all of which goes to Philip, with one exception, which I will get to—my estate is worth about three million dollars in cash and treasury notes and California bonds. It's all detailed in the will that Abner Berman drew up, and which you have; all of it inherited. I have no stock. I want you to be my executor and to pay all costs and taxes out of the estate, and what is left goes to Philip. The one exception is my jewelry, with which you are well acquainted, and I want that, all of it, to go to Eloise—to do whatever she wishes with it, keep it or give it away as gifts, whatever she wishes. After the inheritance taxes are paid, there won't be enough left to divide among the people I love, and none of them really need money. Philip does. His pay is merely a stipend."

"Are you sure you want me to be your executor?"

"Absolutely sure, and I'm also sure that you can't say no to a dying woman."

"I wouldn't dream of saying no."

"Wait. There's a codicil. When my grandfather Thomas Seldon died, he left me a fortune of close to fifteen million dollars, which I neither deserved nor wanted. My first impulse was to give it all away, but Sam Goldberg talked me into setting up a foundation with fourteen million, and he put the rest into bonds, whereby most of my personal fortune."

Harry couldn't keep from saying, "I wish he had put it into equities."

"If he had, and that was in the thirties, I'd be as rich as a Morgan, and no happier than now. Anyway, the fund exists, and the foundation, with all it has dispensed to good causes, is twice as wealthy as it was when I began it. The board did put the money into equities. I'm the director, and the director has the right to approve all gifts; there's a board of six women and men, and Eloise is on the board and so is Abner Berman and Freddie. After I die, I want you to become the director. I have the right to appoint you. And please, please, don't argue with me."

"Now, wait a minute," Harry said. "You're putting me on the spot, but why? Why not Philip? Why not Freddie?"

"Philip is a saint. I'm deadly serious about that. Philip is a saint, and saints can't run a foundation. Freddie has both feet firmly planted in midair, and he doesn't know a damn thing about anything except wine. I love him, but Freddie's Freddie. May Ling has told me a great deal about you. You're a good man, and your politics are like mine, and the affair of Robert Jones is very clear in my mind. I want you to do this for me. Will you?"

He was silent for a long moment. Then he nodded. "I can't refuse you."

"I know that, but I'm not going to apologize, Harry. I have too little time left and too much to get done." She reached into her briefcase and took out several pamphlets. "These will give you a history of the foundation and its holdings, and there's a summary of former gifts, which do sort of make a pattern. Now, once I'm gone, I want the foundation to make a gift of half a million dollars to Philip's church. That will please him, and it will please me, if I'm anywhere to be pleased. Eloise knows about this gift, and she will support you, and I don't think you'll have any trouble with the rest of the board. Now, I'm very tired, and it's taxing to talk. Would you ask Philip to come back?"

FREDDIE BOUGHT HER A WHEELCHAIR. Freddie was not good with words, and there was no way he could tell her how he felt about her. He thought of saying something like, *You're not my aunt, you're my idol, my love, my everything,* and of course he dismissed it as persiflage. When he took her in his arms after she came to Highgate, he could say nothing at all, only clutch her and kiss her. He put his feeling into the wheelchair. It was an electric motorized vehicle, with three speeds forward and a reverse, the absolute latest state-of-the-art wheelchair. "You can scoot all over the place with it," he assured her. "You can even take it down to Harry's place, if you can stand a lecture on wine. You know, Aunt Barbara, he has become the most obnoxious wine peddler that ever was. He's signed up for my seminars at the university, but he's already convinced that he knows more about wine than I do."

"Freddie, thank you. It's a wonderful wheelchair, as such things go. I always wanted a convertible but never dared to buy one. When you convert a rich young woman to social consciousness, it's like converting a pagan to Christianity. No middle way."

Judith had entered the room with Freddie. The still-slim, lovely woman who had married Freddie back in November had gone the way of all childbearers, and now she bulged and walked very tentatively and bent with difficulty to kiss Barbara.

"My dear, when?" Barbara asked her.

"I don't know. I've lost track. I had some pains yesterday and I knew it wasn't real, but Freddie—he bundled me into the car and we drove to Napa and woke up poor Joe, and it was just one of those false alarms, and Joe thinks it won't happen for at least another couple of months. But I'm so big."

"Because you're a big woman," Barbara reassured her. "It's perfectly natural."

"I don't want a basketball player, I want the first black vintner."

"Joe says it's a girl," Freddie put in.

"Oh, worse. She'll be six feet tall, like her mother. Oh, Barbara, darling, why am I complaining? How are you?"

"A bit weak."

"I know." But Judith didn't know what to say, and she struggled to keep back the tears.

Oh, God, no more tears, Barbara said to herself, and to Judith, quickly, "You're not still modeling—I mean, the maternity clothes?"

"Oh no, no, I wouldn't dare go into the City. I might do it on the way, and anyway, it's too much maternity."

"I want you to try the chair," Freddie said. Philip and Freddie helped Barbara into the wheelchair. Freddie watched with small-boy approval as Barbara pressed buttons and navigated about the room.

"Dinner tonight," Freddie said. "Just roll right up to the table."

But she and Philip did not come to dinner that night. At about three o'clock, Eloise knocked at the door. Barbara was in bed, propped up on pillows, and her eyes were closed. Philip had been reading to her from a copy of *Life on the Mississippi*, which he'd found in the living room library. He put the book aside and opened the door for Eloise, who said, "She's sleeping, isn't she?"

"No, I'm not," Barbara replied, her voice weak and low.

"Eloise is here," he said.

Barbara propped herself on one elbow and asked, "Where? Where is she?"

"Right here, darling," Eloise said, walking around the bed and facing Barbara.

"Where?" Barbara demanded.

"Barbara—," Eloise began.

"You're not Ellie. Who are you?"

Eloise looked helplessly at Philip, who went to Barbara and kissed her cheek. "It's all right, baby."

"Why did she say she's Eloise?" And then, glancing at Philip, she said with sudden fear, "Am I sick? Are you the doctor?"

Eloise dropped into a chair, covering her face and her tears with her hands. Philip sat on the bed, his arm around Barbara. She turned to stare at him, and then she smiled. "Philip. Thank God you're here."

"I'm always here."

"Eloise," Barbara said, her voice stronger, "will you please stop crying? You know what happens to me when someone I love weeps."

"I'll stop," Eloise agreed.

"Did you see the wheelchair? Freddie bought it for me. Isn't he a darling?"

"Yes. It's very nice."

"Come here and give me a kiss."

Eloise went to the bed and kissed Barbara. Philip, standing to one side, shook his head and put his finger to his lips. "Don't cry, please," Barbara said.

"Promise. No more. How do you feel?"

"Morphine is wonderful. I have no pain at all. If Joe prescribes it for you, then it's proper medicine. What is Cathrena cooking for dinner tonight?"

"Fish Vera Cruz."

"That's so good. Foolish of me to ask. I can't eat anything. Philip makes me drink milk..." Her voice trailed away, and she closed her eyes.

"She drifts off like that," Philip said softly. "You can stay if you wish, but she may sleep for an hour or so."

"I'll come back later."

At the door, Philip said to Eloise, "I won't try to bring her to dinner tonight. It's too much for her, even with the wheelchair.

You might send over a small dish of that fish she likes so much. Just a small portion, which she probably won't be able to eat, but it would be nice for her to taste it."

"I'll bring it myself."

"Good. She's so fond of you—and I don't know how ever to thank you enough."

"God bless both of you for being here," Eloise said.

THAT NIGHT BARBARA FELL ASLEEP in Philip's arms. He could not sleep, and at about three o'clock in the morning, feeling his arm growing numb, he withdrew it from under Barbara. When he did that, she made no response, and when he kissed her cheek, lightly, it was cold. A spasm of sick terror wracked his body and he forced himself to feel for the vein in her wrist, but could find no pulse. He shook her. "Barbara, Barbara—wake up!"

He got out of bed and turned on the bedside light. Barbara lay on her back, eyes open, her white hair spread behind her over the pillow. He bent over the bed and kissed her lips. Then, without thinking, he made the sign of the cross. He was unaware that he was crying. There was a small mirror on her bedside table. He took it and held it above her slightly parted lips. There was no sign of breath on the mirror.

Philip closed her eyes, pulled up the blanket, and then folded the sheet below Barbara's chin. He could not cover her face. His first thought then was to call Joe, but he stopped himself before he picked up the telephone. What good would it do to wake him at three in the morning? What good would it do to awaken anyone? He had been a priest once, and he had seen enough death to recognize it. He got dressed, and then he kissed Barbara again, and then he sat beside the bed until dawn came.

AT A HALF HOUR PAST SIX, Philip called Joe and told him that Barbara had died.

"When?"

"Last night—at about three in the morning. She passed away in her sleep."

"Phil, you should have called me."

"Why? What good would it have done?"

"How are you taking it?" Joe asked.

"All right, I suppose." *What else do you say,* Philip wondered—*that the best thing in your life is gone?*

"I'll be there as soon as I'm dressed."

"Thank you."

The sun was rising over the hills as Philip walked to the kitchen, the air clean and sweet, a sting in the cold morning air that bit through his sweater. In the kitchen a fire was already going in the big fireplace. Eloise and Adam sat at the table, drinking coffee. Cathrena stirred a pot of oatmeal.

Eloise glanced up as Philip entered, read his face, and whispered, "Oh no—no."

Philip nodded. "Yes, Barbara's gone. She passed away last night, quietly, no pain; she was in my arms."

Adam's face wrinkled with pain. He was very old, Philip thought; an old, old patriarch who rose and walked unsteadily around the table and put his arms about Eloise.

"I want to see her," Eloise said, forcing the words through her sobs.

Adam helped her out of her chair, his arm around her, and they followed Philip back to the bedroom. "The morning's so beautiful," Eloise said, almost in a whimper.

Eloise bent over Barbara's body, stroked her cheeks lovingly, straightened her hair, and then bent to kiss her. "Go, dear one, and wait for me."

Adam said nothing; tears rolled down his cheeks.

"I couldn't cover her face," Philip said. "She looks beautiful. She just went away."

Adam managed to ask Philip whether he had called Joe. He spoke with difficulty, biting his lips.

"I called him. He'll be here soon," Philip said.

"I'll stay with her until he comes," Eloise told them. "I don't want to leave her alone."

"Yes, of course," Philip said. "She fell asleep in my arms, Ellie. She didn't cry out. I woke up, and she was gone."

Eloise sat down, next to the bed. Philip took Adam's arm and led him outside. "There are a few things," he explained. "Her wish was to be cremated, and she wanted her ashes scattered among the vines. I must honor that."

"Yes, I understand." Philip had never seen Adam like this, so deeply affected, his face tangled with pain. "I understand," he repeated.

"We'll leave her in bed until Joe and Sally come. Sally will want to see her. Are Freddie and Judith here?"

"Yes."

"I must call Sam. I'll call him from the kitchen."

Adam nodded.

"Do you want to stay with Eloise?"

Adam nodded again.

In the kitchen Cathrena sat huddled over, weeping copiously. She spoke pleadingly to Philip. Philip's Spanish was indifferent, and he could only make out something about God taking the good. He stood a moment, looking at her uneasily. What could he say?

"You shrived her?" she asked in English.

He nodded, thinking how Barbara would have looked at him if he had ever suggested confession—that expression of loving disagreement. Or was it loving pity?

"That's good," Cathrena said.

"I must use the telephone," Philip said.

Cathrena nodded.

He called Sam at home, and when he answered the phone,

shortly, Philip said, "Your mother passed away last night. Peacefully. There was no pain. She died in her sleep."

Sam's reaction was unexpected. "No, no!" he protested. "Not so soon! Why didn't I do something? I could have done something—why didn't you call me?"

"It was three o'clock in the morning. There was nothing you could have done, Sam. She went as she wished to go."

Sam went on pleading that they should have tried chemotherapy, and that she could have still been alive. Philip throttled his rising anger and said gently, "Come down here, Sam. You'll want to be here."

Then Philip slumped into a chair at the table. "Please, Cathrena, could you give me some coffee?" he asked wanly. "I'm very tired."

It was then that a sobbing Sally entered the kitchen, Joe behind her, and Philip stood up and embraced her. "She's in our room," he told Joe, "with Eloise and Adam. Take Sally there." When they left, he put his head down on the table and wept. There was a bottle of fifty morphine pills in their room. If he washed them down with a glass of water, all the pain would be gone; and then he felt defiled at the very thought. Cathrena brought him the coffee. Freddie and Judith were still asleep. He would have to awaken them, and he would have to call Harry and May Ling. "Everyone will be here," he told Cathrena sadly. "You'll have food for them?"

She nodded.

Then he went to awaken Freddie and Judith.

BARBARA DIED ON THE 18TH OF FEBRUARY. Later, in the spring, Judith's child was born, and they named her Barbara Lavette. She was nine pounds at birth, a plump, beautiful baby and an easy birthing. She had blue eyes and a skin of pale brown, and as Judith put her to her breast, she told Freddie, "I will never model again. I will have three more, just like her. I shall be a mother."

On the 15th of February, a Sunday, a memorial service was held for Barbara at the Unitarian Church. Freddie and Eloise both spoke, and when Philip asked whether anyone else desired to speak, a black man came forward and said simply, "I went to rob her, but you can't rob a person who will give you all that she has. She gave me my life." There were others who spoke, but these few words moved Philip most. When these memorials were done, Philip spoke and said, "For seven months, I was married to a gracious and beautiful woman who, above all things, knew who she was. I think that is the most I can say about her here and now. My church has given me a month for retreat, and perhaps at the end of that time I will know who I am, and my union with Barbara will be complete. I thank you for all the words of grace."

A few months after Barbara passed away, Eloise and Adam had a granite plinth put in the small clearing on the hillside, opposite the bench where she and Eloise would sit and talk and open their hearts to each other. On it, they had engraved a verse from Barbara's book of poems, a verse selected by Philip:

DO NOT LOOK FOR ME HERE,
FOR I AM NOT HERE.
BUT YOU CAN FEEL ME WHEN THE WIND BLOWS
AND YOU CAN SEE ME WHEN THE VINES LEAF OUT
AND YOU CAN SENSE ME WHEN THE GRAPES ARE CRUSHED
AND YOU CAN SEE ME SMILING WHEN THE SUN RISES
AND YOU CAN HEAR MY LAUGHTER WHEN THE BIRDS SING.
SO DO NOT WEEP FOR ME. I AM EVERYWHERE.

Barbara Lavette Carter
Nov. 10, 1914–February 18, 1985